Lisa Plumley

Mad About Max

ZEBRA BOOKS
Kensington Publishing Corp.
www.kensingtonbooks.com

ZEBRA BOOKS are published by

Kensington Publishing Corp.
850 Third Avenue
New York, NY 10022

All Kensington titles, imprints, and distributed lines are available at special quantity discounts for bulk purchases for sales
promotion, premiums, fund-raising, educational, or institu-
tional use.

Special book excerpts or customized printings can also be created to fit specific needs. For details, write or phone the office
of the Kensington Special Sales Manager: Attn. Special Sales
Department. Kensington Publishing Corp., 850 Third Avenue,
New York, NY 10022. Phone: 1-800-221-2647.

Zebra and the Z logo Reg. U.S. Pat. & TM Off.

ISBN 0-8217-7697-5

First Printing: July 2006
10 9 8 7 6 5 4 3 2 1

Printed in the United States of America

1

Max Nolan was on top of the world.

Okay, so technically he was on top of his bed. Not the whole world. But since his bed was in his new apartment, and his new apartment was in the most luxurious loft complex in downtown Phoenix, he figured that was close enough.

Sprawled in the sheets, bare-ass naked and awake with the sunrise, he rolled over. A groan of pleasure escaped him.

Life was good. Sunshine washed over him, as golden and potent as the desert outside. A faint breeze cooled his skin, courtesy of the turbo-powered A/C he'd cranked up exactly the way he liked it—almost arctic enough to frost the windows overlooking his coveted view of Camelback Mountain.

From the nightstand beside him, the tang of gin reached him, along with the waxy sweetness of a half-dozen burned-out candles. Both were remnants from last night. So were the clothes he'd discarded someplace nearby, his aforementioned nakedness, and the martini-fueled aftertaste on his tongue.

Given the crucial importance of his business meeting this morning, downing so many cocktails probably hadn't been his smartest move. But he'd had cause to celebrate. A new town to conquer, a new venture to launch . . . a new beginning, period.

Today was the day that would change everything.

Powered by the thought, Max opened his eyes. His bedroom snapped into focus, designer decorated in minimalist shades of tan, white, and black. The sunshine sliced his plush carpet into rectangles that unwittingly showcased last night's intended debauchery. An empty bottle of Tanqueray. Crushed rose petals. A woman's single black stocking.

A pair of plane tickets. Torn in half.

Oh yeah. Certain things hadn't gone as planned. That was a new experience for him—one he hadn't exactly savored.

Not that it mattered. He didn't intend to be caught by surprise again. Last night was a fluke. Even if it wasn't, he knew he could turn things around today; he always did. He was lucky that way—lucky and persistent.

To some people, those two things—luck and persistence—were equal. Max didn't agree. He took luck seriously, with the same gravity he reserved for financing terms, deal making, and NBA play-offs. Luck was real. As real as the good-morning kiss, cuddle, and argument-ending makeup session he planned to savor approximately ten seconds from now.

Those ripped-up plane tickets meant he had some heavy-duty compensating to do. Only an idiot—or someone utterly unfamiliar with women—would have failed to realize that. Cheerfully pondering the situation, he considered talking it over. Having a long heart-to-heart, trying to explain and apologize. But the way Max saw it, talking was overrated. Especially when it came to making amends. With apologies—as with life—what really mattered was what a guy *did*.

Particularly if he could be creative about it.

And Max considered himself to be *very* creative.

Squinting at the bedside clock, he gauged how long it would take him to shower, shave, and make it to the site of his business meeting. If he got started right now—and skipped breakfast in favor of chugging his usual Ethiopian Yergacheffe on the drive—he could make up for last night's plane-ticket-ripping, tantrum-throwing debacle with time to spare.

With an anticipatory grin, he swept his arm along the sheets in search of Ms. Tantrum herself—his girlfriend of six months, Sarabeth. He'd wake her up, roll her over, and . . . find her gone?

Puzzled, Max took a closer look. Yep. Nothing but acres of rumpled sheets, an abandoned pillow, and a missed opportunity to set things right. Hmmm. That was weird. This definitely didn't fit the master-of-the-universe vibe he had going this morning.

She couldn't have gone far. Sarabeth never went any-place without a wardrobe change, a manicure, or both. Throwing off the sheets and comforter, he padded naked across the bedroom. He cocked his head, listening for sounds of water running in the shower or dishes clanging in the apartment's sleek galley kitchen.

Nada. Confused, he wondered if he'd somehow miscalculated the situation. Was she pissed enough to walk out on him?

That wasn't like her, though. Sarabeth never did anything halfway. There'd be a scene. A dramatic announcement. Something. Besides, she *had* slept with him last night, even if all they'd done was . . . sleep. Much to his disappointment, after the weeks he'd spent out of town—monastically, even celibately—putting the finishing touches on his most recent entrepreneurial venture.

It was true his relationship with Sarabeth wasn't serious. It was fun and frivolous, based on good times and lots of traveling to exotic spots. But Max was a one-woman-at-a-time kind of guy. He'd remained faithful to her anyway. It was just his way.

"Sarabeth?" he called.

The tap of her high heels was his answer. She breezed into the bedroom from behind him, where his customized walk-in closet was. He hadn't heard her rummaging around, but apparently she'd been busy in there, because she strode purposefully past him now with an armload of gray flannel and black wool.

He blinked. "What are you doing with my suits?"

"You'll see."

Her singsong tone didn't quite match her steely expression. It looked a lot like the one she used whenever a boutique salesperson kept her waiting too long. Warning bells clanged in his head. This couldn't be good.

She didn't so much as glance his way as she passed. She merely scooped up a few dropped neckties and then kept going. Miffed, Max put his hands on his hips. Come on. When a guy was standing there naked, a woman was obligated to offer a morning once-over. A perfunctory ogle. *Something*. It was just common courtesy.

"I'm making some changes around here," she informed him, still not ogling. "These are first up."

He frowned at his suits. *Making some changes*. Even said with her trademark honeyed Georgia drawl, those words left him feeling chilled. The same way "meatless hamburgers" did, and movies with wisecracking computer-generated babies in them.

Holding her head high, Sarabeth headed for the living room, her sequined minidress glittering as she moved. In addition to last night's outfit and high heels, she was also wearing last night's moussed-up hairdo and a load of smeared eye makeup. Exactly how long had she been hatching this cockamamie plan? Whatever it was.

Before he could decide, his front door slammed.

What the . . . ? Determinedly, Max followed. No

woman absconded with all his suits, talked about mysterious "changes," *and* failed to ogle him, all in the same morning. It was enough to hurt a guy's feelings.

A weaker guy than him, sure. But still.

He whipped open the front door, intending to stop Sarabeth before she reached the elevator.

"Morning, Mr. Nolan." The doorman, Hank—who usually did not perform double duty as elevator operator—doffed his cap.

Sarabeth, stopping in the midst of entering the elevator, finally dropped her non-ogling attitude—not that Max found much to shout about in the experience. Her gaze slipped down his bare torso toward parts south and then . . . she rolled her eyes.

Hell. Belatedly, he remembered he was still naked. Which explained Hank's averted gaze *and* added insult to injury. His own girlfriend had just rolled her eyes at his nakedness! What was the world coming to?

He picked up the *Arizona Daily* from his doormat. Using the newspaper as a vertical shield to cover his bait and tackle, he ignored Hank's nondoormanlike smirk.

"Sarabeth, wait. Whatever this is, we can talk about it."

"Talk? *You?* Hah!" She tossed her hair, shaking out its expertly highlighted blond length. "You never talk, Max. Not lately. Lately all you do is work. Work, work, work. I've had it!"

She turned to the doorman. "Let's go, Hank. I've got a drop-off to make."

With a subdued thunk, the elevator doors slid shut.

Max stared. Drop-off? What kind of drop-off involved his suits? Sarabeth's laundry service picked up and delivered. She wasn't exactly the domestic type. It was unlikely she intended to visit the Wash 'N' Spin herself.

What the hell was going on here?

He wasn't waiting around to find out. In hot pursuit,

Max jabbed the elevator button. Five seconds later, it lit up.

Staring at that feeble red glow, he remembered that while the building's elevator system might be state of the art and the car itself opulently decorated in marble and gilt, it was still notoriously slow. Which probably explained why Sarabeth had apparently asked Hank to hold it for her.

Aggravated, Max ducked inside his apartment, grabbed a pair of boxer briefs—the first thing that came to hand from his still-unpacked luggage—and yanked them on. Half-hopping, half-walking as he wriggled into his tighty-whities, he headed outside to the terrace to scope out the situation.

Downstairs on the sidewalk, Sarabeth popped into view from beneath the awning. She tip-tapped purposefully to a gaudily painted metal container—it looked like a renovated mailbox gone horribly wrong—and dropped everything in her arms on the sidewalk beside it.

She opened the box's gaping maw, which allowed Max to see it wasn't empty. A few familiar items poked haphazardly from within. Items like his favorite black nightclubbing shirt. His Oxford wing tips. Several of his leather belts. Three button-down shirts. A brown dress sock.

This wasn't the first trip she'd made, he realized. He must have slept through a few of them.

With glee, Sarabeth stuffed one of his suit jackets inside. Then, holding the box open, she paused. He'd swear she tossed a triumphant look straight up to his terrace. Then she busily resumed stuffing.

With a sense of surreality, Max realized the truth.

She was throwing away all his suits. All his shirts, all his ties, all his shoes and socks and . . . everything.

Shit. Flooded with confusion and disbelief, he heard a ping and ran for the elevator. The doors were closing as he reached it, but he muscled his way inside and rode it, clenching his fists, down to the building's lobby.

By the time he hit the sidewalk, Sarabeth was giddily accepting a broomstick from Hank. With gusto, she jabbed it in the metal box, using it as a ramrod to pack in the suits and shirts and shoes. That accomplished, she snatched the final item she'd brought and prepared to slam-dunk it.

His best suit. His favorite suit. The suit he'd planned to wear to his all-important business meeting this morning.

"Not my lucky suit!" Max shouted.

She hesitated a nanosecond. Then, with evident delight, she crammed his suit inside the box. Two surprisingly powerful broomstick whacks later, it sank from view.

No. This couldn't be happening. Gaping in disbelief, he watched as Sarabeth dusted off her hands. Wearing a bizarre grin, she returned Hank's broomstick. She thanked the doorman politely. She sent him on his way.

Max felt dizzy. His lucky suit! His lucky suit . . . gone. On the day that was *supposed* to change everything.

"There." Sarabeth linked arms with him, derailing his horror-stricken train of thought. "Now you *can't* work all the time, because you'll have nothing to wear to the office. You'll have to take me to Aruba like you promised."

"What?" She was crazy. Wrenching free, he jammed his arm in the box. It wasn't designed for retrieval—he could barely brush his fingertips across the compacted clothes inside. "I told you last night, we can't go to Aruba. I have to launch my new venture with Oliver. My plans changed."

"Change them back."

Her childlike tone demanded he comply. Max knew he couldn't. It was impossible. He'd thought she understood that.

"I have to work." Grunting, he fished for his stuff. No dice. He couldn't salvage so much as a necktie. That didn't mean he was going to quit trying, though. "Work is what I do."

"It's *all* you do! What happened to the fun Max? The Max who took me to Miami, to New York, to Paris?" Her drawl beseeched him, sounding—for the first time—spoiled and petulant. "I want *my* Max back. Not the workaholic who showed up an hour late for dinner last night."

Not this again. "I told you. My meeting ran overtime."

"Right. So you *said*. But according to my therapist—"

Sarabeth kept talking, launching into a play-by-play of her latest therapy session. Max frowned. He tried to follow the mishmash of psychobabble that came next, the same way he always did. But this time, a rumbling down the street diverted him.

Thank God.

An ancient truck jerked into view, its cargo area painted in the same vivid pinks and blues as the metal box currently holding his lucky suit hostage. He squinted. That retro, flower-power color scheme couldn't be a coincidence.

He reared back to read the painted words on the box's side: SUCCESSFULLY DRESSED DONATIONS. Oh Christ.

"You're donating all my stuff!"

"Of course." Sarabeth blinked, an unfamiliar high-handed impatience in her expression. "This is your wake-up call, Max. My therapist suggested it. It's me or your . . . work thing. You choose."

"My 'work thing'? Are you seriously telling me you don't even know what I do for a living?"

She sighed. "So long as it gets me to Aruba, who cares? I don't see what you're getting so worked up about."

He couldn't possibly have heard her correctly. Did Sarabeth really see him as nothing but a walking, talking, martini-swilling plane ticket to Partyville? Was that all she cared about?

Numbly, Max watched as the Successfully Dressed truck squealed to a stop in front of the neighborhood eyesore— a dilapidated natural foods store. There was another donation box in front of the place, probably packed with tie-dyed T-shirts.

It looked as if he had a few more minutes. Enough time to give Sarabeth the benefit of the doubt.

"If I don't work," he told her with labored patience, "I won't be able to *afford* Aruba. I won't be able to afford a trip to the cheap seats at a Diamondbacks game."

She scoffed. "I don't even *like* baseball. Problem solved!"

This was hopeless. "Sarabeth, I *need* my clothes. I need my lucky suit. *Today*. My meeting is—"

"Meeting, schmeeting." Brightly, she smiled at him. "Do you think the airline will take Scotch-taped tickets? Or should I send Hank out for some superglue?"

Max searched her expectant face, at a loss as to how to respond. He wondered how he'd gotten to this point. Usually he was good at things. Really good. Freakishly good. That skill was the cornerstone of his business dealings. That—and luck.

"Well, sugar pie? We'd better get going, hadn't we?" Sarabeth, back to her ostensibly sweet self, jerked him out of his reverie. She gestured toward the apartment building.

Max shook his head.

"Don't be ridiculous. You're not even dressed! You can't stay out here in your underwear."

Max didn't care. Mulishly, he crossed his arms over his chest. Sarabeth had backed him into a corner, and it wasn't a comfortable fit. Without his lucky suit, he might as well be nude anyway.

"People will talk!" she protested.

"People with clothes?" He eyeballed the donation box.

It didn't look all *that* sturdy. He figured he could crack it. "Lucky them."

She shot him an exasperated look. "Don't be difficult. Tell you what—let's go upstairs. I'll order some breakfast, and you can hop in the shower. Maybe I'll even join you." She offered a lascivious wink. "We've got lots of time until we have to get to the airport."

"I'm not going to the airport. I'm staying here," Max announced. "I'm getting my stuff back before that charity truck comes this way."

Avoiding the sidewalk cracks in his path—he'd risked enough bad luck today—he strode to Hank's desk. Ignoring the doorman's protests, he grabbed the broomstick. Max was getting his lucky suit back, and nobody was going to stop him.

From the driver's seat of her truck, Lucy Logan took a fortifying swig of her lemongrass chai infusion. Ahhh. There was nothing like a visit to Jade's health food store to start her morning off on the right foot. Just holding the warm cup and inhaling the spicy aroma made her feel contented.

She'd have been happy to linger at the store's cozy café all day, talking and laughing, if not for the need to get on with her donation pickup route. As it was, she'd already made herself late by stopping to admire her friend Victor's new henna mehndi body art. In general, Lucy tried to take life as it came, but sometimes a person had to get a move on.

Unfortunately, today was one of those days.

She propped her drink in the plastic cup holder attached to the door and started the truck. Its engine roared to life, making the duct-taped vinyl seat vibrate beneath her. The radio crackled. She kept it tuned to her favorite alternative music station, ensuring a kick-ass mood while she made her rounds.

Okay. Determinedly, Lucy gripped the steering wheel. She took a deep breath. The whole rig was a lot to handle. Driving it still made her nervous. But she needed to learn how to do *everything* if Successfully Dressed was going to survive.

Of course, if good intentions counted for anything, the shop *definitely* would survive. Thrive, even. She was sure of that much. So . . . no worries. If there was one thing Lucy had nailed, it was good intentions. Also, belly dancing. And skateboarding. And—to be honest—making a truly wicked mai tai.

Hey, a girl had to have her talents.

The big shots at the next stop, a super-ritzy apartment building, rarely donated anything to their pickup site's box, despite the obvious appeal of its eye-catching paint job. But Lucy parked the truck anyway. She figured, optimistically, that it was important to keep her hopes up.

She also figured, realistically, that it was smart to keep the engine running.

She clambered out of the truck and released its rear catch. The cargo bay door slid upward on its track, liberating the familiar scents of musty cotton, damp cardboard, and mothballs. Wrinkling her nose, she peered into the dim interior. It looked pretty empty. She needed *lots* more pickups today.

With that thought in mind, she hotfooted it to the nearby donation box. She'd give this one a cursory check. Then she could move on to likelier prospects farther downtown. Jangling her keys, she unlocked the donation box's rear hatch.

Avalanche! The door swung open, releasing a jack-in-the-box torrent of wool, cotton, and silk. Surprised, Lucy stuffed the overflow back in, then held it in place with her shoulder while she pried out the removable bin.

Wow. This was a real jackpot. Pants without holes, shirts without stains, even a few warm wool jackets. These things would be perfect for the men's division of Successfully Dressed. Apparently, someone inside Big Shot Central had developed a social conscience.

Happily, she dropped the bin on the sidewalk. Plastic scraped against gritty concrete as she hauled the bin into position and mounded all the clothes inside. Everyone at Successfully Dressed would be *thrilled* to see this haul. It exceeded their collection goals for the whole week.

Just as she added the last stray necktie to the pile, footsteps sounded. Then a shrill, "If you go after those clothes, Max Nolan, we're *through!*"

It sounded like a lunatic southern belle. Or a deranged Miss Georgia contestant in the throes of the swimsuit competition. Curious, Lucy straightened. On the other side of the collection box, a statuesque blonde in four-inch heels and a fancy dress stood beside a man in his underwear. Neither had noticed her.

Frankly, though, the underwear guy was hard to miss.

He said something Lucy couldn't hear clearly. Whatever it was, the blonde didn't like it. She reared back, gave a major-league-worthy windup, and then . . . *slap!*

Lucy gasped. The guy clapped his hand to his cheek, just like in the movies. He looked stunned.

"Fine! We're finished!" the woman yelled.

She tossed her hair—with frankly unnecessary theatricality, in Lucy's practical opinion. She gave a "hmmph." Then she clip-clopped away at double speed without looking back.

That was harsh. Especially the not-looking-back part.

"Ouch," Lucy whispered, hugging her donation bin.

The man glanced her way. Caught eavesdropping, Lucy felt embarrassed enough to do what she always did in uncomfortable situations. She cracked a joke.

"Let me guess." Balancing the bin on her hip, she

hooked her thumb toward the departing belle. "You're a briefs man, but she prefers boxers?"

For the first time, he grinned. "Something like that. Just call me a traditionalist."

"Tough luck, traditionalist."

He gave a murmur of assent, his whole demeanor suggesting it was perfectly natural to discuss the issue. On the sidewalk. In the sunshine. With him all muscle-bound and gorgeously tanned, dressed in nothing but a pair of tighty-whities.

With a shrug, Lucy decided to take her cue from him. Live and let live, and all that. In her artsy, freewheeling neighborhood—in her whole life, in fact—that was the only attitude to follow.

Besides, the guy wasn't exactly hard on the eyeballs. He—Max Nolan, she remembered overhearing—was like a men's underwear billboard come to life. Only brainier looking and slightly more talkative. Besides, his boxer briefs weren't *that* revealing. She'd seen more displayed, to less advantage, at her friend Callia's swimming pool in Tucson.

The whine of an engine overrode the rumble of her truck and sidetracked her thoughts, just for an instant. Caught by it, Lucy stared down the palm-tree-lined street. She and the man both watched Miss Georgia zoom away in a showy sports car.

He released a gusty sigh. Absently, he raked his hand through his dark hair, tousling it further. He turned to Lucy.

He shrugged. "Well, that's that."

He didn't sound too broken up over it. Lucy guessed he and the Amazonian blonde hadn't been that close. Or maybe it was just that men moved on quickly. He was probably combing his mental black book for a rebound date right now.

Not that it mattered to her. She pretty much took

things easy. Hefting her bin, she prepared to leave. The radio in her truck blared one of her favorite punk songs, and the windfall in her arms promised good karma for the rest of the day. There was nothing to stick around here for.

That's that, she echoed to herself.

Overall, this had been a pretty good Tuesday morning, though. She couldn't deny that. One yummy lemongrass chai infusion? Check. One donation windfall? Check. One buffed-up hunk with dark eyes and a delicious grin? Double check.

But she had to be on her way. Waggling her eyebrows, Lucy gave Max Nolan one last appreciative ogle. Given the hard time he'd just endured, she figured the gesture might cheer him up.

It did. His lips curved in a surprised smile.

"You know," he said, "you have a really kind face."

He sounded bemused by that observation . . . almost fascinated. A person would think kindness was rare or something.

"Did anybody ever tell you that?"

"All the time," Lucy said. "Whenever somebody tries to sign me up for cell phone service. Or a credit card."

He eyed her sardonic grin. His shoulders relaxed. She thought he might offer a snappy comeback, since—for some reason—he struck her as the guiltlessly glib type. But he didn't say anything else. In fact, he looked sort of gobsmacked. Given the recent turn of events, she didn't blame him.

"Well, back to work." Lucy nodded at her bin, then tilted her head toward her idling truck. "These donations won't pick themselves up. But hey, better luck next time. Don't take any wooden nickels. Or pick up any bottle blondes."

Still wearing that odd expression, he lifted his hand

in a silent good-bye. Oh well. All her jokes couldn't be knee-slappers, could they?

Three minutes later, she'd stowed all the donations securely in the truck's cargo bay. After a restorative chug of lemongrass chai infusion, she put the truck in gear. Bobbing her head to the radio's music, she headed out.

A block later, a flash of white in the truck's massive side safety mirror caught her eye. Mr. Tighty-Whities. He ran in her wake, yelling something. That was weird. In the spirit of open-mindedness—and of appreciating buff biceps—she decided to pull over.

She leaned out the window. Yep. Maybe Max Nolan was crazy; she didn't know for sure. But his entire body—and she could see most of it at the moment—was insanely *fine*.

"What's up?" she asked. "Dying for my phone number? You're going to be bummed, because I don't have a phone."

He looked momentarily flummoxed. *No phone?* his expression said. *No way!* But he regrouped quickly.

"I need to talk to you. It's important."

He wasn't even winded, she noticed. Even after running all this way. And his pursuit of her—so madcap and uninhibited—was the most thrilling thing to happen to her in days.

Obligingly, Lucy cut the engine. She had nothing to lose by finding out what he wanted. And possibly everything to gain. She believed in experiencing life to its fullest.

She jumped to the curb. The early-morning June sunlight forced her to squint to see his face. Max had a dimple near his stubbly right cheek, she noticed. It upgraded his look from tough guy to potentially *mischievous* tough guy. Very cute.

"I got a little . . . distracted back there." He gestured to the corner where they'd met. "Which is completely unlike me, by the way, because I'm usually very focused. I usually get things done."

She nodded. "Mmm-hmm."

"I don't know what happened, actually. One minute we were talking, and the next . . ." He broke off. A goofy grin lit his expression as he gazed into her face. "The next you were driving away."

Awww. He was a romantic, Lucy realized. A freshly dumped, apparently openhearted, chockablock-with-charisma romantic. He must have been so entranced by meeting her that he'd lost track of everything else. She couldn't remember the last time *that* had happened. It was like something out of a movie.

Still, it was better to play it cool.

"Right. Of course. So . . . you wanted to ask me something?"

He nodded. She held her breath, waiting. Deep inside, the secret, sappy part of her raised itself on tiptoes. Any moment now, he'd say something *wonderful*.

"Yeah." Max cleared his throat. He seemed to regain control of himself. He looked her right in the eye. "Will it take you more than two minutes to open up your truck? My clothes are in there, and I need them back."

2

Ms. Social Conscience looked at him as if he punted kittens. For fun. Max didn't know what her problem was. But he didn't need some touchy-feely, New Age wannabe (version 2.0) giving him a hard time. Especially given the morning he'd had so far.

Even if she was—kind of—cute.

"You *what?*" she asked, goggling at him.

"I need my clothes back. This is all a mistake. Obviously." He nodded at his nearly naked self. "Usually I wear my motorcycle boots with this getup."

She didn't smile at his joke. But she did give him another appreciative once-over, as though picturing that underwear-plus-boots combo he'd mentioned . . . and liking it. Max found that encouraging.

"Those things weren't supposed to be donated. So if you could just open up your truck—"

"Sorry. No can do."

"—and give me my stuff back—"

"Nope."

"—I'd really appreciate it."

"Not going to happen."

Why was she staring at him as though she'd kissed a frog—expecting a prince—and wound up with a dose of swamp breath? A person would think she'd expected him to ask for something else entirely.

"Okay. I understand that you and"—he squinted at the side of the truck—"Successfully Dressed are probably pretty hard up for donations. So I'll make a deal with you. You give me back my stuff, and I'll pick out an entire suit—shoes, shirt, tie, the whole nine yards—to donate."

She wrinkled her nose. "Yeah. That's sweet. But I've already got all your stuff, so . . . no dice."

Well, she had him there. But while he admired her savvy maneuvering, Max wasn't a man who went down without a fight. Or at least a little coaxing.

"Come on . . ." He arched his brows in question.

"Lucy," she supplied.

"Lucy." He smiled. "Give a guy a break."

Momentarily, she seemed to waver. Then, "Ha. You'd have gotten further asking for my phone number."

With an air of finality, Lucy crossed her arms over her chest, making the fabric of her gauzy, beaded dresslike . . . *thing* ripple over her body. Max followed its vintagey wrinkles to the jeans she had on underneath. He wished women's clothes weren't so damned weird. He couldn't see her legs. Not that bohemian girls were typically his type.

There was only one thing left to say.

"My lucky suit is in there!"

A grin tilted her mouth. "Lucky suit?"

Max nodded. For a supposedly gentle and kind charity worker, she sure had a double helping of smart-ass attitude.

"I have an important meeting today. I need that suit."

He'd never embarked on a new venture without it. It was his talisman, his good-luck charm . . . his insurance.

"Lucky suit. Seriously?" She gazed at him in apparent awe. Or amusement. On her, they looked a lot alike. "That's a new one. I've never met anybody who was actually *willing* to admit something like that. Which is saying a lot, given who my friends are."

He stared her down. Mentioning his lucky Astros cap right now probably wouldn't bolster his case.

Lucy caught his expression anyway. "You're really gullible enough to believe that? Wow. What a bunch of hooey." With a confiding air, she leaned closer, sending the mingled scents of spices and shampoo his way. "I hate to break it to you, but . . . there's no such thing as a lucky suit."

"All right." He didn't want to do this, but his meeting was in less than an hour. "Let's get down to business. There's a hundred bucks in it for you if you let me look in your truck and take back what I need. Call it a big tip."

Her mouth gaped. "I'm not doing that! Giving back donations is against the rules. So is accepting 'tips.'"

Max scoffed. "Come on. You don't exactly strike me as the 'follow the rules' type. I mean, look at you."

She glanced down at herself. Then at him. Meaningfully. "I'm better dressed than you are."

Ha. That wasn't the half of it.

"You have purple hair," he pointed out.

As if that explains anything, her expression said.

"My friend is a feng shui hairstylist." She tugged a lock of her raggedy cut. "This color—and it's *lavender,* by the way—suits my chi."

He rolled his eyes. Chi? From a girl who claimed *luck* didn't exist? "And a tattoo."

"So? It's small." She turned up her wrist and examined it. "Very tasteful. I really don't see what you're getting at.

"And piercings. Several piercings."

A frown. "Welcome to the twenty-first century, Mr. Tighty-Whities. One eyebrow piercing, a navel ring, and a tongue barbell hardly make me a freak."

"The name is Max."

"So? We're both identified. I'm still not giving you your donations back."

Was it his imagination, or did she seem kind of . . . wounded? Taken aback at the idea, Max studied her for a minute. He didn't think asking for his clothes was unreasonable. And she'd already warned him off her nonexistent phone number. Maybe she was touchy about her job. Or her purple hair. That hair color could *not* have been intentional, no matter what she said.

Before he could decide, Lucy turned, treating him to a backside view of her gauzy-dress-plus-jeans combo. It didn't make sense from this angle either. A dress *or* jeans, sure. But both together? They cancelled each other out. Sometimes he just didn't get women.

Not *often,* of course, but still . . .

Her truck door slammed. Jerked from his reverie by the sound, Max looked up.

"See ya." Lucy offered a perky salute.

Perky didn't quite mesh with her purple hair, piercings, and skin art . . . but then, neither did the vulnerable look on her face. Against his will and completely inexplicably, Max almost felt sorry for her.

She started the engine and put her truck in gear. Screw *sorry.* He had a lucky suit to retrieve or his meeting was going down in flames.

"Wait!" He grabbed the edge of her rolled-down window. "There must be some way we can compromise."

Lucy lifted her gaze from his desperate grasp on her truck. Slowly. Her attention seemed to get stuck on his hands for a minute before wandering to his face.

He did his best to look open. Approachable. It wasn't easy while hanging off the side of a broken-down truck in his underwear. His johnson was getting a flower-power paint job buffing he didn't quite appreciate.

"Come on," he urged. "Talk to me."

Lucy scrutinized him instead. She started out dispassionate and segued pretty quickly—probably thanks to the baby blues he offered—to big-old-softie-at-heart.

She bit her lip. "Well . . . we always need volunteers."

Her tone was grudging. It was also touched with a huskiness Max found ridiculously appealing. Sexy, even. Just so long as he didn't look directly at her purple hair, he could almost convince himself Lucy was his type of woman. He wished he'd gotten a look at her legs.

Pondering the obvious *un*luckiness of that missed opportunity, he tuned in to hear the rest of her offer.

"You know. People to help sort through the clothes," she was saying. Her gestures picked up speed as enthusiasm caught hold of her. "Clean them, hang them—things like that."

He pictured himself sorting and folding. Ugh.

"I don't do my own laundry, much less somebody else's."

Her face fell. But she rallied quickly—something Max felt improbably certain she managed to do a lot.

"Have it your way." She gave a breezy wave. "I sure am going to enjoy giving away that lucky suit of yours. The people who come to Successfully Dressed could definitely use a little good luck, that's for sure. So, hey, thanks a lot."

She couldn't be serious. Nobody kept an accidental donation. And nobody refused a hundred-dollar tip. Especially not a woman with a hole in the toe of her ratty, beaded, ethnic-looking slippers. Shoes. Sandals. Whatever.

She waved a slip of paper. "Don't forget your receipt. Your donation may be tax deductible, you know."

He snatched the receipt and crumpled it in his fist.

Lucy beamed.

She was goading him! Goading him *and* refusing his offer to compromise. With the clock ticking, Max growled in frustration.

Clearly, all the women within a five-mile radius had

gone nuts. If he hadn't known it was impossible, he'd have sworn his famous Max mojo was on the fritz.

Although with his lucky suit being held hostage . . . damn it. Anything was possible at this point.

Hell. "How much volunteering are we talking about?"

Lucy considered it. "A week."

"No way. An afternoon."

"Six days."

"Two."

"Five. I'll set aside your suit for you to buy back at the end. At a proper donation rate, of course."

He eyeballed her. A woman who couldn't even dress herself properly didn't deserve these kinds of bargaining skills. Maybe her eyebrow ring had hypnotized him.

"I don't do ironing," he warned.

"So? I don't compromise my integrity. Do you want your suit back or not?"

The aggravatingly cocky angle of her head only added insult to injury. Lucy thought she had the upper hand. But with the weight of his impending meeting bearing down on him, Max couldn't afford to stand on principle.

Oliver was counting on him, for one thing. His own self-respect was on the line, for another. He needed this venture to go forward. Starting today.

"Four days," he bargained. "And I get my lucky suit now."

Her expression softened. "You really believe in all that gobbledygook, don't you?"

Max didn't want to talk about it. "Do we have a deal? Or would you like some more persuasion first?"

"Persuasion? What kind of persuasion?"

At the teasing note in her voice, his libido offered up a few suggestions, wholly without his permission. Max found himself staring at her lips. He wondered what it would feel like to kiss a girl with a tongue barbell.

"What kind do you like?" he asked.

She flashed another smile. "The kind that shows up on time, works hard, and doesn't mix up the vintage pieces with the general donations. Can you handle it?"

He could handle anything. He said as much.

Lucy scoffed. "Sure. That's what you say now. Wait till you get there." She nodded toward his hand. "The address is on that crumpled wad in your fist."

He fixed his gaze on her face. "I'll find it."

"You'll want to wear some clothes too."

He considered his near nudity. "Spoilsport."

She grinned at that. For a hard-bargain-driving, weird-clothes-wearing, do-gooder donation-truck driver, she had a smile that lit up her whole face. If Max hadn't just sworn off women—and all the trouble they caused—for the duration of his project launch in Phoenix, he might have been susceptible to that smile of hers. As it was, he was hardly affected at all.

Hardly.

Lucy caught him watching her. For a minute, their gazes locked. Max felt weirdly compelled to keep on looking, to soak up all the details he could. There was a slight sideways bend to her nose. He thought it looked cute. Her eyes were green, or maybe hazel. Changeable. Probably she did that on purpose, just to keep hapless men off-guard.

"Okay. See you around," she said.

The next thing he knew, he was standing in his tighty-whities on the sidewalk, watching the Successfully Dressed truck rumble down the street. In a grinding of gears, it heaved past a diner and a florist, then turned the corner. It lurched over the curb in the process.

Lucy was a terrible truck driver.

But then, that was only fair. Because Max was a terrible volunteer. He couldn't remember the last time he'd done something without the promise of being paid for it. Why would he? He was a sought-after businessman with a knack for innovative ideas and an unmatched ability to bring those ideas to moneymaking fruition.

Or at least that's what his press release said. He had no idea what Andrea, his publicist, would have to say about *this* fiasco. Probably that he was a sucker for a pretty face.

The truth hurt.

Not that Andrea necessarily needed to know about this volunteering gig, Max decided as he headed for his loft. Andrea would only try to give it an altruistic spin it didn't quite deserve. Besides, the last thing he wanted to do was explain why his lucky suit was being held hostage in the first place.

Max stopped. Damn it! He still didn't have his lucky suit! Lucy had distracted him just long enough to drive away with it, he realized. Surprised, he stared after the Successfully Dressed truck again.

How did she keep *doing* that to him?

The first thing that hit Lucy when she got back to Successfully Dressed was the smell—the familiar aroma of heirloom clothing, decades-old polyester, and musty shoes. She inhaled a big lungful as she stepped inside the shop. There was nothing else on earth quite like it. It was the embodiment of mystery and possibility and connectedness. Lucy adored it.

The second thing that hit her was a scarf.

"What do you think?" Nieca asked, twisting sideways.

She stepped back, gesturing to the window display. At twenty-six and in her last year of textile studies at ASU, Nieca had recently put herself in charge of the shop's lone mannequin. Not that having a single mannequin limited her imagination in any way. She had, at various times, outfitted the five-foot-six, plastic-and-synthetic, vintage "Suzy" model in women's suits; men's suits; and (memorably) a montage of stick-on shower decals, silk daisies, and pink faux fur.

Lucy plucked the scarf from her face. Suzy wore several more just like it, strapped and tied creatively across her figure. And nothing else. Okay, except for a pair of multicolored go-go boots. Somehow, given Nieca's talent, the ensemble looked like an actual outfit. It looked good.

"Nice." Lucy nodded. "What's the theme this time?"

"It's 'go-go get a job,'" Nieca said. "Get it? The—"

"I hope it's 'kick ass on the Salvation Army,'" Franco volunteered from the back of the shop. He hurried to the display, his faux-hawk vibrating with the movement. "Those losers won't let up about the game next month. It's really starting to bug." He chomped his gum, giving an offhanded wave. "Hey, Lucy. Good haul today?"

"Ummm . . ."

Guiltily, Lucy flashed on the box of men's items she'd stashed at her place before coming here. She hadn't been able to determine which of the gray flannel overload might be Max Nolan's "lucky suit." Frankly, all boring business wear tended to look the same to her. So she'd sort of . . . *diverted* all the items he'd donated. For the time being.

"About average," she said. "You know."

Nieca and Franco watched her. Trying to seem nonchalant, Lucy put her hands on her hips and surveyed the rest of the shop. Shoehorned into a space formerly occupied by a vintage Laundromat, it could be said that Successfully Dressed lacked certain things. Like spaciousness. Level floors. And working A/C. But what it lacked in largeness and coolness, it more than made up for in style.

The walls were plaster, recently and creatively painted by Lucy's artist friend Vincent. The ceiling was hung with one crystal chandelier and several crinkly paper lanterns—except for the corner by the rear office, where the leftover Christmas lights were. The floor was concrete, cracked, and practical.

One row of washing machines remained from the original layout. So did a bunch of irons and ironing boards—with covers quilted by Nieca—and the wall of '60s-era, aqua-colored antique clothes dryers. These days, the dryers' bubble-shaped windows sported collages of ready-for-work outfits instead of spinning clothes. And the wheeled laundry carts nearby—bought for a steal from the previous owner—displayed sensible pumps and men's neckties instead of dirty socks.

Most of the additional space was taken up with overstuffed racks of clothing, cast-off mannequin heads wearing eccentric hats, and shelves of accessories. Every style and decade was represented, from pencil skirts to fedoras, from zoot suits to disco-era spandex—at least in the special vintage collectibles area, at least some of the time.

The truth was, despite the original owner's intentions, the bulk of Successfully Dressed's inventory these days consisted not of designer hand-me-downs but of work wear donated for their target customers—underprivileged women in need of interview and work clothing. That was exactly the way Lucy liked it.

Not that those women were exactly stampeding the place. You could practically hear the crickets chirping.

"Not too busy here, I guess?" Lucy asked.

"Nah, the usual." Nieca adjusted her plastic-framed Elvis Costello–style glasses, then crossed her arms over her chest. "Four legitimate clients, two browsers, and a tourist wanting directions to the science center."

"She seemed disappointed we couldn't point her to a dude ranch." Franco gave a knowing eye roll. "Or a gunfight."

They all nodded. To some people, Phoenix would never live down its Wild West heritage. It didn't matter that, here in the twenty-first century, the city had more to offer than saguaros, tumbleweeds, and kachina dolls. Tourists still wanted what they considered an "authentic" Arizona experience. They were willing to shell out big bucks to a five-star desert resort to accomplish that.

As long as bottomless margaritas and year-round golf privileges were included, of course.

"Hmmm. I seem to recall *somebody* looking pretty hard for a dude ranch when he first came here." Nieca fussed with Suzy the mannequin, adjusting one of her scarves a millimeter to the left. "Wearing a lot of cowboy hats too."

Franco looked affronted. "I was ten years old." He frowned at the jumble of rubber bracelets on his skinny wrist, plucking at one with black-polished fingernails. He kept them short for easy guitar playing. "I'm over it. Besides, you've got no room to talk, Ralphina Lauren. *You're* the one who found me those chaps at the second-hand store. I had such a rash—"

"Don't be a baby. You looked cute!"

"I looked stupid."

"Well. I got an A on that costuming project, didn't I?"

"Hey, hey." Lucy stepped in. "Let's not dredge up the traumas of last week, okay? What's done is done."

This time, they rolled their eyes at *her*. Then their gazes turned speculative. Nieca even quit fiddling with her scarf in mid-head-kerchief formation. With both hands at her nape, she stared at Lucy, her brown eyes wide behind her specs.

"You look different," she said. "Something happened, didn't it? Tell me!"

"No! Nothing happened." Lucy gave a nervous chuckle. "Not a thing. What could have happened?" Briskly, she strode toward the back of the shop. *Don't even* think *about Mr. Tighty-Whities. Don't do it.* She glanced up. "Have either of you seen the inventory book?"

Nieca gasped. "Now I *know* something's up! You just passed by that new Ziggy Stardust concert T-shirt without stopping."

"Or even," Franco added momentously, "slowing down."

Lucy tried to laugh it off. It didn't work.

"You *love* T-shirts featuring tall, androgynous, super-stylish seventies pop stars." Nieca rushed to the back of the shop, a concerned expression on her face. "What's the matter?"

Lucy smiled. "Nothing!" she insisted. "Come on. I'm fine, aside from the ramen noodle overload I've been suffering from lately." Things had been kind of tight in the finance department. "Seriously. I'm fine."

Franco followed, his head-to-toe black melding with the rack of men's suits behind him. "No, you're not fine. You look . . ." He peered closer. "Horny! Hot damn! You met a man, didn't you."

Nieca peered too. She nodded. "A *special* man."

Lucy gawked. How did they *do* that? It was as if her friends reached inside her head, shook up her brain like a Magic 8 ball, and read the results in big block letters.

"Yeah, I know." Nieca nodded, her features perked in an impish grin. "Just like a Magic 8 ball. You told me that one, remember?"

Lucy rued the day. Seriously.

"Come on," Nieca urged. "I brought tofu salad sandwiches today for lunch." They took turns bringing lunches for everyone, rotating the duty to spread out the work and split the costs. Inevitably, Nieca's contribution was vegan. Also garnished. You could take the girl out of fashion school, but you couldn't take the fashion out of the girl. "We can talk about your new manwich while we eat."

"Yeah. You two go ahead." Franco waved toward the back office. "I'll watch the shop."

"No," Lucy said. "There's nothing to talk about."

Nieca snorted. Her reddish braids bobbed with disbelief.

Franco shook his head. "Sure there is. I can tell. They don't call me The Fabulous Franco for nothing."

Lucy and Nieca stared at him.

"The Fabulous Franco?"

"Nobody calls you that."

He winked. "Someday they will, baby. Someday they will."

Franco sauntered away, his skinny ass all but walking itself out of his low-slung black pants as he went. Probably the weight of his multistudded, triple-wrapped, black leather belt had something to do with that, Lucy figured.

But Franco would never get rid of the thing, regardless of its recklessness when pitted against his string bean body. He was obsessed with the '80s. With punk rock. And with his almost-a-Mohawk hair. If he had his way, his fledgling garage band and the Clash would both rock the Casbah again someday.

"Resistance is futile." Nieca grabbed Lucy's arm and hauled her into the office. "Tell me everything."

There was no point in keeping things secret, Lucy decided. Her friends knew her too well. Besides, on the karmic balance sheet of life, juicy gossip always trumped discretion. Everybody knew that.

Still, she felt weirdly reluctant to discuss things. Killing time, she nudged aside a stack of mail, rearranged a glittering pile of donated costume jewelry, then dropped into the salvaged beauty shop dryer chair that served as her desk seating. Its perforated plastic helmet hovered over her head like a halo—not that her thoughts since meeting the hunkalicious Max Nolan had been anything close to angelic.

"I have a crush," she admitted.

Nieca's eyes lit up.

Rapidly, Lucy clarified, "Not that it's going anyplace! I'm way too busy with things here. The *last* thing I have time for is a man. Especially a man like this one."

She paused, sucked into a compelling remembrance of Max's naked torso. His sinewy arms. His sexed-up smile. Something about him had appealed to her right away. Possibly his nudity. Or his I-dare-you demeanor. At least it had until he'd opened his stupid (sexy) mouth and shattered all her illusions about his supposedly romantic chase.

For a second there, she'd really believed . . .

Lucy shook herself out of it. "Besides, he's—"

She gestured futilely, trying to illustrate the extent of Max Nolan's wrongness for her. Despite his endearing dimple. And his nice hands. When he'd laid them on her truck window to stop her, she'd hardly been able to look away. They'd looked big and strong and very, very capable. Just the way she liked them.

"Married?" Nieca guessed. "Gay? Republican?" A pensive expression. "No. Wait. Oh God. He's franchising a Starbucks, isn't he? That's why you didn't want to tell me."

As a devout supporter of independent small businesses, Nieca was horrified by chain stores in general and Starbucks in particular. A Frappuccino had never crossed her lips. She swore one never would.

"He probably *goes* to Starbucks," Lucy admitted.

"'Nuf said. He's not our type."

"*Our type?*"

"Come on." Nieca settled in the chair opposite the desk, curling up beside the reclaimed gym lockers that housed all the employees' belongings while at work. She gave Lucy a no-nonsense look. It was pretty incongruous, coming from her. "You know we have to vet your dating choices. You can't be trusted on your own. Ever since the Seth debacle—"

"That was an accident." Yes, Lucy tended to be a little too trusting sometimes. Sure. Maybe even veering toward gullible, in some cases, due to her live-and-let-live philosophy. She generally expected the best of people and wasn't often disappointed. But it wasn't fair to bring up Seth. "How was I supposed to know he was only dating me to get closer to the Dragon Lady?"

"And to get closer to *Mr.* Dragon Lady. Don't forget that."

Lucy rolled her eyes. "How could I? He practically trampled me trying to get to him."

She shook her head over the memory. As she did, a copy of the *New Times* caught her eye, poking from beneath one of Franco's '80s punk CDs. Grateful for the distraction, Lucy grabbed the alternative weekly.

She didn't want to talk about the shop's official—if absentee—owners. Successfully Dressed was hers now. Hers to run, to handle, to manage. Seth wasn't. Which was all for the better, really. He'd never understood her or her friends.

She turned the pages, scanning the articles.

"You can try to look busy," Nieca prodded, "but I know all the signs. The Ziggy Stardust T-shirt was only the beginning. You're smitten with this guy. Whoever he is." She waited. Impatiently. Then, "Is that new lipstick?"

"Hmmm." Lucy squinted, deliberately *not* puckering her freshly enhanced Va-va-voom Pink lips. So what if she'd gotten an (admittedly uncharacteristic) urge to primp today? "I wonder how we can get featured in here. We can use all the press we can get, now that the Dragon Lady is out of the picture."

The "Dragon Lady"—aka, Cornelia Burnheart, professional society maven—had provided the shop with plenty of media exposure while she'd been fully involved with Successfully Dressed. But these days, getting attention was considerably harder.

"Maybe I'll invite one of the *New Times* reporters to dinner," Lucy mused. "Jade's having a macrobiotic potluck next week. That might work. I can try some of that . . . what's it called? Networking."

Nieca made a face. "Eat this." She unwrapped a tofu salad sandwich on wheat and shoved it across the desk to Lucy. "Your low blood sugar is obviously causing you to hallucinate. You're talking business. Including the lingo."

She shuddered, then took a bite of her own lunch.

"I *have* to talk business. It's my job now. Besides, it keeps me from talking about tighty-whities."

Whoops. She hadn't meant to say that. Whatever barrier prevailed for most people between their private thoughts and their blurted-out confessions just didn't exist for Lucy.

"Tighty-whities, huh? Interesting. I would have pegged you more as a hemp boxers or commando type when it comes to men." Nieca grinned. "What's his name?"

Lucy swallowed, feeling restored. There was nothing like a good tofu salad sandwich. She hoped nobody would mind Ramen Noodle Casserole Surprise—again—tomorrow when it was her turn.

Blithely, she shrugged. "Doesn't matter. I'll probably never see him again."

She considered Max Nolan, his residence at Big Shot Central, and his look of horror when she'd suggested volunteering. The man might be hot, but he wasn't exactly brimming over with generosity. Plus, he'd tried to bribe her. That was not a point in his favor.

"He's not my type."

"*You* have a type?" Nieca looked skeptical.

Lucy never had before. Diversity had always been a big attraction for her. Also availability. And sometimes well-kept dreadlocks. But when it came to Max Nolan and his aggravatingly obvious *lack* of interest in her . . .

Yeah, Lucy decided. She had a type, all right. Starting

today. And it *wasn't* self-absorbed, supermacho, ridiculously superstitious businessmen.

"Like I said, I'll probably never see him again."

"But it would suck if you didn't. Right . . . ?"

Not taking the bait, Lucy bit into her sandwich again. Casually, she turned the *New Times* pages.

"Come *on!*" Nieca wiggled in her chair, practically bursting with pent-up matchmaking tendencies. "Throw me a bone, will you? My designs are going nowhere, school is predictable, and this place takes up all the rest of my time. Except for my TV boyfriend, Jon Stewart—who at *least* is faithfully there for me every night at eight—the closest thing to a love life I've got is yours."

"Wow. Still faithful to Jon, huh?" Lucy shook her head. "You've got to get out more."

"Hey. All I want is a guy who can crack wise now and then. And maybe write me a poem or two."

"Poetry? Seriously?" Lucy looked at Nieca in surprise. Mushy, gushy romantic stuff wasn't really her thing. But her friend only shrugged in acknowledgment. "Well, poetry's a long shot, but . . . wait, I've got it!" She glanced down. "Here's a personal ad. At least this guy can write. That's a start."

"Fine. *Don't* tell me about your secret hottie." Morosely, Nieca twisted the stems of her parsley and oregano garnish into topiary origami. "Who needs another vicarious love life, anyway."

"This guy." Still perusing the paper, Lucy pointed to an ad. "Because his version of a real-life love life is downright scary. Seriously."

On the verge of describing all the reasons why, she glanced up to make sure Nieca was listening. The forlorn expression on her friend's face brought out every ounce of Lucy's natural softheartedness. She couldn't stand to see her pal unhappy.

Even if Nieca's self-professed poetry jones doomed her to romantic disappointment.

"Okay. Tell you what," Lucy compromised. "If a big-business type shows up to volunteer"—*as if*—"that'll be him. If you want, you can have first crack at hooking us up."

Nieca brightened. "Really?"

If Lucy had thought there was a chance in hell Max Nolan would actually show up, ever, Nieca's matchmaking zeal might have worried her. As it was . . .

What were the odds? Probably a gazillion to one.

The man wore Calvin Klein boxer briefs, after all. Designer clothes. She'd glimpsed his printed waistband when she'd been checking out his abs. Nobody like Max Nolan would ever set foot inside Successfully Dressed.

I don't do my own laundry. Much less somebody else's.

"Yes. You can pimp me like crazy. No problem." Lucy gave her friend a reassuring shoulder squeeze. She liked it better when everyone was getting along. "Okay? Happy now?"

Smiling, Nieca nodded. Vigorously. "Don't worry. If this guy really is wrong for you, I can be a major pit bull too."

"Uh-huh. Right." Lucy took in Nieca's petite-but-curvy figure, her braids, and her happy-go-lucky expression. "Let's just hope it doesn't come to that, okay?"

A pause. Then, "He's a businessman, huh? Kinky." Nieca waggled her eyebrows playfully. "Well dressed? Nice suits?"

Lucy flashed on broad shoulders, powerful arms, and a midsection taut enough to lick cream from. Yum. As fantasy fodder, Max Nolan was . . . well, pretty close to perfect.

"I wouldn't know." Casually, she turned another page. "So far, I've only seen him in his underwear."

The silence that fell next didn't faze her at first. Then,

prodded by Nieca's uncharacteristic lack of commentary, Lucy glanced up. Her friend stared, openmouthed, at her.

So did Franco, from the doorway.

"*So far?*" he repeated. "What kind of player *is* this guy, Lucy?"

"Oh, I dunno. The usual kind?"

Franco wasn't amused. "Because if he's planning on hurting you, he'll have to go through me first."

Nieca poked him meaningfully in the ribs.

"Me and Nieca," he amended.

Right. "What are you going to do?" Lucy asked, stifling a smile. "Knock him unconscious with your belt studs?"

"If I have to." Franco raised his chin. "Yes. Somebody has to look out for you, you know."

"*I'll* look out for me. Besides, he's not going to—hey. Quit smirking, you two. I'm not *that* gullible."

"You're easily hurt," Nieca reminded her.

"Remember Seth?" Franco added.

Geez. One hot hunk in tighty-whities and half her staff jumped up to yellow alert. "I'm busy. I'm not looking for a relationship, okay? So you two can just chill already."

They shared a look. "She's wearing lipstick," Nieca said.

Franco's eyes widened. "Red alert. *Red* alert."

Lucy escaped the madness by heading for the store-room to sort shoe donations. Max Nolan wasn't coming to volunteer, and that was that. She—and her fantasies—were perfectly safe.

3

Oliver Pickett calculated the probability of his partner's being late to their crucial Phoenix start-up meeting—based on experience, weather conditions, and traffic—at approximately twenty percent. If including potential hangovers, the odds rose to twenty-two percent. If including the Sarabeth factor ([wardrobe changes] $\times$ [mood swings] $\pm$ [Max's libido] = [time runs backward]), the odds increased to forty percent.

Still, Oliver wasn't seriously worried until the handshakes and small talk outside his office degenerated into mumbling and complaining. The natives were getting restless. Although the likelihood of Max's being involved in a punctuality-impairing accident was less than two hundred to one, Oliver buzzed his new administrative assistant anyway. Just in case.

"Marlene. What's happening out there?"

Her phone headset crackled. He pictured her cupping it with one manicured hand for privacy. "One of the lawyers just looked at his watch. The donuts are gone. It's getting ugly."

Oliver dismissed the watch comment. Lawyers charged by the hour. They were statistically likely to develop time fixations.

The donut issue was more serious. "I thought the people from the real estate agency were bringing three dozen. At one and a half donuts per person—per fifteen-minute-noshing increment—that's a paltry consumable rate of—"

"Look," Marlene interrupted. "The clients are inking mustaches and devil horns on your picture in the company portfolio. If Max doesn't get here soon, we're screwed."

Marlene was an earthy type, not the sort of person Oliver typically hired. But her employment test scores had impressed him to the point of taking a chance. He should have known he'd live to regret ignoring those three-to-one odds.

Still, meeting clients was definitely *not* Oliver's forte.

"Max will be here." Hoping he sounded more assured than he felt, Oliver went to his office window. He squinted at the sun sparks shooting from the downtown traffic, three floors distant, as it crawled through the June heat waves. No sign of Max's red sports car. "He knows we're meeting to close the property acquisition today. He'd never—"

More crackling cut him off. A thud. Then, urgently, "The APR has just gone through the roof. I repeat, the APR has just gone through the roof."

Their code phrase. Marlene had chuckled when he'd explained it during their new-employee orientation, but nobody was laughing now. Oliver gripped the phone in one suddenly damp hand. With the other, he loosened his tie.

"Maybe you're mistaken." But he heard more muttering through the phone line, and a thump sounded outside his deluxe office door. That thing was constructed to dampen any sound. If his impatient visitors were *that* rowdy . . . "Sit tight, Marlene. And don't worry. I'll be right there."

"Ten-four. Roger that. Over and out."

Click. He really needed to speak with her about getting carried away with the code. Those phrases were not on the approved list.

But for now, Oliver had a job to do. At the door, he paused. He sucked in a deep breath and counted to ten. It didn't help slow his pounding heart or curb the rate of perspiration dampening his armpits. Damn it. All the signs were there. It was happening again.

Oliver steeled himself. Biofeedback be damned. He was going in anyway. For Marlene.

What most people didn't know about him—what most people didn't see beneath his brainpower, his calm appearance, and his reliable, custom-made navy suits—was the crippling shyness that had kept him from going out on his own. The shyness that had plagued him since boyhood and kept him under its thumb all through college and business school and life beyond. He hated it, but he couldn't change it. Now only Marlene's need for a potential defender could have made him face it.

But he still wished he'd have reached Max on his damned cell phone so none of this would be necessary.

Oliver contemplated the scene to come. His idea of hell was a room full of strangers with no corners to hide in. That was pretty much what he was facing now. One on one, he could function pretty well. With, he'd estimated, at least ninety-three percent efficiency. But when faced with a crowd, all his statistics went out the window. So did his self-confidence.

He hesitated, selecting several more colorful swearwords for Max. When he saw his partner, he would whip off his sweaty tie and strangle him with it. How could he do this to him?

No amount of self-help, hypnosis, or triple-malt Scotch had ever cured Oliver's disability . . . although he had learned to compensate for it. When it came to facts or figures or written negotiations, he rocked the house. No false modesty required there. But when it came to interpersonal relations, Oliver suffered complete meltdowns.

Except with Max, whom he'd known nearly all his life.

Those qualities made the two of them perfect business partners. Oliver saw to the details, Max to the networking. Together they'd cobbled together a series of groundbreaking developments in industries ranging from high tech to hydroponics, from winemaking to wool-spinning. Wherever there was a need for innovation, Max and Oliver were there, and had been since business school.

But today, the asshole had let him down. Which could only mean one thing.

Somehow, Oliver had miscalculated the Sarabeth factor.

Girding his courage, he grabbed the doorknob. He plastered a smile on his face, reminding himself of the research study he'd read, which had proved that people formed a greater number of positive first impressions of smiling people. Then, feeling as prepared as he was likely to get, he entered the melee.

By the time Max walked into the suite of central-corridor offices he and Oliver had leased, he was thirty minutes late. The dubious "driving techniques" he'd practiced to get there had left him seriously unnerved, not to mention white knuckled and in dire need of coffee. Usually, he was a confident and expert driver, but without his lucky suit . . .

Christ. Without that, who could expect a man to function normally? Nobody had expected Michael Jordan to sink a three-pointer without wearing his baby blue Tar Heel shorts under his Bulls uniform, had they? No. They hadn't.

The reception area was deserted, so Max strode to the

boardroom with his cell phone to his ear. The sounds of shouting and thumping drowned out the voice of his contact on the other end, forcing him to end his call early. Apparently, in his absence, all hell had broken loose.

Curious, he fisted his phone. This meeting was supposed to contain two real estate agents, a handful of lawyers, and the family members who were selling Max and Oliver their Phoenix-based properties. So why did it sound as if a football team was scrimmaging down the hall?

Adrenaline pumping, Max took the few remaining strides to the boardroom. He loved this part of the business. Lived for it. The final negotiations, the meeting-and-greeting, the deal-sealing handshakes and backslapping. He liked meeting people, and he liked doing business. Since he'd been a kid hawking Space Invaders video game lessons, he'd sought out ways to turn boring solitary activities into new and improved social ones—and he'd succeeded every time. Max relished a challenge.

Inside, the boardroom buzzed with noise and activity. No one noticed him at first. Every adult in the place seemed in the throes of a full-on sugar high. Papers flew, cell phones rang, and one of the lawyers tapped text messages on his BlackBerry. Nobody appeared happy. As Max might have expected, their deal looked on the verge of complete collapse.

He spotted Oliver. His partner hunched near the windows at the far end of the room, cornered by two frustrated-looking members of the Ruiz family. Their properties—former convenience stores that dotted the valley like freckles on a redhead—would form the test-market locales for Max and Oliver's new venture.

At least they would, if Max could salvage this situation.

A harried-looking Marlene approached the doorway, bearing a shiny coffee urn in her arms.

"Save yourself." She jerked her head toward Oliver. "If you can, save him too. The poor fella means well."

Max pursed his lips. He gauged the situation. He nodded, sure of only one thing. "No problem."

Sighing with evident relief, she edged past him. "Try telling Oliver that. His face will turn purple."

Grinning, Max watched her go. He waited a precise amount of time, then leaned sideways for a better look at her legs.

As both of them had known she would, Marlene caught him. She guffawed in her good-natured way, making all the laugh lines in her face stand out in bold relief.

"I know, nice legs for an old broad like me, right? Now go." She shooed him inside. "Work your magic, hot stuff."

Feeling cheered, Max turned back to the boardroom. He didn't like working without a net. This time, he guessed, his natural talents would simply have to be enough.

Less than an hour later, Oliver stood in the reception area, weak-kneed with relief as he watched the last meeting participant shake hands with Max.

"Don't forget about that Little League game," Mrs. Ruiz cautioned him, her face wreathed in smiles. "Ricky will expect to see you there."

"I wouldn't miss it," Max assured her.

More small talk followed. Then, on a stream of smiles and laughter, the meeting officially ended. The participants strolled down the exterior hall, and the elevator zoomed downstairs. The office door creaked shut, leaving Oliver alone with his partner.

And Marlene, of course. But since she hadn't quit glaring at him for an earlier coffee-spilling incident, Oliver figured she didn't want to be counted as part of any group he was in.

Nevertheless, this was the moment he'd waited for. Loosening his tie, Oliver rounded on Max.

"Why are you dressed like that?" he demanded. He waved his hand at Max's open-collared shirt, casual shorts, and flip-flops. In an office setting, his hairy legs looked twice as Cro-Magnon. "The Ruizes's daughter was checking you out! So, in fact, was Mrs. Ruiz—much to Mr. Ruiz's chagrin. Are you mental?"

Max's smile dimmed. "Oliver, hang on, buddy—"

"I can't *believe* you were late today. Today, of all days." He felt his blood pressure rising. "What happened this time? Did Sarabeth break a fingernail, or what?"

"Sarabeth dumped me."

"Oh, that's too bad!" came Marlene's sympathetic voice from across the room. "You poor thing! I knew that girl was no good for you. She's got 'withholding narcissist' written all over her—anybody could see it."

Oliver ignored her. This was no time for pop psychology. "Damn it, Max. You nearly torpedoed this whole deal."

"Ahhh." He had the nerve to grin. "But I didn't."

Right. Technically, this wasn't the first time Max had charged in like Sir Galahad to save the day, either. That was true. But that didn't mean Oliver had to like it. *He* contributed to their partnership too, damn it.

"The deal didn't go off the way we planned, though, did it?" he pointed out. Max only shrugged, looking aggravatingly oblivious to how much this change of plans unsettled Oliver. "And another thing! I still don't have your expense report, you dickhead. Is it finished?"

"I don't know. I'll check." Max strolled to Marlene's desk. He rested his forearms on it, offering her a friendly look. "How is that expense report coming along, Marlene?"

"One box of Cuban cigars away from being finished, boss."

"Excellent. Nice work."

"Thanks." Marlene blushed to the roots of her teased-up, mile-high hair. She fiddled with her jar of pens. "Anything for you, Max. I'm happy to do it."

Max looked her up and down. "By the way, I like your hair like that. It looks good. Sexy."

The two of them smiled, seeming utterly relaxed.

Oliver *never* felt that relaxed. Especially around women. Even women old enough, as Marlene was, to be his mother.

"Really hot," Max elaborated, touching a hair-sprayed curl.

Oliver groaned, barely resisting an urge to smack his forehead. "Jesus, Max. That's hardly appropriate. Don't you know that the rate of sexual harassment suits is rising every single—"

"It's a Frost 'N' Glow kit." Marlene primped, plainly loving the attention. "My niece Veronica did it for me."

"Don't change a thing." Max framed her face with his hands, like a photographer composing a picture. "You'll break my heart if you do. Gotta run. I've got papers to sign."

"I'll just bet you do, hotshot." A wink. "Thank God you got here in time, that's all I have to say. You've got a gift. A gift for bringing people together. That was something to see in there." Marlene angled her head toward the boardroom. "Really impressive."

"Aw shucks, Marlene. I only did my part. You'll give me a big head if you go on talking like that."

"I mean it! You deserve it. Well done, stud."

They both laughed.

Dumbfounded, Oliver stared. The sheer ridiculousness of Max's charisma never failed to leave him speechless. If he'd possessed a mere one-tenth of Max's machismo, plus one-sixth of his personal charm, he'd have spent the past fifteen years of his life getting laid. Period. Screw business; bring on the ladies.

"You're too kind, Marlene," Max said.

He reached—as usual—for his cell phone, the universal sign he was getting down to business. He turned toward his office. It adjoined Oliver's and was theoretically identical in layout and design, but somehow Max's digs felt . . . swankier.

"Oh, wait! I almost forgot." Marlene crooked her finger to motion Max closer again. As he propped his hip comfortably on her desk, she pulled something from her drawer. "I saved a donut for you," she cooed. "I hope you like maple frosted."

Oliver frowned. He *loved* maple frosted.

"My favorite." Max grinned. "If I weren't an honorable guy, I swear I'd steal you away from that husband of yours."

Marlene tittered like a schoolgirl.

"All right, all right. Break up the love fest." Oliver snapped his fingers. "We've got work to do."

Leisurely, Max rose. He looked as if he'd never heard the word *work* and couldn't be expected to spell it, much less actually practice it.

Marlene just looked forlorn. "Lunch later, Max?"

He hesitated. For a minute, an uncharacteristically pensive expression crossed his face, which was—Oliver noticed for the first time—*unshaven*, damn it. Max seemed on the verge of confessing something, but then . . .

"I'll have to take a rain check. Something came up."

Marlene pouted but handed over the donut all the same.

Oliver shook his head. He'd just *bet* "something came up." Something like an illicit assignation with Max's inevitable Sarabeth replacement. Given his knack with women—with everything, frankly—he'd probably tripped over a stunning brunette on his way to work today. He'd probably had to scrub her lipstick prints from his too-casually-attired chest before joining the meeting.

Max stuck the donut in his mouth. He gave a wolfish moan of appreciation—probably learned at the brunette's feet—then headed for his office. The cheerful swagger in his step only bothered Oliver all the more. He liked Max. Really, he did. But sometimes . . . sometimes his friend's *ease* got on his nerves.

He faced Marlene. She looked surprised to see him there.

"Oh, are you still here?"

"Very funny." Oliver leaned on her desk, trying out the gesture. He waggled his eyebrows suggestively. "Got any more goodies in your drawers?"

The telltale menthol aroma of Vicks VapoRub roused Max shortly after he arrived in his office. That had to mean Oliver was nearby. Wearily, he lifted his head from the cradle of his arms. He tried to look as if he hadn't been dumped, late, and only partially successful in this morning's exploits.

"Hey," Oliver said. "We need to talk."

Max glanced up. Surprise widened his eyes. "Holy shit, Probability Man. That might be a shiner you've got going."

Gingerly, his partner touched his face. In contrast with his dark curly hair and pale skin, the bright hand-shaped imprint on Oliver's cheek really stood out.

"Marlene and I had a misunderstanding about the donuts."

"Yeah. So I see." Max shoved his maple frosted across the desk. "Have mine. I'm not hungry."

He hadn't been hungry all morning, he realized. In fact, he felt weird and out of sorts and vaguely unlike himself. Probably due to Sarabeth's freak-out. Not to mention his run-in with Ms. Do-Gooder and her incredible purple-haired bargaining skills. He couldn't remember the last time a woman had one-upped him. Grudgingly, he had to respect her for that.

Oliver reached for the donut, then blanched. "It's got a bite out of it."

"So? Pour on some of that sanitizer crap you use and chow down. It's still good." Max looked his friend in the eye. He had to own up to his mistakes—that's what a man did. "Sorry about this morning—things got out of hand. I didn't mean to leave you hanging. I got here as soon as I could."

"It's all right." Oliver shrugged, moving his gangly body to the chair opposite the desk. As always, he looked on the verge of doing anything except what he was actually doing—standing when he was sitting or frowning when he was smiling. "Things worked out. Except for that alteration in the investor clause, of course."

Max didn't want to talk about it. "It'll be okay."

"Sure. *If* we can secure some additional investors to re-assure the Ruizes this venture has merit. Otherwise—" Oliver hooked his thumb to the door and whistled—the universal sign of *we're out of here.* "Back to the drawing board."

"I can get investors," Max assured him.

But right now, he didn't much feel like it. As far as he was concerned, the last-minute change to their deal signified only one thing. His luck was already vanishing.

He had to get his suit back.

"You'll need to schmooze your ass off to keep this deal hammered together," Oliver warned him. "No more stunts like the one you came up with today. I mean it."

"I pulled it off." He gave his friend a *back off* frown, not feeling in the mood for Oliver's buttoned-down philosophy on life. "That's what counts. In the end, I always deliver."

A reluctant nod. "But this venture is different. You weren't quite on board with the idea from its incept—"

"I said I'll do it."

Max stood, needing to move. To do *something*. He hadn't had the heart for more phone calls, despite his usual habit of keeping his cell phone glued to his ear for 24/7 networking. The solitude of his office—until Oliver had arrived—had felt too good. He rolled out the kinks in his shoulders.

"Fine," Oliver told him. "See that you do 'do it.'"

At the window, Max gave a rueful grin. He'd give Oliver credit for one thing—he didn't back down. The man might be soft-spoken, obsessed with facts, and as gentle as a Teletubby, but he was no pushover. Some people saw Oliver's reticence and judged it as snobbishness or stupidity, but Max knew better. He knew they were wrong. Oliver was brilliant with everything except people, and even that would come along eventually.

Plus or minus a few black eyes along the way.

"So, are you going to tell me what's up?" Oliver asked.

Stalling for time, Max gazed at the city sprawled below him. Like L.A., Phoenix was a conglomeration of suburbia and downtown, with pockets of high rises and office buildings. Palm trees dotted the landscape, and so did cacti. Multiple freeways snaked through the grid of the city itself, connecting it with the outlying commerce- and industry-centric neighboring towns.

At first glance, Phoenix didn't look like one of the fastest-growing urban areas in the country, but Oliver's research had told them it was. Max intended to capitalize on that. Capitalizing on opportunities was one of the things he did best.

"Sarabeth left me." He staved off Oliver's polite commiseration with a wave. "Yes, after all those trips, all that jewelry, all that late-night clubbing. Blah, blah, blah. Don't bother with the pity routine. I know you didn't like her. The timing was bad, though."

"Yes. It was."

Wincing, Max splayed his fingers over the window glass. It felt frigid beneath his palm, cooled by the air-conditioning. It was true he hadn't exactly handed over his heart to Sarabeth, but . . . "Jesus, Oliver. Have a little sensitivity, will you?"

"Eh, you'll bounce back. You always do."

Max thought about it.

He gave a grunt of assent.

Oliver knew him better than anyone else—probably better than his family, whom he only saw a few times a year during his infrequent sojourns back to Austin. When it came to close ties, Max liked to keep them loose. Loose and comfy.

"In the meantime," Oliver continued gleefully, "you can spend *all* your energy on work. Work, work, work."

Max eyeballed him. "Careful. You'll piss your pants with excitement."

His partner gave him the finger. Max returned the favor. With that out of the way, he surveyed his credenza. Usually Marlene kept fresh, pitch-black brew in his coffeemaker, but today the pot was empty. He picked up a bottle of water from the assortment nearby and swigged.

An instant later, he spewed the whole mouthful.

"What the fuck is *that?*"

Oliver pulled an elaborately innocent face. "Water. For our project. Remember?" He offered Max a bundle of tissues. "Samples from potential suppliers have been arriving for weeks, ever since we leased this space. This is the overflow supply."

Max wiped his mouth, then his shirt. Water beaded on his credenza and dripped in the silence to his rug. He glared at the bottle in his hand.

Poultry flavor.

"You might have warned me, asshole."

"And miss the look on your face? Not hardly."

Max put down the water bottle, coughing up the dregs

of improbably meaty-tasting liquid. He swabbed his tongue over his teeth, reminded of Thanksgiving turkeys and Dog Chow. It was a heinous combination.

"We're not making a dime selling that shit. It's foul."

"Millions of pet owners will prove you wrong," Oliver disagreed. "Or I should say, 'pet guardians' will prove you wrong. That's the new PC term, I understand. Pet guardians. Their pets are like children to them. Itty, bitty, precious little—"

"—furry, stinky—"

"—spoiled children. They'll be flocking to give them some of this"—Oliver peered at the deceptively ordinary-looking bottle—"vitamin, mineral, and antioxidant-fortified water with authentic poultry and bacon flavor."

"Bacon too? Ugh." Max stuck out his tongue, wishing he could scour it with a gigantic Altoids mint. "I'm not buying it. I *like* bacon. That had to be some kind of vegetarian soy crap in there. That's it. It was soy crap flavor."

Oliver looked amused. "Here. Try one of these."

It looked like the mint he'd just wished for. Gratefully, Max popped it in his mouth.

"It's a new formula with chlorophyll and mint extract to kill germs," Oliver explained, his scholarly air firmly in place. "Very effective as a doggie breath aid."

Max spat. The bogus mint pinged from a display of monogrammed pet carriers.

He stared. "Holy shit. It turned green."

"Yes." Oliver leaned closer. "It did. Interesting. Saliva-activated coloring agents, more than likely. Eighty-seven percent of dogs are droolers, you know."

"You're enjoying this, you bastard."

But Max said it good-naturedly, and Oliver accepted the rebuke in similar spirit. With a loopy smile—like the one he wore while explaining the odds of something as obscure as picking a watermelon from your nose—he rose from his chair.

He approached the credenza and swept his arm toward the objects arrayed on it. Max recognized his friend's windup into Mr. Professor mode. He wished he had a mute button. The only interesting thing about business was succeeding at it.

Right on cue, Oliver drew a preparatory breath. "These products are really very simple. Let me explain."

"You should hire a hot game-show hostess to do that," Max observed. He crossed his arms over his spotty, poultry-scented shirt. Now he'd have to scrounge up another one from his unpacked luggage at his loft. "The hand gestures look kind of prissy on you, pal."

"Bite me." No one but Oliver could have made the rejoinder sound quite so precise. Or so jolly. "If you'd paid the slightest attention to the information I've compiled, you would have known what all these things were— along with their suggested retail prices, markups, selling points, and discount schedules."

Those details were Oliver's arena. They both knew that.

"Okay, okay," Max said, finally catching on. "You're pissed because I was late. I get the picture." He warded off further boring, blah-blah detail talk with both palms. "I'll find us some investors. I promise."

"You promise?"

Uncomfortably, Max shifted. He didn't take a promise lightly, and neither did his partner. He nodded.

As though gauging the value of his word, Oliver gave him a serious look. Thoughtfully, he rubbed his suit-clad wrist over his temple. The movement was typically uneasy and habitually *Oliver,* through and through. His sleeve, too long for him, flapped with the gesture.

That sleeve was what did it. All at once, Max flashed on the day he and Oliver had met. He'd come around the corner from the lunchroom, filled with third-grade light-heartedness. He'd been thinking of not much beyond how

He-Man could trounce Batman if they ever mixed it up. Then he'd spied a skinny kid on the ground near the jungle gyms, just sitting there, not bugging anybody, drawing with a stick in the dirt.

Later, he'd found out that Oliver had been drawing congruent triangles, inspired by a fifty-page peek ahead in their *Fun with Geometry!* book. But at the time, all Max had known was that Jimmy Truemore, the jerkface, had come by and stomped all over that kid's drawings, for no reason at all. Then he'd laughed and shoved that kid in the dirt.

Max had always hated bullies. So it wasn't surprising that several sweaty and jumbled minutes later, he'd found himself in the principal's office with a bloody nose, a set of scraped knuckles, and a friend for life.

Starting on that day, Oliver had been the only one who'd ever stuck by him.

"Hey." Max pointed to a froufrou collection of pink pet collars. They looked like something a Las Vegas showgirl would wear—if she were furry and walked on four legs. "I haven't seen these before. What are they?"

As he'd expected, Oliver launched into a long-winded explanation involving Swarovski crystals, hand-dyed ostrich feathers, and—if Max heard him right—aromatherapy.

Through the whole thing, Max nodded attentively. He even chimed in at the "coordinating quilted pet carriers" part. Because talking like an expert made Oliver happy. And seeing Oliver happy . . . well, that kind of made up for the crappy morning Max had had so far.

"What about these?" he asked during a lull.

Oliver flashed him a delighted look and took off on another detail-crammed ramble. Stretching his arms out, leaning back in his chair, Max propped up his feet and listened with satisfaction. At least something in his world was going well.

Oliver's voice came back into range. ". . . which is why

it's crucial that we secure every one of those properties," he
was saying. "With local investors to bolster our position."

Hell. Or not.

"I'll get on it," Max assured him. "Don't worry."

Silence.

Max glanced up. Just as he'd feared, one look at Oliver
told him his friend *was* worried. This time, for more reasons than one, Max had to deliver.

4

"If you take off the jacket and try this cardigan, it makes two outfits in one." Lucy draped a pink cotton sweater over her customer's shoulders. "The suit is perfect for a job interview, and the sweater dresses down the skirt so it's just right for an ordinary workday. What do you think?"

They both examined the combination in the mirror. Propped in a corner near the fitting room, its elaborate gilt frame was dressier than most items in the shop. The woman reflected in it, a single mother named Tracee, made a face.

"I don't know . . . it's so 'old lady' looking. It's not me." She wriggled her shoulders, shrugging to dislodge the cardigan. "Thanks for trying to help, but it's getting late, and—"

"Wait! It can be you." Urgently, Lucy held up both hands. She wasn't letting Tracee go yet. "Just hang on."

Lucy headed for the Successfully Dressed accessories shelves, taking a discreet peek through the front window as she did. It had been two days since her run-in with Max Nolan. Not that she was counting. Or that she was expecting him to *really* volunteer. She was just saying, is all. Two days.

She returned to the mirror with a simple leather wrist cuff, a wide belt, and a funky turquoise pin. She showed Tracee how to fasten the cuff on her wrist, then how to pin up part of her skirt hem for a fresher, jagged silhouette.

"See? It's still work appropriate, but now it's a little edgier. Younger."

Tracee nodded. She bit her lip. "But what about the suit jacket? It looks like something my mom would wear. Ugh."

Lucy asked her to trade the cardigan for the jacket. The maneuver wasn't simple, since Tracee had to keep one eye on her toddler and another on her ponytailed three-year-old. They'd been roaming the store, hiding beneath the racks and making the clothes shimmy as they ran past them, since they arrived.

"Put that down! Not in your mouth." Tracee groaned, shaking her head. "I should've gotten a babysitter while I did this, but I'm gonna need one every day if I get a job, and—"

"Babysitters are expensive." Lucy paused in mid-tuck to give her a commiserating pat and a smile. "It's okay. There's nothing in here that's not kidproof. Besides, they're both so cute. Just look at those smiles."

"Yeah." Tracee's tense shoulders relaxed as she glanced at her children again. "You're right." She gave a gusty sigh. "You're really nice, you know? Usually I shop at the dollar store, but you can't find stuff like this in there. Even if you could, *I* wouldn't know how to put it together for a real job. I've only ever worked for minimum wage, like at McDonald's, and there you get a uniform. It smells like french fries, but—"

She broke off, staring in the mirror. Lucy made one last adjustment to the belt, then stepped back.

"There. See?" She smoothed down the jacket, then gave Tracee a reassuring squeeze to both arms. "With a belt over the jacket, it fits you much better. I took out the shoulder pads too. That boxy cut is what made it look too old to you."

The woman gawked. "It looks like a whole new suit!"

"Yep. And all for a grand total of . . ." Lucy hesitated, performing the necessary calculations in her head. They all went out the window when she saw Tracee swivel to sneak another thrilled glimpse in the mirror. "Nine dollars."

"Nine dollars!" Tracee wheeled to face her. "No way. You can't give me all this for nine dollars." She grabbed a hanging tag. "This says fifteen-fifty, just for the jacket."

But with that jacket, Lucy knew, Tracee would feel confident. She would ace her upcoming job interview.

Lucy wanted to see her succeed. Plus, Successfully Dressed wasn't exactly doing blowout business lately. Nine dollars was better than nothing, wasn't it?

"We're having a special today. The only catch is, you have to come back on Friday and tell me how your interview went."

Tracee gave her a skeptical look.

Lucy recognized that look. She'd seen it too many times on women who'd been left behind, left out . . . left to fend for themselves with few resources and even less hope. If she could make a difference for only one of those women, she figured her job was worthwhile.

"I mean it," she said sternly. "First thing after your interview, I want to see you in here with a full report. We're having an . . . um, special Successfully Dressed cocktail hour, and everyone who buys an interview suit this week is invited."

Tracee's face broke into a smile. "Ohmigod, you are *too* nice!" She grabbed Lucy for a grateful hug. When she leaned back, she swiped tears from her eyes. "I'll do a good job on that interview, I swear."

"I know you will." Lucy bundled the cardigan in her arms, then smiled as Tracee pivoted, model style, one more time. "You'll be great. Let me just get you a couple of our résumé and interview tip sheets while you change."

"This is too much." Pausing at the fitting room's curtained entrance, Tracee glanced down at her children. The little girl stood, wide-eyed, with the fingertips of one hand in her sticky-looking mouth. "Doesn't Mommy look pretty?"

Her toddler boy nodded. He pointed. "Purty."

"And when I get my first paycheck, I'll come buy a whole bunch of stuff in here!" Tracee told Lucy. "I promise."

"I hope you do." Clutching the sweater, Lucy headed for the cash register. "I'll start wrapping this up for you," she called over her shoulder.

She turned to find Nieca in her path, shaking her head. She held an armful of skirts, a pair of beat-up but salvageable slingbacks, and a tape measure.

"I guess we have a weekly happy hour now?"

Lucy nodded. "Sort of." Not wanting to elaborate, she nudged aside Franco, who'd been inking a skull and crossbones on the cash register's zero key.

He looked up. "Hey. Are you crying again?"

"Again?" Determinedly, Lucy searched the shelves below the register for the résumé and interview tip sheets. She blinked fiercely. "I don't know what you mean."

Bingo. She found the tip sheets, then lay two on the sweater. She started bagging the whole ensemble.

"We all know you're a soft touch when it comes to the hard-luck cases," Franco said. He yanked a black bandanna from his back pocket and handed it to her. "Here. Before she sees you."

"They don't take the discounts if they think they made you cry," Nieca pointed out, angling her head toward the fitting room. "Aside from which . . . what's got into you? Cocktail hour? You don't know squat about 'cocktail hour.'"

That was true. Lucy straightened, giving an offhanded

wave. "How hard can it be? A few drinks, a few friends—"

"It gets even better than that," a man said from the other side of the cash register. "Wrap it up, and I'll show you."

Lucy recognized that voice. Her smile—intended to show Franco and Nieca she was okay—froze on her lips.

Slowly, she raised her gaze.

It was just as bad as she'd expected. Max Nolan stood twelve inches away, and he looked—if anything—even better dressed.

"I'm surprised you came with me." Max offered Lucy a smile. He lowered his attention to his cut-crystal tumbler of bourbon, then ran his index finger around its damp rim. He sucked his fingertip clean. "Your coworkers seemed ready to give me a polygraph test, fingerprinting, *and* the third degree before they let me take you away."

"Yeah." Lucy forced her attention from his fingers. Something about the way he used them was positively mesmerizing. "I guess Nieca and Franco can be a little protective sometimes. They care about me. That's what friends are for."

Max gazed into his bourbon. For a moment, he looked troubled. She nudged him with her shoulder, hoping to jolly him out of it. Maybe he missed having cocktails with his own pals.

"If I met *your* friends, they'd probably call security." She mimed holding a walkie-talkie to her mouth. "Alert, alert! Purple-haired suspect is on the loose."

His mouth quirked. "Maybe." He swallowed his drink.

She fiddled with hers, testing the glass's condensation-slippery sides. She couldn't believe they hadn't had anything on tap here. No place was too fancy for Budweiser.

"I'm surprised you waited for me," she said. "It took

me a while to get Tracee settled and turn things over to Nieca."

Max shrugged, as though he hadn't minded killing time outside her fairly grungy downtown vintage clothing store when he could have been someplace like this. Someplace filled with cozy leather banquettes, deluxe dark paneling, and the muted strains of a piano playing in the corner.

The bar at the opposite end of the room was long, brass ornamented, and probably made of endangered tropical wood. The mirror behind it reflected bottles of liquor Lucy had neither tasted nor seen before. The clientele was subdued, the service impeccable, and the sense of privacy in their secluded alcove absolute.

On someone else, the atmosphere might have seemed cheesy. On Max, it seemed retro-cool and drop-dead sexy. Lucy ran her hand over their table's lush red cloth, enjoying its fineness in spite of herself. All kinds of illicit things probably went on beneath a tablecloth like this one.

Holding hands. Accidentally touching knees.

Feeling a palm slide subtly beneath your skirt, rising to your thigh, making you squirm. . . .

Whew. Clearing her throat, Lucy fixed her gaze on the candle flickering at their table's center. It cast elegant shadows on Max's hand as he cupped his empty glass. His wrists looked capable, too, she noticed. Flexible enough, in fact, to navigate around the droopy edge of that tablecloth.

Too bad she was wearing cast-off sailor pants with her halter top, miles of beaded necklaces, and clogs. Her pants made that palm-slide maneuver impossible. Next time she'd wear a skirt, Lucy decided. Maybe the new sequined miniskirt they'd gotten in yesterday. It would be perfect.

She felt her gaze drawn to Max's hands again. Mmmm. . . .

He caught her looking and arched his brow.

She grinned. So what if he knew she liked the way he looked? The way he handled his . . . hands. Lucy had the confidence not to get all goo-goo eyed and fluttery. Come on.

"You know, *somehow*," she mused, surveying their surroundings, "I doubt this is going to be as instructive as you promised. This probably isn't the kind of happy hour shindig we'll be able to throw at Successfully Dressed."

Max gave a thoughtful rumble. "I don't know about that. Everything's possible if you want it bad enough."

Something in his voice, some catch of emotion, caught her attention. Lucy looked at Max carefully. He'd shaved recently. Showered, too, by the soapy fresh smell of his skin. He'd rummaged up some clothes, and his button-up shirt and dark jeans were none too shabby—even if they weren't officially "lucky." And even if they were kind of ultraconservative.

Damn, ultraconservative was hot.

She grinned at the very unlikeliness of her—her!—thinking such a thing. Even while knocking back fancy imported beers. Max Nolan wasn't here to be friendly, she reminded herself. He was here to weasel out of his volunteering commitment. Lucy would have bet her last pack of ramen noodles on that.

Still, his weaseling wasn't entirely unexpected. She'd been waiting for it. And there was no reason she couldn't enjoy herself while Max meandered to the point.

She was still positive she'd seen some kind of reaction in his face when they'd met. She knew *she'd* felt something. Maybe it was time to find out where that something could lead them.

Besides, life was about as much fun as a person made

it. With that philosophy in mind, Lucy ran her finger over her eyebrow ring and smiled at him.

"So . . . what makes a good cocktail party?" she asked.

He jerked. "Did you just run your foot up my leg?"

She loved his astonishment. It made her feel wicked.

"Don't worry. I took off my shoe first. See?"

She leaned sideways in their booth and nudged her foot—sans clog—higher. The toe ring she'd bought at last year's crafts fair twinkled in the candlelight. So did her favorite sky blue toenail polish. Experimentally, she wriggled to his knee.

Another few inches, and . . .

"Hey!" Max gawked at her foot.

"So, do you need lots of drinks? Or just a few?"

"Uhhh . . ."

"A bartender, or just a handy friend?"

"I, uh—" He broke off, seeming about to grab her foot. "You're really flexible."

"Yoga. It does wonders."

Lucy widened her eyes in sham innocence—the better to scope out the fit of his jeans. She wondered if their underwear-first acquaintance meant she could skip a few steps in the courtship process. You know, just to be efficient about things.

Efficiency was her watchword.

At least tonight it was.

Because if she had to wait for him to weasel, she was at least going to enjoy herself. Feeling a flicker of anticipation, she nudged her toes higher.

Warmth. Soft denim. Rock-hard thigh muscle. *Very* nice.

Their server appeared. "Another bourbon, sir?"

Max froze. He looked from his near lapful of Lucy's beringed toes to the server's polite and inquisitive face.

"Yes. Please."

She had to give Max credit. He only sounded a *little*

breathless. He was probably a pro at surreptitious toe groping. Just her kind of guy. Open to all possibilities.

"Right away, sir," their server said.

After he trundled away, Max returned his attention to her. He looked amused, attracted, and most of all . . . daring. Lucy had the unexpected feeling that she may have been playing with fire.

He arched his brow. "I underestimated you."

"People often do." She gave a breezy wave. "It's the freckles. They have that 'sweet and innocent' effect."

"Freckles?" He leaned nearer. His slid his arm along the top of their banquette, his biceps barely brushing her halter-top-exposed shoulders. "I don't see any freckles."

Maybe not. But from this vantage point, Lucy saw plenty of *him*. Such as his fascinating eyes, dark and deep. His mouth, wide and compelling. His nose looked simultaneously too big and yet perfect for his face. Max had thick brows and angled cheeks. If Lucy hadn't known better, she'd have sworn that intent expression on his face meant he was interested in her.

Plus, he smelled really good. Downright lickable.

"That's because I don't really have any freckles," she confessed. "It was all a ploy to get you to come closer."

"Good ploy. Does it work for you often?"

"I don't know. I'm winging it. It's how I do things."

"Tell me more."

"I don't believe in planning ahead," Lucy said. "What can you really plan for, anyway? Nada. If you try, life comes along and wallops you with a surprise. The way I see it, all you can do is keep your head on straight, make sure your intentions are good, and enjoy the ride."

"Hmmm. You don't strike me"—he lifted his gaze to her lavender hair—"as the 'head on straight' type."

"Geez, enough with the hair already. It's pretty."

"On you? Yeah."

A flutter coursed through her. Okay, so Max might not

have been full of sweet talk on the street in his underwear. But maybe the guy was worth taking a chance on.
Just for fun.

Enjoying the idea, Lucy smiled. "Aside from which,
'head on straight' is really the *least* important part of my
philosophy." She tried to maintain a serious expression.
"Good intentions, and especially *enjoyment*"—she wriggled her toes suggestively against his thigh—"are
critical."

Their server chose that moment to arrive with Max's
bourbon. Lucy waited impatiently while he served it. His
gaze dipped to her foot. His otherwise neutral expression
flirted with distaste, then smoothed again. Feeling
weirdly chastised, Lucy let her foot slip from Max's lap.

This lounge might be deluxe, she realized, but it sure
wasn't her kind of hole-in-the-wall, friendly neighborhood place. All of a sudden, she felt a lot less entranced
by the ritzy atmosphere. Also, she couldn't find her shoe.
She felt around with her big toe, searching for her discarded clog.

Max glanced at his empty lap. He raised his brows.

She shrugged, an unwelcome self-consciousness stealing through her. She hadn't noticed before, but every
other woman in this place was blond, sophisticated, and
not engaged in foot-to-thigh getting-to-know-you maneuvers under the table.

"Did I do something? *Not* do something?" Max
reached for her hand. "What's the matter?"

"Nothing." Lucy extricated her hand and quaffed her
beer. She thumped the glass on the table. *Thud*. She
imagined heads turned at the sound, but suddenly she
didn't care. She *determinedly* didn't care. "I'd better get
going. Was there something you wanted to tell me?"

Max looked at his empty hand. He seemed surprised.

"Come on. I don't have all night." Technically, she did,
but that wasn't the point. "What's your excuse going to

be? Too much work to do at the office? An allergy to dust? Traumatic childhood memories of wearing hand-me-downs?"

She bit her lip, still fishing for her clog. She encountered nubbly carpet, the table's center post, and something that might have been a fuzzy gum wrapper.

"I *do* have a lot of work to do," Max said, "which is why I came to the shop to—" He broke off, his look of confusion deepening. "What are you doing under there?"

"Searching for my shoe." Frustrated, Lucy flipped up the tablecloth and ducked her head and shoulders beneath it. She saw Max's legs stiffen to her left and couldn't help but grin. "Don't get your hopes up. I'm only down here to get my shoe."

An instant later, Max hunkered in the dimness beside her. He didn't fit. His shoulders barely squeezed into the space between the banquette and the table post, leaving their bodies only inches apart. He peered at the carpet.

"I don't see it. Maybe it slipped under that booth."

He angled his head toward the banquette next door.

She stared at him, unable to believe he'd actually joined her under the table. Him. Mr. Traditionalist. "Maybe."

"It'll be okay there for another minute or two."

His gaze flickered over her face. It settled, with something close to fascination, on her lips.

"Huh? Why would it take another—"

Max touched her chin with his fingers, leaned nearer, and kissed her. In the dimness. Beneath the table.

Lucy stilled. *Wow.* "Why did you—?"

He did it again, this time smiling first as he brought his mouth to hers. Maybe Max had a privacy fixation, she thought fleetingly. That would explain why he'd chosen to make his move here. Beneath a table. Although that was unlikely in a guy who would go outside in his tighty-whities.

"There's something about you, Lucy. I can't explain

it. I thought maybe if I tried out your 'winging it' philosophy . . ." His smile dazzled her. "How am I doing?"

"Pretty good. For a newbie." Maybe Max had noticed the waiter snub her and was trying to cheer her up, she reasoned.

"I'll have to keep trying, then," he said.

His next kiss felt warm and light and sweet . . . more of a prelude to something deeper than the full-on, straight-to-slobberfest some men used. She had to admit, Max had a knack for this stuff.

Lucy felt charmed.

But then, in this position, that light-headed sensation might have been due to all the blood rushing to her head.

"Smart," she said. "Softening me up before weaseling."

Popping her head from beneath the table, she gulped in fresh, cool, *non*-carpet-shampoo-scented air. The dip in temperature restored her equilibrium.

Max's appearance, seconds later, upset it all over again.

He brandished her street-fair clog like a conquering hero.

"Believe me," he told her with a wicked look. "If I were softening you up, you'd know it."

He had fluff in his hair, dust on his shirt, and no chance in hell of being the kind of guy she usually went for. He didn't even play an instrument. Or live with his mother. And he hadn't yet asked her for a loan ("just until my DUI lawsuit pays off"). He was wrong, wrong, wrong for her.

Although he did seem to appreciate a no-holds-barred woman who could keep up her end of a flirtation. Like Lucy. That was something, wasn't it? Then, of course, there was that kiss. . . .

They both knew this wasn't going anywhere anyway. Max hadn't even stayed inside the shop to chat with her friends. He'd preferred to wait outside and talk business on his cell phone.

This was nothing but a windup to a bunch of excuses for not volunteering. No matter what Max said. Any minute now, he'd trot out some business obligation or other and try to renege on their deal.

But in the meantime . . .

"Weaseling?" Max repeated. He looked as though her statement had just registered with him. "I *don't* weasel."

"Right." She accepted her clog from him and slipped it on. "That's why you haven't been back for your lucky suit yet."

His mouth twisted. "I've been working."

"Mmm-hmm." Here it comes . . .

"But it hasn't been going especially well lately," Max admitted. His gaze dimmed, probably in remembrance of his lost lucky suit. "Anyway, my partner is counting on me. I can't spend all day at a thrift store."

"Mmm-hmm." She wasn't giving an inch.

"Tell you what," he said, looking inspired. "I'll pay you instead. A really whopping donation, in return for my suit."

Lucy scoffed. She planned to turn down his "donation," of course. Just on principle. She had to. But she couldn't help wondering . . . exactly *how* "whopping" was he talking about?

She wavered. After all, Successfully Dressed *was* in dire financial straits. It had been ever since the Dragon Lady had decided owning a vintage clothing store wasn't as much "fun" as she'd expected. She'd essentially washed her hands of the place, leaving Lucy in charge for the first time in her life.

"Come on," Max coaxed. "I've seen your shop, remember? It's obviously struggling. Be reasonable. I'm sure you can use the money."

She snapped out of it. *Reasonable?* He might as well

ask her to start charging full markup for all the clothes. Or stiffing Nieca and Franco on overtime pay.

She'd worked hard to keep Successfully Dressed going. How dare he talk about her shop that way. As though it was on its last legs.

"You promised to volunteer. I expect you to keep your word." Besides, she could always sell his stuff for cash. Lucy hadn't wanted to do this, but he'd pushed her. "Be at the shop tomorrow morning, or your blue suit gets it."

She tossed some money on the table to pay for her beer. She didn't believe in anything but going Dutch—especially with a guy like Max. She tilted her head, waiting for his answer.

The only sounds were the piano music and the subtle crackling of ice melting into bourbon.

Then, "Are you threatening to off my suit?"

Lucy lifted her chin. It was hard not to grin at the un-abashed look of astonishment on his chiseled features.

Thank God Max actually owned a "blue suit."

She'd been guessing. Stupid boring business wear.

"Just be there, okay? I've got to go."

She slid from the booth and hurried away, head held high. She felt Max's admiring gaze on her butt the whole way, though, and Lucy hadn't even hit the door before she started reliving that kiss. Damn it. When it came to Max Nolan—and his ideas of "winging it"—things might not be as easy as she wanted them to be.

5

Nieca almost twisted an ankle in her Doc Martens as she bolted across the sales floor at Successfully Dressed. Potential customers were few and far between these days, and she was bored with picking out suits for interviewees. The woman who'd just walked in promised a different kind of clientele. At least if her fuchsia snakeskin Gucci bag could be believed.

Nieca believed. Handbags didn't lie.

"Hi! How are you?"

Gently, she steered the woman to the meager vintage collectibles area. It had been bigger when the Dragon Lady had run the place, but since her defection, donations were way down. Her la-di-dah society pals seemed to have forgotten Successfully Dressed existed.

"You *have* to see this Dior dress," Nieca gushed. "It's looking for just the right owner, and I think you might be it."

"Oh, no, thank you. I'm actually only here to find out—" A gasp. "This is a real Dior!"

Nieca grinned. Even though Lucy wanted to focus on ordinary work wear, and Franco wanted to start selling guitar strings and used CDs to augment their selection, Nieca knew their future lay in fashion collectibles. Like the Dior.

"It certainly is. One of our favorites." She reached for the full-skirted dress, then paused. She scrutinized her customer. "I'd say you're about a size 6 in vintage?"

Silently, the woman nodded. She wore lots of jewelry, a to-die-for pair of Ferragamo flats, and an outfit Nieca would swear she'd seen in British *Vogue* two months ago.

This one was a real catch.

"Then you're in luck! The fitting room is back here."

Gaily, Nieca led the way. She watched with satisfaction as the woman ducked inside. Lucy wasn't here yet, and Franco was in the back changing CDs on the sound system. For now, she had the whole place to herself. *Let the revolution begin.*

Everyone would thank her in the end. She was sure of it.

The curtain rustled. Jolted back to the crucial matter of the Dior, Nieca leaned closer. "How's it coming? Do you need a hand with anything?"

"I'm fine," came the muffled reply. "This is . . . oh my God. It's fabulous. I never *imagined* . . ." The words ended on a sigh.

Nieca grinned. She loved making couture dreams come true. It was the next best thing to developing her own designs.

"I'd love to see it when you're ready," she said. "That particular piece has been here since we opened. It's from the private collection of one of our wonderful local benefactors."

Wonderful was stretching it, considering they were the Dragon Lady's friends. Nieca dropped a few names anyway. It couldn't hurt, especially if the woman was a local.

". . . friends of Cornelia Burnheart," she finished.

She couldn't *wait* to see Lucy's face when she told her about making this sale.

The curtain screeched across its rod. The woman stood there in the Dior, needing a zip up the back.

"Did you say Cornelia Burnheart?" she asked.

Nieca nodded. "Have you heard of her?"

"Well, I'm new in town, but . . ." Wearing an unexpectedly shrewd expression, the woman extended her manicured fingers for a handshake. "I'm very interested in learning about the local social scene. I'm Andrea Cho, publicist at large."

With his cell phone headset firmly in place, and himself firmly ensconced in the storage room at Successfully Dressed, Max picked up a woman's shoe. Halfheartedly, he examined it.

He didn't know much about feminine footwear, but he did know this clodhopper was seriously ugly. He tossed it to the discard pile and kept going.

"You're right, Jerry," he said into his phone, "and that's why this venture is so perfect for you. The potential is—"

He went on, giving a snapshot of the project. The L.A. real estate mogul was interested in branching out into a franchising opportunity. If Max played his cards right, his and Oliver's new development idea would be right up his alley.

Jerry wasn't local. And the Ruiz family preferred local investors. But after almost a week's worth of making calls and taking meetings, Max figured he was in no position to be picky. He'd been having more trouble than he'd expected breaking into the piggybanks of the Valley's elite. So far, his contacts weren't quite panning out the way he wanted.

And Oliver was counting on him.

He picked up a skirt from the pile of donations. Max didn't know much about women's skirts—other than how to get women to shimmy out of them in a hurry—but he did know this one was dowdy. He couldn't imagine himself sliding his hands up the thighs of a woman wearing that sandpapery thing.

Into the discard pile it went.

"Right. I'll see you then," he told Jerry.

They confirmed their next meeting, then Max hung up.

Pausing between phone calls, he surveyed the work he'd completed so far. Successfully Dressed's storage room was depressingly gray, in contrast to the color-packed sales floor. That fact was made all the more obvious by the glaring fluorescent lighting.

Despite the dismal conditions, he'd done a good job— probably better than Lucy and her staff of punk rock, arty misfits expected. He had a substantial pile of discards and a smaller bundle of keepers, and he was well on his way to being finished with sorting the day's donations.

Who said men couldn't multitask like women? Hah.

Satisfied, Max hit the speed dial on his phone. His next contact was out. So was the one after that. He left messages and kept going down his list. It was weird— usually he got on the inside track to the people who mattered in any given town right away. Then, inevitably, success followed.

In Phoenix, apparently, things were different. Frowning, Max tried his next potential investor.

While on hold, he kept sorting. Jesus, people gave away a lot of crap. Most items had rips or stains or other defects. All of them were *used,* a realization that made him shudder.

He wasn't particularly fastidious, but he was pretty sure handling other people's dirty laundry wasn't an entrepreneur's dream. He didn't know how Successfully Dressed survived on donations like these.

He flashed on the pickup bin outside his building. Beyond considering it an eyesore, he'd never given it a moment's thought. If Sarabeth hadn't crammed all his things in it, who knew how long it would have taken him to notice it.

Who knew how many other people had done the same thing.

His phone beeped, signaling he was done holding. An administrative assistant came on the line to warn him that his potential investor was in meetings all day.

"That must make your job tough," Max told her. He picked up a prim, button-up top. Too starchy. He tossed it to the discard pile.

"Oh, it does." The admin sighed. "It's only my first week on the job, and there are so many things to juggle!"

He empathized with her, still sorting. Sometimes assistants just needed to be listened to. He gave a murmur of agreement. More small talk ensued while he pitched orange shoes, a checked jacket, and a parrot-print shirt to the discard pile in rapid succession.

"Anyway, I'll make sure Ms. Martinez gets your message right away." The admin's voice had warmed considerably. "Don't worry about a thing, all right?"

Max thanked her and hung up. That was some progress, at least. He selected a pair of baggy-looking pants from the rapidly diminishing donation pile, made a face, and hurled them to the no-way-in-hell group. Next to hand was a long scarf, printed in leopard-pattern silk. Max rubbed its sleek texture between his fingers, considering it.

He'd dated lots of leopard-print-wearing women. Usually, sophisticated women were exactly his type. Today, though, memories of a certain set of beringed, blue-frosted toes came to mind instead. He still couldn't believe Lucy had all but toe groped him with her yogafied feet, right in broad candlelight at Rocco's, his new favorite bar.

Lucy was unlike anyone he'd ever met. When he'd told her last night there was *something* about her, he'd meant it. He'd surprised her with that confession, Max suspected.

Hell, he'd surprised himself too. He didn't usually go

for brash bohemian types, with their hearts on their sleeves, their silver rings in their eyebrows, and their weird clothes.

But Lucy . . . Lucy had gotten under his skin somehow.

She wasn't impressed with his job or his money or his car. Hell, she didn't even know he had a car. She didn't want anything from him except his service volunteering . . . and maybe an occasional something extra. Like his kisses. Lucy hadn't seemed to mind those last night, he recalled with a grin.

At least she hadn't until she'd bolted from the bar.

His smile dimming, Max wondered what had happened to scare her away. Usually, he had a way with women. He always had. He loved them and got along with them, and he liked to think he understood them. At least as much as was possible, given that they rarely made sense. But with Lucy . . . hell. He didn't know.

He still wasn't sure what had made him kiss her. Under a table, of all things. It had been an impulse, pure and simple.

The thing was, Max didn't usually follow impulses.

He followed plans.

Just like his current plan—to volunteer for a few days, get back his lucky suit, then get the hell out of Vintageville.

He picked up another donation. It looked like a limp rag, something he wouldn't have washed his Lexus with. Scrunching his nose, he held it at arm's length and unfolded it. Ugh. Who the hell donated panty hose? Large, fake-suntan-color panty hose?

In fact, what women still *wore* panty hose?

Nobody he'd dated, that's for sure.

And not Lucy either, Max learned as he tossed the hose over his shoulder. He turned to make sure they'd hit the discard pile and came face-to-calf with the longest, lithest, most wonderfully naked pair of legs he'd ever seen.

He followed them upward, where they eventually disappeared from view—to his disappointment—beneath the hem of a white spangly miniskirt. Craning his neck, Max peered higher.

In a black T-shirt with a silk-screened dragon, an armload of jangly bracelets, and a mouthful of red lipstick, Lucy looked like a prom princess from the waist down—and a juvenile delinquent from the waist up.

Especially with that hair. And those piercings.

Bizarrely, he liked it. All of it.

Until she opened her mouth.

"What's the matter with all this stuff?" She prodded the discard pile with the toe of her unlaced, green canvas high-tops. "It looks perfectly good to me."

"It's not," Max told her seriously. "I wouldn't look twice at any woman who was wearing any of those things. And I *definitely* wouldn't put the moves on her."

Lucy's mouth gaped. "You wouldn't . . . Oh, come on, Casanova. You can't be serious."

"A person's got to have criteria." He stood, stretching out his crimped back with the motion. "Those are mine. Hey, how about a coffee break?"

She consulted the time clock near the back door. "You were late getting here again today. And you've only been back here for twenty minutes."

That was twenty minutes too long, as far as Max was concerned. To prove his sincerity, he took off his hands-free headset. He offered her a coaxing smile.

"Let's go. It'll be fun—we'll just duck out for a minute. I know a great espresso shop right around the corner."

"Hmmph." Lucy crossed her arms over her chest, spoiling his view of her cute . . . dragon. "I know that shop. It almost put my friend Jade out of business when it opened. I can't believe you patronize it."

"Why not? It's good coffee."

"They demolished three houses to build that place— not to mention that massive parking lot to go with it." Lucy shook her head. "I knew the owners. One had lived on this block her whole life."

"Progress marches onward." If Max had his way, his new venture with Oliver would change the face of down-town too—and the whole Phoenix area. For the better. "Your friend probably got a good price for her house. Probably more than it was worth, since development raises property values."

"That's not the point! Some things should be treasured, not just . . . *thrown away*." Lucy scooped up several of the items Max had sorted, including the orange shoes and the leopard scarf. Defiantly, she dumped them on the keeper pile. She glanced up at him. "Don't you get it? The ends don't always justify the means."

Max shrugged. As far as he was concerned, they usu-ally did. "That corner property is better used for the espresso shop. Lots of people benefit from it, not just one woman."

She stared at him for a long moment, a startling amount of perception in her level gaze. Especially for a nouveau hippie in a sequined skirt.

"Maybe you'd better try laundry duty."

"Yeah," Max agreed. Anything to escape the stinky confines of the donation piles. "Laundry duty probably requires a big, strong man, right? To load and unload those massive washing machines out front? No problem."

"No." Lucy rolled her eyes. "It requires less brain-power. Come on, He-Man. I'll show you where the industrial-strength detergent is."

Following her sexy sashay into the Laundromat-turned-clothing-store part of the shop, Max beamed.

Lucy might talk crazy, and she might look kind of crazy, but she understood the appeal of a man's boyhood hero. He-Man ruled. Any woman who realized that was all right in his book.

Lucy leaned against the cash register table, hands propped at hip level. A few customers browsed the racks. Franco helped a woman select an outfit for applying to culinary school, his wild gestures appearing to charm his customer more than alarm her. That was good. It took a certain kind of person not to be scared away by a skinny, six-foot-four, faux-hawk-wearing punk rocker, but when Franco met his sort of clientele, he was wonderful at customer service.

The whole shop smelled of acrid, soapy detergent. Near the ancient washing machines, Max Nolan labored to mop up the results of his first attempt at laundry. Even though Lucy had explained the whole procedure, down to demonstrating which fill line to use on the plastic detergent cup, Max had typically decided he knew better. Two minutes after he'd turned on the clothing-packed machines, they'd had a soapsuds avalanche.

He swiped the back of his hand over his brow and kept mopping. Lucy followed the wet arc of the mop head, lifted her gaze to his hands holding the handle, then followed the muscular lines of Max's arms upward. His biceps flexed with each push. His shoulders worked to swivel the mop. Beneath the white undershirt he'd stripped down to for mopping, his chest looked broad and strong, sprinkled with exactly the right amount of dark, curly hair.

"Mmm, mmm, mmm." Nieca shook her head, joining Lucy at the register. "I can see why you wanted Max to 'volunteer.'"

Lucy smiled. "I wanted him to volunteer because he said he'd do it. I like a man who keeps his word."

"You like a man who's got to-die-for muscles and knows how to use them." Another appreciative *mmm*. "Don't we all?"

"He was a total washout in the donation-sorting department," Lucy confided. "He hardly wanted to keep anything."

"He's selective, then. Good. That would be a nice change for you. You need a man who's discriminating."

"I'm not looking for a man." Trying to snap herself out of her juvenile ogling, Lucy glanced around the shop. She needed more business, it was true, and yet . . . "I've got *way* too much to do as it is. I thought convincing the Dragon Lady to let me take over this place would be the hard part, but now . . ."

She must have been crazy, Lucy thought. What did she know about running a charity-slash-vintage clothing shop?

She'd never been in charge of anything in her entire life. Now, although Cornelia Burnheart officially retained ownership of Successfully Dressed, Lucy was responsible for donations, scheduling, payroll, maintenance, ordering, taxes . . . so many things she'd never counted on.

At least she *meant* to make a success of the place, though. Which was more than could be said for her flighty former boss. Cornelia, a socialite with a penchant for collecting vintage clothing, had launched the shop on a whim—and had managed it with all the success her non-forethought implied.

As far as Lucy was concerned, the Dragon Lady's lack of good intentions had doomed her to fail.

"Now you're well on your way to making a go of this place," Nieca said loyally. Her smile, framed by her usual red braids and geek-chic glasses, brimmed with caring.

"Who knows? Success might come from a direction you're not even expecting."

It took a minute for Lucy to decipher her friend's eager expression and sparkling eyes.

"Like your super-duper Dior sale?" Lucy hesitated, realizing she'd hit the mark when Nieca nodded. "I don't want to be a buzzkill, here, and I'm really happy about all the money you brought in for that, but . . . you know we can't count on getting any more donations from the DL's friends."

Suddenly silent, Nieca ground the toe of her Chinese slipper against the rubber mat underfoot. She didn't look up.

"Besides," Lucy went on, feeling awful to burst her friend's bubble, "it's just as well if we clear out the vintage collectibles area. We're supposed to be serving underprivileged women, remember? When they wander over to the collectibles and see the whopping price tags on some of that stuff—"

"Why can't we do both?" Nieca gave her a pleading look. "The money we make on the good stuff will help bolster the—"

"Bad stuff?" Lucy shook her head. "I don't want to do that to our customers. Making them feel like second-class citizens will only discourage them from coming here."

Nieca rolled her eyes. "I'm starting to feel nostalgic for the Dragon Lady days. At least then we got to work with fabulous clothes. And shoes. And handbags."

Lucy pointed to a nearby rolling cart. "We have shoes."

"Sensible navy pumps don't count."

"And handbags."

"Those old things?" Nieca made a face. "If you'd just let me make a few solicitation calls to the DL's buddies—"

Lucy shook her head. They'd been over this. "Franco does the solicitation calls. He's got experience at it, because of booking gigs for his band. And he's requesting regular donations, not designer wear. Remember?"

They'd all agreed on this plan. When Lucy had first taken over at Successfully Dressed, coming up with brilliant business tactics had been her top priority. She'd held a big company meeting, first thing, to discuss strategy.

Well, okay . . . so she'd held a sangria-fueled heart-to-heart, followed by hugs to seal the deal and a rollicking vegan fiesta to celebrate. But that was practically the same thing.

Then, she and Nieca and Franco had all been on the same wavelength. Now, Nieca suddenly seemed intent on turning the shop into one of those snooty boutiques where the collectibles were kept in locked display cases and everyone talked about "Mainbocher's wasp-waisted dresses" and "Norma Kamali's *darling* parachute jumpsuits."

Lucy didn't care about fashion elitism. Getting dressed was supposed to be fun, not exclusionary. She liked clothes, but as far as she was concerned, they didn't have to be expensive or hard to find or intimidating to look good.

And speaking of looking good . . .

"No," Lucy breathed. "He's *not.*"

"Oh yes." Nieca sounded delighted, having just noticed the same thing Lucy had. "*He is.*"

They both watched, transfixed, as Max peeled off his undershirt. He grabbed it over his shoulders and tugged its water-spotted cotton over his head. For a few tantalizing seconds, his abs flexed as he pulled. His shirt sailed toward the open maw of one of the front-loading washing machines.

It made it inside.

"Yes!" Max pumped his fist like a free-throw shooter.

Unaccountably, the boyish gesture made Lucy smile. There was more to Max Nolan, she suspected in that moment, than slick business success, sexed-up cocktails, and a half-baked belief in lucky suits.

Nieca nudged her. Her knowing gaze shot from Lucy's still-smiling face to Max, who was now clad only in low-slung shorts and flip-flops—the vacation-worthy remnants, he'd confided to her, of his nonwork wardrobe. He wrung his mop, seeming hilariously focused on accomplishing the task perfectly.

His intensity only charmed Lucy all the more.

"You really like him, don't you?" Nieca asked.

Reluctantly, Lucy averted her gaze.

"You do!" Nieca's triumphant squeal made both Franco and his customer turn around. She waved them both away, then hunched closer to Lucy. "You can't fool me. Your face is all red. It's a dead giveaway. Next thing you know, you'll have a love zit."

Stubbornly, Lucy crossed her arms. She found herself sneaking another peek at Max's buffed-up bod and frowned.

"There's no such thing as a love zit."

"Oh yeah? Try telling that to your face in about a week. I know you, remember? Every time you fall for a guy, you get at least one huge, honking zit, usually on your nose."

Hesitantly, Lucy touched her nose. Did it feel just a little bit . . . swollen? "That's ridiculous."

"It's the hormones." Nieca gave a knowledgeable look. "They'll get you every time. Every time you're hot for a guy."

Damn that Magic 8 ball effect. "We're not in ninth grade anymore. I'm not going to get a love zit just because I happen to find one well-developed, intelligent, witty—"

"Aha!" Nieca crowed.

"—aggravating, stubborn, Big Shot Central–dwelling—"

"Lucy's got a cruuush," Nieca singsonged.

"—*playboy* moderately . . . appealing." Lucy shut her mouth.

"Well. Let's just test your theory, shall we?"

Wearing a flip, know-it-all grin, Nieca put both hands to her black mesh bra. She'd worn it in plain view beneath the Betty Boop–style gingham shirt she'd left unbuttoned and knotted at her waist, so it was a simple maneuver to boost her cleavage. She smoothed her floral miniskirt over her hips, smacked her lips together, then sashayed toward Max.

The jerk watched her coming, leaning on his mop handle while he enjoyed the view. Groaning, knowing full well what was coming next, Lucy covered her eyes.

Pretty soon, though, peeking between her fingers proved unsatisfactory. She lowered her hand. Just as she'd suspected, Nieca was laying on all her best flirtatious moves. She tossed her head, then puckered her berry-colored lips.

Max leaned nearer. Nieca laughed at something he said, then gestured coquettishly to the mop bucket.

Oh no. She wasn't . . .

She was. Nieca bent over, ostensibly trying to lift the bucket in a helpful manner—but really offering Max what had to be a full monty view of her thong panties and tattooed butt cheeks. Nieca had never been shy, but this was outrageous.

Lucy fumed, heartily wishing she'd never been informed of the Tinkerbell inked on Nieca's right cheek and the Peter Pan illustrated on her left. Maybe there *was* such a thing as too much closeness between friends. Also, Lucy recalled semiwistfully, too much tequila.

But if Max was too dumb to see through these girly maneuvers . . . Well, then he wasn't even worth ogling anymore.

By the time Nieca breezed back to the cash register, Lucy had her head down, pretending to double-check receipts.

"He passed. Not even a *hint* of interest." Nieca folded her arms and leaned on the counter. She shook her head. "Any man who can resist me has *got* to be way into you."

Lucy rolled her eyes. "Next you'll be telling me *Max* is going to get a love zit, too."

"Well, then you'd know for sure, now wouldn't you?" Nieca beamed, then picked up a handful of blank price tags. Before heading out to affix them, she cast Max a thoughtful glance. "Just remember, Lucy Goosey. The next move is up to you."

6

The next move is up to you.

For the next two days, those words rolled around in Lucy's head. They pestered her over breakfast and nagged her over dinner. They mocked her when she stepped inside Successfully Dressed each day, and they clamored incessantly when she glimpsed Max's broad shoulders, easy smile, or capable hands.

The next move is up to you.

She counted down the days left in his volunteering agreement, without even meaning to. She savored each moment they spent together, without even trying to. And when she considered how little time she had before their two worlds diverged again, Lucy's pesky antimantra all but dared her.

The next move is up to you.

Damn it.

She'd never been afraid to make a move. Nieca knew that. Lucy considered herself both forthright and energetic. She was anything but shy with men (or anyone else), and she knew how to get what she wanted. But this time, what she wanted was . . . weird. A traditional guy? For her? It just didn't happen. Never had, never would.

She didn't even like regular guy hangouts like sports

bars or football games or big-budget action movies. She liked neighborhood hot spots and spending time at craft fairs and going to art house films with her friends.

She liked eclectic. Edgy. Free and easy living.

Still, she persisted in being attracted to Max.

Maybe she was coming down with something.

Yeah. That was probably it. A fever would explain her interest in Max . . . and her persistent, tantalizing fantasies—er, *fever-induced hallucinations*—about him. Because ordinarily, her needs were pretty straightforward and very simple.

Friendship. Clean sheets. A better mastery of the Ustrasana pose in yoga. Regular stuff. These days, though, as Lucy spent more and more time with Max, she found herself needing new things. Like a masculine grin. An oh-so-casual touch. And a more thorough understanding of the man who'd come to volunteer—usually while wheeling and dealing on his cell phone—and had wound up setting her whole world off-kilter.

Lucy didn't understand how it had happened. But being around Max made her feel . . . well, stupid. Silly. Hot and bothered. The sight of him made her giggly, and a word from him made her blush. More than once, she caught herself mooning around behind him on the sales floor, then whirling around abruptly whenever he spotted her.

She doubted he was fooled by the "what a fascinating ceiling" maneuver she'd patented at sixteen and was appalled to find herself dragging into service again. But every time she tilted her face studiously upward, she just couldn't help it.

Max made her feel giddy.

He'd mastered sorting, mopping, and operating the massive industrial steam iron. Now he excelled at dragging huge basketsful of donated clothing to the machines, expertly sorting them, and getting them started washing.

For her part, Lucy never tired of watching him work.

She figured it was because of the way he did it—with full, Zen-style absorption and sheer tenacity. Anyone could tell Max wasn't a typical laborer. Yet he often shut off his cell phone and dived into the task at hand, no holds barred. His focus and (admittedly) unexpected capacity for hard work fascinated her as much as his nimble fingers did.

"Hmmm. You look like a super spy dismantling a bomb," she observed, leaning against one of the display tables. "So full of concentration. Are you always this intense?"

Max shrugged. He grunted as he shouldered one of the ancient washer doors closed. "Are you always this curious?"

"Most of the time, yeah." He had a habit of answering a question with a question, she'd noticed. Today, Lucy felt determined to make *him* talk for a change. "Take you, for instance. We've been working together all week long, but I hardly know anything about you. At least not anything *real.*"

He gave a noncommittal sound. "What do you want to know?"

To begin with . . . "What's your family like? Where did you live before coming here? What made you move into Big Shot Central?" Lucy sucked in a breath, all the questions she'd been wondering about coming faster now. "Don't all those suits of yours chafe? How come your hair's cut so short? Was it an accident? A drunk haircut? Are you a TV person or a book person? Do you like champagne? Have you ever been moshing?"

She ignored his grin. You never knew about a person's background. Lucy had learned not to judge anyone by appearances.

She waited. No answers were forthcoming.

"Don't you want to know what I *do?*" Max asked, looking amused as he wheeled his laundry cart. "What my job is? How much it pays? How many bonuses I get every year?"

She waved him off. "Nah. Your job's not who you are. It's what you do. Besides, what *I* want to know is, how do you feel about tofu? Where do you celebrate holidays? Have you hugged your mom lately? Do you like puppies?"

"Take a breath," he suggested.

"Is the stock market as phony as it looks? Do you own stock?" She followed him to the next washer and watched him load the clothes. She had a terrible thought. "I hope you're not one of those fly-by-night types who cons little old ladies out of their social security checks. That's very wrong. I know you're self-employed, but everyone needs limits."

Beside her, Max pushed buttons, spun the dial, and got the washer going. Lucy stared at his muscular forearms and tried not to drool. When contrasted against the machine's vivid aqua color and the shop's eclectic interior, Max looked twice as out of place, even in his so-called casual shorts and open-collar shirt, but that didn't matter a bit. He was still hot.

His big feet slapped with confidence across the crooked floor. He muscled open another doddering washer.

She refocused. "What's your business partner's name? How did you meet him? In school? *Private* school? College?" She groaned and grabbed his arm. "Tell me you're not a former frat boy. I'd have to ditch you right now, out of sheer principle."

He frowned into the washing machine's empty tub. "How many clothes go in one of these again?"

Sighing, Lucy grabbed an armful of donations. Franco had driven the Successfully Dressed truck this morning. He'd come back with a paltry haul, a triple espresso from the café on the corner, and a phone number for a potential date. She suspected hanging around with Max was corrupting him.

It was a concept she understood all too well. Max's influence was hard to resist. So was the impulse to help him.

"There." With her example load stuffed in, Lucy brushed her palms together. "About that many. Just enough to fill the washer barely halfway, so everything can agitate freely. It's bad for the fabrics if there's too much friction."

Max raised his brow, giving her a suggestive look. "Too much friction? How can there be—"

"There just can be. Trust me." For a moment, she drifted into a rousing daydream about rubbing against Max and testing her theory. They could even wear clothes, to make it a realistic study. At least at first. "Now, about my questions—"

He grinned, as though he'd guessed exactly what she'd been fantasizing about. Then he pushed his rolling cart under her nose, just like a Krispy Kreme baker with a donut and a dieter. Lucy caught sight of the remaining items inside the cart.

She gasped. "Are those new donations? *Vintage* donations?"

"They're pretty decrepit, I guess. Yeah."

Reverently, she lifted one of the pieces. At the luxurious, satiny feel of the fabric, excitement gripped her. All thoughts of interrogating Max flew from her head as she examined the vivid print. "I think this is a genuine Pucci!"

Imitations abounded, though. Without the trademark guarantee of Emilio's signature embedded within the pattern, she couldn't be sure. She peered closer.

"I was manning the front for Franco when that stuff came in," Max explained. He jerked his thumb toward the shop's front door. "He told me to dump any new donations in with what we already had and give out a receipt."

Lucy raised her face to his. "You did the right thing. This is a *major* windfall." She selected another piece, this one made of pink plastic patent leather in a distinctly squared-off shape. "A Courrèges jacket! I can't believe it—this is like a museum piece! I'll need Nieca to take a look to know for sure, but—"

She broke off, her excitement dimmed. With these items in their inventory, they'd be idiots not to move toward the vintage collectibles market. But that would leave her other customers, people like Tracee, out in the cold.

"But . . . ?" Max edged nearer. "What's the matter?"

"Nothing." For now, Lucy decided, she'd defer the decision. Their entire business plan didn't have to be decided in one day, did it? "I'll just take these back and . . . store them till later. They'll need special cleaning."

She left a thoughtful-looking Max behind. In her office, she wrapped the vintage pieces inside a massive donated caftan, tucked the bundle in a cranny of her desk, then straightened. Her heart pounded. Her hair stuck to her clammy temples. With trembling fingers, Lucy nudged the strands back in place.

She wished none of this subterfuge was necessary. Why couldn't she and Nieca just agree?

"Hmmm. Nice to know you're fallible, after all."

She whirled to find Max filling the doorway, all dark eyes, dreamy muscles, and uncomfortable perceptiveness.

She tilted her chin. This was none of his business anyway. "I don't know what you're talking about."

His gaze shot to her drawer. "Sure you do."

Cheerfully, he kicked the door shut. The one-way mirror on her office wall quivered in reaction. So did Lucy—and all the knickknacks hung beside the mirror.

She had several artisan friends who crafted sculptures

and pottery and wall hangings. Lylia, who did glass blowing. Vincent, who painted in oils. Meggy and Lou, who wove hemp place mats and made beautiful beaded baskets.

Oblivious to her collection, Max filled the whole space with his presence.

"Well, it's simple. Just look at you." He spread his arms, doing exactly that. "You run a charity shop. You give discounts to single mothers. You eat organic Twinkies and volunteer for food drives and hug everyone you meet. Hell, you probably recycle your stuff *and* your neighbors'."

"So? My neighbors are busy."

"All I'm saying is, given all that, it's good to know you're not perfect." Max leaned on her desk. He gazed down at her with his patently self-assured expression. "Otherwise, I wouldn't be able to explain my attraction to you at all. I don't go for 'perfect.'"

Hmmm. Did that mean he went for . . . *her?*

Flummoxed, Lucy gawked at him. "You think I'm doing something sneaky . . . and you're happy about it?"

"Not happy. Just relieved."

"Relieved?"

"If I decide to corrupt you, I won't feel guilty."

"Ahhh." At his teasing grin, she shook her head. Now she was on familiar territory, and she felt tremendously relieved. Max wasn't really talking about the Pucci or the Courrèges, or her hiding either of them. "You descended-from-the-Mayflower types really *are* freaky. Guilt is a waste of time."

His brow rose. "You never feel guilty?"

Lucy wondered when—and why—*he* had. "No. As long as my intentions are good, I don't worry about the outcome."

Max looked skeptical. "Good intentions don't count for squat. I know that much for certain."

"We have a fundamental difference of opinion, then." Still feeling quivery, Lucy moved toward him. Her new position left her almost as tall as Max, since he lounged against her desk. Boldly, she stepped between his spread legs. "Not that it matters, since you'll be out of here in approximately"—she consulted her mod desk clock—"three hours, and we'll never see each other again. In the meantime . . ."

She put her arms around his neck.

He looked surprised. "In the meantime?"

"In the meantime," Lucy explained, feeling a tingle of anticipation, "we should probably spend this time more wisely. Now that you know I'm not too perfect for you."

The next move is up to you.

She lowered her gaze to his mouth, remembering what it had felt like against hers. The only thing wrong with their previous kisses had been that they were too brief.

"Ahhh."

Catching on, Max skimmed his hands over her rib cage. He watched their seductive progress along her ruched pink top. He studied her hips in her patchwork denim miniskirt, then examined her face. A grin flashed over his.

"This wouldn't be a ploy to distract me from wondering why you hid all those old clothes in your desk, would it?"

If that was the excuse she needed to keep them plastered together from knee to hip to chest . . . maybe. Right now, Lucy felt just thrilled enough not to mind.

"If it was, would you care?"

She stood close enough to feel his breath on her mouth, close enough to feel their body heat mingling. She eased her hips forward a little, letting herself relax. There was a lot to be said for flirtation as a tension-reduction technique, Lucy realized. She should recommend it at her next yoga class.

"Hell, no," Max answered. "Do whatever you want, so long as it keeps you right there."

He proved his words with a squeeze of her waist. His hands felt big and powerful and deft—every bit as good as she'd imagined they would. She wanted more, more, more . . .

The next move is up to you.

Hazily, it occurred to her that this was crazy. Unwise. Probably not included in the How to Run a Nonprofit employee handbook—especially the one for managers. But just at that moment, Lucy couldn't bring herself to care. She'd wanted Max for what felt like weeks, and now he was with her.

Reveling in the realization, Lucy shot a quick glance over his shoulder to her one-way mirror. At this time of the afternoon, the shop ordinarily stood vacant. Today was no exception. Franco had stepped outside for his usual four o'clock cigarette, and there were no customers to be seen.

"We'd better make this quick," she said.

Max knew exactly what she meant. He rumbled his agreement, tipped her head back, and kissed her. This time when their lips met, it felt neither sweet nor light—but it definitely felt hot.

"Glad I'm not corrupting you," he murmured.

"Don't corrupt me some more," Lucy demanded.

She moaned and crowded against him, wanting more. She clutched his shoulders and kissed him back, and as their mouths came together again, she realized she'd been wrong. She'd thought Max was good.

He was *great.*

And he was a quick study, too, having instantly come up to speed on her getting-together plan. Still not satisfied, intent on deepening their kiss, she angled his face in her hand. A half-day's growth of raspy beard met her fingertips. The deeper contact she wanted came next.

Max groaned his approval, then stretched his mouth wide. His hands dropped to her derriere, cupping and squeezing. Shivering, it occurred to Lucy that Max made out exactly the same way he did everything else—with delicious intensity. It seemed as though he couldn't get enough of her. The desire swimming through Lucy's veins left her feeling the same.

She lurched backward and grabbed his shirt. He needed to lose that shirt, and soon. It meant there was still far too much fabric between her body and his.

Urgently, she worked her way through the buttons. It was impossible to unfasten very many of them with her hair falling in her eyes and Max—*oh God*—kissing his way down the side of her neck. He peeled her top from her collarbone and kissed there, too, just as she triumphantly managed his fourth button.

The heck with the rest. Panting, Lucy yanked his shirt upward. She caught a glimpse of familiarly tanned skin, curly hair, and nice, taut muscles, and then—

"Let me do that," he rumbled.

His cooperation elated her. After one quick move, his shirt flew to her desk. Eagerly, Lucy kicked off her comfy vintage moccasins. One landed on her massive to-be-filed stack of dreaded paperwork, the other skittered beneath her beauty-shop reject of an office chair.

She wanted to shuck even more clothes. Her skirt and top were only in the way. But Lucy was, at heart, sort of a traditionalist herself. She liked being undressed. It was only gentlemanly of a man, as far as she was concerned, to offer.

Max seemed preoccupied with kissing her. She decided to give him another, oh, thirty seconds or so to get started. In the meantime, she enjoyed her fill of touching him.

He felt amazing—all hard-ridged muscle, taut energy, and irresistible warmth. She smoothed her palms over his shoulders and chest, then hurriedly caressed his back. He liked it; she watched his Adam's apple bob as he swallowed hard. His dark eyes fixed on her face. In them, Lucy saw desire and urgency and, fleetingly . . . vulnerability?

His hands on her breasts pushed the thought from her mind. Beneath her top's shimmery fabric, her nipples tightened. Her whole body arched closer, needing more. She *really* wished Max would get with the program and get her naked.

As an offer of encouragement, she kissed him again. The answering sweep of his tongue dispelled every doubt she might have had. This, *now,* was all that mattered. Surely he felt the same. No man who kissed her with this much intensity, who touched her with this much urgency, was only fooling around.

"We should go somewhere," Max panted. "Do some—"

"I *am* doing something."

She grabbed his belt buckle and pulled. All of a sudden, she was all thumbs, possibly because of the hazy, crazymaking effect of his continued stroking. He cupped her breasts and murmured something blushingly complimentary about them, then grazed her nipples with his thumbs. Why she'd decided today would be a good day to wear a bra, Lucy didn't know.

"Stupid bra," she grumbled, then rubbed seductively against him. Full-body contact was better than fighting with clothes. "Come on. You rub on me too. Our clothes are bound to burst into flames sooner or later."

"Then they'll be gone, at least."

Lucy paused, beaming up at him. "You get me," she marveled. "I don't believe it."

"Me either," Max said, still panting. He shrugged, his gaze focusing on the giant safety pin she'd used to ornamentally close the punk-rock-style gash in her top. His face took on a devilish slant. "Let's not fight it."

Gleefully surrendering, Lucy kissed him harder.

Being with Max felt wonderful, heady . . . beyond exciting. He kissed her with blatant desire, touched her with thrilling expertise, coaxed her higher and higher on the spiral of eyes-closed, head-back, screaming-to-the-stars thrill ride she'd jumped onto. She wasn't wild, and she tended more toward free-spirited than freewheeling. But somehow, right now, clearing her desk and straddling Max on top of it sounded like a really excellent idea.

Lucy was about to suggest it when his hands slipped to her bare midriff and rose. She squealed, a sound Max swallowed with another kiss. His palms roved higher, pushing her top upward at the same time, and the friction of his skin on hers felt as necessary as breathing. Warmth tingled from the places he'd touched. Lucy couldn't begin to keep up. His hands swept to the small of her back, and her top rose another few inches.

Aha. Max was a stealth undresser, she realized dreamily. If she hadn't been alert for telltale movements, she might have missed his maneuvers altogether. She might have found herself buck naked, surprised, and disappointed to have missed the whole experience. After all, Lucy believed in living life to its fullest.

She also believed in equal nakedness. Keeping that philosophy in mind, she examined Max's belt buckle with new determination. It couldn't be that tricky. Unfortunately, her examination led to ogling, which led to touching, which led to a long, kissing-accented span of wishing Max wasn't leaning so she could squeeze his butt. She knew from following him around the shop that he was leaning on a really, really *fine* butt.

Max kissed her again, deeply, and Lucy lost all sense of goal-orientedness altogether. Which wasn't particularly surprising. She'd always been a moment-by-moment kind of person. Even when faced with a hot, sexy, surprisingly sweet—

The back door crashed open, bashing into the office wall. A hoarse sputter sounded, then rapid footsteps.

"Sorry, sorry! Don't mind me. Carry on."

Franco rushed from the alleyway into the office, outfitted in black leather pants, a skinny rhinestone-embellished western shirt, and (of course) his studded belt. His faux-hawk gleamed darkly. The aroma of French cigarettes hung all around him. He shielded his eyes with one hand and waved to them with the other—presumably to encourage them to continue.

Lucy stared at Max. They both stared at Franco.

He gave another strangled exclamation. "Left the door open." Backtracking to the back door, he kicked it shut with the toe of his scuffed boot. "Just pretend I'm not here, okay? Good. I'm leaving now. Have fun."

Max released her. Lucy's top slid back in place, and her patchwork denim skirt seemed to sag in defeat. She stepped back a pace, her whole body still thrumming with eagerness.

Franco saw them separate. He frowned, then made get-together gestures with his hands. "Don't mean to spoil the mood. Keep going! Have fun!"

It was too late. Even as Franco hurried, grinning, to the sales floor and shut the office door behind him, Lucy realized what she'd almost done. If a customer had seen her, or—God forbid, the Dragon Lady—she'd have put her job at risk.

Lucy needed her job. Just a couple of months ago, when Cornelia Burnheart had decided it wasn't "amusing" to sell vintage clothes anymore, she and Nieca and Franco had almost wound up on the street. None of them had huge savings; each of them lived pretty much paycheck to paycheck. The DL's announcement that she'd decided to abruptly close Successfully Dressed had shaken them all.

Only Lucy's fast-talking determination had convinced

their would-be philanthropist boss to keep the place open—and keep them in paychecks, however meager. She couldn't afford to blow it now. Her friends were counting on her.

Wishing her stupid heart would quit pounding so hard—it clearly hadn't gotten the message yet—Lucy gazed up at Max.

"This was a mistake. It can't happen again," she said.

He smiled, his clothes askew and his hair ruffled. He looked ready for anything but calling it quits. "Sure, it—"

"I'm sorry." Lucy wrapped her arms around him and hugged him, trying to infuse Max with all the gladness he'd made her feel just a few minutes ago. "I really liked making out with you. Thanks for understanding."

Then she straightened her shirt, smoothed down her skirt, and marched out of her office, reluctantly leaving Max gawking after her for the second time that week.

7

"And then she just left you standing there, boner in hand?" Oliver shifted his attention from the Xbox game displayed on Max's plasma TV, shaking his head. "Unreal."

"You don't have to sound so happy about it, numbnuts." With gusto, Max shot down Oliver's guy. Ha. The ass deserved it for jubilating over Max's personal heartache. "She *thanked me for understanding*," he repeated for the third time that night. "Thanked! Me! For understanding! As if I were some kind of wussy, never-been-laid, polite . . . *you*."

"Hey. I resent that."

"Truth hurts, pal."

Thirty seconds went by, punctuated by the sounds of their on-screen fighters grunting, swearing, and otherwise digitally raising hell. Max and Oliver hunched over their game controllers, each of them intent on scoring in their long-standing rivalry.

The screen went still. The red-lettered statistics screen superimposed itself on their game.

"You paused it!" Max complained. "You know that screws up the—"

"I've been laid," Oliver informed him archly. "I've

been laid plenty. In the dark, in the daytime, upside down—"

"Upside down? How does that work exactly?"

His friend gave an awkward head bob. "It just does."

"Hmmm. Must have been at Star Trek space camp." Max jabbed him with an elbow. "With that exchange student you told me about. You know, the one with the hairy pits and buck teeth."

Oliver offered him an expletive and unpaused the game.

"Damn it!"

Caught off-guard, Max was forced to focus on the game for the next several minutes. He bobbed and weaved, yelled and swore, and laid on the body English every man knew helped ensure victory. Also, he wore his lucky Astros cap, so he was bound to . . .

"Damn it!"

"Take that, sucka!" Oliver crowed.

"For the last time, you're *not* Shaft."

"Sixteen thousand points. And she didn't have buck teeth. It was a slight overbite. Looks aren't everything, you know."

Max grunted and swilled some Dos Equis. "Now you sound like my crunchy granola girl." He affected a Lucy-style falsetto. "Thanks for understanding. That was *really* good making out, honest."

Oliver shrugged. "I wouldn't mind if a girl said that to me. She sounds sweet."

She *was* sweet. That was part of the problem. Lucy's mysterious behavior with those old clothes notwithstanding, Max knew she was way too kind and gentle and *giving* for him. He'd seen her hug her mail carrier, for Christ's sake, then invite the grizzled, sunburned guy inside the shop for organic carrot cookies and tea. Lucy wore her heart on her sleeve. Max wasn't quite sure if his heart was even functional.

He didn't need it for deal making, after all.

Frowning, he snagged his beer between two fingers and stalked to the window. Across the cityscape, the sun meandered toward the distant mountains, getting ready for another spectacular Arizona sunset. They might not have subways or monuments in Phoenix, but they did know how to throw a kick-ass sunset. Morosely, he stared outside at the shimmering heat.

"Lighten up, pal," Oliver said. "At least your volunteering time is finished, right? No more trooping over there when you could be making contacts, no more parking tickets"—a whopper had garnished Max's Lexus convertible on his first day of volunteering—"no more wasting time. Right?"

Max made an evasive sound. He *had* been determined not to waste time here. That was part of the reason he'd sworn off women, he remembered vaguely. After Sarabeth, it had seemed a smart move. So he shouldn't be thinking about Lucy at all.

But he was. Because even though Lucy had tried to end things between them on a positive—if frustratingly platonic—note, something still felt unfinished.

The weird thing was, as much as Successfully Dressed and the whole downtown milieu wasn't his scene, Max knew he'd kind of miss it. He'd miss walking into the shop and seeing Lucy smile at him. He'd miss pretending not to see her following him. He'd miss baiting her with some deliberately non-PC, non-touchy-feely remark and watching her leap to the defense of whatever cause lay at hand.

"Only nine percent of the population volunteers." Oliver rattled things around—probably alphabetizing Max's video games. "Did you know that? Given the typical involvement in volunteerism, I'd say you've done your lifetime stint. Personally, I'm glad. Business is slipping, and Marlene won't shut up about needing your 'golden touch' to straighten things out."

Max turned. "What day is it today?"

"Friday. You've got that Little League game for Mrs. Ruiz's son tomorrow, and—oh hell. I recognize that look."

A nod. "We're going out."

Oliver blanched, holding up both hands. "Hey, I know you're pissed about how things ended with Lucy, but that—"

"She thanked me for understanding." Max didn't think the heinousness of that could be overemphasized. Who was he, Dr. Phil? "She 'liked' making out with me. *Liked!*"

"So what? Face it, Max. Not every woman is going to go crazy for you." Oliver shrugged. "Welcome to my life."

Max downed his beer. He headed for his closet.

"You know I hate going out!" Oliver called, trailing him. "This is revenge for me beating you at the game, isn't it? I never win, and you can't handle it." He smacked his forehead. "You were distracted. Damn it. I should have known."

Rifling through his recently returned clothes—courtesy of a certain purple-haired, outrageously happy-go-lucky girl—Max paused to give his lucky suit a fond glance.

He *had* been distracted. Today. In Lucy's office. She'd caught him off-guard. That was the problem.

All during his volunteering stint, he'd been trying to leave her alone. Trying to keep things on a professional basis so that Lucy—a certifiably *nice* girl, unlike the ones he usually got involved with—wouldn't get the wrong idea.

But what was wrong, he asked himself now, with finishing what they'd started? Nothing, that's what.

He hurled a shirt and jeans on his bed. A belt. His money clip, filled with twenties for tips.

Oliver gawked at them, looking pasty. "You're serious."

"Don't have a panic attack. It's just a cocktail party."

His partner crossed his arms. Sweat rings dampened his armpits. "Have fun. I'm not going."

"'Course you are." Max offered him an anticipatory grin, knowing he was bound to get his way sooner or later. He always did. "You're my excuse. You have to meet the whole crew."

Surrounded by all her friends, Lucy clutched her recyclable plastic party glass and looked around. Successfully Dressed was hopping. Somehow, word had gotten around about their first cocktail hour, and not only were all the invited interview suit buyers there, but so were Jade and Victor from down the street, several of her neighbors, and assorted passersby.

Franco and Nieca had stayed to help out, and Jade had donated refreshments from her health food store. Even now, people clustered near the makeshift buffet, scarfing pigs in blankets, edamame, and baba ghanouj. Ordinarily, Lucy loved a party—especially one with free munchies, given the sad state of her finances and the echoing emptiness of her refrigerator—but tonight she felt weird. Out of sorts.

And not just because her overfriendly FedEx delivery man, Crewcut Charlie, kept pinching her butt.

Scooting sideways to get beyond arm's reach, Lucy kicked herself for bringing Max's suits and shirts and stuffy business wear to work today. It had been his last volunteering day, so technically she'd owed them to him. But now she wished she'd hung onto them longer—maybe even delivered them to his place at Big Shot Central. Then she'd have had an excuse to see him again. As it was, all she had was a glass of punch, a shop full of pals . . . and a bunch of hot, steamy, cherished memories.

Although, Lucy told herself cheerfully, that was more than some people had. She ought to count herself lucky. Besides, if tonight went off well, it might mean increased business for Successfully Dressed. They could definitely use it.

She'd almost convinced herself that everything had worked out for the best—seeing Max leave included—when Franco stopped by. He took one look at her face and opened his arms to her.

"Poor Lucy. Had to let her dreamboat go."

There was no use protesting. Lucy stepped into his skinny embrace and immediately felt better. Franco patted her head with the hand that wasn't holding his drink.

"There are lots more investment bankers in the sea," he murmured, squeezing her tightly. "You'll find another one. No matter how kinky it might be to try."

She didn't have the heart to tell him Max wasn't an investment banker, but an entrepreneur—especially since she wasn't entirely clear on the difference herself. Max had only shared the barest details about his work— something having to do with putting exclusive retail "pet boutiques" on every street corner—before changing the subject.

Franco hugged her, seeming determined to bolster her flagging mood. It shouldn't have been all that comforting to be held by a man who probably had only twenty pounds on her—and those, stretched out several more inches—but it was.

"I miss Max too," Franco said. "Just like you do. He explained football to me! Nobody's ever had the patience to do that before. My dad will be totally psyched this Thanksgiving. And Max said he liked my belt too."

Jointly morose, they separated to glance down at it.

Lucy sniffled. "Who wouldn't? It's so you."

They hugged again, then separated, smiling.

"Go on," Lucy said, giving her friend a little shove toward the other side of the shop. "You're missing the whole party. Go mingle. Have fun. I'll be fine."

"Sure?"

"Absolutely." Fondly, Lucy watched Franco head for the other side of the sales floor. It was easy to keep track of his faux-hawk, especially in a crowd of mostly shorter people.

A minute later . . . "How are you holding up?"

Lucy glanced over her shoulder to find Nieca there. "I'm okay. How are you? Enjoying the—ooof!"

Her friend's commiserating embrace nearly knocked Lucy off her feet. As hugs went, Nieca's were hundred proof, backed by her voluptuous figure and bolstered by her general air of joie de vivre. Despite her sometimes tough stance, Nieca had a big heart. It was one of the things Lucy loved most about her.

"You can't fool me," her friend said, voice muffled. "If your shoulders were any more hunched, you'd be a turtle." She released her, then peered at her with concern. "Are you going to be okay? Franco told me about your hot desktop nookie this afternoon—"

"It was an accident! Sort of."

"—and, knowing you, if you've already reached the stage of wanting to get horizontal with Max, then you're pretty well head over heels for—"

"I'm fine. And *you* should be enjoying the party." Lucy pointed at the shop mannequin, searching for a diversion. "Just look at all those people crowding around Suzy! You came up with a fabulous ensemble for her tonight."

Nieca wasn't biting. Not even when it came to her "job seekers in space" Pierre Cardin theme. "Do you want to talk?"

"About what?" Batting her eyelashes, Lucy sipped her punch.

"Oh, I don't know. Maybe about . . . how I've never known you to jump a guy in your office before?"

"It didn't used to be my office," Lucy pointed out. "It used to be the DL's. So, strictly speaking, I didn't have the option before." *More's the pity.* "Besides, I'm fine."

"Say it another dozen times. Maybe someone will buy it. Someone who doesn't know you the way I do."

"Sheesh, Nieca." Lucy rolled her eyes. "Between you and Franco, you'd swear I need a keeper. I'm not picking out wedding rings with Max. I'm just having a little fun with him!"

She took in Nieca's skeptical gaze.

"Maybe I felt like taking a walk on the wild side, okay?" Lucy elaborated. She was a free spirit. She didn't need to fall in love with a man to want to sleep with him. "I'm an adult. I'm fine."

Damn it. There it was again. *Fine.* What was that, some kind of verbal tick? Fine, fine, fine, fine, fine.

Nieca gave her another assessing look.

"Don't look so worried!" Lucy said. "Come on. Let's talk about something else. Have you tried Jade's mango salsa yet?"

"Yes," Nieca grumbled halfheartedly. "It's delicious."

They lapsed into silence, Nieca shooting Lucy concerned glances and Lucy doing her best to ignore them.

So she'd gotten a little hot and heavy with Max today. So what? That didn't mean they were destined to start picking out his-and-hers bath towels. It didn't mean anything except that Max was a really wonderful kisser with a propensity toward stealth undressing and a brainteaser belt buckle.

"So . . . any luck with the people from the *New Times?*" Nieca asked, perking up. "We could sure use some positive press."

"No." Lucy sighed, thinking of her hopes for media coverage of the shop in the alternative weekly. "I sent an invitation to the address in the paper, but I never heard anything."

"Maybe next time." Nieca offered a reassuring shoulder squeeze, evidently having decided to scrap the subject of Lucy's love life . . . for now. "After all, this party sure looks like a hit. I think it's even drawing in people from the street."

They both glanced around, watching the customers mingle with the neighborhood businesspeople. The starving artists congregated around the appetizers, happily munching.

"I wouldn't be surprised if a few of our customers get jobs from people they meet here tonight," Lucy mused, watching Tracee chat with Jade. "All of the résumé and interview flyers I put out are gone already too." She smiled. "Maybe this was a better idea than I thought."

Nearby, another customer shook hands with Crewcut Charlie—who, despite his pinching habit, might have some leads on jobs with FedEx. Watching them, Lucy felt wonderful. Maybe she *wasn't* in over her head. Maybe she really *could* stay on top of everything—and ensure Nieca and Franco's paychecks, the way she'd promised.

Just so long as she remained focused and—

"Hey." Nieca nudged her. "Isn't that Max?" She squinted. "And who's the Geeky McGeekerson with him?"

As near as Oliver could determine, the odds of his enjoying this event were approximately a million to one. Which wasn't saying much, since they'd started at a hundred thousand to one when he and Max had climbed into Max's sports car and zoomed past every semifamiliar Phoenix landmark to arrive in the heart of what was, to Oliver, another world.

Here, the tastefully landscaped and luxurious grounds

surrounding new high-rises and shopping centers gave way to scraggly grass, concrete, and water-thrifty desert plants. The stucco houses huddled low to the ground. The billboards above the streets were in Español, and on the way here, Oliver was sure he'd counted six tattoo parlors and eighteen dive bars.

They'd heard the party before they'd gotten there, thanks to what sounded like ancient Kinks music booming from the sound system. They'd smelled it before they'd officially arrived too. Exotic patchouli and candle wax scents hung in the air, interspersed with the aroma of garlic-laden edibles. Joviality spilled from the shop's lighted windows, and several leather-wearing people hung outside, smoking.

After running that gauntlet, he'd need to Febreze the hell out of himself when he got home, Oliver realized as he followed Max deeper into the party. Maybe bathe in the stuff. He had several economy-size bottles, purchased at a thirty-two percent discount from his favorite price club.

Wishing he were anywhere but here, silently cursing out Max for dragging him to a (non-work-related) get-together, Oliver shoved an errant rack of sparkly clothes from his face. He looked around, desperately trying to get comfortable.

The place was weird. Colors popped at his overstimulated brain, and the sounds of people talking rattled him. Everyone seemed to be having fun, but Oliver knew he was not one of the chosen people. Socializing did not come easily to him and never had. There wouldn't even be any potential investors here.

Forcing himself to straighten his spine, he sucked in a deep breath. *Look casual,* he commanded himself. *Approachable.* He fingered the hastily scribbled list of potential current events conversation starters in his pants pocket, knowing it was probably already crumpled and moist from handling.

Max slapped him on the shoulder. "Hey, have fun."

"Wait! Don't . . . leave yet."

Too late. Max shouldered his way through the crowd with exactly the easy confidence he always displayed, leaving Oliver behind. Damn it. Since they'd been kids, Max had insisted that Oliver would outgrow his shyness— would learn to love talking up the ladies and making jokes with the men. No matter how much Oliver insisted, "No, that's *your* version of a party," Max remained staunch in his belief that someday Oliver would simply snap out of it.

Miserable, Oliver followed a few paces behind. He kept Max in view for reassurance, not wanting to be stranded at the party. It wouldn't be the first time Max had hooked up with a woman and left Oliver to find his own way home. His research of the emergent Phoenix taxi and public transit systems had convinced him they would not be likely getaway options.

"Hi," he mumbled as he passed people. "Hello."

He nodded as though he knew some of them, then kept going. It was better to remain in motion. Otherwise, Oliver was liable to find himself plastered against one of the vintage washing machines he'd seen, drink in hand, a frozen smile on his face, superglued in position for the night. Hard experience had taught him to stay out of corners at parties, as much as his entire being urged him to hide in one.

Multiple piercings, tattoos, dreadlocks, and unusual hair colors abounded. Determined not to stare at them, lest he find himself in an ass-kicking situation, Oliver kept his gaze focused straight ahead. Max and his black shirt wove through the crowd, looking carefree and secure. Damn them both.

Suddenly, Oliver collided with something soft. "Ooof!"

A woman turned. "What's the matter, curly? Don't get out much?" She gave him a once-over. "Are you lost or something? The insurance adjustors' meeting is across town."

"I'm sorry, I . . ." Oliver trailed off, gawking. "I . . ."

"Hey." Recognition flashed over her features, then assessment. "You're the guy who crashed with Max."

"I, er . . ."

Hell. Speak, he commanded himself.

Nothing emerged. Since he was staring at his dream girl, that wasn't surprising. Oliver knew it instantly. Even though it had never happened before, he recognized the sensation of falling head over heels. Hard.

Unfortunately, he also recognized the probability that his feelings made it twice as likely he would make an ass of himself. Maybe two-point-three times more likely.

"Geeky McGeekerson," she announced, nodding as though reading his mind and viewing all the percentages there.

She folded her arms over her chest, pushing her tantalizing cleavage higher. Her skin gleamed, revealed to advantage in her skimpy dress and accented by jewelry unlike any Oliver had seen before, featuring razorblades and talismans. She tilted her head, drawing his attention to her reddish braids, her amused expression, her horn-rimmed eyeglasses.

At the sight of them, something inside Oliver zinged. He loved girls in glasses. Especially this girl. Admittedly, hers were freaky glasses, like the ones in fuzzy black-and-white movies. But they made her look smart, and that made Oliver believe, just for a fleeting instant, that they might have something in common.

"I guess I ought to be nice to you," she said, her voice sounding rich and throaty and sexy. "Seeing as how we're practically going to be in-laws someday, anyhow."

He wanted to ask her what she meant, but she took his arm before he could open his mouth. Her breast jiggled seductively against his biceps, and her hips brushed his companionably as she hustled him to the punch bowl at the other side of the room. Oliver stood by dumbly, feeling a keen sense of disappointment as she released him to dip up a drippy cup of red liquid.

"It's an all-ages party, because of the interview-suit mothers and their offspring. That's why we don't have anything stronger." She raised the cup, tongued a drip from its edge, then handed it to him. "*Salud!*"

Oliver gripped the cup, his whole body alert with the knowledge that his dream woman had actually *licked* it. Her manner felt impossibly intimate. Oliver felt hopelessly hooked. He had to speak to her. Tell her how he felt.

Miraculously, he managed a smile. "We should get married."

She patted him. "Very funny, smooth talker."

"Do you . . . know anyone here?" Oliver forced out.

Yes! He was engaging in small talk. Even without his list! She seemed surprised to have finally had more than four consecutive words from him and stood looking at him now with new appreciation. At least to Oliver, it seemed that way.

His heart pounded. His mouth felt simultaneously parched and drooling. He knocked back some sticky-sweet punch and felt his blood sugar soar. Yes, that was better. A hundred percent better. But he was never letting go of this cup. Never.

"Anyone? Try everyone. I practically *live* here."

Her laughter enchanted him. So did her teasing eyes, her fluid gestures, and the arresting structure of her face. She was a goddess. She was perfect and yet not perfect . . . perfect, Oliver decided, for him.

"You practically live here, huh?" More small talk, even if it was a little faltering. He felt like a socializing *genius*. Max had been right! "I guess that means—"

"Speaking of which," she said, "I see someone I know."

She gifted him with a smile, then another squeeze of his biceps. Oliver wished mightily that he'd spent the Surgeon General–recommended sixty minutes per day at the gym this week.

"So, I'd better run. Good luck with that 'getting married' thing." She swiveled. Her backside was amazing too.

"Wait!" Oliver touched her. Beneath his hand, her bare shoulder felt warm and smooth. Exquisite. His stomach lurched painfully at the thought of losing her. "What's your name?"

"Nieca." She looked puzzled. "But then, I'd have thought Max would have told you all about me already. Doesn't he ever talk to his friends about his other friends?"

Fuck. Max had gotten to her first. Despair crushed Oliver like a gigantic, people-filled, Acme party anvil.

He didn't have a chance.

"Max doesn't talk to anybody," he said. "Not seriously."

"Oh. That's too bad." Nieca crinkled her nose. Adorably.

Then the woman Oliver had always wanted—and hadn't known it until now—walked away from him . . . probably forever.

Lucy couldn't stop staring. *Max was here.* Max was here, he looked incredible, and he was headed her way.

She stood rooted to the spot, the whole party receding around her. Nothing seemed to exist except Max's face, Max's wind-tousled dark hair, Max's tall, strong body. He cut a swath through the crowd, dressed in a lean, dark shirt and a pair of jeans, his gaze fixed intently on her. Something unfinished and wildly exciting whooshed between them.

"I'm going to pretend my invitation got lost in the mail."

He leaned nearer, offering something between a hug and an enticement to mambo. He put his hand on her hip as though to steady them both amid the swirling crowd. "I know you didn't mean to leave me out of the fun."

His husky voice—and the promise inherent in his tone—made goose bumps rise on her arms. Grinning with excitement, Lucy rose on tiptoes and put her face near his. Two could play the "this party's too crowded" game. She steadied herself with a hand on his shoulder, then gave a subtle caress.

"You know the fun doesn't start till you get here, Max. At least that's what everybody tells me." She leaned back just enough to catch a good view of his mouth. Ahhh, memories. "It turns out you made a big impression with the clientele. Everyone's been asking about you."

He grinned. "I may have advised a few customers here and there."

"Also, Franco has two dates next week, more phone numbers than he can handle, and big plans to watch football this Thanksgiving for the first time ever. You're his hero."

Max inclined his head modestly. "Glad to help."

"Nieca swears the washing machines will revolt without you here to keep them in line. I don't know what you did, but they've never worked so well. She's bummed your volunteering is over with."

His gaze met hers. "What about you?"

She eyed him, trying to gauge his seriousness. "Me? Well, I heard the mail carrier say it won't be the same around here without you to haul in the heavy stuff."

"It was only a few boxes. Franco will help next time."

The party surged on. They only stood there, unable to look away. Lucy felt her old giddiness return, tempered this time with the knowledge that it would only be temporary, *could* only be temporary, if she was going to save Successfully Dressed and everyone's jobs along with it.

She was having enough trouble as it was, and Max was simply too distracting. It was just as well he'd be back at Big Shot Central soon.

"So." She sipped her drink, searching for something to say besides the obvious—how *fine* he looked . . . and how happy she was to see him. "Did you feel like slumming tonight, or what?"

Max looked intent. "What about you?" he repeated. "Do *you* miss me yet?"

She hesitated. If she told the truth . . .

Who was she kidding? She always told the truth.

I feel as if I've waited a lifetime for you to walk through that door.

No way. Maybe a diversion was in order.

Lucy gazed up at him, hoping her feelings didn't show as readily to Max as they did to her friends. "Not as much as I'm about to," she said. "Enjoy the party, Max. I'll see you around . . . and take care."

Then, using every ounce of job-saving fortitude Lucy possessed, she said good-bye and lost him in the crowd.

8

The door to Max's loft apartment burst open, slamming against the wall. He followed it with Lucy in his arms, dropping his keys and not caring a damned bit. With one foot, he managed to swing the door shut again. Short of breath, hot, and taut with anticipation, he pressed Lucy against the door and continued what they'd begun in the elevator.

"Wait," she murmured, craning her neck between kisses. "I want to see what your place . . . mmmm."

Her next moan shot straight to his groin, making him even harder than he already was. He couldn't remember the last time he'd wanted a woman this much—the last time he'd been cross-eyed with desire and longing and need. The last time he'd shaken with the raw necessity of getting closer to another person. He ducked his head and shoved up Lucy's top, then unhooked her bra.

Max couldn't wait long enough to remove either piece of clothing. He held them up with one hand, then sucked her nipple in his mouth and tongued her, groaning with the intense pleasure of finally tasting her. Her skin felt sleek, her body warm and inviting and wonderfully curved, and he spread both palms over her shoulder blades to arch her forward, to give himself access to everything he wanted.

Almost.

"Ahhh, you're incredible," he whispered, hearing the huskiness in his voice. He dragged his lips across her breasts in a frenzied arc, feeling as if he'd waited a lifetime to pull Lucy in his door, push her against it, and give her all the pleasure he could. "You feel so good."

She buried her hand in his hair, yanking just hard enough to let him know she was on the verge of losing control. She panted in his ear, her breath as hoarse as his own. Writhing against him, Lucy heaved him nearer by his belt, plastering them both against the door.

It thumped beneath them. Max didn't care. He could wake his neighbors, they could call the police . . . just so long as he could stay with Lucy, just like this.

Well . . . nearly.

"Take off your panties," he said, kissing her neck.

God, she felt good. So smooth, so eager, so . . .

"I'm not wearing panties," she answered. "Kiss me harder."

He did, nearly coming undone at the thought of Lucy naked beneath her little denim skirt. Max lowered both hands to her butt and squeezed, catching her gasp of surprise with another, wetter, deeper, and—as requested—*harder* open-mouthed kiss.

Never let it be said Max Nolan didn't aim to please.

Wiggling his fingers, he found her skirt hem, then the bare backs of her thighs. He groaned, pulsing with an elemental need to lift her skirt, hear her gasp, make them both come in the next three heartbeats.

He lifted her. "Wrap your legs around me."

Lucy moaned and raked through his hair, seeming beyond the ability to comprehend his suggestion. She tipped her head back against the door, eyes closed and face flushed, looking hotter than he'd ever imagined.

Somehow, she'd taken off her top and her bra—or he had. He couldn't remember, having lost track during all the kissing. In the low glow of his spot lighting, her bare breasts quivered.

Seduced by the sight, Max hitched her higher against him and leaned over to kiss her. She seemed to catch on then, clamping both legs around his middle with a limber strength he hadn't counted on, but should have. Her thighs gripped his hips, taut and smooth and steady. Damn, there was a lot to be said for yoga-practicing bohemian girls. Especially this one.

Her tight nipple rolled against his tongue, inciting Max to near riot below his beltline. God, he wanted her. Usually, he possessed more stamina than this, but somehow, with Lucy, things were different. She pushed her hips against him, demanding more. That was what he wanted too. More. Soon. Now.

Now that he had Lucy in his arms, he'd carry her to the bedroom and do this properly. He'd—

Some low sound penetrated his lusty fog. Max blinked and cocked his head, trying to hear it in case they were about to be arrested for indecently loud enjoyment.

". . . how we got here," Lucy was saying, panting, "but when you caught up to me, all I said was, 'You look nice.'"

Vaguely, he recognized her words. Their meaning followed a few gasps later. She wanted to talk? About how he'd followed her at the cocktail party? Talk? Now?

"Yeah," he managed, wanting to make her happy. If Lucy wanted to talk, he would . . . savor the sight of her as he caressed her thighs, her knees. Wow. This position afforded leverage, not accessibility, but he loved it anyway. Wait—where was he? Back at the shop. "That's all you said," Max agreed. "But it was the *way* you said it."

He couldn't explain it. Right now, he damned sure didn't want to try. But he did remember it had been sweet. Affecting. Irresistible. There was something about the way Lucy looked at him. Something he knew he needed.

"It might have helped," Lucy said, "that you remembered me doing this." She grabbed his belt buckle, her wild purple hair brushing over his chest. She wriggled and slid down his body, changing their position as she struggled with the buckle. "Doing *this!*" No dice. Her feminine bravado wavered. She bit her lip and added her other hand to the mix. "Doing—"

"Oh no you don't. Not this time." Max caught hold of her wrists, pinned her arms over her head, then kissed her. Deeply. "This time, *I'm* calling the shots."

"Fine. Then take off your pants."

There wasn't much to argue about in that suggestion.

He grinned. "You read my mind."

"And then give them to me. Because later I'm having my artisan friend melt down that damned belt buckle."

He didn't care. That was how crazy, how *ready,* he felt.

While Max unbuckled, Lucy kissed him. By the time he realized what was happening, his fly was open, and Lucy had her hand on his naked chest, doing something to his nipple. Maybe sizing it for a piercing—he didn't know and didn't care. With her other hand, she clutched his shirt, whirling it overhead in a windup. He caught a glimpse of her face, exhilarated and sexy and unique, and knew right then that there was no one else in the world he'd rather be considering getting pierced for.

His shirt flew across the room.

Something tottered. Tipped. Crashed.

Lucy's hands went to her mouth. "Oh! I'm so sorry!"

She bolted away from him before he could stop her. Following the sound, she headed in the semidarkness toward the sofa. Through the windows, moonlight trickled across the terrace and into his loft, mingling with the subtle "lighting scheme" his designer had insisted on.

The combination offered just enough illumination to

let Max know he *definitely* wanted to follow. The smooth expanse of Lucy's back, so graceful and feminine and so, well, *naked,* was nearly as intriguing as her front . . . especially at the place where her low-riding skirt hung on her hips. He wanted to kiss her there. Right there. And elsewhere. Over and over.

She leaned over, giving a distressed sound as she spotted the thing that had tipped over. A midcentury modern lamp.

"It doesn't matter," Max said. "It's just a lamp."

"But maybe it's expensive." Lucy hunched, reaching for it. She set it on the end table where it belonged, then scanned the room, her eyes widening. "Because this place looks like—"

"I don't care. It's fine."

But he was too late. She'd already gotten an eyeful of his apartment, and for the first time, Lucy seemed distracted.

"Hey, this is . . ." Frowning, she straightened. "*Nice,* but did you just move in? It feels so impersonal in here. No pictures, no *stuff.* Like you haven't unpacked yet, or—"

"This is the way it always is."

Max didn't want to talk about it. Softening his refusal with a smile, he caught Lucy round the waist, then pulled her to him beside the coffee table. He kissed her. Her bare breasts rubbed against his chest, encouraging all the same rampant, up-against-the-door feelings he'd been having a few minutes ago.

"Hey . . . remember me?" he murmured.

As a reminder, Max pressed her hand to his open fly.

Lucy's eyes widened. Her expression of amazement was one he knew he'd remember forever. Just like her, it was unexpected, endearing . . . and sexy as hell.

"Hello, Mr. Wonderful." Her grin flashed. "I'll never forget you now."

She caressed him, then nudged his jeans fractionally lower. Her fingers closed around the length of him, and Lucy gave another delighted sound. Sucking in a breath, Max looked down. The view of her hand moving against him, framed by his open fly, was the most erotic thing he'd ever seen.

Helplessly, he tightened his grasp on her shoulders. "Oh God, don't stop. That feels so . . . ahhh."

His knees threatened to buckle. He'd thought that only happened in the movies, yet here he was, wobbling. Moaning, Max swallowed hard and gazed at Lucy. She looked directly back at him, plainly loving what she was doing and clearly intent on making him crazy for as long as he allowed.

Or not.

From somewhere, he mustered the strength to stop her. To drop to the sofa. To pull her, with a kiss for encouragement, on his lap. The air between them felt heavy with anticipation, hot with need, musky with desire. Lucy balanced on her knees and straddled him, and at the sight of her there, so beautiful and so giving and so *open*, Max nearly lost control.

Her position was an invitation he couldn't refuse. As though sensing that fact, Lucy leaned forward, clad in her rucked-up skirt, her belly ring, and nothing else. Her hips swiveled and her breasts chafed his chest as she kissed her way from his mouth to his ear. She nipped his earlobe, making him shudder and awakening him to a sensitivity he'd never been aware of before. She pinned him to the sofa and whispered to him, making him ache.

"Touch me, Max. Please. Right here."

Like him, she put his hand exactly where she wanted it—beneath her skirt. She felt hot and slick and ready, writhing beneath his every stroke. Her next kiss, when she gave it to him, was rough with impatience and need.

Max met her in every way. In this, at least, they were a perfect match.

He stopped for a minute to protect them both, then paused to cup her face. He gazed at her seriously, absorbing the slant of her nose, the dark gleam of her eyes, the luscious, crooked pink of her open mouth.

"I had to come back for you," he said, explaining as best he could. "I knew things weren't finished with us yet."

Lucy nodded. She lifted slightly, positioning herself. Her thighs quivered. "Let's finish," she urged. "Now."

Silently, he nodded. He clutched her hips. The denim of her hitched-up skirt offered a wicked contrast to her softness everywhere else. Max couldn't get enough. So when first he pulled Lucy down on him, when first he felt the tight, welcoming embrace of her body, it was all he could do not to thrust again and again in a frenzy of longing. Something about Lucy's face as he entered her, though, something tender and brash in equal measure, made him slow down. For her.

It didn't last long. Because next Lucy clutched him with her head thrown back and her breath coming faster. She moaned, coming closer to the edge. She rode him with eager enjoyment and urged him to love her, and Max simply couldn't hold out.

The two of them were joined in a molten clasp, the room filled with their cries. His whole body tensed, need pushing him further and further, and as he lifted his gaze from Lucy's body to her face, Max knew something incredible and strange and unforgettable was happening. Heart hammering, he cupped her face in his hands. Her eyes were deep and lovely, her body hot and generous, and as Lucy stilled, then shook in ecstasy above him, she did something surprising.

She smiled. Smiled as though she'd never been happier, smiled as though Max was responsible for everything good in this room, in the world, in between them. She panted and smiled, her whole face glowing, and Max knew he'd never seen anyone more beautiful than Lucy in that moment.

An instant later, he tipped over the edge himself, coming with a mindless roar that would definitely wake the neighbors, even if nothing else had. Wracked with shudders, Max could only hold on to Lucy, could only tip his head back and thrust again and again, needing to prolong this feeling for as long as he could. Gasping, breathless, he pulsed with fulfillment.

"Wow." Lucy grinned down at him, her hair askew and her smile still wide. Her body gleamed with sweat, as did his, and her legs quaked around him. "That was amazing."

She sat back, giving him a teasing inner squeeze. Max groaned, not trusting himself to move. Something had just happened between them. Something . . . different. He couldn't puzzle it out, not with most of his blood pooled south and his mind spinning, but he felt . . . weird. Changed.

Wonderful.

Christ. Widening his eyes, he gazed up at Lucy.

"Want to go again?" she asked, still grinning.

That was when it hit him. The difference was *Lucy.* And the weird feeling was . . . uncertainty. Holy shit.

For the first time in his life, Max Nolan didn't have the faintest idea what to do next.

His heart rate picked up speed. This time, it had nothing to do with wanting, and everything to do with needing.

Needing . . . Lucy?

No. Screw that. The last thing he wanted was—

"No, wait." Lucy made a face, swiping her purple hair from her cheek. "I forgot. I have to go back to the party—I'm supposed to be giving out gift certificates at the end of the night."

Her face downturned with disappointment, she leaned

over him in an intimate caress. Her soft, lingering kiss worked magic on Max, rousing him before any man had a right to be roused, making him want her to stay. Stay, stay . . . stay.

Lucy straightened gracefully, her gaze pinned to his face. He thought he glimpsed a vulnerability there . . . a question.

She wanted him to ask her to stay.

Hell. This was more than he'd counted on.

"Yeah. I've got to go back for Oliver," Max agreed, feeling like a heel just for saying it. He eased his words with a caress, then tried for his usual carefree smile. He had no idea whether he pulled it off or not. Jesus, that never happened to him. "He gets mad when I leave him stranded."

Silence fell. He and Lucy stared at each other, still joined, but not for much longer. Max stiffened, feeling freakishly reluctant to make the first move.

As soon as he did, Lucy would be gone.

He needed her to be gone, he reminded himself. Her bighearted gaze, so speculative and so full of life, was doing things to his heart he'd never experienced and wanted no damned part of. Trying to resist, he glanced away first.

"I guess we'll have to take a rain check," she said.

Despite her light tone, they both knew that wouldn't happen. Unaccountably confused, Max nodded.

"I'll drive you back."

Not much later, Lucy gathered her things and kissed him good-bye. She touched his cheek and gave him a smile. She slid out of the passenger seat of his Lexus and left him alone.

They'd both agreed—at Lucy's instigation—it would be better to rejoin the party separately.

"Well," Max said, staring at his steering wheel as he

waited for a parking spot to open up outside Successfully Dressed. "*That* didn't go off exactly as planned."

Ensconced in the passenger seat of Andrea Cho's gigantic, gleaming SUV, Oliver brooded at the lighted instrument panel. Unfamiliar Phoenix streets whizzed past, a blur of light and darkness. Andrea drove the same way she did everything else—double speed and to the point—but that was all right with him. He just wanted to get away from the scene of his heartbreak.

Damn Max. Damn him and his I'm-so-charming-and-effortlessly-talkative vibe. Damn his knack with the ladies and his idiot inability to leave a single one of them alone. Damn his opportunity to know Nieca first and shove Oliver right out of the running.

"We could have waited for Max, you know." Andrea braked at a red light, her satiny dress shimmering in the reflected glow. She looked at him through no-nonsense, almond-shaped eyes, as though seeing all his secrets. "I wanted to talk to him, anyway, but he disappeared."

Oliver just *bet* he'd disappeared. Probably, Max had stumbled into a horde of Playboy Bunnies and hadn't been able to extricate himself yet. What a problem.

He folded his arms. "You can talk to me."

"Sure, but Max is the one I usually—"

Oliver set his jaw. "You can talk to me."

"Okay. Fine."

Andrea set the SUV in motion again, the tires wheeling through the sultry night. All that nonsense about the desert cooling down after sunset apparently referred to the walloping twenty-degree drop from one hundred fifteen to ninety-five. Still hot enough to make Oliver, most recently based on a project in San Francisco, pretty damned surly.

Or maybe watching his dream goddess walking away had done that. It was a fifty–fifty split, odds-wise.

"I guess you and Max got my message," Andrea began, "since you were both at the Successfully Dressed cocktail party."

Actually, Oliver hadn't expected to see her there. It had been a stroke of dumb luck that he'd stumbled upon their publicist while making the rounds, looking for that bastard Max, who'd left him marooned again. Oliver's inconvenient tango with love at first sight had made him lose track of his friend just long enough to get separated. And for what?

"Speaking of which, before I forget"—Andrea plucked a scrap of paper from her visor and handed it to him—"you should tell Max to be more careful with his receipts. I found this one in his building's lobby when I was dropping off contact lists."

Oliver unfolded it. Successfully Dressed donations.

"Naturally, I was curious when I found that." Andrea nodded to the receipt, then squinted through the windshield as she turned the corner. Her SUV's A/C blasted them both. "We both know Max isn't exactly the charitable type."

Oliver snorted. "Not when it comes to women, at least."

Andrea slanted him a curious look.

"Never mind." Oliver shook his head. "You were saying?"

"So I went down to the shop to check it out. You know, to find out if there'd been some sort of mistake, or to see if Max was up to some new venture. It's important for me to have a thorough understanding of my clients."

Oliver gave a thoughtful sound. He felt ninety-eight percent certain Max's only new venture involved spreading his machismo far and wide. And shutting out Oliver. Dickhead.

But since they still had a business to run together . . .
"Max spent a few days volunteering. He's finished now."

"Oh no. He can't be finished." Andrea braked in front
of Oliver's building, a renovated 1930s complex with
orange trees between the units and a golf course sprawl-
ing behind the main grounds. "Given what I've found out
about Successfully Dressed, it's going to be crucial in
getting your new venture running in Phoenix. I know
Max has been unusually stymied making contacts, but
that's all about to change."

Andrea reached in the backseat, shoved aside a Successfully Dressed shopping bag, and withdrew a binder.
She dropped it on Oliver's lap with a nearly soprano-
inducing thunk.

"What's this?" he asked.

"That is the key to getting the local investors you need
to make the Ruizes happy." Andrea, never one for false
modesty, seemed extremely pleased with herself. "Have
a look. You'll see what I mean."

Skeptically, Oliver flipped open the binder. In the
feeble glow from the streetlight, he saw a series of names
and figures and detailed records. Right now, the only
thing he wanted to do with this binder was drop it on
Max's big, fat head. He didn't give a damn about who
had contributed what to—

"Holy shit," he said, turning a page.

"Exactly." Andrea smiled. "Can you take it from here?"

Oh yeah. Feeling better already, Oliver closed the
binder and cradled it to his chest. "I'll handle everything."

Lucy swooped through the shop on a burst of energy,
scooping up used punch cups and tossing them in a
wastebasket for later recycling. Seen in the sunny light
of another June morning, Successfully Dressed looked a
little the worse for wear after their inaugural cocktail

party—and so did Suzy the mannequin—but right now Lucy felt equipped to handle everything.

She'd handled Max last night, hadn't she?

Yes, she had.

Literally.

Reminded of her bold behavior, Lucy grinned. She picked up an abandoned hors d'oeuvre plate, feeling light enough to spin around the room with it. Max had been wonderful last night. She'd enjoyed herself to the fullest, and she knew he had too.

At least he had . . . until they'd finished. Then, in the swanky subdued lighting of his posh apartment, Max had just looked freaked out. And very eager to see her leave.

That, Lucy admitted, had been a disappointment. A part of her had been hoping . . . No, she should have expected it. It didn't take a rocket scientist to realize Max wasn't exactly a by-the-numbers, let's-have-a-cuddle kind of guy. He wasn't looking for anything long-term.

But then, neither was she. Right? So things had worked out nicely between them. Hadn't they?

Yes. Even if this morning, she *did* wish . . .

Nah. Fiercely, Lucy made herself count her blessings. She'd had a fabulous night with a charming man, and she'd pulled off a successful event for her shop too. She really couldn't ask for more.

Besides, with her Max-centric curiosity out of her system, Lucy figured she had a good chance of concentrating on work again. After all, she wouldn't be wasting time following Max around anymore. She wouldn't be spending her days mooning over him, ogling his butt, longing for one of his smiles. That was all for the good. She'd taken charge, assuaged her yen for Max, and then moved on. They'd both be happier now.

Although she *did* wish he'd asked her to stay.

No, she didn't. Being with him had been incredible. Hotttt. Impossibly erotic and unbelievably fulfilling. But it had also been—of necessity—temporary. That was just the way it was, and Lucy believed in accepting things as they were. It was a philosophy she'd always found very freeing.

Cleaning at a slower pace, Nieca followed, her eyes shielded with her glasses. Her braids hung limply, and her red hair seemed slightly less vibrant than usual. Even her sundress and combat boots lacked their typical sense of fashion irony.

Frowning, surprised she hadn't noticed those details right away, Lucy halted. "What's the matter?"

Gloomily, Nieca scrubbed at a gooey patch of spilled punch. She swiped her hand over her forehead. "I came home to an eviction notice last night. If I don't come up with my back rent, my landlord is giving me the boot." Her depressed gaze met Lucy's. "And my student loans are coming due soon too."

Lucy gave her a hug. "No problem. I'll give you an advance on your paycheck. Just don't worry, okay?"

"But I'm *already* advanced on my—"

"You're good for it, right? It's not as if you're going to skip town on me. Come on. At the very least I know you wouldn't leave Suzy looking like that."

They both glanced at the shop window. In her usual place, the mannequin posed in a 1940s negligee, a grunge-style flannel shirt, round-toed pumps, and—horror of horrors—leg warmers.

They shuddered.

"Cretins. Flannel *and* round-toed pumps? Ridiculous."

Lucy smiled, happy to see Nieca's feistiness returning. "I don't know who re-dressed Suzy during the party, but they're definitely *not* up to your fashion caliber."

"Oh, Luce." Nieca sighed. "You're really being nice about this, but you can't afford to keep giving me early paychecks. This place isn't doing *that* well yet, and you're not exactly a financial wizard. If the Dragon Lady decides to pull the plug after all—"

"She won't. Sooner or later, we'll make this place a hit." Determinedly, Lucy hefted her wastebasket again. "It'll just take time, that's all. I'm not worried."

But one look at Nieca's face told Lucy her friend *was* worried. This time, for more reasons than one, Lucy had to find a way to deliver. She'd promised to make Successfully Dressed a hit. Somehow, she had to do it.

Otherwise, Cornelia Burnheart might change her flighty socialite's mind—again—and sell the whole shop out from under them all. They'd be jobless. Paycheckless. Hopeless.

Yikes. The stakes were really sinking in.

"You're not worried," Nieca chimed in breezily, "because, unlike me, who only met Captain Geekazoid last night, you're on a post-hookup high." She offered a teasing grin. "I can tell. So come on, spill."

Lucy hesitated, eagerness battling with discretion.

"A lady never tells," she said.

Then she flounced away, hoping Nieca hadn't glimpsed the stress puckers that had surely bloomed on her forehead.

For the first time ever, Lucy needed to learn to strategize. But how?

9

Max hurtled into work on Monday morning at seven forty-five sharp, briefcase in hand and sunglasses on. A dozen steps took him from the lobby to the glass and steel confines of his office, where things were predictable. He liked it there. He knew what to do, how to do it, and what would happen next.

Except today.

Today, Oliver slouched in the Eames chair opposite Max's desk. And as if the slouching weren't bizarre enough for a straight arrow like Oliver, his partner had a distinctly menacing air about him too.

Max glanced over his shoulder, sure he'd wandered into the wrong suite of offices.

"You missed Ricky Ruiz's Little League game," Oliver said.

Hell. He was in the right place.

"Yeah?" Max dropped in his desk chair, whipped off his sunglasses, then snatched some message slips. He scanned them. "You missed your calling as a Girl Scout den mother."

All he wanted to do was grab some files, pick up his cell phone, and bury himself in work. *Real* work. Work that didn't have to be postponed for volunteering. Work that would keep him from thinking about a certain bohemian girl with laughing eyes and a smile that made a man feel ten feet tall.

And a whole lot less alone.

Not that Max needed stuff like that. Other guys might need mushy-gushy, touchy-feely crap, but he was different. He'd already learned that lesson well enough to—

"Bite me, Nolan." Oliver straightened in his chair, both hands clasped between his bent knees in an unusual show of coordination. "Going to that game was your responsibility. *Your* contribution to the business. Your *only* contribution to the business. Or are you too 'busy' these days to schmooze the people you're supposed to schmooze?"

Taken aback at his partner's biting tone, Max frowned. This wasn't Oliver's usual Monday morning shtick. Neither was the way he kept saying "schmooze"—as though it might be contagious. Max didn't like it.

"So I missed one game. Big deal."

"It is a big deal. To *our* deal."

"And what's with all the 'busy' talk, anyway?" Max tried to moderate his tone. To smile. "What the hell does that mean?"

"Oh. I think. You. Know."

High-handedness had never been Oliver's thing. More confused than ever, Max stared at him. "Yeah. I don't. But whatever, pal." It occurred to him that Oliver was probably pissed about the cocktail party. "Speaking of busy, where the hell did you disappear to on Friday? I looked all over the place for you."

I'll just bet you did, Oliver's expression said.

"I left with Andrea Cho," he said with dignity.

"Ahhh." Max couldn't help but grin. This was more like it. "So *that's* what's going on. You found a girl you like—"

Oliver's sharp look told him he was on the right track.

"—and you're all shook up over it. No wonder. Jesus, you had me going there for a minute." Relieved, Max surveyed his friend with new eyes. He nodded, happy for him. He'd always known Oliver would snap out of his head-trip "shyness" routine. "So you and our publicist are . . . ?"

"Working to dig up leads for our pet boutique venture. Like you're supposed to be. Like you're *going* to be."

Max spread his arms, indicating the files awaiting him and the hands-free cell phone headset he'd left on his desk, right beside the entrepreneurial award they'd won last year.

"Right. Working. That's why I'm here. So if you'll go do whatever picky-ass stuff you do"—he leavened the jab with a smile, waiting for Oliver to protest—"I'll get down to it."

Oliver only sat there, arms crossed.

If anything, he seemed more constipated than ever.

Perplexed, Max tilted his head. It hadn't been *that* much of a jab. What was Oliver's problem? "Look, I shouldn't have left you at the party alone. Okay? It sounds as if it all worked out pretty well for you and Andrea in the end, anyway. Are we good?"

More sitting. With fifty percent more glaring.

"Come on," Max coaxed. He wasn't in the mood for babying Oliver, given the weekend he'd had, but if that's what it took. . . . "Cut me some slack. All I want to do is wipe last week from my memory and get down to business."

At that, Oliver perked up. "Why?"

"Why get down to business?" Max hedged. "Because that's what I do. What I've always done."

Oliver looked on the verge of refuting that assertion when Marlene entered his office, sporting a sassy smile and a mile-high beehive.

"Rough weekend, hot stuff?"

Wearily, Max scrubbed his face with his palm. Shaving this morning hadn't been a picnic. After two days of growth, his stubble had been like barbed wire. But Marlene didn't need to know that. Although she might have some advice about Lu—

Hell. *Advice?* What was the matter with him?

He propped his chin in his hand and gave her a grin. "I can't remember. Now that you're here, everything seems better."

"Awww. Sweet." She slid a mug of steaming coffee across his desk, then leaned her elbows on his leather blotter. Her motherly, semiflirtatious gaze whisked over his suit jacket, shirt, and tie. "I've gotta say. You on a bad day is probably better than most men the rest of the time."

"You're an angel, Marlene."

On the other side of his desk, beside a newly delivered cardboard display of beef-flavored doggie toothpaste, Oliver snorted. Max didn't care. At least somebody in this place wasn't pissed at him. Also, he really needed that coffee. He sipped. Groaned.

"Nobody brews up a cup of heaven like you do. Thanks."

He winked, feeling fortified. Marlene blushed.

"You probably haven't had breakfast yet, either." She plunked down a paper-wrapped bagel and four grape jelly packets. "Heavy cream cheese, just the way you like it."

"Mmmm." Max squirted jelly on the cream cheese, surveyed the whole mess with satisfaction, then took a bite. He clutched his stomach in ecstasy. After licking his lips, he gestured to his partner. "Hiring Marlene was a brilliant move, Oliver."

"You're disgusting. That food is so third grade."

"So's your mamma."

"Come over here and say that."

"Boys, boys." Marlene put out her arms, giving them identical disapproving looks. "What's got into you two?"

"Ask him." Oliver jerked his chin toward Max.

"Beats me. But he can't have my bagel."

"Fine," their admin said. "You're on your own."

Shaking her beehive, Marlene clip-clopped out. Not even their expensive carpet could muffle the high heels she preferred with her zebra-striped skirts. She sashayed past Max's wall of additional awards, reminding him—painfully—of all he and Oliver had accomplished together. She shut the door.

Stubbornly, Max went back to his bagel. He wished he had six packets of jelly. Grape was his favorite. He eyed Oliver.

His partner glared at him.

Chomp. Chomp.

Oliver's fingers twitched.

"Mmmm." Max rolled his eyes. "That hits the spot."

Oliver leaped up. "At least move the wrapper over. Grape jelly stains are hell to get out of leather desk blotters."

Max grinned. "Knew I'd get you." He lifted his elbows, showing the napkin he'd surreptitiously moved atop his blotter.

"Asshole."

"Tell me what's really bugging you." Max edged his sloppy bagel sideways, jelly wobbling. "Or the blotter is history."

For a minute, Oliver seemed about to relent.

Then, "You're going back to Successfully Dressed."

"The hell I am." Of all the things in his life, Max felt most certain about that. He needed distance from that place—and the people in it. "Next item on your agenda?"

"You're going back to Successfully Dressed," Oliver repeated with a distinctly (Max had to be imagining things) devilish gleam in his eyes. "You're going back, and this time, you're accomplishing something."

Accomplishing something? That was low.

As far as Max was concerned, getting his whole world-view screwed up was "accomplishing something." Feeling twisted up in knots over a ridiculously cute girl hippie was "accomplishing something." And feeling all weekend as if he might never be the same again was sure as hell "accomplishing something."

But given what a jerk Oliver was being, Max decided he'd rather chew through his coffee mug than admit the truth. He steepled his hands and enunciated with agonizing clarity.

"Nothing in the world can make me go back there."

To Max's amazement, Oliver's devilish gleam turned downright fiendish.

He stared. Clearly, he'd arrived at work this morning in an alternate universe. Next thing he knew, Oliver would announce he *didn't* know the odds of winning Boardwalk in Monopoly—something he'd figured out when they'd both still been crazy for Transformers. Then he'd throw away his infrared-equipped multifunction graphing calculator, shave his head, and take up Speed Dating.

"You don't want to go back?" Oliver jutted his jaw, the macho gesture at odds with his fidgety movements. "Too bad."

He went to the credenza and came back with a thick binder. He dropped it on Max's desk with a thud, sending message slips and mail flying.

Max eyed it. "What's that?"

"*That* is the key to your gold mine of a thrift store," Oliver said. "You know all those people you've been trying to get in contact with? Your potential local investors?" A meaningful pause. "The ones who won't take your phone calls?"

Speaking of low . . . "You don't have to sound so damned happy about it."

"They're all in there." Oliver angled his head toward the binder. "Andrea researched Successfully Dressed, and then I did a little digging over the weekend myself. You know what we found out? That little shop's benefactors are some of the wealthiest women in the Valley—women with resources and funding. Not to mention links to their *husbands'* resources and funding."

No kidding? As though unable to resist, Max found himself reaching for the book. He opened it to the first page.

"You're going back there," Oliver announced with certainty. "I'll hold down the fort here. Happy volunteering."

He turned to leave.

"Wait." Max stilled, his hand on the opened pages. Almost every contact he'd tried—and so far, mostly failed—to make in Phoenix was listed. If he could reach them through Successfully Dressed . . . "No. No, the hell with it. I don't need this. I'll get investors the usual way. My way."

Oliver arched his eyebrow.

Max stared him down. He didn't want to buckle on this. He'd put business first most of his life. This time, maybe things could be different. Maybe *he* could be different.

"You're not Superman, Max. We need to finish this and move on. *I* need to finish this."

Frowning, Max swiveled his chair. He should have known that particular piece of pie-in-the-sky philosophy wasn't going to fly. Not for him. Also, there was something new in Oliver's demeanor. Something determined and almost . . . aggressive?

"I, for one, would like to make a splash with this particular project," Oliver went on. "I want it to be big."

Hmmm. "All our projects are big."

"Bigger than big. Starbucks meets Wal-Mart big. Huge initial IPO big. Just do it, Max. Okay?" Oliver's tone harkened back to their Thundercats and Galaxian days, catapulting Max to playgrounds and fistfights. "Do it for me."

That was all it took. "Fine. I'm in."

"So we're all clear, right?" Glancing up from her clipboard, Lucy focused on Nieca and Franco. She turned to Penny, one of their part-time senior citizen volunteers. "We'll all meet up for our first practice on Wednesday night, at the municipal park near Penny's house. It's lighted, so we can be there after sunset when it's cooled off."

Penny nodded. Her close-cropped silvery hair lent her an angelic appearance—one that was only augmented by her colorful blouse and rouged cheeks. She really was a sweetheart. She was also invaluably helpful with their older customers, who sometimes felt more comfortable with her assisting them.

Nieca agreed. "I'll spread the word to the other part-timers and the staff of the soup kitchen down the street." They were banding together with other small charities for the event. "Also, I'm pretty sure I can borrow some bats and gloves from my brothers. That'll get us outfitted, at least."

"I'll bring the Gatorade and PowerBars," Franco offered. His band members were temporarily joining their team, which lacked a certain . . . athleticism but more than made up for it in enthusiasm. "We'll need sustenance, for sure. Maybe some tunes too."

"And I'll bring the killer attitude." Penny's eyes gleamed. "The rock 'em, sock 'em, beat-the-pants-off-'em . . ." She waved her fist, setting her beaded Chico's bracelets jangling. "The Salvation Army won't know what hit 'em!"

They all stared at her.

"It's a charity baseball game to raise donations," Lucy reminded her gently. "Not a cutthroat competition."

"Says you," Franco scoffed. "With the trash talking we've endured till now?"

"Yeah, right," Nieca added. "Charity. Ha."

"Bring 'em on!" Penny cried. "We'll rip their heads off!"

Her enthusiastic outburst morphed her from sweet granny to ruthless competitor in an instant. It was quite a phenomenon.

"Penny," Lucy began, laying her hand on her arm. "I—"

"Oh, settle down, boss." Penny grinned, waving her off. "I'm old, not decrepit. I go to Curves four times a week." She straightened her already impeccable posture. "I'm probably in better shape than you three."

Doubtfully, Lucy, Nieca, and Franco looked at each other.

Then they shrugged. Penny had a point. Aside from yoga and bicycling to work, Lucy didn't exactly reach for the burn. Nieca thought exercising anything except her sketch pad and sewing needle was idiotic. And Franco still had traumatic memories of middle school gym class to overcome.

"Freakin' dodgeball," he muttered, eyes darkening.

"It's true," Penny said. "In fact, I beat my husband at arm wrestling just last night." She made a Popeye-style muscle, beaming proudly. "Four tries out of five."

"Penny, Walter is on crutches."

"So? A temporarily sprained ankle doesn't affect his arm strength. I'm telling you, if you let me at those Salvation Army folks, I'll give 'em what for."

In her younger years, Penny had been one of the first vanguard of working women, pitching in with her bow-tied blouse and hugely shoulder-padded navy suit to break through glass ceilings everywhere. Apparently, retirement hadn't blunted her competitive edge.

"Oookay." Needing to move on, Lucy clapped her hands together. "Now that that's settled . . ."

They moved on to a few more items on their weekly Monday morning meeting agenda. Nieca reported that interest in the shop's vintage collectibles had shot up, with the sale of a handbag to "Andrea, the publicist with the Dior and the Gucci bag," leading the vanguard. Nieca tended to bond with people over their accessories.

Franco reported that the Successfully Dressed donation pickup truck was "making weird noises" and probably needed an oil change "or something." Penny reported (demurely) that, with her granddaughter graduating from sixth grade next week, she'd need to adjust her working hours.

"No problem," Lucy told her. "Give Taralynn a shout out for us, okay? Or maybe we can all go to the ceremony?"

They spent some time discussing it, then reminiscing about grade school. They snacked on the sesame and apricot muffins Lucy had brought from Jade's health food store and discussed those too. Meetings were fun. It was all in the attitude you brought to them.

While Lucy scanned the agenda, everyone fell silent.

"I could really go for a triple espresso," Franco mused.

They all gasped. Nieca's gaze shot to the perfectly good chamomile tea on the rickety corner snack table.

She remained silent. Lucy knew why. Franco didn't miss espresso. He missed Max.

Somehow, Max had made himself a part of their group, even during the short while he'd volunteered. Evidently, Lucy wasn't the only one who'd felt it.

"Well. I guess that wraps things up here." She rose, straightening the sheer antique chemise she'd layered atop her black tank top, purple leggings, and Indian sandals. Her wrist bangles clanked as she grabbed her clipboard. "I'll just go unlock the front door. It's almost time to open."

No one disagreed, so Lucy made her getaway, feeling proud of the way she'd skirted the issue of Max and his completed volunteering stint. If she'd thought there was a chance in hell someone like him would come in on a part-time basis, like Penny, she might have handled things differently. As it was, she didn't want to mislead her staff. She didn't want to give them—or herself—false hope. That wouldn't be fair.

Bustling to the door, she used her master keys to unlock it. She swung it wide, then stepped to the gritty sidewalk beyond. Warm air and sunshine met her there, replacing the beloved smells of aged fabric, laundry detergent, and ink. In a minute, she'd go back inside. She'd go in, turn on all the multiple oscillating fans they used to keep cool instead of pricey A/C, and get to work. But right now . . .

Right now, she missed Max too.

And she didn't want anyone to know it.

Least of all . . .

"Hi, gorgeous. Need any volunteers?"

Standing around between customers, Nieca folded her arms and watched Max drop the suit he'd brought to donate in the sales floor bin. Beside her, Lucy paced.

"That's one of Tom Ford's menswear designs," Nieca observed, squinting. "I can't believe Max is donating it."

"I can't believe he's back here," Lucy muttered. "Suit or no suit."

"What? Of course he's back here." Nieca rolled her

eyes. Sometimes Lucy could be really dense about men. "He's into you. It's obvious."

"Here! Of all places!" Lucy shot a frustrated-looking glance toward the man outfitted in casual pants and a tailored, open-collar shirt. He wore both with striking ease. "Doesn't he have some high-powered work to do?" She paced faster. "What does he want, anyway? Is he slumming? Is he delirious?"

Franco yawned. "He said he wants to volunteer again. *You* said he could."

"You're right. I did. I must have been possessed."

Lucy kept on with the staring, even as she paced faster. She was totally into the guy, Nieca realized. This one might be serious. Happily, Nieca shifted just enough to catch Franco's eye. They nodded.

This didn't come as a surprise to either of them. Lucy's dodging the subject of mighty Max at their meeting hadn't fooled *anybody.* They'd talked about it at length after Lucy had skedaddled away. Even Penny had suggested their boss should "get some action with the studmuffin."

"I can't have Max around," Lucy dithered, wringing her hands. "He's too distracting."

Nieca sighed. Lucy, for all her faults, was not really a ditherer. This was *very* serious. It must be love.

"He's helping," Franco said. "Look."

They did. Max smiled at the customer he'd corralled, then gestured to the skirt suit she'd picked out. He said something they couldn't hear, making his customer laugh. And blush.

"He already managed to unload that orange pencil skirt we've had for weeks," Nieca observed. "And in only twenty minutes on the floor too. I think you should keep him around."

"He doesn't even have *time* to volunteer!" Lucy narrowed

her eyes with apparent suspicion. "He's got an ulterior motive. He must have."

Suspicion *really* wasn't like Lucy. She had it bad. Poor thing. They had to help her.

After all, Lucy didn't have much experience with normal, good-times, nonheartbreaking relationships. She always fell so hard for the wrong guys. But this was different.

"Yeah. He's motivated to get next to *you*." Franco gave Lucy a one-armed hug, jiggling her as though to jolly her up. "Trust us, Luce. The man is here to win your heart."

While they watched, Max turned. He saw Lucy watching him, and the knowledge transformed his whole face. If anything, he looked even yummier. His eyes lit up. He waved.

Lucy wiggled her fingers back at him. Giggled.

Then she crumpled against the cash register, groaning.

"Awww." Much to her embarrassment, Nieca couldn't hold back the girlish sound. She frowned to cover it, then discovered she sucked at her usual aura of sarcasm today too. Alarming. "He's like your very own Gucci-clad Prince Charming!" she heard herself gush.

"Totally," Franco agreed, thoughtfully overlooking Nieca's sentimental faux pas. "Now you don't have to go investment banker fishing just to get your freak on."

Lucy shook her head. "There must be something else going on. Last week, Max couldn't wait to get out of here."

She bit her lip, still watching him. She also tugged at her hair with her free hand, rearranging those fierce lavender strands artfully around her face without even seeming to notice.

Primping. That was all the proof Nieca needed. She caught Franco's eye again, and once more they shared a nod.

"Max is here for *you*, Lucy Goosey. And we'll prove it."

Lucy groaned. "Oh no. You're going to get totally

naked this time, aren't you? Nieca, no. I seriously don't—"

"No, it's my turn," Franco interrupted. "You just wait and see. We'll prove to you that Max is worthy."

"Franco, I don't think—"

"Don't worry about a thing," Nieca assured Lucy. "We'll take care of all the details."

Then she grabbed Franco and headed out back for a cigarette break. Co-conspiracy could be fun. If practiced correctly.

In the storeroom that afternoon, Lucy lounged against a partially crushed box of industrial hangers. It turned out that cardboard made for a surprisingly good bed, especially when cushioned properly.

She turned her head and caught Max watching her from his identically reclining position beside her. Since her head was pillowed on his biceps and they were both still breathing hard, that wasn't entirely surprising. Except for the fond—almost sappy—expression on his face.

Probably, she looked the same way. Wow.

"I don't know how this keeps happening." Breathlessly, Lucy put her hand over her heart. Since she was nearly naked, it was easy to feel its still-galloping rhythm. "All I did was offer to show you how to hang and display the new arrivals."

"Yeah. But it was the *way* you offered."

Max leaned sideways and kissed her. His mouth descended on hers gently. Tantalizingly. Just as she had earlier, Lucy found herself swept away by the sensation.

There was just something *irresistible* about Max. Something she'd never encountered before with any other man. She wanted to be with him. Wanted to hear him talk, to see him smile, to feel his body over hers.

Which probably explained how they'd gotten here, making fast and fabulous whoopee during the shop's downtime.

"We can't keep doing this," she protested. Her whole body tingled pleasurably with the aftereffects of their lovemaking. Her arms ached from clutching Max so tightly, and her big toe had a cramp from trying to balance in their awkward position, but Lucy couldn't quite bring herself to care. "We're supposed to be working. *I'm* supposed to be working."

"This wasn't exactly what I had planned when I got here today either." Max looked pensive for a minute. Then, characteristically, he brightened. "No problem. We'll stay late tonight to make up for it."

"Working late? With you?" Lucy slid her hand down his mostly naked torso, pushing aside her discarded chemise. It had landed atop him at some point. She whirled her fingers over his chest. "Something tells me that wouldn't be smart."

"And here I thought you were dedicated."

"I am! I just—oh!"

"Let me see if I can persuade you." He grinned.

"Oooh!" She squirmed as his fingers crept up her thigh. He stroked her softly, sparking the same tempting sensations she'd enjoyed a few minutes ago. Max's next kiss felt so deep and soft and affecting, it was all Lucy could do to hang on to him and enjoy it.

A familiar sense of giddiness bubbled up inside her. She loved this. Loved being with Max. Loved the naughtiness of slipping away with him . . . loved the way he'd insisted on cuddling with her afterward, despite their less-than-ideal surroundings.

Twenty panting minutes later, Lucy clutched him in an entirely *non*cuddling fashion, toes curling. She quivered in his arms. Everything just felt so . . . *ahhh*. Blissful.

Max sure did have some talented hands.

When she could see straight again and had regained enough muscle control to do it, Lucy gave him a swat on the arm. She couldn't help but laugh. "We're supposed to be stopping!"

"Sorry. Call that a bonus round. I got carried away." Max's mischievous grin and tousled hair made him look completely nonrepentant. "You just feel so good."

"Mmmm." Lucy burrowed next to him again.

He held her close, then kissed the top of her head.

"I've completely lost my appetite for non-purple-haired girls," Max announced. "All I want is you."

And all she wanted was him. Morning, noon, and round the clock. But since this was completely casual between them, she figured a few hot and steamy encounters were okay. Sighing, Lucy let herself enjoy the wonderful feeling of lying in Max's arms. It was a good thing they were on the same wavelength. Even if he did sometimes tease her with stuff like that "all I want is you" comment. She figured Max was so naturally flirtatious, he just couldn't help it.

She stared at the water spots the last monsoon storm had left on the storeroom ceiling, feeling contented. If a person was going to have a no-strings-attached fling, Max was the perfect guy to enlist. Hunky, generous, talented, and drop-dead sexy. Also, completely uninterested in commitment.

Beside her, he rummaged in his tossed-away pants. He came up with something small and wrapped. "Here. For you."

Curiously, Lucy accepted it. The aroma struck her first—sugary, fake, and (she gasped) familiar. "Dubble Bubble!"

Wide eyed, she clutched the gum in her fist. It was her favorite. Her most longed-for secret vice and—despite her otherwise macrobiotic tendencies—her most treasured treat.

Max smiled. "You said you liked it."

"Liked it? I *love* it!" Wriggling to accommodate her disarrayed clothes—like the legging still hanging from one knee—Lucy brought the gum to her nose. She inhaled. Her mouth watered just contemplating all that rubbery, delicious, super sweetness. "Here. I'll share."

She flopped happily again and unwrapped the gum. One persistent pinch divided it. She offered half her artificially colored, pretty pink treasure to Max.

He blinked. "No, it's yours. Your favorite."

"So? Everything's better shared. Open up."

Seeming confused, he shook his head.

What was his problem? "Okay, then. Let me kiss you."

She did. Then, for a chaser, she popped the gum in his mouth. Max's eyes widened, but he chewed gamely.

"Isn't it amazing? So good. Mmmm."

This was the life. She couldn't believe Max had remembered her offhand comment to him about Dubble Bubble. She'd only admitted her craving for the stuff because he'd been giving her a hard time about her organic Newman-O's chocolate cookies. Even Nieca and Franco didn't know about her hidden vice.

Nobody did, it occurred to her. Weird that she'd trust Max with her secret. But then they had hit it off, hadn't they?

Bowing to the inevitable, Lucy squirmed into her clothes a few minutes later, pausing occasionally to savor her gum. She gave a sigh of appreciation, then went on getting dressed. Tank top? Check. Leggings on both legs? Check. Chemise? Uh . . .

She glanced up to see Max dangling the vintage garment. He wore a strange expression, one that almost seemed . . . tender. And a little uncertain. She couldn't be sure, since *uncertainty* and *Max* went together like Top Ramen and peanut butter.

Lucy had learned that one the hard way.

Max hadn't made a move to get dressed. He'd apparently spent this whole time watching her.

He smiled. "You like it?"

"The gum?"

His rumble of assent gave her a thrill.

Sheesh, she was really over the moon for this guy. Even his voice made her want to lunge for him.

Lucy restrained the impulse and cupped his jaw in her hand instead. *Casual,* she reminded herself. *Friendly.*

She smiled back. "I love it. Thank you."

And it was then, looking at Max as he tried not to grin wider in that macho way of his, that Lucy finally got it. Maybe, just maybe, Max really *had* come back for her.

There was only one way to find out.

By getting more of Max.

Starting just as soon as she got some work done.

10

Oliver paused beneath the awning outside Successfully Dressed on Thursday afternoon, his arms loaded with several reference documents, worksheets, and the Andrea Cho Public Relations giveaway pens Andrea had insisted he bring today. His laptop hung from his shoulder, making him feel lopsided.

Beside him, Max doffed his sunglasses and grinned at the mannequin in the shop window.

He pointed. "Look. Nieca strikes again."

Oliver squinted. The mannequin wore a bizarre getup involving a snorkeling mask, laced-up moccasins, a tube top, and sequined shorts. Helium balloons were tied to her elbows. Gold stars—like the ones Oliver had earned in grade school—festooned the floor all around her.

One star glittered from the tip of her plastic nose.

"If there's a theme," Oliver mused, "I don't get it."

"You don't have to. That's Nieca's genius."

"Oh. I suppose *you* get it?"

"Hey, relax." Max elbowed him, offering up a reassuring smile. "You're giving a workshop, not facing a firing squad. Don't let those nerves get the better of you."

On the verge of telling Max *he* was getting the better of him, Oliver found himself nearly smacked in the face with the shop door. He stepped back, juggling his things. Geez. Max obviously couldn't wait to get in there and start flirting with the woman who *should* have been Oliver's.

Nieca. A vision of her smart-girl demeanor, glowing skin, and curvy body imposed itself on him before Oliver could stop it. She was so right for him. He knew it.

He'd never tried fighting Max for a woman before. Had never seen the need. With pathetic odds of success like those staring him in the face, a man would do well to just back off. Especially a man like Oliver. But this time . . .

Determinedly, Oliver stepped inside. A sea of colors and shapes assaulted him, gradually resolving themselves into clothing, bright antique washing machines, and paper lanterns twirling in the breeze from several oscillating fans. He also spotted tinsel and Christmas lights. In June. It was a wonder this place survived with such lackadaisical management.

"It'll be awhile before everybody gets here. I set up the workshop for three o'clock." Max moved with assurance between the overstuffed clothing racks. He paused, frowned at a Brady Bunch shirt, then moved it to another rack. He waved toward a slightly open area near the cash register. "You can set up over there. I'll see if Franco has the chairs ready to go yet."

Oh no. Oliver wasn't falling for that again. Doggedly, he followed Max toward the back of the shop. Here, the clothes got even weirder, and the shoes were displayed in those rolling carts his mother used to use at the Laundromat. He glimpsed a mirror in the corner beside a strung-up curtain. He paused.

His reflection stared back at him, overburdened with equipment and overdressed in a suit. Overall, not bad. Maybe a seven-point-five on a ten-point scale. Maybe a seven. His dark curly hair looked as if he'd stirred it with a latte foamer.

Frowning, Oliver patted his head.

A voice drifted toward him, instantly familiar.

"Yes, Mrs. Callahan. Your de la Renta would be ideal." A pause. "Wonderful! Yes, yes. I understand. Of course, we do accept shoes in good condition. Yes, handbags too!"

Nieca. She was nearby.

At the thought, Oliver's whole body switched to red alert. His laptop slipped an inch lower, unbalancing him. His palms sweated. His papers ruffled. He thought he might pass out.

This was what he got for trying to get tough with Max, he realized desperately. For forcing Max into volunteering again. It had been a momentary lapse of reason—one Oliver heartily regretted. He should have known playing hardball would come back to bite him in the ass. He wasn't a hardball kind of guy. He preferred bowling.

No. He had to get a grip. He had to make the most of this situation. For Nieca. Because while it was a fact that when Max had asked him to come here today, Oliver had been reluctant, he also really, really wanted to see her, despite the very likely odds, approximately three to one, that he would break out in a rash the moment he laid eyes on her.

"Well, please *do* tell your friends, Mrs. Callahan," came Nieca's voice again. It sounded exactly as throaty and exhilarating as he'd remembered . . . albeit with a new tension he didn't quite understand. "I'd love that. Yes. Buh-bye."

Before he could chicken out—or break out—Oliver followed that sound. He rounded the corner to the shop office, nearly colliding with Max. His partner seemed dumbstruck—although that was understandable. He was looking at Nieca, after all.

She was a vision. A vision in white pants, a crazy-print

tube top, and those eyeglasses. Her braids looked adorable. *All* of her looked adorable. Oliver felt smitten.

He shouldered past Max—to the victor went the spoils—and extended his free hand. "Nieca. How are you?"

His formality seemed to shatter whatever spell had existed between her and Max, although tension still crackled in the air. Oliver figured that was because he'd arrived to break up their vintage-shop-volunteer tête-à-tête.

Score one for the shy guy.

"Hey, McGeekerson." With a smile, Nieca slipped her hand in his. She actually seemed happy to see him. "Long time, no see. How's the insurance adjustor business?"

He felt his face heat. Damn it. "I'm not really an—"

"I thought Franco made the solicitation calls," Max interrupted, gesturing to the phone Nieca had been using. "Lucy was pretty clear on that."

"—insurance adjustor," Oliver forced out, talking over Max for possibly the first time ever. His heart pounded. He couldn't quite figure out why Nieca was sitting in a cast-off beauty shop hair dryer chair. "I'm an entrepreneur."

"Yeah?" Nieca lifted her brows. "You'll have to tell me about that sometime."

Oh God. It was working. She was interested. Interested, right under Max's good-looking, insufferably oblivious nose.

Oliver preened, gazing into her eyes with delight. Desperately, he tried to summon a follow-up.

He was still working on it when Nieca withdrew her hand, leaving him bereft. She met Max's suspicious gaze head-on.

"FYI, that was just a social call. To an old friend."

"An old friend who just happens to have some spare vintage designer wear lying around?" Max asked. "Designer wear like the stuff Lucy *doesn't* want to sell in here anymore?"

Nieca narrowed her eyes. "Actually," she said tightly, "solicitation calls aren't the part-timers' purview."

Purview. She had a lovable vocabulary too! Those glasses hadn't misled him. Oliver felt more psyched than ever.

She rose, offering him and Max a brief smile. "I'll go see if Franco is still unloading the chairs he borrowed. He was supposed to have things already set up for you."

She sashayed out. Oliver knew that nobody in the world had ever exited a room so gracefully, so sexily, so stunningly.

He sighed. Then he came to.

He kicked Max on the shin.

"Hey!" His partner glared. "What the hell? Why did you *kick* me?"

"Because my hands were too full to punch you. Get off her back, will you?" Oliver glared back. "You made her leave!"

Frowning, Max rubbed his leg. "Have you been sniffing toner cartridges again? What's the matter with you?"

"Nothing *you'd* understand," Oliver said with dignity.

Then he left to chase down Nieca before his workshop began. By the time he caught her, he knew he'd have something to say.

He hoped.

The battle was on. And all at once, he felt more than up for it.

Max stuck his head outside Successfully Dressed's back door. In the alley behind the shop, Franco labored in all his rangy, punk-haired glory. He bobbed his head as he shuffled folding chairs, keeping time with the music blasting from the MP3 player strapped to his skinny arm. While Max watched, Franco leaned a set of chairs against the truck, then went back in the cargo bay for more.

Propping the back door open with the coffee can of loose change that always stood nearby ("You'd be surprised how many people leave money in their donation-clothes pockets," Lucy had told him), Max went outside. His shin still throbbed, but his mind was clear. He couldn't wait to get going.

Lucy would be so surprised.

Max hadn't known her for long, but it didn't take an Einstein like Oliver to realize Lucy needed help. She was way too softhearted to be an efficient manager. She was clearly in over her head with the shop. As long as he was going to be around, Max figured he might as well try lending a hand.

He lifted his palm in greeting. "Hey, Franco."

Franco spotted him and plucked out his earbuds. "How's it going? Almost done here. Do you think this is enough chairs?"

Max surveyed the two dozen arrayed around the truck. He nodded.

Grunting, Franco repositioned two of them. "I called in a few favors while I was out picking up donations." He grinned, then stroked his faux-hawk affectionately, making sure it still stood straight. "Anything to help out a friend, right?"

Max wouldn't know. Of necessity, he'd kept his friends to a minimum. He nodded anyway. "Good job."

"Yeah. Anything for a friend." Franco stopped, giving Max a weird look. An overly casual, just-between-us-pals look. "So . . . is that why you came back for more volunteering? To make new *friends*? Or maybe to make *particular* friends?"

Particular friends. Did Franco know about Max's binder? About his mission to line up local investors for the Ruizes?

Max shrugged. "Everybody likes friends."

Franco gave him the eagle eye. "Friends like Lucy?"

Ahhh. "Where is Lucy, anyway?" A change of subject would be useful about now, Max decided. "Does she know—"

"Nah. She doesn't know about your plan." Franco slapped his hand on the nearest stack of chairs, jangling the batch of nightclub bands on his wrist. "Your secret's safe with me. In fact"—his expression turned crafty—"*any* secret of yours is safe with me. So if there's something you want to tell me . . ."

Again, Max wondered—could Franco have guessed what Max was up to? What he really needed from Successfully Dressed?

"I'll help you carry those inside." Max grabbed an armful.

Franco trailed him, also hauling some chairs. They wended their way through the office to the shop sales floor.

There, a few people browsed. Oliver and Nieca chatted near the used necktie bins. A pair of women who looked familiar to Max—former customers he'd helped, most likely—waved to him. They'd probably come for the workshop.

"Where's Lucy?" he repeated, looking around for her as he and Franco set up chairs in mostly tidy rows.

"Don't worry. She's occupied." Franco grinned. "Jade concocted a relationship 'crisis' and called her down to the health food store. Lucy's always up for helping somebody."

"Jade? Lucy's friends are in on this too?"

"Sure. Why not?"

"Because the best way to keep a secret is to *not* tell anybody." It seemed pretty freaking obvious to him. Feeling unsettled, Max shuffled some chairs. He didn't understand Lucy's whole close-knit, artsy crowd and their constant "sharing." As far as he was concerned, keeping things to yourself was smarter. "Who else knows about this?"

"Jade, Victor, Charlie . . ." Franco ticked off the names on his fingers. "The guys in my band, the mailman, Lucy's mom . . ."

"Okay. Enough." Clearly, Max was working with amateurs, but he appreciated their help. "Never mind. It's no biggie."

Franco peered at him. "You look like it's a biggie."

Christ. Did he? Feeling suddenly suffocated, Max yanked at his collar. He'd have to speak with his laundry service about shrinking his shirts.

Just because he wanted Lucy to be happy, just because he wanted to help her, didn't mean he was desperate to please her. Max was still focused on his long-term goals. Taking care of business was what mattered, he reminded himself.

"I'm fine."

Franco didn't look convinced. "Okay, tell you what," he offered with a generous air. "If you want, I'll wait to grill you about your financial details, job prospects, and income potential till later. Okay?"

Max gawked. "Huh?"

"Nothing." Wearing a secret smile, Franco leaned nearer. "But just because you taught me what a cover-two defense is, I'll tell you this much. You're doing pretty good."

Franco gave him a jolly "rock on" sign, then winked and went outside for more chairs.

Good at what? Max wondered, thoroughly baffled.

"Fresh-baked dog biscuits?" Nieca repeated, staring at McGeekerson. "Customized catnip bouquets? *Poultry-flavored* bottled water?" She shook her head, trying not to guffaw, since the guy looked so freakishly sincere. "That's messed up."

"No, it's not," Geeky said. "Pet owners—pet *guardians,* I should say—take their pets' well-being very seriously. And they want to treat them specially too. Just like any other member of the family."

"But little sweaters? Designer booties? Poochie sushi?" Nieca couldn't believe some of the stuff he'd told her since following her to the sales floor in all his nervous but well-dressed glory. "Come on. You're kidding me, right?"

"No. It's all part of our business model." Earnestly, Geeky nodded toward Max, who was setting up chairs across the room. "We identify a market and come up with a concept to fulfill its needs. Then we finance stores in test markets, sell the idea to franchisers, and move on to the next thing."

She angled her head, studying him. "Without even sticking with the previous thing? It all sounds crazy to me. How can you make any money at that?"

Geeky's face lit up. "Well, it's like this . . ."

He launched into a facts-and-figures-loaded explanation that clearly got his motor running. He spouted percentages and recited market research. He described striking big-ticket financing deals and identifying obscure but lucrative niche markets. He gestured, calling Nieca's attention to his arms and hands and abundance of energy. He smiled and nodded.

He distractedly ran his fingers through his hair to make a point. He even touched her shoulder for emphasis, then started stammering. He actually—and she couldn't believe she found herself thinking this—seemed kind of cute.

For a geek.

"What's your name, McGeekerson?" Nieca asked.

He stopped in midmonologue. Swallowed hard. "Oliver."

She took his arm. His whole body seemed to quiver beneath her touch, something Nieca found surprisingly appealing. Obviously, the man had vitality to spare. Plus a little something going on upstairs too. He was a regular novelty.

Maybe she could use a change of pace.

"You've got a workshop to conduct, and I've got some more phone calls to make." She walked him toward the cash register, noticing almost against her will that he felt a lot more solidly built than he looked. Hmmm. "But it's been nice talking to you. Maybe I'll see you again sometime. You can tell me more about cat raincoats and faux-Impressionist pet portraits."

Oliver gulped. "They're actually very well done. Oil—"

"Easy, there." She smiled up at him. He had nice eyes too. Gentle eyes, despite his crazy talk. "I'm flirting with you. Don't ruin the vibe."

He paused, looking a little green around the gills.

"Would telling you about our pet grooming service with optional fur coloring and highlighting ruin it?" he blurted eagerly. "It's all part of the potential expansion plan I just came up with. Pet Du Jour grooming salons."

With a flourish, Oliver held up his arms. He unfurled a massive imaginary banner. "For the *chic* pampered pet."

Nieca rolled her eyes. That was the most ridiculous idea she'd ever heard. But for some reason, she didn't want to say so. Oliver might be crushed.

So all she said was, "You've never had a pet, have you?"

He offered a crooked smile. "Pets cause sixty-two percent of common allergies. Statistically speaking, I'd—"

Stopping him with her fingers on his mouth, Nieca studied him. He was nice. Actually nice. Once a person got past the jitteriness and the stammering and the head-to-toe (presumably) neon-red blush. She didn't know why she hadn't noticed before.

"Do you like dogs?" she asked.

Beneath her hand, he nodded. His eyes searched hers. *That settled it,* Nieca decided.

"Then I guess I like you," she told him.

Oliver's gaze darted to where Max and Franco labored to set up chairs for this afternoon's workshop. He probably thought she and Franco were an item. Silly man. Franco was like a brother to her. A tall, galumphing, music-obsessed brother.

She smiled, letting Oliver know he had nothing to worry about. "So try to keep up with me," Nieca said. "Okay?"

Then she left him behind and headed for the office. In the few minutes before Lucy came back, she still had time for more phone calls . . . and more developing of her plan to save the shop.

Strolling down the sidewalk with a fresh lemongrass chai infusion, Lucy shook her head. She still didn't know why Jade's crush on the guy who supplied her with organically grown alfalfa sprouts had required a full-on SOS. Or why, of all things, it had helped to have Lucy stand beside her in the produce section, watching the grizzled supplier unload sprouts.

Slooowly. Carton by carton.

"Just look at the way he handles them," Jade had whispered, crowding closer to Lucy. "So decisively. So manfully. So . . . excitingly!"

"Ummm. Manfully. Uh-huh." Puzzled, Lucy had crossed her arms. "I guess so, Jade. Listen, is he married or something? Because otherwise, I'm not sure I see what the crisis is here."

But Jade had only shushed her, then spent the rest of the time enchanted by her fella's burly sprout handling. Every time Lucy had tried to make an excuse and slip away, her friend had grabbed her for another analysis of his occasional glances, his gregarious "hey, ya," his symmetrical stacking skills.

"A man like that can stack my sprouts anytime," Jade said.

Lucy's disbelieving look hadn't even fazed her. It had taken all sixty-seven cartons and a smattering of awkward small talk before Lucy had managed to duck out. Even now, she worried that Jade didn't feel sufficiently supported in her unrequited affection for her produce delivery man.

But the truth was, Lucy had done her best. And when it came right down to it, she had work of her own to do.

Summertime wasn't exactly heavy traffic time in downtown Phoenix, what with the reduction in tourism and the overall oppressiveness of sidewalks hot enough to fry tofu on. She needed a gimmick. A special attraction of some sort to help draw in customers. Supplying clothes to her job-seeking clientele was one thing, but the shop required other shoppers—spendthrift impulse shoppers—to stay open.

Maybe she'd book a palm reader, Lucy mused as she passed the florist's shop. Palm readers were always entertaining. A palm reader would probably draw a big crowd.

She sipped her infusion and pondered some more as she walked, then paused to inhale the incredible yeasty aromas wafting from the artisanal bakery next on her path.

Or an astrologist! Her customers would probably find it useful to have their charts drawn up.

After all, nobody should go job hunting while Mercury was in retrograde. That was just crazy.

Yeah. She knew more than one person who practiced astrology. In fact, her friend Naomi practiced numerology too. If Lucy simply tapped her network of friends and neighbors, she could revitalize what Successfully Dressed had to offer *and* help provide necessary exposure to the people she loved too. That was definitely a goal worth pursuing.

As a matter of fact, several of her friends made items that would be wonderful for Max's pet boutiques. Glazed ceramic dog food bowls, hand-carved cat posts, patchwork-quilted pet beds—all of them one of a kind and made with care. How could Max say no to stocking unique arts-and-crafts pet supplies?

Feeling certain and energized about her future, Lucy went on her way. When she reached Successfully Dressed, the bell over the door tinkled. The antique-lace-and-soapsuds scent hit her, leaving her happy, as it always did, to have returned. She'd found a home of sorts here. That was one reason the shop's success was so important to her.

"So that's why mutual funds are a good investment," a man said, his voice carrying clearly across the sales floor. "If you find yourself temporarily unemployed, they can provide a buffer to shield against potential . . ."

Probably someone on a cell phone, Lucy guessed. Loud talking cell phone users were everywhere, even in less-than-ultrapopular thrift stores and—

Lucy stopped in surprise. A whole crowd of people, mostly women, stood near the cash register, listening to someone she didn't know. Someone who *didn't* happen to be using a cell phone. He appeared to be giving a . . . seminar?

The crowd shuffled aside as Lucy came closer, revealing rows of folding chairs set up in front of a lectern. Behind it, the man gestured to a graph he'd projected from his laptop computer onto . . . one of the shop's cache of vintage Victorian petticoats?

Lucy peered closer. Yes, that span of white ruffled fabric strung and clothespinned between the Better Business Wear and the Skirtsapalooza sections was a petticoat, standing in for—she guessed—a traditional screen. The man pointed at the graph, then clicked something in his hand. The image switched to a pie chart showing various budget categories. He went on talking.

What was going on here?

Flummoxed, Lucy edged around the crowd. They seemed rapt with attention, including Tracee in the front row. Even her two children sat placidly on the seats on either side of her, looking transfixed—probably by the changing charts and graphs.

The man noticed her. "Please, come on over." He gestured toward the nearest row, his expression patient and welcoming beneath his dark curly hair. "I'm afraid we underestimated the turnout today, but there's always room for one more."

Heads turned to watch her. Caught beneath their attention, Lucy knew she had to do something.

"Actually," she began, "this is my shop, so there's always room for me here. But you—"

Suddenly, Franco and Nieca swooped in on either side of her. Before Lucy could do more than register that fact, they actually *lifted* her by her arms and carried her away.

11

"*What* is going on here?" Lucy demanded, stuck in her office against her will. She extricated herself from Franco and Nieca's grasp, then put her hands on her hips. "I can't *believe* you actually *forced* me off of my own sales floor."

"Yeah. Cool, right?" Franco beamed.

"Thank God for Franco's stint as a bouncer," Nieca added, angling her head toward her partner in crime. "I'd never have thought of that elbow lock maneuver on my own. Very effective."

That was it. Her staff had gone bonkers.

"What," she repeated stiffly, "is—"

"It's a surprise." Max stepped in from the opened back door, looking handsome and relaxed and pleased with himself. He glanced at Franco and Nieca. "Good idea to keep a lookout out back. And nice work, you two. Who knew you'd both be so good at subterfuge?"

Her staff—her friends!—beamed beneath his praise.

Keep a lookout. So that's what he'd been doing.

And subterfuge? Huh?

Speechless, Lucy could only stand there as Max nodded to Franco and Nieca, then sauntered around them to come near her.

He looked her up and down. She didn't think *unmistakable male appreciation* was quite appropriate in this situation . . . but she liked it all the same. Damn it.

Max touched her arm, then kissed her hello. When he pulled back, his eyes sparkled. His dimple worked its magic.

"You must be a bundle of trouble at a surprise party."

"Wha . . . ?"

"Because you almost blew poor Oliver's concentration out there. He doesn't deal well with unexpected events."

"Oliver?" Max's business partner? She'd heard of him, of course, but Max had been notoriously closemouthed about letting her into the rest of his life. Oliver included.

Now that she realized it, it kind of hurt her feelings.

"I heard him stop, then invite you to join the workshop." Max pursed his lips, considering her. "Maybe you should have. God knows, everybody needs help with their finances."

Thoroughly befuddled, Lucy gawked at him. "Not me."

Nieca snorted. "Two words: art collecting."

Okay. So Lucy did have a teensy soft spot when it came to buying her friends' artwork. Who wouldn't? Those gallery openings could be pretty dismal for the artists involved. It didn't hurt anybody to pick up a new painting or patchwork quilt or handwrought bowl. Or twelve.

As though he knew her weakness—but found it inexplicably endearing—Max smiled. "You need help. I'm here to help. I'm happy to do it."

"Do *what*?"

"A financial workshop," Max said. "For your customers."

Franco nodded. Nieca grinned.

Everyone was in on it, Lucy realized. Except her.

"If there's one thing I know," Max added, "it's how to convince people they need something. All week,

I've been talking to people about Oliver's financial workshop—"

So *that's* what he'd been murmuring to customers about! All at once, Max's heads-down, private conversations with the shop's clientele made a lot more sense.

"—convincing them to come back today, and to bring a friend." Leaning sideways to peer through the open office doorway, he surveyed the crowd on the sales floor with satisfaction. "It looks as if it worked."

There was only one thing Lucy was still stuck on. Aside from the fact that she'd been excluded.

"*Help?* I don't need 'help' from anybody! I've done a good job with this place"—*for somebody with no experience in management,* she amended privately—"and I'm getting better all the time. What makes you think you can just come in here with your big-deal business sense and your Big Shot Central chutzpah and fool around with *my* shop?"

Max frowned. "The place is packed. For the first time in almost two weeks."

Lucy bristled at the implication she was failing.

"Word is getting around," he added good-naturedly. "Half the challenge in getting business is getting people in the door. If my experience has taught me anything, it's that—"

"That you should *sneak* around?" Distraught, Lucy stared at him. It hurt that Max thought she was incompetent. Hurt that he'd somehow—and even if only temporarily—turned her friends' loyalties away from her. "That's low, Max."

He seemed confused. "Look, the results speak for themselves. If you'd just—"

"No." Lucy raised her palm to stop him. Wearily, she released a breath, uncomfortably aware of Nieca and Franco's bewildered glances. "Maybe your intentions were good—"

At that, Max's expression turned stony.

"—I don't know. But I do know that making a success of this shop is important to me. I've got some ideas of my own, ideas I thought of on the way here, and they're really—"

To Lucy's horror, her voice cracked. Tears welled in her eyes. They choked off her voice and made her nose burn.

"Really *good,* I think," she tried again, "so I just—"

It was no use. Before she embarrassed herself any further, she clutched her lemongrass chai infusion and shoved her way out the back door, looking for any place where she could be alone.

Max's first throw pinged off the stucco archway of the sheltered house in front of him, then dropped to the graveled yard. Grabbing more ammunition, he tried again.

This time, he hit the window. Gently, with enough force to make a *ping* but not enough to break the mullioned glass. Apparently, they'd constructed the tiny 1920s houses in central Phoenix out of sturdy stuff, because his calling card didn't so much as cause a stir.

He knew Lucy was home. Light shone from the stained glass transom over the front door and from the window he'd chosen as his likeliest target. Winding up with more ammo, Max gave another toss. It pinged harmlessly—and almost noiselessly—from the sill, then dropped to the ground beside a trailing bougainvillea branch covered in vivid fuchsia bracts.

Drawing in a breath for patience, Max adjusted his ammo box. He scanned Lucy's house, taking in the low, red tiled roofline; the cozy windows; the swirling khaki stucco. Several homemade-looking pots of geraniums hunkered along the porch rail, soaking up the sunset. A variety of handcrafted wind chimes dangled from the eaves, and a bike—complete with wicker basket—leaned against the porch wall. By the front door, a sisal mat lay, sporting an image of either a fire-breathing dragon or a heartburn-suffering pizza eater. He couldn't tell for sure.

All in all, from the outside, the place looked a lot like Lucy. Cute. Unusual. Inexplicably welcoming.

It hadn't been easy to find it, though. By the time Max had reassured Oliver, gotten the necessary information from Nieca and Franco, and wrangled himself from the clutches of the eager crowd of workshop attendees, he'd lost Lucy's trail altogether. He'd spent more than an hour in his Lexus, combing the nearby neighborhoods, before realizing that Nieca's instructions—"left at the florist's, right at that old blue building, two blocks toward the take-out Thai place"—had left him hopelessly confused.

Thank God for Oliver's mastery of Google, online mapping, and the remote capacities of Max's automatic dashboard GPS system. He knew there was a reason he loved his Lexus. Aside from its 4.3-liter, 300-horsepower V8 engine, double-wishbone suspension, and ability to go from zero to sixty in 5.9 seconds flat. Which was pretty sweet too.

He selected more ammo and weighed its heft in his hand. He could have simply knocked on the door, he reasoned. But where was the romance in that? *Ping* went the window again.

This time, someone flipped aside the deep red curtain. Lucy's face appeared behind the glass, curious and open. For some reason, the sight of her made Max's heart flip over.

She cranked open the casement window. Surveyed the spent ammo lying on the gravel beneath the sill. Grinned.

"Dubble Bubble is a treat, not a cure-all." She angled her head, studying him. "Do you really think a few pieces of bubble gum will smooth everything over?"

He didn't know. He hoped like hell it would.

"No." Max showed her the box in his arms. "But I hoped a thousand-piece box of it might be a starting point."

His goodwill gesture didn't go over as well as he'd hoped. The curtains swooshed closed, then Lucy disappeared from sight.

Max stood in the yard, bereft. He felt like an idiot. He didn't know what he'd expected when he'd turned up with fifteen pounds of bubble gum, but it wasn't this. Usually he was good at romantic gestures.

But then this wasn't entirely romantic, was it? a part of him prodded. It was business. Aside from everything else, the bottom line was that he needed Lucy's cooperation to continue making contacts via Successfully Dressed.

Shoving aside the thought, Max frowned at the house. Seeing Lucy in tears had done something to him today. Something new and not at all welcome. Remembering it made his gut twist. She'd looked so vulnerable, so betrayed. . . .

He'd obviously screwed up with his surprise workshop plan. Evidently, Lucy didn't like surprises. Okay, Max told himself, regrouping. Next time he'd come up with a better way to help her. A way she couldn't object to.

After all, it was his job to get people to agree with him. No matter what it took. That was what he excelled at.

He stepped toward the front door just as it swung open.

Lucy stood on the threshold, arms crossed. Her gaze zipped over his pants and shirt, his face, then his armful of (let's face it) bribes. "Come on in."

The moment Max sat, he realized Lucy's patched, girly, flower-upholstered sofa was going to eat him alive.

His ass sank lower than his knees, leaving his legs propped in front of him like a stork in a Barcalounger. His back slumped. His arms encountered sixteen pillows and a discarded sneaker. He felt pretty sure the demon sofa's gravity-sucking cushiness was never letting go of his nuts.

It was all worth it, just to see Lucy smile at him.

"Comfy?" she asked.

Max plucked the fringe from one of those fuzzy crocheted blanket things out of his nose and nodded. "Nice place."

Lucy scoffed. "It's a dump, compared with yours."

"I know, but it's . . . just like you." He gestured to the ten-by-twelve living room jammed with knickknacks, more flowery furniture, and tables from a variety of eras. Everything looked homemade, inherited from benevolent relatives, or on the verge of Dumpsterville. But it all had warmth and style and vivid color. "It's unforgettable."

"It's what I can afford."

"So's my place. See? We're even."

She frowned. Damn it. He usually excelled at making up with women. What was the matter with him?

He didn't even feel like himself, Max realized. His shoulders were in knots and his mouth felt dry. His hands even shook as he nervously grabbed his knees, hovering stork-style. If he hadn't known better, he'd have sworn he was as desperate to snag Lucy as Oliver was to hook up with Andrea.

Not that that seemed to be going very well. Poor Oliver.

"I can't believe you let me in," he heard himself say.

For a minute, Lucy studied him. "It's simple. I don't believe in giving up on people."

He'd never heard of a philosophy like that.

"What if you didn't believe in the person to begin with?"

She crinkled her forehead. Her gaze, clear and straightforward, met his. "Why wouldn't I believe in you?"

Max shifted. "I didn't say *me*. I didn't even mean me." He picked up a pillow, concentrating on its satiny texture and lumpy embroidery. "It was a rhetorical question."

"A rhetorical question about you."

He frowned, wanting to escape that damned knowing gaze of hers. Lucy didn't know him. Nobody did. He tossed aside the pillow, his mind made up. "Let's go get a drink."

"I don't like your version of drinks."

She'd seemed to like it when she'd had her foot almost in his lap at Rocco's, Max reflected, but he'd sidestepped her questions, and that was what mattered. He smiled. "Don't hold back, Lucy. Tell me what you really think."

"Okay. I think you're uncomfortable. I think you'd rather talk about anyone or anything but yourself. I think you don't especially like my place." She drew in a breath, giving him a look that brimmed with understanding. "I think you're alone too much."

On the verge of disproving all that mush—then sweeping Lucy away to find out what her bedroom was like—Max froze.

I think you're alone too much.

His smile felt wobbly. "I think you're imagining things."

Urgently, Lucy sat beside him. The sofa did not, he noticed, clutch at her nether regions like a six-foot-long jockstrap. Nor did it bury her in pillows. It only . . . *enveloped* her, seeming perfectly made to keep her comfortable.

"I've seen your apartment, remember?" She curled up to watch him with warm, sympathetic eyes. "It's empty. Completely bare of anything personal or meaningful or beautiful."

"My decorator would disagree. So would my checkbook."

"Money doesn't make things beautiful. People do." Lucy grabbed one of the pillows, a puke-green velour one with tassels. She shoved it in his arms. "Here. Take this. Start with this one thing to cozy up that mausoleum of yours. You'll see what I mean."

"Either that or I'll go blind."

She rolled her eyes. "Funny. I'm serious."

Max pushed it back. "I can't take this. It's yours."

"Not anymore." A gentle push.

Against his will, he clutched the pillow to his chest. It felt kind of nice. Soft. What the . . . ? He shook his head. "I've never taken anything from a woman."

"I'll bet you've never taken anything from anybody."

How the hell did she keep doing that? Was her house wiretapped directly into his brain, his memories . . . his stupid heart? Nobody knew about—

"My rivals in business would disagree." He stood.

"Oh puhleeze . . ."

Decisively, he set down the pillow. It looked better, more right, on Lucy's sofa than it had in his arms, anyway.

He extended his hand to her. "How about that drink?"

Giving the pillow a thoughtful look, Lucy shook her head. Her gaze rose to meet his. She grabbed his hand and hustled them both out of the living room. "I've got a better idea."

Dragging a wooden bat across the baseball diamond to the grassy space beyond, Lucy sighed. Warm air rose all around her. Insects buzzed around the brilliant halogen lights surrounding the field. In their glow, her makeshift Successfully Dressed team struggled to complete their second postsunset practice.

She tipped her bat against the dugout wall. Inside, it felt sheltered and smelled of earth. Outside, Max stood in the twilight, hands in his pockets, watching her.

He smiled at her approach.

She wondered why he hadn't joined everyone else at the edge of the chain-link fence. There, the people who weren't batting—along with friends who'd come to watch the practice—laughed and joked. Their boisterousness carried across the park, making the whole endeavor feel worthwhile.

Even if Lucy sucked at batting.

"Hey, don't worry," Max told her when she reached him. "You'll do better next time."

His eyes were full of empathy, despite the fact that she'd dragged him off to this practice on impulse. She didn't think he was especially adept at *impulse*. Although he was very good at other things. She nodded, accepting his encouragement.

He continued, looking ultraserious. "I mean it. That pack of moths can't possibly come rampaging back to throw off your swing next time."

Lucy made a face. "Hey. They were *big*."

"I know!" His eyes sparkled. "Big, furry . . . I think I saw fangs on the ringleader."

"Ha, ha." She leaned beside him, propping her shoulder against the dugout's exterior wall. Max felt a solid presence beside her—strong and steady and sure.

She wondered how right she'd been about him earlier. Because just now, Max seemed utterly invulnerable. Completely carefree and smart and sure. Manly. But when she'd met him coming to her front door tonight . . . well, then the sheer *need* she'd glimpsed in his face had affected her.

Probably in ways that were unwise, even for her.

Maybe she'd imagined it.

"So . . . what are you doing all the way over here?" She gestured to the other side of the field. "I expected to see you charming the pants off everybody on the team. Or maybe rearranging the stuff in the dugout for top efficiency."

Her jab at his interfering business ways—which, frankly, had grown rampant lately—didn't even hit home.

Max shrugged. The look in his eyes seemed faraway. "I'm not wild about baseball fields."

"Why not?"

He looked at her. "Long story."

"We've got all night." Lucy touched his arm. "Tell me."

Her touch seemed to snap him out of it. Max put his head near hers. His mouth caught her attention, show-cased as it was by his hard jaw, his jutting nose, his deep, dreamy eyes.

"Ever get lucky in the backseat of a Lexus?" he asked.

Tingling at his husky tone, Lucy considered it. "I don't know. What's a Lexus?"

To his credit, Max only gawked for an instant. "A car."

"Oh. I don't pay much attention to cars." She waved her hand, half-listening to the sounds of the practice. The *thwunk* of the ball hitting the mitt. The swoosh of the bat hitting empty air. The occasional crack of the bat actu-ally making contact, and the resulting whoops and hollers from the bystanders. "I can't afford one. I've got a bike instead."

His disbelieving stare was the same one she usually encountered. The seductive slide of his palms down her sides was new, though, as Max pulled her against him and cradled her from behind. Her backside fit thrillingly against his groin. He was not, she discerned with a whoosh of eagerness, interested in discussing bicycling.

She pretended an overriding fascination with baseball.

Unfortunately, she didn't comprehend any of the activities she saw on the field. She barely recognized the players.

Max's cheek rasped against hers. His lips teased her ear. "The backseat of a car is bigger." He nuzzled the nape of her neck. "Allowing for more movement, more agility . . . more everything. Want to try it?"

Goose bumps sped along her arms and legs. Despite the hot weather, Lucy felt herself shiver. How many times had Max held her this way? How many times had he made a wicked, sexually charged suggestion like this?

How many times had she, ultimately, succumbed?

Not nearly enough, she decided and followed him to the parking lot.

Fogged-over windows made following the progress of a baseball practice really tricky, Lucy discovered. She sat up, her clothes half-off, and tried to smudge away a bit of the condensation on the rear window.

Max's strong arm pulled her back on the leather seat beside him. It was a cramped fit, but delicious.

"Not so fast," he commanded in the semidarkness. "I'm not through with you yet."

She smiled. "If *that* wasn't 'through' with me, I don't know what is." Her whole body hummed with the after-effects of the fast and fabulous lovemaking they'd just shared. "I'm not sure how I'll find the strength to crawl out of this car."

"Then don't."

Max's voice rumbled in his chest, sounding self-assured. As though he took her acquiescence for granted, he wrapped both arms around her and squeezed tightly. Lucy didn't protest.

"I don't know how your girlfriends cope with this supersized snuggling routine of yours," she teased, enjoying the closeness between them. She arched her back and kissed his cheek, then ran her hand over the corded muscle of his arm. "It's getting pretty lengthy. Every time—"

"Snuggling routine?" Max sounded about to laugh. "I don't have a snuggling routine."

"Sure you do." It was one of the things she loved about

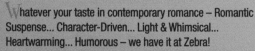

To start your membership, simply complete and return the Free Book Certificate. You'll receive your Introductory Shipment of FREE Zebra Contemporary Romances, you only pay $1.99 for shipping and handling. Then, each month you will receive the 4 newest Zebra Contemporary Romances. Each shipment will be yours to examine FREE for 10 days. If you decide to keep the books, you'll pay the preferred subscriber price (a savings of up to 30% off the cover price), plus shipping and handling. If you want us to stop sending books, just say the word... it's that simple.

If the FREE Book Certificate is missing, call 1-800-770-1963 to place your order.

FREE BOOK CERTIFICATE

Yes! Please send me FREE Zebra Contemporary romance novels. I only pay $1.99 for shipping and handling. I understand that each month thereafter I will be able to preview 4 brand-new Contemporary Romances FREE for 10 days. Then, if I should decide to keep them, I will pay the money-saving preferred subscriber's price (that's a savings of up to 30% off the retail price), plus shipping and handling. I understand I am under no obligation to purchase any books, as explained on this card.

NAME_____

ADDRESS_____ APT. _____

CITY_____ STATE_____ ZIP_____

TELEPHONE (_____) _____

E-MAIL_____

SIGNATURE_____

(If under 18, parent or guardian must sign)

Offer limited to one per household and not to current subscribers. Terms, offer and prices subject to change. Orders subject to acceptance by Zebra Contemporary Book Club. Offer Valid in the U.S. only.

Thank You!

CN076A

Be sure to visit our website at www.kensingtonbooks.com.

ll..l.lll....ll.l.l.l.l.l.ll.l.l.l.l.ll.l

Zebra Contemporary Romance Book Club
Zebra Home Subscription Service, Inc.
P.O. Box 5214
Clifton NJ 07015-5214

PLACE
STAMP
HERE

being with him. "Whenever we're, um, together, you insist on staying like this"—she illustrated by nudging closer, improving their awkward car-bound position—"for a long time afterward."

He snorted, plainly disbelieving.

"Okay," Lucy offered, willing to play along, "if you want to be delusional about it—"

"You're the one who's delusional." Max moved, bracing himself on his arms above her. His face, rugged and handsome enough to take her breath away, hovered over hers. He kissed her. "But then, maybe you're complaining. In which case I'll have to prove you wrong. Or maybe . . . teach you a lesson."

His wolfish grin promised his "lesson" would be enjoyable.

"Oh no," Lucy deadpanned. "Anything but *that*."

Then, giggling, she pulled him down and got busy all over again.

They made it back to the field just as practice was breaking up. Max didn't think anyone had noticed him and Lucy slip away, but he double-checked anyway by looking at everyone as they tromped across the park. Not a smirk, a surreptitious thumbs-up, or a leer among them. Perfect.

Not that he cared about his own reputation. But Lucy . . .

He didn't want to see her hurt by some jackass making assumptions. To be honest, Max had made some less-than-stellar decisions in his life, but hurting someone like Lucy would not be among them. Not if he could help it.

Even if she *was* crazy enough to call him a "snuggler." Which was ridiculous. Because Max didn't snuggle. He took, he conquered, he enjoyed, he moved on. But he didn't snuggle.

At least, he never had.

One of them was imagining things.

Putting it out of his mind, he moved across the field, waving good-bye to the volunteers he recognized. He shook hands with a few he'd just met. Before long, everyone had meandered to their cars or carpools or bus stops, laughing and chattering as they went. They seemed as close-knit a group when away from the shop as they were inside it. Max didn't get it. They genuinely seemed to care about each other.

Like a family.

Aside from Oliver, he didn't really *have*—

"Don't just stand there daydreaming, snuggles." Grinning, Lucy hefted a mesh bag of baseballs and tossed it his way. "Help me pick up."

As he might have expected, she'd volunteered herself to cart the practice supplies back and forth. How she'd planned to do that on her bike, Max didn't know. He was learning, as he spent more time with her, that Lucy routinely took it upon herself to help everyone around her—whether she was prepared for it or not.

Just like she'd done with Successfully Dressed.

He plucked an aluminum bat from the ground, then added it to the two tucked under his elbow. "Why didn't you ask me to be on the team?" he asked.

Working beside him to shag balls, Lucy stopped. She seemed baffled by the question. "You're not a real volunteer."

Max didn't know what the hell that meant. He spied a penny on the ground, then pocketed it for luck. "I could be an asset. I could bring a lot to this team."

"Maybe."

Her doubtful tone bugged him. "For all you know, I'm a major league slugger."

Lucy laughed. "You're a major league *something,*

that's for sure. Charmer, kisser . . . who knows what else."

"I mean it." She made him sound shallow. One-dimensional. For the first time, Max wanted to impress someone with his finer qualities. Wherever they were. Hell, he'd dredge up a few. They had to be in there somewhere. "Let me be on your team."

"You don't even like baseball fields. You said so."

Well, there was that. . . .

No. Screw it. "I said I'll do it."

Her contemplative look searched him up and down. He wished he had an extra supply of sincerity stashed in his kneecaps.

"Okay. Whatever." Lucy smiled. "Wait till you get a load of our uniforms."

12

For the next few weeks, Oliver toiled in the office while Max frittered away his days at Successfully Dressed. He insisted he was making progress—and making contacts—but Oliver wasn't so sure. From where he sat, a few blocks northwest, it looked a lot like Max was just making time. With Nieca. The bastard.

Surrounded by financial reports, bathed in the glow of his laptop's screen, Oliver stuck his ballpoint pen in his mouth and stared out the window. An image of Nieca came to him, glorious and golden and sassy. She was everything he wanted.

And everything he couldn't have.

He'd tried competing with Max. After his second financial workshop (which had seemed another resounding success), he'd even mustered the *cojones* to ask Nieca out for a latte at the coffee shop around the corner.

Inexplicably, she'd snorted and refused.

Maybe coffee was gauche. *So* last year.

He should have asked her out for body shots instead.

Ha. As if. He wasn't even sure what body shots involved, but the idea sounded risqué enough to intrigue him.

Lost in contemplating it, Oliver relaxed in his chair.

He pictured Nieca, holding a shot glass. Him, holding a salt shaker. The two of them, coming together—

"Delivery for you, boss."

Marlene sashayed into his office, bringing with her a waft of perfume. She held a cardboard box in her arms.

Ever chivalrous, he leaped up to help her. Gratefully, she relinquished the box, just as whatever it contained gave a *wiggle* and a sneeze.

Oliver almost dropped the box in surprise. He stared. "This is a dog."

"Close, genius." Marlene grinned. "It's a puppy."

Then it couldn't be for him.

He peered. Nestled in a blanket, the puppy had shaggy fur—patchy in spots—oversize paws, and a pair of chocolate brown eyes. They stared back at him trustingly. Gleefully.

Maybe a *little* hesitantly.

Oliver shoved away the box. "Send it back. There must be some kind of mistake."

Marlene clutched it. Puppy claws skidded across the cardboard. Snuffling could be heard, as could—Oliver would swear—a sort of mewling. The pathetic sound would have broken a lesser man. But not Oliver. It was true he was shy sometimes. That didn't mean he was a total pushover, destined to take somebody's abandoned mutt.

He resisted the urge to look inside the box again.

Marlene's accusing glare followed him across the room.

"I mean it. It's not mine. It can't be." He gestured to the reception area. "If you hurry, you can still catch the delivery person."

He strode blindly to his desk and grabbed a P&L report.

"What kind of numskull do you think I am?" Marlene

asked. "This is *yours,* you big old fraidy cat. The card says so."

Oliver stilled. "Card?"

His admin sighed. "Sometimes you brainy types really need a keeper, don't you?" Carefully, she set the box on the corner of his desk, then detached the card on its side.

A small furry head peeped over the cardboard. Then a tiny thump sounded as the puppy flopped sideways, too uncoordinated to manage the maneuver for long.

Oliver felt a bizarre kinship with the thing.

"To Oliver," Marlene read, sounding exasperated. "From Nieca. I saw this little guy and immediately thought of you. Maybe it was the runty legs."

Marlene guffawed. Damn it. He was *definitely* adding more weight to the leg press machine at the gym this week.

But the note sounded exactly like Nieca. Exactly like the woman who'd talked and laughed and even flirted with him. Him! Despite his better judgment, an irresistible excitement gripped Oliver. He'd have bet anything on the odds—approximately four to one—that he knew what was coming next.

Just kidding, Oliver mouthed.

"Just kidding," Marlene read.

Holy shit! He actually understood his dream woman.

"I hope he'll help you think up more crazy ideas for those pet boutiques of yours. Anybody who likes puppies deserves to succeed." Marlene raised her eyebrows, shooting him a disbelieving look. "Call me sometime. Love—"

"Give me that." With a shaky hand, Oliver grabbed the note. Yes. There it was, in pink gel ink. *Love, Nieca.*

Followed by her phone number.

She'd called him Oliver too. Not McGeekerson.

For the first time in his life, he was winning.

Feeling hot all over, Oliver stared in disbelief at the

box. The puppy stuck his snout over the top and sniffed at him.

That was the most adorable dog in the world.

Marlene shook her head. "I've never seen a puppy used as a man trap before. Who is this Nieca person?" she demanded, clearly suspicious. "How well do you know her?" She paused, putting both hands on her ample hips. "Exactly what are her intentions toward you?"

At his admin's protective tone, Oliver grinned. "I don't know. But I hope they're completely disreputable."

Lucy strode into Successfully Dressed after a morning spent driving the donation pickup truck, her head down and her hair flopping in her eyes. Welcomed by the comforting smells of vintage polyester and laundry detergents, she edged past a rack of blazers. If she was lucky, she could make it to her office before anyone saw her.

"Hey, Lucy. What's up?" Franco asked.

His voice reverberated over the sound system, amplified by the microphone he'd cadged from a gig. His vibrant Union Jack T-shirt made him look like a gangly Brit refugee, but he wore a smug grin that told her something was different.

Franco was clearly bursting to share something. She couldn't just motor past under those circumstances. Giving in, Lucy pulled her trailing scarf a little higher and waved with her other hand. "Hey. What's new?"

"*I* had a date."

"Ahhh. Did it go well?"

"If you call another date lined up for Saturday night 'well,' then, yes." Franco grinned, spinning an old vinyl LP—no doubt by one of his '80s faves—between his palms. He set it on the turntable. "I was playing it cool. You know, not calling right away. But apparently I'm irresistible."

Lucy felt glad for him. He'd been having sort of a dry spell lately. She smiled. "We all knew that already."

"Well, you'll just have to share the wealth, Lucy Goosey." Franco preened, fluffing his faux-hawk. His impish expression was pure Franco, gawky and lovable through and through. "Because I think *this* one might be The One."

Lucy gasped. "Seriously?"

"Well . . ." He pondered. "Or one of The Ones. I haven't decided yet." Franco gave an offhanded wave, still beaming. "Apparently *your* smokin' love life is rubbing off on all of us."

Yeah. On that subject . . .

"Gotta run." Yanking up her scarf, Lucy hurried to her office. Over her shoulder, she called, "Good luck!"

God knew, all of them could use it.

At the threshold to her office, Lucy skidded to a stop. Her vintage Chuck Taylors squeaked against the concrete floor, and her eyelet lace miniskirt—very early Madonna—swooshed around her thighs. She dropped her scarf against her vintage menswear pinstripe vest and inhaled.

A prickly sense of dread crept up her spine.

"Is that Shalimar I smell?"

Nieca, already inside with a cup of chamomile tea, nodded. Glumly. "Yes. The Dragon Lady was here again. While you were out getting donations."

Dispirited, Lucy sank on her makeshift chair. The hair dryer hood almost clonked her on the head, which didn't surprise her, given how her day had progressed so far. "Why? Why does she still pretend to care about this place?"

A shrug. "Probably because she's still footing the bill."

"But she agreed to let me run things!"

Which, Lucy reminded herself, was something *she* intended to do with one important difference. Unlike the DL, *she* intended to make good on her good intentions and make the shop a hit—not abandon it when the going got rough.

"Sure, she said you could handle it on a trial basis," Nieca reminded her. "Or until she gets bored again."

They stared at each other, reliving that awful morning when Cornelia Burnheart had cheerfully announced her intentions to close the shop. "Oh, in a week or so," she'd said. "Whenever I can get someone to come haul away everything. I have a cruise to catch, after all. Priorities have to be maintained."

Apparently, ordinary priorities like groceries, utilities, and rent for her employees hadn't occurred to her.

Feeling queasy, Lucy stared at her cluttered desk. It overflowed with papers, sticky notes, Franco's CDs, and their team roster for baseball. Near her potted aloe vera plant, one of Jade's recipes for miso soup languished beside a swivel-up lip gloss. Several weeks' worth of the *New Times* back issues tottered by the phone, reminding her—belatedly—of her plans to garner media attention for the shop.

She still had a lot to do, Lucy realized. If she failed, she'd be letting down her friends and herself.

"Well, the DL's visit doesn't matter," she announced firmly, "because I'm bringing in an astrologer *and* a numerologist next week—a special attraction. Tell all your customers. Franco too. Okay? We have to spread the word. Half the challenge in getting business is getting people in the door in the first place, you know."

Belatedly, it occurred to Lucy that that sounded like something Max would say. She hoped he wasn't rubbing off on her. Mr. Busy McBusinessman.

Nieca eyed her warily. "What day? Because we have the weekly cocktail party for our interview-suit buyers on Friday, and Oliver's next financial seminar on Thursday. That doesn't leave much time open for—"

"Saturday. Saturday at noon."

"No good." Nieca pursed her lips. "That conflicts with Max's session on how to handle a job interview."

All of a sudden, Lucy felt as if control of her shop was slipping away from her. She'd never been less in touch with the plans that affected her job. And she could date all her newfound disconnectedness to one man's arrival.

"His what?" she asked.

"Max is offering a seminar series about interviewing. It's really good. He gave me a preview." Nieca's face brightened. "I swear, if I ever switch jobs, I'm totally using his hints."

Lucy frowned. "What makes Max such an expert?"

"Come on." Nieca put her hands on her hips and rolled her eyes. "*You,* of all people, shouldn't have to ask that. Near as I can tell, Max is good at everything."

Gritting her teeth, Lucy shoved aside a few items on her desk. Maybe if she got better organized . . .

No. It wasn't a lack of organization that was bugging her. It was Max. Max and his aggravating, know-it-all interference.

He might have the muscles of a steelworker and the charm of a diplomat, but he acted as if he owned the place. He'd been suggesting "improvements" in the way she managed things ever since showing up for his second volunteering stint. His buttinsky behavior was seriously starting to cramp her style.

Lucy believed in a "live and let live" philosophy. She didn't impose her ideas on other people. So why couldn't anyone—especially a certain tall, hunky, backseat Romeo—extend the same courtesy to her? Huh? Was that so much to ask?

"Never mind," Lucy said, waving her hand. "I'll take

care of Max myself." She narrowed her eyes, relishing the thought.

Nieca chuckled. "Right. I'll just *bet* you will."

"Not like that. I mean, I'll bring him in line. I'm the boss. *I'll* set the schedule around here."

Max would simply have to accept her authority. Simple as that. Easy peasy. It was time she exercised her influence anyway, Lucy decided. Otherwise, she'd never succeed.

Maybe, she admitted to herself grudgingly, she'd been a little *too* laissez-faire up until this point.

"*You're* going to take on Max," Nieca said.

"You don't have to sound so incredulous."

"Okay." Stifling a grin, her friend crossed her arms over her chest. "But before you get all dominatrix on his ass, there are two things you ought to know."

Lucy raised her brows. She practiced her new authority-figure demeanor by folding her hands calmly atop her desk.

"One," Nieca said, holding up her index finger, "the DL is coming back later today to discuss her 'inspirations' for the shop with you."

Not again. Lucy almost groaned but held back the impulse through sheer force of will. Even if being in charge killed her, she was going to nail it. End of story.

"Yes? And what else?"

"Two"—Nieca's grin grew even wider—"you might want to slap some concealer on that big, fat love zit on your nose before Max gets here." She flounced to the doorway, saucily holding her teacup aloft. "And you thought I wouldn't notice. Ha!"

Max slunk into Successfully Dressed, his head down and his collar turned up. He hadn't worn his shirts this way since his brief stint as a middle school prepster.

Then, it had looked ridiculous. Now, it probably looked worse.

So much for being older and wiser.

Stubbornly, he made his way to the storage room and loaded up a few carts of donated items. He manhandled them to the washing machines, keeping his back to the sales floor.

It was a good thing he hadn't had to go to the office today. He hadn't felt this embarrassed since he'd glimpsed Kaitlyn Kramer's red polka-dot panties beneath her skirt and gotten his first-ever geometry class boner. Skulking out of class with his textbook plastered to his frank and beans hadn't been much fun. Neither was this.

Franco and Nieca called out greetings. Max raised his hand to them and returned the favor, keeping his back turned. He shoved in the piles of clothes, sorting them expertly into machines by color and fabric as he went. It occurred to him that, after this, he'd probably become fully capable of doing his own laundry at home instead of having it sent out.

He made a face. Nah. Life was too short.

Arranging the washer dials, Max mulled over his tactics for the day. He'd made a few important contacts so far, but he'd only progressed about a third of the way through Oliver's binder. A lot more work remained to be done. The trouble was, every time Max saw Lucy, he got distracted. There was something about her smile, her voice, her legs in those miniskirts she liked, that made his mind—and his hands—wander.

Yesterday, he'd even wound up making friends with Lucy's butt-sucking sofa during a trip to her place to, ostensibly, retrieve one of her account books. Max had offered to help her "check figures." At the time, he'd meant it. But Lucy had insisted there was something special about his invitation.

"It was the *way* you said it," she told him, pulling him

down amid her cast-off sneaker and her fuzzy fringed blanket.

Afterward, Max had even found himself smuggling home the dorky puke-green pillow she'd tried to give him. As a memento. He'd awakened this morning—not that he'd admit it to a soul—with the thing tucked under his cheek.

And he hadn't gone blind looking at it either.

In fact, he'd kind of liked it. Especially its softness.

Forgetting where he was and what he was doing, Max turned. He felt the goofy grin on his face an instant too late to stop it—not that he could have, since Lucy stood there waiting for him.

She smiled back. Then her eyes widened. Her gaze zoomed in on his face, then closer . . . closer. She covered her mouth with her hand. A muffled expletive followed.

He was still staring at Lucy's retreating back when Nieca sauntered up. She gave him a knowing nod.

"I knew it. You've got one too."

Self-consciously, Max touched his nose. The hideous, honking zit that had blossomed on it overnight seemed to pulse beneath his fingertip. It felt like a neon beacon, beckoning everyone within fifty yards to gawk at his face.

This was *not* a feeling he'd have preferred to relive.

Then . . . "Too?" he repeated.

"Yup." Nieca looked him up and down, seeming inexplicably pleased with herself. She nodded again. "You're done for, pal. The love zit is always the most telling sign."

"Love zit?"

But Nieca only leaned forward conspiratorially, not offering any further explanation. "Tell me, Max. Exactly how serious *are* you about Lucy? Because if you break her heart, I'm going to snap off your Mr. Happy and slap you around with it."

Max winced. "That's pretty graphic."

"Yeah? Well, that's how much we love Lucy around here. She's a special girl." Nieca jabbed him in his shirt-front, probably denting his chest hair. "Now that it's official, don't screw up. Hear me?"

Max wasn't quite sure how a pimple made things "official."

Then he spotted Lucy, scurrying past with a scarf half around her face and an armful of donated purses. Her scarf slipped. A vibrant pink zit glowed from her nose, re-minding him, inexplicably, of the mannequin, Suzy, with the gold star on her nose. He gawked. Stared at Nieca.

"Uh-huh. I think you're feelin' me now," she said.

Then she sauntered away, leaving him wondering. In a world where winning didn't count, sharing was the rule, and everybody wore somebody else's old clothes, Max figured just about anything could happen. Including him . . . falling for Lucy.

It was for the safety of his crotch, after all. Ouch.

Tapping her toe against the floor, Lucy watched as Max and the Dragon Lady moved toward the racks of in-terview suits. They kept their heads together, talking like old pals. She snorted.

"Takes one to know one, I guess," Lucy told Franco, shaking her head. "Maybe they're neighbors at Big Shot Central."

"I dunno." He squinted after them thoughtfully. "Maybe Max is just trying to help you, Luce. I'd think you'd be happy to have the DL off your hands for once."

Well . . . there was that. Lucy had spent most of the morning listening to Cornelia Burnheart jabber on about "the Winston gala" this and "the Diamond Jubilee benefit" that. It seemed the woman's most pressing concerns—aside from Botoxing her forehead into perma-plasticity—were what to wear, which jewelry to match with what she wore, and who might see her in all her resulting froufrou glory.

"I've simply *got* to get down here to the shop more often," she'd simpered at one point, examining the place with a vaguely confused air that suggested she'd needed a map and driver simply to remember where it was. "It's just chock *full* of atmosphere, isn't it? Plus, Harold says it's a fantastic tax shelter. Whatever that means." A twitter. "I let him take care of all those *boring* financial details."

With the help of her live-and-let-live mantra, Lucy had managed a smile. "Let me show you the shoes."

"Shoes?" Cornelia had surveyed the dilapidated, crammed-full baskets with a delicate moue. "My goodness. I had *such* good intentions for a fabulous shoe display, remember? Remember, Lucy?" A jab with her bony, ultra-dieted elbow. "It was going to be *filled* with my old Ferragamos." A sigh. "Oh well. Que sera sera."

That was when Lucy had nearly lost it. It had taken her three hours to scrub, spray-paint, and fill those carts. Hearing all her hard work dismissed so casually had tipped her right over the edge. She'd gritted her teeth, opened her hands into claws behind the DL's back. . . .

That was when Max had swooped in, all charm and benevolence beneath his hunkorific exterior. He'd tucked Lucy protectively behind him, then hurriedly extended his hand. Cornelia, enchanted, had taken one look and all but smacked her lips.

"What do you suppose they're talking about?" Lucy asked Franco now, suspiciously—if semigratefully— watching.

He examined them. "Max is probably telling the DL how to buff the lip prints off her ass."

Narrowing her eyes, Lucy followed their progress. Max's tour of the shop seemed to be going much better than hers had. The DL hadn't quit laughing, squeezing his biceps, or making goo-goo eyes at him since they'd started. If successful entrepreneurship depended on heating up bored socialites, then Max definitely excelled at it.

Unable to stand it any longer, Lucy escaped to help a few customers. A newly divorced woman who was reentering the work force for the first time in sixteen years. A married mother of three who'd just graduated from night school and wanted an interview suit. A pair of giggly ASU students who were looking for early Betsey Johnson skirts, and a man who'd offered to buy the mini disco ball in the fitting room.

The bell over the shop door tinkled. Max and Cornelia Burnheart stood framed in the doorway, smiling. She put her hand on his arm, cooed something in her snooty voice, then air-kissed his cheek. He executed a similar maneuver as though it were completely natural to him, then waved her down the sidewalk.

The DL hadn't even said good-bye to her, Lucy realized. It just went to show how low on the totem pole she ranked. Who was she, anyway? Only the person who'd sweated and strained and contracted tennis elbow helping haul and hang racks of clothes for Successfully Dressed's opening. Only the person who'd endured hours of socializing with the DL's fluff-brained friends as they'd dropped off their donated "treasures." Only the person who'd stepped up, without even realizing she'd planned to, when Cornelia had threatened to close the shop.

Lucy had been the one to hire Nieca, to find Franco, to line up volunteers like Penny. While the DL had lounged in the back, enjoying the "kitsch factor" of the hair dryer chair, Lucy had made phone calls and helped customers. She'd learned how to evaluate vintage pieces, how to price them, how to sell them.

This wasn't her first job in retail, and it probably wouldn't be her last. But Lucy was proud of how well she'd done and how hard she'd worked to make Success-fully Dressed fit into the neighborhood. It was a part of things now, as much as the artisanal bakery, the tiny hardware store, and the mom-and-pop grocery on the corner were. As much as Lucy's little house was.

Both of them felt like home now.

Max strode to meet her, seeming pleased.

"That CC Burnheart." He shook his head, grinning. "She's fascinating. Did you know she and her third husband, Harold, have lived in Milan, the Côte d'Azur, *and* Des Moines?"

"Mmmm." Lucy pretended an overriding interest in a button-down Oxford shirt. "You two did seem to hit it off."

A pause. "You don't like her?"

"What's to like?" She shrugged. "Two pounds of makeup, lots of blond hair, and a pair of 'enhanced' double-Ds don't exactly make a person worthwhile."

"You're jealous." He sounded amazed.

"Of the DL?" Lucy scoffed. "Hardly."

Max only leaned against the rack and studied her. "What do you know?" he mused. "You *do* have a flaw."

"What I have is an inability to meet people on a completely superficial basis."

"Right. And it bugs you."

"That's ridiculous." She released the pale blue shirt she'd been folding and stared at him. "It does not."

"It does. Because you like getting along with everyone, and you can't get along with CC."

"CC. Hmmph. Nobody around here calls her that."

"Lucy." Max caught her arm, looking surprised. "She's not an alien life form. She's a person, just like you and me. She might look different, or sound different, but if you look past the outside—"

"Wait a minute. *You're* lecturing me on being open-minded?"

Max angled his head. His dimple flashed, making

him seem boyish and happy. "I guess you're rubbing off on me."

"Right." She moved to the next rack, feeling inexplicably bothered. Once again, Max had excelled in an area Lucy couldn't *quite* get a handle on. Just like he'd been right about hosting Oliver's financial seminar, he'd been right about how to handle Cornelia too. "I'm *such* a wonderful influence."

She snorted.

"Hey."

She kept moving. Something about this hurt her, and Lucy didn't want to feel hurt. Not when she needed to be strong.

"Hey," Max repeated, gentling his voice. He caught up to her behind the couture section and put his arm around her waist. He tipped up her chin. His gaze, deep and insightful, met hers. "I mean it. Because of you, I'm different."

Lamely, Lucy gestured to his pants and turned-up shirt. "Yeah. You don't dress like a banker anymore."

"It's more than that."

Skeptically, she eyed him. He didn't let her go.

Instead, Max brought his mouth to hers. He kissed her, softly, then leaned back and gazed into her eyes. He kissed her again, bringing his hand to her cheek and holding her to him with a tenderness she wouldn't have credited to a man so rugged. There was something new in the way their lips met, in the way they leaned together, lingering when the kiss was through.

Max rested his forehead against hers, the gesture intimate even in their noisy surroundings. "Believe me. I'll show you. Tonight."

Just like that, Lucy could hardly wait.

13

Lucy stood trembling beneath Max's hands, his grasp on her shoulders light as he helped her into position. The blindfold covering her eyes flopped against the side of her neck, its pattern familiar to him. On such short notice, he hadn't been able to think of anything more innovative than one of his softest Charvet silk neckties, wrapped around Lucy's temples and fastened in the back. Its knot was as secure as he'd dared make it.

Semidarkness surrounded them, broken only by moonlight. The only sounds to be heard were occasional passing cars and the faint buzz of distant lives being lived across the city.

As though he were blindfolded, too, Max felt his other senses heightened. Touch, enhanced by the silky feeling of Lucy's bare skin beneath his fingertips. Smell, enlivened by the scented oil she always wore, cinnamony and sensual. Hearing, lured by the raspy sound of Lucy's breath as she waited to learn what he had in mind.

"You said you trusted me," Max reminded her.

She nodded, serious beneath her blindfold. "I do."

He couldn't believe he was doing this. He'd sworn he never would again, but it had been so long. Too long. At times, he'd even wanted it . . . so much. But until now, until Lucy, he'd refused to so much as consider trying again.

Drawing in a deep breath, he gave a signal. Light flooded them both in a circle of brilliance, clear as day. It was time.

Max peered at the supplies he'd brought, then selected an item. Gently, he opened Lucy's hand, then put it within her grasp. Her whole body seemed taut. He felt her confusion as he wrapped her fingers securely.

"Ready?" he asked.

"Max . . . I . . ." She straightened. "Yes."

"Good." He untied her blindfold, held it in place while he edged around to her front, then removed it. It crumpled in his fist, soft as silk but not as soft as Lucy. "Surprise."

She blinked. She took in the field of green grass surrounding them, the chalked dirt under their feet, the chain-link fence nearby. The lights. The bases. The bat in her hand.

"The baseball field?" she asked.

He grinned. "What did you *think* I meant when I said we'd probably make it to third base tonight?"

They both knew what she'd thought. Especially given her wicked smile. And if Lucy went on looking at him that way, so delectably and so meaningfully, Max knew he might wind up abandoning his good intentions altogether.

He plucked his Astros cap from his back pocket and stuck it on her purple-haired head. She clapped her free hand on it, looking surprised.

"That's a very special, very lucky hat," he warned her sternly. "So don't screw around with it. Hear me?"

She lowered her hand—at least partway. It swooshed into a smart-alecky salute instead. "Yes, sir, Mr. Lucky, sir."

"Funny." Max had never tried sharing his good luck before, he realized. But with Lucy . . . well, she needed it. And he . . . he was starting to need her too.

He frowned to cover the realization. "All right. Back up, listen up, and quit trying to distract me." He put his hands to her curvy hips, repositioning her at home plate, and nearly succeeded in distracting himself. "We've got work to do."

The minute the phone call came, Nieca knew she'd done the right thing. She cradled the receiver against her ear, nodded, then smiled.

Twenty minutes later, she drove through the gates of a swanky foothills apartment complex. Here, the cicadas hummed, and the night felt perfumed with orange blossoms. Nieca inhaled appreciatively, then gathered her things and strode toward one of the complex's art-deco-style buildings. She didn't bother to ask directions. Generally speaking, she knew where she was going. Tonight was no exception.

At the end of a long, shadowy sidewalk bordered with lush and mature landscaping, she spotted him. Oliver. Her heartbeat quickened, and she found herself moving faster in her platform shoes. They gave her the height she needed to meet him face to face—something she liked and somehow, curiously, needed.

He didn't see her at first. He was busy with the tiny bundle in his arms, cradling it and saying something to it. Then the clomp of her shoes alerted him, and Oliver glanced up.

His buoyant expression delighted her.

"I hear someone needs a helping hand," Nieca said.

He was strong enough to agree. His nod was all she needed.

"Come inside." Oliver moved aside, letting her pass.

A hush enveloped her. Astonished, Nieca stood in the foyer, hardly able to comprehend the sense of welcome she felt. Unlike the city outside, Oliver's apartment seemed an oasis of calm, a cool contrast to the sultry summer night, but somehow warm all the same. She pondered it, the designer within her trying to decide if the effect owed itself to the cozy caramel fabrics he used, the cushy furniture, the warm woods, or the unlighted stone fireplace. The color scheme looked spicy and inviting, coaxing her to move farther within it.

She wanted to hug the whole place.

Still gawking, Nieca heard the heavy oak door shut, sensed Oliver's nearness as he noiselessly crossed the plush carpet.

"Have a seat," he said, moving past her. "I have everything set up over here."

Something was different. Alerted to the possibility, Nieca studied Oliver. Dressed in dark pants and a blue linen shirt with the sleeves rolled up and the top few buttons undone, he was all easy casualness. His shoulders seemed broad, even without the sleek designer jacket he'd dropped at one edge of the sofa. Nieca sidestepped a pair of enormous monk strap men's shoes, her interest piqued even further.

Big feet. Broad shoulders. And even, bizarre as it seemed, a rock-solid sense of confidence. If only Oliver hadn't had that geeky mess of curly hair. . . .

"Spike won't eat. And he'll only sleep if I hold him, like this." Oliver demonstrated, nodding toward the furry bundle in his arms. "I don't know what to do."

Neither did Nieca. At least with her feelings.

She came nearer, glad to confirm that her shoes put her, if not face to face with Oliver, at least eyes to chin. Sometimes being short was a real pain in the ass.

"Spike? That's a lot of name to live up to for such a little dog."

Oliver lifted his shoulder. "I'm an optimistic guy."

Just then, Nieca believed him. Intrigued, she examined

the bundle in his arms. "What's that thing you've wrapped him in?"

"One of my sweaters. He peed on the blanket he came with."

Nieca touched it. "This is cashmere."

"It's working. It's making him happy." Oliver crooned this last word to the puppy he held, probably unaware of the sweet, singsong tone of his voice. "That's all I care about."

"It's expensive cashmere," she protested. Sure, the puppy had been a gift, but . . . still. "Don't you have any respect for fabrics? For designers? For the people who combed hair fibers off the bellies of obscure Mongolian Kashmir goats just to make this stuff?"

Oliver smiled. Remarkably, she found him stunning when he smiled. "Quiet. You'll scare Spike."

She was starting to scare herself. She *never* went for nerdy guys. Something was wrong, because Nieca wanted to move closer, to soak up Oliver's presence, to make him smile again.

"What's wrong with you?" she blurted. "You're so— so—"

"So . . . ?" He raised his eyebrow.

"So normal!" *So sexy.* No, she hadn't just thought that, even on the inside. "Or at least not as geeky as before."

For a long moment, Oliver only watched her. "You did say I should call you. In your note."

She nodded. "Right. I did."

As though that explained it all, Oliver fell silent. The puppy in his arms slumbered on, oblivious to its ultra-expensive multi-ply bed. After awhile, Nieca started to worry she'd offended Oliver—the man who, until now, had allowed her to flirt outrageously with him and had only stammered in return.

"But usually you stammer. Or blush," she explained. "You shake and sweat and trip over everything you say."

Oliver's careful regard continued. It was seriously starting to unnerve her. Nieca jabbed at him again, trying to get on safer, more familiar ground.

"What's the matter, geeky? Stuck for a comeback?"

That got him. "Stuck for a comeback? Here? At home? With you?" Wearing an unreadable expression, Oliver shook his head. "Not anymore. I'm over it."

Over it? Over *her?* Damn it. She'd thought of the puppy maneuver too late. Usually she was so good at seduction.

Floundering, Nieca stared as Oliver hunkered down to check his supplies. Nestled amid the tartan plaid blanket in a padded wicker dog bed, she spied a hot water bottle, a gently ticking clock wrapped in flannel, and a small bowl of water. There was puppy food nearby. Toys too. He'd thought of everything to make a new puppy feel welcome.

She wasn't needed here at all, Nieca realized.

She had nothing to offer.

Oliver glanced up. The surety, the comfortableness, in him made him seem like a new man. A man she could respect as much as she—suddenly—wanted to get closer to.

Only . . . just as suddenly, Nieca wasn't sure he'd let her.

What had she gotten herself into?

Oliver angled his head to the sofa. "You might as well get comfortable. I want you to stay all night."

"All night?" She stared at him. "Did you just invite me to . . . ?"

Stay all night reverberated in the air between them.

"No! Not that." Oliver blushed . . . although a certain speculation did show on his face. Just for a minute, all his old awkwardness returned. "You know. To help with Spike."

Ahhh. Feeling better, Nieca sat on the sofa. She patted the cushion beside her. "Let's get a closer look at the little guy." Oliver sat. "Wow. Big feet, huh?"

* * *

Lucy lost track of how long she spent on the baseball field with Max, learning how to throw, how to catch, how to wield a baseball bat for maximum effectiveness. All she knew was that she saw a different side to Max that night . . . an endearing side that made her fall even harder for him than before.

With enduring patience, he showed her how to position herself at home plate. He laughed and joked, making her feel less gangly as she gripped the bat. He touched her hands, her arms, her shoulders, demonstrating how to execute a proper swing. And when she finally managed to hit a grounder—to golf-club it, really—the expression of delight on Max's face made her feel as proud as if she'd smacked a home run.

"Okay, slugger." He grinned, thunking the ball in his mitt with practiced confidence. He gave an elaborate windup. "Let's see you hit one *above* kneecap level this time."

Unfortunately, Lucy couldn't. No matter what happened, as soon as the ball veered toward the strike zone, she ducked.

"Damn it!" She lowered her bat to her side. "Give up, Max. I'm just not a sports person. I'm not athletic."

Max winked. "Tell that to my ribs. I'm pretty sure I pulled a muscle that time on your sofa when you rolled me over, pointed to that page in the Kama Sutra, and started kissing my—"

"Keep talking like that and I won't *want* to bat."

He tossed the ball in the air. High in the air. Caught it. His whole demeanor seemed content. "Come on. One more."

"Hang on." Suddenly inspired, Lucy closed her eyes. She imagined the ball as a glowing bundle of positive energy, pictured herself wanting to swing at it, saw it sail away into the darkness beyond the field lights. She got ready. "Okay."

An instant later, a familiar *whoosh* flew over her head.

"Damn it!" She slumped. "No matter what happens, I'm afraid it's going to hit me."

"Shake it off," Max instructed in his best drill sergeant voice. "If it hits you, you'll be fine."

"I'll be hurt! Who wants to get hurt?"

"Getting hurt happens. Quit dwelling on it."

Aghast, Lucy stared at him. The bat felt leaden in her hand, more of an impediment than a tool. "You're supposed to promise not to hurt me."

"I can't." He tossed the ball in his mitt again. "Like I said, it happens. The more you fear it, the more likely it will be. You'll stiffen up, try to protect yourself . . . and put yourself right in the ball's path."

"*That's* your philosophy? Hurt happens?"

Max spread his arms. "You've got my lucky hat. What more do you need?"

One look at him told her he was serious. "Fine. Throw."

He eyeballed her as she brought the bat to her shoulder, then assumed her best batting stance. Lucy narrowed her eyes and focused. She wanted to hit that ball. Wanted to learn, so she wouldn't let down her team. She was the worst batter of them all—and that was really saying something, given the dubious "skills" of Franco's bandmates. She nodded.

Max hesitated. A grin crossed his face, deepening his dimple. "You're cute when you're determined."

"Be quiet and pitch."

"Your nose gets all scrunched and your cheeks turn pink."

"Come on." Her palms ached from gripping the bat.

"Adorable."

"Max!"

He pitched. Lucy's adrenaline revved. The ball came toward her, a slow and easy arc against the dusty dirt field.

An instant later, she crouched at home plate, swearing.

The ball hit the chain-link fence behind her, then dropped to the ground and rolled, joining the two dozen or so already littering the dirt. Frustration shoved through her.

"I don't get it!" Lucy cried. "I really, *really* want to hit that ball." She dropped her bat, pacing. "Every time, I *mean* to hit that ball. And then, when it comes toward me . . ."

Max strode toward her. "Wanting it doesn't matter. *Doing* it does. You can do it."

He was wrong. On both counts. She shook her head. "Everything starts with having good intentions. With meaning well. If you haven't got that—"

"Good intentions don't count for squat. I sure as hell didn't get where I am by meaning well." He scooped up her bat with one lithe movement, then pressed the ball and mitt in her hands. "Let's try something else."

Lucy was still puzzling over a statement so mind-boggling as "good intentions don't count for squat" when Max traded places with her at home plate. He angled his head, motioning for her to assume the pitcher's position. Gamely, she did.

"Okay," Max said, the bat poised near his broad shoulder. "Throw the ball as hard as you can, the way I showed you. The way we practiced. Remember?"

Nervously, Lucy nodded. She bit her lip. Hefted the ball. The mitt felt clumsy on her left hand, big and bulky and leathery. She'd probably be kicked out of PETA just for holding it.

"As hard as you can," Max repeated earnestly. "I want you to try to hit me."

Lucy stopped. "What?"

"Try to hit me. On purpose." He let the bat fall to one side and thumped his chest with his fist. "Right here. Do it."

"No! I'm not going to hurt you. *Especially* on purpose."

He sighed. "That's the part you don't get. 'On purpose' doesn't matter. If it happens, it happens. I'll survive."

He was still wrong. Lucy knew it. "On purpose" made all the difference to her. That old saying about how it was the thought that counted really resonated in her world.

She shook her head. "No way. Let's quit."

"If you quit now, you'll never learn."

"Yes, I will! I want to—"

"Wanting to doesn't matter. *Doing* matters. Now do it."

He was insufferable. Screwing up her courage, Lucy tried a windup. She was just getting the hang of it when she imagined herself walloping Max upside the head and knocking him unconscious. How would she drag him back to his car?

As though reading her mind, Max frowned. "Quit making excuses. Excuses are for losers."

He was really starting to make her mad. "I'm not a loser."

"Prove it." He got ready again. Expectantly.

"You're a lot nicer when you're volunteering," she groused.

"There's no room for nice in baseball. Throw it."

"Stop telling me what to do!" Lucy remembered something else. Something she'd meant to tell him before all the kissing had started this afternoon. "And while we're at it, stop taking over my shop too. *I* make the decisions at Successfully Dressed, not you."

Max stared her down. He whirled the tip of his bat in the air, making MLB-worthy circles and swirls. He posed again.

"So you can quit telling me how to organize my books, rearrange my sales floor, schedule my time, and advertise!"

Still nothing. He waited, poised like granite.

"I might not be a big shot like you, or a fancy socialite like Cornelia, but I *mean* well, and that matters more."

Max yawned. He swept the bat in a practice arc. "Hit me."

He wasn't even listening! Lucy was pouring her heart out, and he didn't even care. All at once, Lucy saw red.

She hurled the ball straight at him.

An instant later, a tidy *thwack* sounded. The ball zoomed into the stratosphere, disappearing beyond the lights.

Max gave her a smug smile. The jerk.

She grabbed another ball from the bucket beside the mound. Wound up. Threw it with all her might, directly at his big, broad, stupid chest.

Another home run. Max stretched his neck. "Come on. You throw like a girl. Try to put some gusto behind it."

Lucy flung the next few balls fast and furiously. Anger and frustration poured out through her fingertips as she hurled one ball after another, aiming them at Max's chest, his belly, even his aggravating handsome face.

He pounded every one, no matter how wildly thrown.

Gaping in astonishment, Lucy watched the umpteenth ball soar into the night and disappear from view beyond the lights.

"We're going to have to shag a lot of balls later," Max observed. "You've got a strong arm. I guess you're motivated by trying to take my head off."

He'd known. All at once, Lucy felt ashamed.

"I've got to go," she said, and bolted for the grass.

He'd be damned if he'd follow her, Max decided.

Lucy was going off to sulk. To pout. Then, inevitably, to blame him for something. Max knew it. Women were like that. Hell, *people* were like that.

He still didn't know what he'd done wrong. He'd proven it was possible to bat without getting knocked out cold by a rogue ball, the way Lucy had feared. He'd demonstrated good form, bashed a few balls out of the park, gotten limbered up. He'd remembered exactly how good it felt to swing a bat—at least he had once he'd gotten Lucy to pitch to him.

She was stubborn and unreasonable. He knew she'd been meditating or some crap when she'd closed her eyes earlier. What kind of bullshit maneuver was that? You couldn't wish upon a star and get a home run in return.

It only went to show how incompatible he and Lucy were, Max told himself as he watched her sashay-stomp across the grass. Lucy was all about good intentions and not hurting anyone. Max knew it was better to screw good intentions and just get the job done, no matter who got hurt. They'd get over it. Everyone did.

Near the bleachers, Lucy wavered. She looked to both sides, glanced to his Lexus in the parking lot, then stiffened her spine. He read her like a book. There was no way in hell she was going to let him drive her home unless he groveled first.

Fuck that. He'd meant well. He'd done what needed to be done, shown her baseball wasn't freaking *deadly*. Scowling, Max deliberately looked away. Lucy could hitchhike home for all he cared. She could grab a ride on the Care Bears Bus of Sharing with all the other pie-in-the-sky, purple-haired hippies.

Where did she get off, telling him to leave her shop alone? If anyone needed help—needed it desperately— it was her. It wasn't Max's fault he was uniquely equipped to provide it.

She didn't have to like it. She just needed to let him do it. Just like she'd needed to let him take those wild pitches.

Against his will, Max grinned. Jesus, but Lucy had an arm on her. She'd pelted him with balls willy-nilly. The fire in her eyes had been kind of cute—until she'd almost windpiped him. Then he'd had to get semiserious about hitting.

The ache in his arms felt good. Necessary.

Cooled off some, Max looked up. He scanned the field, feeling almost ready to talk Lucy out of her snit. He could do it—he had a million times before, with women of all kinds. It didn't matter if things felt a little different with Lucy. He was still the same man he'd always been . . . mostly.

She was nowhere in sight.

Confusion gripped him. He dropped his bat and strode forward without even meaning to, following the path she'd taken. The area near the bleachers stood empty now, and so did the parking lot beyond, except for his car. There was a bus stop nearby—he'd pinpointed it as Lucy's likeliest destination—but she wasn't there.

Christ. Walking faster, Max reached the bleachers. He studied them in the semidarkness, feeling a weird sense of . . . guilt? . . . wash over him. Had he pissed off Lucy enough to make her do something crazy?

Like, for instance, *actually* hitchhike home?

She was just gullible enough to do it, he thought, with her aren't-people-super? mantra and her trusting ways. He should have known better than to take his eyes off her for a minute. But she'd pissed him off with her know-it-all talk about good intentions—not to mention her refusal to pitch to him.

He'd had a plan, damn it. Didn't she trust him at all?

Veering sideways, Max lurched toward the other side of the bleachers. He searched all over them, growing colder by the second. It didn't matter that the hot summer night still simmered all around him. Without Lucy—

A dark shape near the back of the bleachers moved.

Max stopped, idiotic hope surging through him. The shape coalesced into a stubborn profile, curvy shoulders, some sort of yoga-looking hunch . . . *Lucy*. She sat with her back to the bleacher support post, arms hugging her drawn-up knees.

She'd never looked better.

He stomped nearer. "What the hell is the matter with you?"

She jerked at the sound of his voice. She lifted her face toward his, her features glowing in the light reflected from the aluminum bleachers. "Oh yeah. You probably want your hat back."

His lucky Astros cap hit him in the chest.

He didn't care about his stupid hat.

"I looked all over for you!"

Lucy shrugged. "I've been thinking."

Max gawked. "Thinking? Here? In the dark?"

She nodded.

She was so weird. He just didn't understand her.

More and more, he wanted to.

He was hopeless.

The sight of her stooped shoulders twisted him in knots, made him ache in ways baseball never had. Max eased beside her on the grass, fully expecting Lucy to pointedly move a foot farther away, just to aggravate him. That was what women usually did. They made a point in the most obtuse way possible.

Confusingly, Lucy stayed put. "I'm sorry I tried to pummel you with baseballs. It was mean of me."

On the verge of reminding her he'd told her to do exactly that—sort of—Max hesitated. He looked at her. This time, he saw her for who she was. Lucy. And he realized how important it must be to her that he try, somehow, to get it.

A long moment swept past. Lucy remained silent.

But her silence wasn't accusatory or demanding. It was just . . . there, in the moment. Exactly like Lucy.

"I'm okay," Max heard himself say. Gruffly. He butt-scooted closer. "I forgive you."

Lucy turned her head. Her warm gaze swept over him, startling in its perceptiveness. She seemed to hesitate.

"You're really good at baseball."

Max felt humbled. Ridiculously so. He couldn't

remember ever hearing that before, not even when he'd needed it. Warmth suffused his chest.

"I mean, unusually good," she continued. "I don't know much about sports, but even I can tell that. Those were some crazy pitches I threw. You hit every one without breaking a sweat."

The warmth inside him spread.

Trying to tamp it down, he grunted. He ran his fingers through the grass. It felt dry and cool, cooler than the summertime air around them. The sensation grounded him.

She didn't know. Didn't know anything unless he told her.

"So . . ." Lucy nudged him. "How come a guy who hits like you doesn't like baseball fields?"

He should have known she'd remember that.

Max shrugged. "Unhappy memories."

She nodded. "You still came here to help me, though."

"Yeah, well . . ." He stared straight ahead, the same way Lucy did. It made talking easier. A tuft of grass came loose in his hand. He twined two blades together, examining their length with a frown. "I said I'd changed."

Companionably, Lucy plucked some grass too. She flipped over a few blades, whistled through one, then peered toward the bus stop. She seemed perfectly content to stay there, lounging against the deserted bleachers all night. She didn't ask anything from him. She didn't pester him or coax him or try out some psychobabble crap on him. She just . . . sat there with him.

Maybe that was why Max found himself talking instead.

"I must've been on dozens of fields like this one. Hundreds." He shook his head, remembering. The tang of the grass, the bite of the dirt, brought it all back. "From the time I could swing a bat, baseball was all I loved to play."

At the admission, something inside him eased. He leaned more comfortably against the bleacher post, then imitated Lucy's whistle. They both smiled.

"You must have been really good," she said.

He nodded. "Good enough for a few good games. A few championship seasons. Baseball was the only thing I did just because I loved it. Not to win. At least at first."

He felt Lucy's questioning glance.

"Playing to win was what made me stay away from baseball fields. I haven't been on one for years."

"Why?"

"Because the better and harder I played, the more I resented my parents for not coming to see me do it. At first, I thought if I won, they couldn't be 'too busy' for those Little League games." His *own* missed games—the ones he'd been supposed to attend for Ricky Ruiz—flashed through his mind. Damn it. "They always meant to come. That's what they said. But meaning to didn't mean anything to a kid looking up to a row of empty bleachers."

"I'm sure they wanted to be there," Lucy said softly.

"But they weren't. Which one matters more?"

She touched his hand. Max didn't want her sympathy.

"It's *not* the thought that counts," he said, needing to make her understand, to make her comprehend the lesson he'd had to grasp the hard way. "It's the *doing*. That's what matters in the end. That's what people remember."

"It was a long time ago."

Scowling, he looked at her. "Yeah. But *I* still remember. I remember what my family didn't do. Those baseball games weren't the first time they screwed up." *Or the first time they all but abandoned me,* he thought. He refused to admit something that candy-assed out loud. "They sure as hell weren't the last."

Lucy's clear-eyed gaze met his. "At least they *wanted* to be there. Wouldn't it have been worse if they hadn't?"

"The result would have been the same. Me. Alone. So what difference does it make?" Max shook his head. "None."

"I don't believe that." Urgently, Lucy wriggled on the grass, turning to face him with her legs crossed. She twined her fingers with his, squeezing. "It's like with Successfully Dressed. Cornelia started the shop on a whim. She never thought it through, never really *intended* to make it work. Because of that, she was doomed to fail. Don't you see?"

"Maybe she should have read her horoscope first."

Lucy's face fell. "I'm serious. Don't make fun."

How could he help it? "Then start making sense."

Huffily, Lucy released his hand. "Fine. I'm only trying to help. The whole point is, you shouldn't judge your parents for not being there for you. They obviously meant well, only you were too young to realize it."

"I was twenty-nine the last time I invited them to a franchise-opening party. They meant well that time too . . . all the way until the point when they found something more important to do. They didn't show."

It had been his last invitation. A guy didn't have to get kicked in the head too many times before he quit trying.

And just started doing.

Doing without.

"Okay. It's clear you're hurt," Lucy said, "but—"

Screw this. Max didn't know why he'd started spilling his guts in the first place. He got up, then held out his hand to help Lucy. "Come on. We've got equipment to pick up."

"But we're talking!" She swatted grass from her rear end.

"Not anymore." He should have known trying to explain himself was a waste of time. Actions spoke louder than words, anyway. To prove it, he gave her a smile. "The faster we shag those balls, the faster I can show you what *else* a blindfold is good for. Back at my place."

Lucy frowned. But a blush crept up her neck all the same.

Sensing he was making progress—and feeling inexplicably relieved about that fact—Max moved nearer. He put one hand around Lucy's waist and let the other slide toward her luscious backside, "helping" with her grass removal job. Thoughts of his past slipped away, seeming less important by the minute.

He kissed her neck, loving her softness.

"Or we can try out this cozy spot beneath the bleachers," he murmured, feeling Lucy squirm beneath his touch. Her breath came faster. So did his. "You can be the cheerleader. I'll be the quarterback."

He kissed her. His hand tangled in her hair, tipping her head back so he could better explore her mouth. Lucy arched against him, rising on tiptoes to get closer. He loved the way she responded to him. It made him feel . . . *needed*.

"Someone might see us," she whispered.

"I don't care." Max needed her too, needed . . . just *needed*. He put her palm over his hammering heart and offered a smile. "I just scored the game-winning touchdown. Help me celebrate."

"Give me an M," Lucy said, wearing a silly, sexy smile. "Give me an A. Give me an X." She swiveled her hips, making him crazy. "What does it spell?"

"*Just love me,*" he growled, then carried her down to the grass before either of them regained their senses.

14

After her baseball date with Max, Lucy knew what she had to do. She had to teach him that people really *were* good, that they *could* be counted on, that being together with everyone you loved was what really mattered. She knew it was the truth. And judging by the lost look on Max's face when he'd described being disappointed by his family, he needed to know it too.

So when Max suggested spending a little of Successfully Dressed's cash reserves to spruce up the sales floor and buy a new exterior sign to attract customers, Lucy agreed. When Max suggested more signage inside, more advertising, more determined efforts to contact the *New Times* and other local papers for media coverage, Lucy agreed. And when Max suggested hosting a runway fashion show to celebrate the shop's gala reopening, Lucy agreed to that too.

See? People—people like her—really *were* good at heart.

Not that Max didn't do his share too. He kept on volunteering, with a dogged persistence to learn and contribute that continually amazed her. He helped customers and hauled all the heavy stuff. He even endured

Franco and Nieca's continued "love-worthiness" tests, despite their increasing wackiness.

"So if Lucy told you she was crazy for a man in plaid," Franco asked skeptically, holding up a pair of baggy, garish, donated golf pants, "would you wear these?"

Max glanced to Lucy, his brow arched in question.

She shook her head, unable to hold back a grin. Grandpa pants were sexy on no man.

"Yes. Yes, I would," Max told Franco. Firmly. Then he actually grabbed the pants in question and shelled out six bucks for the privilege of taking them home in one of Successfully Dressed's new redesigned shopping bags—courtesy of her artisan pal Adam, who specialized in recyclable paper art.

"Just in case," Max explained to Lucy with a wink. "I wouldn't want to miss out on anything because I didn't have the right pants."

"How about this?" Nieca piped up sometime later. She positioned herself in a seductive pose near the ladies' sundresses, leaning sideways on the rack. "I'm a whole troupe of Playboy Bunnies, hot for your bod. Lucy is . . . Lucy." She gestured to Lucy, her eyes sparkling behind her glasses. "Ordinary, bland, *not*-stacked upstairs, Lucy. So when I invite you back to the grotto for a marathon groove session, what do you say?"

"Hmmm." Max put his hand to his chin, stroking it thoughtfully. His eyes sparkled, too, as he lingered over a sideways view of Lucy's "not-stacked-upstairs" figure. "I say, no thanks. I'm a one-woman man."

"No problem," Nieca purred, stroking her imaginary bunny tail. "We'll take you on one at a time, big boy."

She winked, then puckered up for a kiss.

But Max only laughed. "Nobody measures up to Lucy."

Even Victor got in on the act, storming into the shop with his muscles flexing beneath his custom henna mehndi body art, his bald head making him look fierce. He growled and grabbed Max by the collar, lifting him clear off his feet.

"Lay off my woman. Lucy's mine, you punk."

Several shop customers shrieked and moved a safe distance away from the fracas, but Max only met Victor's scary countenance stare for stare. Which probably wasn't easy with his feet dangling five inches from the floor. At six foot seven, Victor intimidated most and towered over nearly everyone.

"Let's take it outside," Max said, jutting his chin.

They'd made it all the way to the sidewalk, Max still dangling but seeming more than ready for the challenge, when Lucy intercepted them.

"Come on, baldie," Max said. "Let's see what you've got."

Lucy charged up to them. Looking up to see their mutually belligerent faces gave her a crick in her neck. "Victor, cut it out. Can't you see Max isn't scared of you?"

Another growl. "He ought to be scared."

"Of your breath, maybe." She waved her hand and rolled her eyes. "More Thai-style tofurkey for lunch? Whew!"

Max angled his head at her. "You *kissed* this meathead?"

Victor roared. People gathered at the fringes of the cracked sidewalk, muttering and pointing.

"Victor!" Lucy hissed. This "test" had gone too far. "You're causing a scene. Put him down right now!"

"It's all right, Lucy." Max's voice sounded strained, probably due to Victor's ironfisted grasp on his collar, but his attitude was one hundred percent willing and ready. "I'll fight for you. There's no way this assmunch is getting you back."

At that, Victor dropped him. A broad smile spread over his face, and he surveyed Lucy and Max with satisfaction.

"Awww. That's all I needed to know, pal. Good luck you two."

Victor gave Lucy a friendly good-luck pat on the shoulder that nearly toppled her over. She sighed and shook her head. "This is getting crazy."

But it wasn't, she learned, even getting close to being finished. Jade got in on the act next, proclaiming to Max—in secret—that Lucy could never "fall for a carnivore—she's hot for vegetarians only." It had taken Lucy almost a week to realize why Max had started mainlining cheeseless veggie pizza, tempeh enchiladas, and split pea soup.

"If I could only find an organic beer," he'd moaned one night at his place, surveying his sleek industrial fridge in despair, "I could almost handle my craving for T-bones."

The whole story had come tumbling out. Lucy hadn't even been able to pretend to be surprised. Her friends were nuts. Well-meaning and inventive, but nuts.

"We're telling you," they said, coming to her in groups of twos or threes to report on their latest "tests" for Max. "He is so head over heels for you, it's a wonder he hasn't been drafted into the Cirque du Soleil Men's Division!"

So, gradually, Lucy found herself weakening. She talked to Max more, skirting the issue of his baseball-loving past but covering almost everything else. Her trips through Spain. Her relationship with her family. Her plans to tie-dye her bedroom comforter and her inability to apply nail polish without looking like Bozo afterward. She confided in him about her paycheck-to-paycheck existence, her embarrassing fondness for game shows ("everyone seems so hopeful!") . . . even her dreams for her shop.

"What I really want to do is expand Successfully Dressed all across the Valley," Lucy explained earnestly, lingering in bed with Max one long Sunday morning. "Someday, that is. You know, I realized the other day that

if I can find locations near bus stops, it'll be a lot easier
for women to get to us."

Max rolled over and propped his head on his hand, listening to her describe how tough it was for unemployed
women to maintain car payments, find money for gas,
wrangle access to repairs. The whole idea of people who
couldn't just hop in their sports cars seemed alien to him.

"I'll help you," he said, his gaze solemn.

And he did. He studied bus routes and stepped up his
efforts to outfit their interview-suit customers, talking
with them at length about their needs, their issues, their
most far-fetched wishes. He coached Franco on cold-
calling for donations. He assisted Nieca with getting a
mannequin companion, Rocky, who posed in the window
demonstrating men's work wear with Suzy—sometimes
in fairly risqué tableaus that garnered *plenty* of attention.

Max even helped Lucy draw up rudimentary expansion plans, showing her how prioritizing certain aspects
of Successfully Dressed could help the shop grow into a
franchise.

"Is this what you do with your entrepreneurial projects?" Lucy asked him, impressed with his knowledge and
planning despite her own tendency toward a "winging-it"
philosophy.

"Sort of." He squeezed her hand and kissed her.
"Minus all the goo-goo eyes and the kissing and the
sneaking away to the storeroom. Hubba hubba."

Looking at his grinning, cheerful face, she could see
why Max had proved an irresistible investment opportunity to so many people over the years.

In return, Lucy did her part too. She showed Max how
to make a good sangria, how to throw a potluck fiesta,
how to relax with friends with no agenda in mind. He
seemed new at it and sort of confused by the prospect of
not having to network every minute.

"Just relax," she urged him, squeezing his hand. "These people are your friends now too."

But he'd only glanced around her cramped houseful of artists, Successfully Dressed staff, and neighbors. A longing lit his eyes . . . as did a certain amount of bafflement. "They hardly know me. I'm never in one place long enough to—"

"So? Be in the now. Go on."

Twenty minutes later, she'd spotted Max grilling chipotle veggie kebabs. Later, he'd learned how to finger paint—outside the lines. Even better, not one iota of business talk was spoken. There was still hope for him, Lucy realized, and felt far more encouraged by that fact than she should have.

At Max's place, things were different. However luxe and expensive his loft was, to her it still felt chilly. Bereft of hominess and cheerfulness and vigor. Lucy took to sneaking things in with her—a snug crocheted afghan here, a scented beeswax candle there, several knick-knacks, pillows, and two wind chimes. With enough handmade, comforting items in place, she knew she could wipe out the generic atmosphere and ultra-expensive sterility Max's decorator had instilled.

She refused to believe it really reflected *him*.

She was smuggling in a framed photo of Max and her and Franco and Nieca at Successfully Dressed, each of them wearing funny donated hats, when Max came around the corner and caught her. He shook his head.

"Aha! I *knew* it was you." He glanced at her contraband picture frame, with its embellishment of seashells and brilliant paint job. "My decorator would have a heart attack."

"It's just a photo," she protested, arranging it more artfully on one of his lacquered modern tables. Lucy stepped back, examining it. "For a guy who knows a gazillion people, you have depressingly few mementos."

"I've never wanted any," Max insisted. "Don't need any."

But the photo stayed . . . and so did everything else.

Lucy was making progress . . . and, increasingly, falling in love. There was no doubt about it. How could she not, when Max was starting to fit so perfectly into her world?

Lucy *did* want to succeed, Max realized. Despite her freaky art-school accoutrements, despite her piercings and tattoos and purple hair, and despite her outrageously unautocratic demeanor, she was ambitious.

Just like him.

It was the first *real* thing, as far as he could tell, that they had in common. Aside from a shared appreciation of whipped cream, hot sex, and snuggling. Yes, snuggling. So shoot him—maybe Lucy's whole snuggling allegation wasn't so far off the mark. Realizing that he and Lucy *were* similar, even in such a small way, made him feel almost jubilant . . . despite the knee joint he'd tweaked while showing Lucy how "bouncy" his mattress could be. His deluxe loft apartment had its advantages, damn it. If only she'd admit it.

More and more, though, Max felt comfortable in Lucy's world. It felt weirdly welcoming there. And the more time he spent with Lucy, even when they weren't naked and sweaty, the more Max wanted to be with her. All at once, he understood why everyone was so crazy about her. Lucy had a way of making a person feel good. Really, really *good*. About everything.

Max wanted more. Needed more.

Since he was . . . well, *him,* he knew he'd get it.

He didn't know how it had happened. But sometime when he hadn't been looking, his time with Lucy had expanded into something different. Something—and he

couldn't believe he was even thinking this, it was so
mushy—beyond sex. Beyond fun. Beyond everything
he'd ever known.

Not that the sex wasn't still fantastic. It was. But all of
a sudden, when he held Lucy in his arms, he wanted . . .
more. He wanted her laughter and her husky conversations
and even her far-fetched, woo-woo, let's-all-hold-hands in-
sights into the world. Being with Lucy made Max feel as
though goodness still prevailed. Even for him. Which was
nothing short of a miracle.

Of course, he had to put up with a lot of those damned
homemade knickknacks she kept sneaking into his place.
And he kept tripping over the fringe on her blankets and
pillows too. But as long as Lucy came with them . . . hell,
who was he kidding? He kind of liked them too. Even the
photo.

He caught himself gazing at it, in a completely pathetic and wussy fashion, more than once.

But the plain truth was, he'd never felt so included
before. So *needed.* Charged up by the feeling, Max re-
doubled his efforts to help Lucy with Successfully
Dressed.

Miracle of miracles, she let him.

He didn't know why she'd changed her tune about his
"interference," and he didn't care. It wasn't in his nature
to question good fortune. Over the years he had, frankly,
gotten used to enjoying his share of it. All that mattered
was that things were going his way again and Lucy was
happy.

Max's networking attempts to connect with the shop's
wealthier benefactors fell by the wayside, forgotten in his
eagerness to install the new lights, to talk with Andrea's
media contacts about Lucy's success, to see Lucy do an
impromptu happy dance over the new welcome mat he
bought for the shop.

Volunteering at Successfully Dressed, as cumbersome

as it had been at first, had turned out to be a good thing—in ways Max had never expected. He found friends. He found purpose. He found a pair of baggy plaid golf pants that were going to make a perfect gag gift for Oliver at Christmastime.

Life was good. During the days, he had laughs and plans and more work than he could handle. During the nights, he had Lucy. There was nothing else he wanted.

Well . . . except to get Oliver off his back.

"Missed another one of Ricky Ruiz's Little League games," his partner would scold during Max's infrequent visits to the office. Or "Pet boutiques, remember? How about those benefactor contacts? How's it coming?"

"Good. Fine. Great," Max would reply, then duck out again with a wink for Marlene and a wave for his friend. "Don't worry! I've got it covered."

He always meant to. And they always believed him.

Because who would have bought the idea of Max Nolan, fast-talking entrepreneur extraordinaire, actually blowing off work?

Nobody, that's who.

Max almost felt guilty about it. The feeling passed whenever Lucy smiled at him. He'd spent most of his adult life working. Working, working, working. Sarabeth had been right about that much, at least. Now, he decided, it wouldn't hurt a damned thing if he turned his attention elsewhere for a while.

Successfully Dressed, at first so dingy and decrepit, now welcomed him with open arms and a myriad of possibilities. CC Burnheart took Max under her scrawny wing, introducing him to everyone and anyone who mattered in Phoenix. He blithely used those contacts to further promote Successfully Dressed—or to obtain new donations—and didn't give a second thought to the investors he was supposed to be lining up.

There'd be time for that later.

He was still Max Nolan, able to talk anyone into anything, wasn't he? When the time came to exploit his new
contacts, he would. Until then . . .

"Come on out," he coaxed Lucy, glancing impatiently
toward his walk-in closet. "I want to see you."

"Promise you won't laugh?" Lucy called.

"Well . . ." Max hesitated, pretending to consider it.
"How funny do you look? I might be irresistibly tempted."

Lucy came around the corner. The sight of her wiped
the grin from his face. The only thing he felt irresistibly
tempted to do was hug her. Or maybe kiss her senseless.

Just because she'd tried something new. For him.

"Well?" Lucy prompted. "Pretty ridiculous, right?"

Biting her lip, she posed in the slinky dress he'd helped
her choose from Successfully Dressed's designer vintage
section—an area that, surprisingly, had burgeoned lately.

A sexy length of white fabric dropped from her shoulders in a way that promised easy removal. It nipped in
at the hip with a silver clasp. It showcased Lucy's curvy
figure, her sleek skin, her yoga-perfect posture. As
dresses went, this one was seductive, sophisticated, and
drop-dead gorgeous. It looked exactly as good on her as
Max had suspected it would.

He'd always had an eye for *stunning*.

"Okay, fine. Fine." Obviously uncomfortable with his
silence, Lucy grimaced at herself. "I tried it. I should
have known traditional wasn't exactly my thing. I'll go
change, then we'll hit that supper club you told me about.
No problem."

Forehead puckered, she headed for the closet. She
made it three steps, moving gracefully—if unsteadily—
in her silvery high-heeled sandals, before Max caught up
with her.

"There *is* a problem with that," he said.

Lucy's lips quivered. She seemed on the verge of tear-
ing up. Once again, Max realized he'd treated her like

any other woman—like any woman he'd dated who would have loved a designer dress, just because it *was* a designer dress—instead of like Lucy. Unique, incredible Lucy. But he was learning fast.

He tipped up her chin. Smiled. "You can't go change, because *I* want to be the one to take this off you."

"Hey. It's not *that* bad. It's just not me."

"Hmmm." Max pretended to ponder that. "Sexy, smooth"—he punctuated the word with a slow stroke of her hip, feeling the cool silver buckle beneath his palm— "irresistibly gorgeous. Yeah. I'd say that's you."

Lucy's smile flashed. "Irresistibly gorgeous, huh? Nice try. That's pretty suave, even for you."

"Suave? Then I'm not making myself clear." He pulled her into his arms, gazing down at her sternly. His heart felt full, filled to overflowing. It was a weird and unexpected sensation. "You take my breath away."

A pause. "Oh. Maybe you should try yoga. The Ujjayi Pranayama is very effective for improving breathing patterns."

Max loved the funny way her eyes widened when she advised him, the endearing way she nodded for emphasis, the fact that Lucy wanted to help him at all.

"You're special," he told her, still trying to explain. "With or without that dress."

"Hint taken. Be right back."

"No. I—"

But he was too late. Somehow, his Max mojo had deserted him, leaving him unable to make the simplest statement stick with its target. Lucy swerved toward his walk-in closet.

There was nothing else for it. Max stopped her, determined to make Lucy understand. Her confused gaze met his, then dipped to his hand on her arm. "What's the matter?"

"Not a damned thing. Let me show you."

Lucy needed to learn how special she was. Max could think of only one way to do that. With actions, not words.

Silently, he eased her down on his custom suede divan, then knelt between her thighs. Shucking his own suit jacket, he regarded Lucy with mingled affection and eagerness.

"We're going to be late," she said, brow furrowed again.

Max didn't care. Not when he could gently skim his hands from her sexy stilettoed feet to her knees. Not when he could slowly raise her dress, firmly part her thighs, and lower himself between them. He brought his mouth to the tantalizing warmth he found there, helpless to prevent a moan. She felt so good.

Lucy gasped. She stiffened against the divan. "Max . . ."

"You won't need these."

He tugged. Her panties eased downward, white and skimpy and completely impractical. Just like her. Smiling, Max tightened his grasp on her thighs. Postponing his enjoyment, he took a moment to look at her. She looked so good.

"Our reservation," she began breathlessly. "We really don't have time . . ."

Her words ended on a hoarse sigh. Max had always felt it was rude to interrupt a man while he was intent on giving the most pleasure possible. He explained that philosophy to Lucy in vivid detail, changing positions now and then to keep things interesting. She tasted so good.

"Mmmm." He paused, adding a swirling lick he couldn't resist, then glanced up at her. "Are you sure you're getting all this? Is everything clear?"

Lucy's eyes fluttered open. "Yes. No. Don't stop."

"I love a woman who knows what she wants."

In fact, it occurred to him then, he loved Lucy.

"Good," she moaned. "Then . . . just . . . keep . . . ahhh."

"My pleasure," Max rumbled, and for a long time afterward—time he couldn't begin to keep track of—it was his pleasure. He savored Lucy's openness, her trembling, her panting breaths. He savored *her,* as genuinely as he could, and knew that if his feelings about her didn't make themselves known to her this way—this *closely*— one or both of them was doing things wrong.

Lucy's cries reached a crescendo, her thighs quaking near his ears. Max held her more tightly. He needed . . . needed *this,* as she trembled with pleasure beneath him. Blunt satisfaction burst through him, startling him. He didn't care about himself. Only Lucy. Lucy, Lucy. Her fulfillment was all that mattered.

When she sagged against the divan moments later, regarding him through languid eyes, he could not have asked for more. A smile enlivened her features, beautiful and bright.

"Wow." As though she'd guessed all the intimate, tumultuous emotions he'd been trying to express, Lucy held him to her. She sighed. "You don't say much . . . but you sure do know how to communicate."

Her smile felt like a good-luck charm. Max's heart expanded a fraction more, threatening to overwhelm him. He thought he might laugh, bawl, pound his chest. Something. He wasn't himself anymore. If this didn't work out between them, he realized abruptly, he'd be a wuss for life.

That's how much Lucy was getting to him.

"For you, I'd talk all night," he said. "I promise."

He'd never made promises before, either, it occurred to him. Unless offering good times and mutual fun counted . . . and for the first time, Max realized, they didn't. Not for him. Or for Lucy.

Those things weren't nearly enough anymore.

"In that case," Lucy said, fanning herself elaborately as she grinned wider, "I promise to listen. Very carefully."

What if those things were all he had to give?

"Hey, why the long face?" Lucy peered at him, rising partway from the divan. Her new position put her in fuller view of him. Her gaze dipped, then her eyes widened. "Ahhh. I see what the problem is."

Max hoped like hell she didn't. He froze.

"C'mere," she coaxed, crooking her finger in his belt. She tugged. "I'm not finished with you yet. I feel a 'conversation' coming on."

Her vixenish expression left little doubt what she meant. And while a part of Max reacted with predictable enthusiasm at that realization, the rest of him worried.

What if Lucy needed more? More than him?

She managed his belt buckle with finesse, then spread open his fly. His whole body throbbed in reaction.

For the rest of the night, he didn't think about a thing.

15

Nieca shut the office door behind her, her hand on the envelope she'd stuffed in her shorts pocket. She pulled the chain on Lucy's desk lamp, then squinted through the one-way mirror to make sure the dim, after-hours sales floor of Successfully Dressed was empty. It was.

Carefully, she pulled out the letter. She'd recognized the New York return address immediately. All day, Nieca had been dying to read it . . . but with the shop undergoing a general sprucing up and the employees and volunteers working overtime to implement Max's renovation plans, there hadn't been time. Especially with their former interview-suit buyer, Tracee, stopping in for a preclosing shopping spree to celebrate her new job at the insurance company around the corner.

Nieca drew in a deep breath and unfolded the letter. A few quick glances . . . *thank you for your inquiry* . . . blah, blah . . . *at this time, unfortunately* . . . She stopped, dumbfounded.

They'd turned her down.

She couldn't believe it. She'd been so sure that *Vogue*, of all publications, would see the value of what Successfully Dressed did and give them the publicity they needed. The publicity that would keep the shop open, wherever the DL's "business" vagaries happened to take her. The publicity that Lucy, for all her talk, had been too distracted to garner.

Damn it. Disappointed but not nearly down for the count, Nieca stared across the office. Okay. There was still a chance one of the other magazines she'd tried would come through for them. *Elle, Marie Claire,* even *Lucky.* Exposure in any one of them would mean everything to the shop.

To Nieca, sure. But also to Lucy.

She wanted so much to succeed—they all knew that. And they all—Nieca, Franco, and Penny included—were grateful to her for taking on the job of managing the shop. But ever since she'd done so, Lucy had been in so far over her head, she should have been blowing bubbles. Despite her good intentions, Lucy needed more than enthusiasm and a few tarot card readers to serve as "special attractions."

She needed help. They all did.

More determined than ever to get it, Nieca searched through Lucy's top desk drawer. She needed a few more sheets of Successfully Dressed stationery to use for additional letters. This time, she'd target smaller, regional magazines—publications that might be more open to featuring a vintage shop like theirs.

No dice. There wasn't a scrap of paper to be found, probably due to Lucy's latest visit to her feng shui hairstylist. She always came back from those appointments with new ideas about rearranging. Expanding on the usual places, Nieca tried the other desk drawers. Then the side cabinet.

A crumpled caftan tumbled out, practically in her lap.

Frowning, Nieca picked it up. This didn't belong in the office. All the donated clothes went to the storeroom first. Then they were cleaned, ironed, and sent to the sales floor.

A flash of white caught her eye. Then a distinctive print.

Pucci.

A quick check told her it was authentic. And it didn't require a last-year textiles student to recognize the vintage Courrèges jacket right beside it, tucked into the folds of the ordinary polyester caftan. Nieca stared in disbelief.

These things were worth a fortune.

Lucy had been holding out on her!

No wonder Franco had been jabbering on last week about "missing donations" from an elderly lady. He must have meant these items. Probably he'd taken them in and written a receipt . . . and Lucy had stashed them here, in her office.

Because she didn't want to sell designer items.

She wanted to cater to one kind of customer only.

She didn't care about Nieca's vision of the place at all.

Or, frankly, about Nieca's impending rent payments—which usually required advances on her salary, something she didn't want to accept anymore. As generous as those advances were, they definitely put a crimp in her self-sufficiency.

A sense of betrayal stabbed at Nieca, as uncomfortable as her cute but toe-crunching ballerina flats. She'd always believed she could win Lucy over to the wisdom of offering both designer vintage *and* interview suits. But now . . .

Now she knew better.

Staring at the stuff arrayed before her, Nieca knew there was only one thing to do. And she had to do it immediately.

At the sound of a knock on his front door, Oliver started. So did Spike. He gave his puppy a reassuring murmur and a pat, then picked him up and carried him to the foyer. Spike seemed nervous if left alone for too long. Oliver couldn't stand those plaintive puppy-dog looks.

Leaving behind the newspaper he'd been reading, he crossed his living room in slippered feet. He secretly hated uncomfortable dress shoes, but they were necessary for keeping up business appearances. God knew, his damned partner wasn't doing anything toward that goal these days. Max had stayed away from the office lately, probably brooding over the fact that Nieca preferred Oliver to him.

Oliver still couldn't believe it. Stealing the spotlight from Max was unprecedented. The odds had to be at least fifty to one against, maybe more. Not that he was complaining. Ever since Nieca had given him Spike, they'd had opportunities to spend more and more time together.

Oliver had, to put it bluntly, loved it.

He opened the door, admitting a burst of hot evening air and the scent of just-watered landscaping plants.

"I need advice," Nieca told him from his threshold. "And you're the smartest person I know to get it from."

As though he'd conjured her with his thoughts, she edged past him in a bundle of sweet-smelling energy, leaving him to close the door. Her legs looked lithe and limber beneath a pair of shorts. Her tank top slipped from one shoulder, baring her smooth skin. Her braids whooshed over that skin, drawing his attention to her face.

She waited expectantly, lips pursed.

For a moment, all Oliver could do was stare in wonderment. What was a woman as remarkable as Nieca doing here? With him?

Any minute now, she'd tell him to snap out of it. She'd probably snap her fingers at him too. For effect. But Oliver didn't care. She was here, and that was all that mattered.

"Look, Spike." He pointed the puppy toward Nieca. "It's your favorite person in the whole wide world."

She sighed, then flopped on his sofa. Her lips trembled. "I'm not *anybody's* favorite person. Not tonight."

"You're my favorite person," Oliver said. "All the time."

Her skeptical gaze met his. For a moment, Nieca seemed to waver. To contemplate . . . something. But then she rolled her eyes with all her usual sarcasm seemingly intact.

"That's sweet, Oliver. But I have real troubles."

To his horror, she burst into tears.

She seemed as surprised by her outburst as he was. She fluttered her hands and swabbed at her eyes, making her glasses crooked. Then she gave up and hunched over to hide the whole spectacle from him, still blubbering.

Oliver stood immobile, completely out of his depth. Seeing Nieca that way, so vulnerable and so unexpectedly open, affected him in ways he'd never experienced. All at once, she didn't seem like a goddess anymore. She seemed like a woman. A woman he wanted to care for.

Except he didn't have the vaguest idea how.

"Wait! Stop!" he cried, rushing toward her. "I'll—"

You'll what, Einstein? he thought suddenly. *Solve everything?* For the first time in his life, Oliver really didn't have a clue. He couldn't believe his brainpower had deserted him just when he needed it most.

He paced, listening to Nieca's heartrending sniffles.

"I'm sorry." She waved her arm, making him dizzy. "I never cry, I swear. I don't even know why I came *here,* of all places. It's just that, somehow, I could only think of you."

Her words dissolved into more bawling.

Oliver didn't consider himself a typical man. He didn't fear intimacy or commitment or conversation. He didn't freak out over ordinary things like calling when he was

going to be late for a date—he *had* had a few—or opening a door for a woman. He didn't break into a cold sweat
at the thought of being "tied down" or of having children
someday. So he was doubly surprised to find himself
panicking over Nieca's tears.

He paced back and forth, casting her anxious looks.
Every time a strategy occurred to him, it seemed more
idiotic than the one that had preceded it. Why wasn't
Max here? Max always, *always* knew what to say and
what to do, damn him.

The thought galvanized Oliver.

Screw Max. He, Oliver, would come to Nieca's rescue.

He flew to the kitchen. Nieca's snuffly explanations
followed him all the way there, something about Lucy
and Successfully Dressed and *Vogue*. Something about
Courrèges, whoever the hell that putz was. Oliver felt,
just then, that he could probably take him, especially if
he had hurt Nieca.

He returned bearing a filled glass in his free hand and
a box of tissues tucked beneath his chin—all he could
manage while holding Spike. He sat beside Nieca and
dropped the tissue box between them, intently trying to
understand her problem.

She kept on talking, swabbing occasionally at her eyes.
She accepted a tissue, honking unconcernedly into it. She
took the glass from him, then drained it in one swallow.

Nieca sputtered. "What *is* that?"

"Milk." Oliver blinked. "It'll calm you down. Unless
you have dairy allergies, which approximately thirty-
three percent of people do, according to the latest
studies. On the other hand, for all its faults, milk does has
valuable calcium to offer. About forty-five percent of the
RDA in a cup that size. Would you like some more?"

"No! I don't want—" Nieca broke off, looking on the
verge of demanding a Jack Daniels straight up, or

something equally hair curling. She softened, inexplicably. "Anything."

"So." Oliver studied her, resolved to get to the bottom of things. "Tell me more. Lucy hid those vintage pieces, and now you think she doesn't trust you or your judgment. Right?"

Nieca only gawked, her grasp slack on her empty glass.

Hell. He'd gotten it wrong. Oliver regrouped. "You wanted to surprise Lucy with a whole new vision of Successfully Dressed, to garner national media exposure so she'd feel like a success, and all your paychecks would be assured." He bit his lip, remembering more. "But now that you've found those hidden designer clothes, you wonder why you bothered. Am I close?"

She angled her head, looking at him the way kids in gym class used to whenever he'd attempted to climb that damn rope. He wasn't a freaking Marine, and he hadn't been one at fourteen either. He tried again, resolutely.

"Also, with your rent coming due again, you're worried about your finances, hence your interest in making sure the shop does well. If 'the DL' decides to close the place, you'll be out on the street." He paused, decided not to pursue the subject of who the "DL" was, then immodestly added, "That one I can *definitely* help you with. I'm kind of a budgeting savant."

Nieca opened her mouth. Closed it again. She put down her glass on the side table, then did a double take at the plastic party glass already sitting there. It was the one she'd filled, licked, and given him on the night he'd met her. The one Oliver had been unable to throw away, despite the overall sappiness and probable unsanitariness of keeping it. He'd never intended for her to see it. But although she moved on quickly, she didn't speak or seem particularly reassured.

Despair swamped him. He wanted so much to help

her, but he was blowing it. Filled with desperate urgency, Oliver looked down at Spike. The puppy wagged his tail. Inspiration struck.

Carefully, he lay the puppy on Nieca's lap. He closed her arms around Spike to keep him secure. "There. Look at Spike," he commanded. "Nobody can feel bad while holding a puppy."

Nieca glanced down. Peacefulness suffused her face.

"I wish we could share him," she blurted.

Oliver wanted nothing more. Well, almost.

"Hold still," he told her, gathering his courage for his final move. "Because I have only one strategy left, and if it doesn't work, I'm sunk."

Curiously, she turned her face to his.

"Predictably, you didn't follow directions."

She rolled her eyes again, oblivious to his distress. But she'd quit crying. That was progress, so Oliver felt heartened.

He scooted closer on the sofa, then bravely took her in his arms. At first, Nieca felt rigid against him, poised to safeguard Spike on her lap—or to keep Oliver at a distance.

He wondered if he'd overstepped his boundaries. He wasn't a man who ignored boundaries. Ever. His own, or anyone else's. He was respectful that way. But surely Nieca knew she could protest. Didn't she? Maybe he should make that clear.

Although this *was* his last-ditch effort. He felt loathe to bring on its untimely demise. Also, Nieca felt incredible . . . if a little too ironing-board rigid.

Magically, by degrees, Nieca softened. She breathed out. For a long time, they sat that way, just hugging. Oliver had never experienced anything more moving.

"Thank you," she murmured against his shoulder.

"I didn't do anything." Jubilation shot through Oliver, lending him enough bravado to stroke her hair. Her braids crinkled beneath his fingertips, feeling wonderful. "I wish I could have done something more, made a plan.

Maybe if you start over from the beginning? I'm usually very adept at—"

"You did *everything*," Nieca disagreed. She separated from him just enough to raise her face to his. Behind her fogged-up glasses, her eyes gleamed richly. "You listened. You really, *really* listened to me. That helps a lot. It's so . . . wow."

He didn't comprehend how listening to her problems was better than solving them. That was crazy. Crazier than cavalierly ignoring a body's need for milk. But he nodded all the same. Oliver wasn't a ladies' man, but he knew when to go with the flow.

Nieca tilted her head sideways, studying him. She grinned. "That milk routine needs work, though, Casanova. Seriously."

He grinned back. "Casanova" beat the crap out of "Geeky." He was so glad Nieca had quit calling him nerdy names. That, combined with the fact that she'd given him Spike *and* had visited several times to help with the puppy *and* had signed her note to him "Love, Nieca," had made Oliver's confidence soar.

"That's only the L-tryptophan talking," he explained. "With the help of a few enzymes, it's converted into serotonin in your body, which makes you feel calmer. Calm enough, even," he joked, "to browbeat me over it."

Nieca sobered. Her gaze roved over his face, then inexplicably lingered on his wild, curly hair. She shook her head. "I'm sorry to dump all this on you. I'll leave."

"No!"

She stopped in the midst of disengaging herself. Oliver knew he had only one chance at this. He had to make it good.

"I mean . . . stay awhile." He lowered his gaze to her lips. Although they were no longer pursed—to hold in sobs, he realized with a belated stab of regret at his own ignorance—they still looked luscious. Lovely. Perfect. "Stay with me."

Her brow lifted.

"And Spike," he added hastily, pointing to the dog. He lowered his voice in what he hoped was a macho way. "Stay. Really. We need you."

Nieca still seemed puzzled. "What for?"

"For this," Oliver told her.

Then he lowered his mouth to hers.

He half-expected her to shriek, to slap him, to burst out laughing the way Allison McCaffery had in ninth grade when he'd kissed her in the Taco Bell parking lot. His and Allison's days of post–Math Club "hanging out" had ended that afternoon. But all Nieca did was turn suddenly still . . . and then kiss him back.

It was a tentative gesture, a mere brushing of their lips together. But it was all the encouragement Oliver needed. He lifted his gaze to hers, blinked at the enormity of the emotions pinwheeling through him, then kissed her again. This time when their mouths met, he knew he would never get enough. Kissing Nieca felt like heaven wrapped up in cashmere—the fabric he'd taken to wearing ninety-eight percent of the time—like probability melded with certainty. He needed and wanted, and for once in his life, Oliver *got*.

Almost, very nearly, Oliver *took*.

"Wow." Nieca admired him through new eyes. "That was—"

"Not nearly enough."

He kissed her again, this time leaning them both back against the sofa. Its downy cushions embraced them. Oliver felt his heart pounding, his mind whirling, but for the first time in his life, all he could think about was his body and what it was feeling. *Wowee* was the extent of his intelligible thought, and he didn't mind a bit. Nieca arched against him, burying her fingers in his hair, and he didn't mind that either. He wanted her to touch him more and more and more.

"It feels better than it looks," she murmured puzzlingly, sounding surprised. "Soft and curly and . . . what do you know? Hmmm. I think I'm a convert."

"A convert to what?" Her lips were delicious.

"You." A smile crossed her face. "Kiss me again, Oliver."

Before he could, a tiny rumble interrupted them.

They glanced down. Spike mewled again, plainly disgruntled at being ignored. The puppy squirmed in Nieca's lap, then clumsily climbed her chest to nuzzle her neck.

Oliver wanted to travel the same path. Soon.

Nieca clasped Spike's chubby, furry body, her smile broadening. She sighed. "This must be what it's like to be parents. Always interrupted in mid-kiss."

"It's not so bad," Oliver observed, although he was dying to march the puppy to its bed and continue what he'd started. There'd be time for that later, he suddenly felt sure. "It's nice to be needed."

Matter-of-factly, Nieca nodded. "Nice to be loved."

They stared at each other, burgeoning possibilities seeming to stretch between them. Oliver pictured long dog walks; shared training sessions; a beefy, candlelit "first doggie birthday" cake from one of his and Max's pet boutiques.

If he and Nieca played their cards right, those things could be theirs . . . and more.

"Are you thinking what I'm thinking?" he asked.

Her eyes gleamed behind her smart-girl glasses. "Yes. Double veggie burger with onion rings. And a Cherry Coke."

"Huh?"

She gave him a tender look. "After a crisis, I always get hungry. Ask anybody. You want to go get something to eat?"

"But . . ." Oliver gestured feebly to the sofa. His visions of Nieca and him testing out the cushions' vaunted multispring resiliency vanished like so many miscalculated odds.

Nieca saw his undoubtedly crestfallen expression. "Come closer. You're not understanding me."

Obligingly, he did. Her gaze roved over his face, his shoulders . . . his arms, with their threefold increase in strength due to his stepped-up gym workouts. Oliver had hoped Nieca would appreciate his new musculature—but not as an instrument of potential burger-with-the-works conveyance.

"You'll need a veggie burger too," she said. "Maybe a triple decker. To keep your strength up. For later."

He hardly dared to hope. "For . . . later?"

Nieca's smile made him tingle all over. It held eighty-two percent more sexiness than ever before, all aimed at him.

"I'm seducing you, Oliver. Try to keep up."

"Keep . . . up?" His breath whooshed out of him.

"Yeah. It's what boyfriends do."

Oliver cleared his throat, trying to tamp down the eagerness inside him. Currently, it was busy encouraging him to leap on Nieca, kiss her all over, and possibly wag his tail.

"Four out of five adult males don't use the term *boyfriend* until after the fourteenth date," he said.

She rose her brow. "And the fifth?"

"He holds out until the honeymoon, at which point the redundancy involved makes it not count. Technically."

"And you?" Nieca regarded him through hopeful eyes.

"Me? I'm dying for a triple burger with lettuce and extra ketchup—it's got powerful antioxidants, you know." Oliver rose and held out his hand to help her up, mindful of their puppy and unable to prevent an ear-to-ear grin. "Let's go. You don't want to keep your new boyfriend waiting."

16

At their final practice before the impending charity baseball game, Lucy stood with her mitt in hand, sugar-buzzing on a wad of Dubble Bubble and surrounded by her teammates. Pumped by their filled pledge sheets and by their long-standing rivalry with the Salvation Army, everyone was ready to go. Lucy was not. She peered out past the blob of brightness created by the field lights. Max had promised to meet her here, but there was no sign of him yet.

"Hmmm." Resigned to starting without him, she took her place. It wasn't like Max to be late, although he had promised her a surprise tonight. Maybe it was taking extra time.

She gripped her ball and wound up. Thanks to her practice session with Max, she'd uncovered her singular baseball talent.

Pitching like a banshee.

"Awww, Lucy! Lighten up!" her third hitter called, dispiritedly lowering his bat to home plate. "We're supposed to be practicing hitting, not striking out."

"Yeah! Save it for those scumbag losers we'll be playing!" Penny yelled, waving her fist. Her silvery pixie-cut hair gleamed in the brilliant lighting, as did her *killer*

Chihuahuas T-shirt. "Grind 'em into the dirt! Losers! Wahoo!"

"Hey." Franco tuned in, pausing in the midst of artfully arranging his special lucky batting socks around his ankles. He'd gotten inspiration for them from Max. He finger-combed his faux-hawk, looking thoughtful. "Was that a ball or a strike? I still can't tell the difference."

One of his bandmates leaned nearer. "Dude, it's only a strike if the umpire goes *huuuuggghh*." The guttural sound ended in a chortle. He shrugged. "Without that old guy going *huuuugggghh* and waving his arms, you can't tell."

Knowledgably, they both nodded.

The theory sounded reasonable to Lucy. Her dad definitely got worked up when the umpire went *huuuugggghh* during televised games. Or when her mom dusted the set when the bases were loaded.

She regarded the hitter. "I'm sorry, Charlie. I got kind of carried away. We'll have a do-over, okay?"

Everyone nodded. Even Penny. Do-overs were necessary.

From the corner of her eye, Lucy spotted someone climbing up the bleachers. Not Max, as she'd hoped, but Andrea Cho, the PR expert with the designer accessories. With her was a petite redhead carrying a notebook and a tote bag. Lucy waved.

Maybe spectators would rev up everyone's enthusiasm.

Except Penny's, of course. If she got any more revved, she'd have to sign up for the WWE senior division.

Three batters later, it was time to switch pitchers. Lucy relinquished her mitt and headed for the dugout, her arms and shoulders aching from the unusual exertion. She could hold a downward-facing dog yoga posture for eons, but hurling a baseball challenged her. Still, she felt optimistic. Their team was really coming together, their new expertise due—in no small part, she reasoned—to the sage-smudging ceremony her friend Amber had practiced last week.

"Okay, come on everybody!" Lucy shouted, cupping her hands over her mouth. Then she clapped enthusiastically. "You can do it!"

"Hey, Lucy."

Max. At the sound of his voice, she whirled around. She smiled when she saw him, feeling a familiar flutter as he leaned nearer to kiss her hello.

"I hope there's still room for another player."

"Another player? Is that your surprise?" she asked. "Sure. There's always room for one more per—"

Lucy stuttered to a stop, gawking. A man as tall as Max, clad in a recognizable purple and turquoise uniform, stepped to the forefront. Genteelly, he offered a handshake.

"I hope pros aren't excluded, ma'am."

"I . . . you're . . ." She closed her mouth. Opened it again. Blinked. "You're a Diamondbacks player." Everyone in town recognized those uniforms, those caps, that logo. Heck, since the D-Backs had won the World Series a few years ago, everyone in the U.S. probably recognized their members. "You're—"

"Yes, ma'am." Stopping her before she could blurt out his name, he lifted his cap and grinned his famous smile. "Max, here, says ya'll could use a hand."

Lucy goggled. "Yes, we . . . ahhh. Uh-huh." She nodded.

It wasn't that she was a huge baseball fan. Although she did admire athleticism, the same way she did other personally impossible feats—like balancing a checkbook or cooking paella.

On any given game day, she could more likely be found combing the farmer's market with Jade, recuperating from one of Franco's gigs, or checking out DVD rentals for obscure foreign films with Nieca. But seeing this player in the flesh was like coming face to face with a celebrity. Lucy was no more immune to that than any other girl.

Her dad would go *crazy* when she told him.

Max grinned. "With the game coming up soon, I figured the team could use a ringer." Looking pleased, he gestured to the superstar Diamondbacks player. "So I pulled a few strings and called in a few favors."

A ringer? Strings? Favors?

Just like that, everything changed. Lucy felt her smile dim. Trying to hide it, she squeezed the player's impressive biceps. "Thanks *so* much for coming. It's really nice of you. If you want, maybe you can warm up now, then sign a few autographs after the practice?"

"Sure thing, ma'am. Thanks kindly." He tipped his baseball cap, then strode away to introduce himself to the meager batting lineup.

As their new star player traversed the field, his athletic build loomed starkly at odds with those of the team's largely lumpy, out of shape, sunlight-starved members. The field lights gleamed off his official cap, further setting him apart.

"I'm sure he'll be willing to wear one of your team uniforms for the actual game," Max observed, arms crossed over his chest. "As long as you can find one big enough."

Lucy regarded him. Max seemed tickled pink, bouncing on his heels while he waited for her reaction.

"You're kidding me, right?" she asked.

"About the uniform? No, I—"

"Max, I can't believe you did this. It's outrageous, even for you."

His smile wavered. "Outrageous in a good way, right?"

"I can't let a famous Diamondbacks player be on our team, especially under these circumstances!" Lucy crossed her arms to match his pose. "Do you want to tell him, or should I do it?"

"What do you mean? I thought you'd be thrilled." Max gestured to the batter's box. "With a power hitter like him on your team, you'll win for sure."

She couldn't believe Max still thought winning was most important to her. "It doesn't matter if we win. We'll earn our sponsors' pledges whether we win or not."

He seemed confused. "Then why practice?"

"Well, because it's fun, I guess. And because we don't want to *completely* embarrass ourselves," she admitted. "Plus, we've kind of had a rivalry going with some of the other charities, thanks to Franco's trash talking."

Max raised his eyebrows.

Lucy shrugged. "He's mouthy but lovable."

"And you're stubborn but lovable." Trying out a smile in an obvious—and engaging—bid to change her mind, Max moved closer. "Come on. Let him play. Won't it be nice to win for a change?"

For a change? "With a ringer? No, it won't."

"Lucy—"

"You still don't get it." She shook her head. "I don't want you to pull strings for me. I don't need you to. How can you spend all this time with me and not understand what I'm about? I don't want to win unfairly."

His mouth hardened. "You don't know what the other team will have up its sleeve."

"Sure I do." Seeing the lineup shorten, she grabbed a bat and stretched with it held over her head. "One tattoo artist, two ASU students, a potbellied pig, and a bunch of volunteers."

Max seemed to debate asking her about the pig. He shook his head. "Why not have an advantage?"

"Because it's not fair. I don't want to crush the other team, I just want to play them." Deliberately, she softened her voice. She didn't want to argue. "Look, it's almost my turn to bat. I have to practice my visualizations first or I'll duck again." She closed her eyes, getting ready.

"Lucy." He caught her arm. Tugged her nearer. Pressed a kiss to her upturned mouth, which she *definitely* hadn't visualized happening. "I'm helping you. Please, for once in your life, just let me."

"I *have* been letting you help me! What do you think all the changes at Successfully Dressed are about?"

"Succeeding at business." As though it were obvious.

"They're about taking your advice," she disagreed. "Making you see that—" *That people can be counted on to be good and generous.* No, she didn't want to spill that much. Lucy shook her head. "It doesn't matter. The point is, this is going too far." She waved her hand toward the Diamondbacks player. "I can't do it. Not if it means abandoning all my principles and—"

"Oh, for Christ's sake!" Max interrupted. "Don't get all high and mighty on me. It's not always about you." Impatiently, he turned her to face the rest of the team assembled along the chain-link fence, in the field, and near the dugout. "Don't you think *they* deserve a say in who plays with them? Don't you think *they* might like to win? Most people do, you know."

Lucy scanned all those familiar faces. Crewcut Charlie, with his lumbar belt on. Franco, with his lucky socks. Penny, with her homemade DON'T MESS WITH SUCCESSFULLY DRESSED banner strung along the fence. Her friends *did* get kind of down every year when they (inevitably) lost. Maybe she owed it to them to try another approach.

Nieca batted, then trotted in the wrong direction to third base. She stomped the bag, cheering. "Woo-hoo! A shortcut!"

"Good going, Nieca!" Franco's bandmates shouted.

"Keep it up!" Penny yelled. "They'll never see it coming!"

"Steal home!" Franco added, gesturing wildly.

Nieca did, nearly colliding with the next batter. Everyone whooped and hollered, patting her on the back.

No, Lucy decided. For everyone's sake, she had to take charge. She owed them her best efforts.

Soberly, she turned to Max. She took his hand in hers.

"I know your heart's in the right place, and I do appreciate that," she told him. "But this just won't work."

"Hey, Lucy!" her friend Adam called. "You're up."

Casting Max a regretful look, she hefted her bat. "Gotta go. It's nothing personal, okay?"

"Nothing personal," he repeated tightly. "Right."

For a moment, Max's pensive look made her hesitate. Then he smiled and waved her off to the batter's box. "Hey, I should have known better," he said. "Go on. Have fun."

Max watched the practice, feeling weirdly discouraged. Although everyone on the team had welcomed his ringer with broad grins and open arms, Lucy remained aggravatingly immune to his star power. She was friendly, sure. She was always friendly. But she seemed staunch in her unwillingness to accept any "unfair" advantage in the upcoming game.

He'd only been trying to help her. He'd thought bringing on a D-Backs player was brilliant. What the hell was wrong with Lucy that she couldn't see that?

He'd only wanted to give her more—more than just himself.

"Nice work." Andrea Cho stood at the fence beside him, her sleek publicist's aura as polished as ever, despite their sporty surroundings. "I can get a lot of mileage out of him."

She nodded to the Diamondbacks player.

Max felt vindicated. At least somebody still recognized his contributions. "He's willing to do interviews. I already briefed him."

Andrea gave him an admiring gaze. "You haven't lost your touch, I see. You've had me worried lately." She held out her hand to the redheaded woman beside her, who stepped forward. "I want you to meet Beryl Naughton. Beryl's with the *Arizona Daily* newspaper. I've been telling her about your new altruistic ventures with local charities."

Introductions were made all around.

"It's really not about me," Max said a little later, partway into their exchange. Just as he'd expected, Andrea *had* been busy spinning his volunteering into positive press coverage. "Lucy Logan is the one who's spearheaded efforts at Successfully Dressed."

"That's Max," Andrea interrupted with a tight, ultra-whitened smile. "Always modest to a fault." She chuckled. "Go on, Max. Don't be shy. Tell Beryl about how you've been volunteering to help out-of-work single mothers."

"Again, that's all Lucy's doing." Max gave the journalist a slightly less Day-Glo smile, warming up to their chitchat. Just beyond them, the baseball practice continued. "She stepped up when other people would have turned a blind eye to the issues of women returning to the work force, struggling to find transportation, training, and opportunities."

Andrea elbow-jabbed him. "But *you're* the one who's planned the grand reopening of the shop, who's reinvigorated a foundering charity, who's made connections with important people like Cornelia Burnheart—connections that keep Successfully Dressed thriving. You're the one who, although new to Phoenix, is rapidly becoming an asset to the community."

Beryl looked impressed. "You've really dug into the

Valley's charity scene," she said. "That's a unique spin on successful entrepreneurship. I'm sure our readers will be interested to know more, especially since the same man who plans to reshape pet boutique franchising also seems to have the community's best interests at heart." She scribbled in her notebook. "Cornelia Burnheart, you say?"

With a glance at his publicist's taut smile, Max relented. He could work Lucy and her staff into this interview—and give them all the proper credit—but he was clearly going to have to include himself. Otherwise, there'd be no coverage at all.

"That's right. CC has become a good friend of mine. She's the start-up woman behind Successfully Dressed." He steered himself and the two women toward the bleachers where they'd be more comfortable. He cast a backward glance toward the practice, where Lucy struggled to bat, then kept going. "As a matter of fact, several of CC's friends are major benefactors. Let me tell you about it. . . ."

The rest of the week was a blur to Lucy, jam-packed with preparations for the upcoming gala reopening of Successfully Dressed. Along with Franco, Nieca, Penny, and Max, she worked to clean, refurbish, and rearrange the shop. Everything had to be perfect.

"Hmmm." Lucy gazed at the corner where the designer vintage was kept, taking in the spotlit and attractively displayed garments. Usually, she gave Nieca free rein with this area, because of her interest in collectible couture. "I could *swear* we've gotten in a bunch more designer stuff."

Beside her, Nieca shrugged. "We can't help what people decide to donate. Maybe a bunch of those society types have been cleaning their closets . . . totally, uh, spontaneously."

Franco agreed. "It's probably a bitch to have a garage sale at a mansion. All those people driving their Bentleys on the grass, parking in the solid gold fountains, haggling over the prices of the couture."

"Yeah." Pondering it, Lucy distractedly touched the nearest item, a brocade de la Renta gown. "Still . . ."

"You know, if we put up a partition right here"—Nieca stepped sideways, pointing to a demarcation in the floor—"we could make two separate shopping areas with individual entrances. So *everyone* feels comfortable shopping here." She gave Lucy a meaningful, hopeful look. "All we'd have to do is unblock that door and hang another sign."

They all contemplated the unused door, which had painted-over glass in the same distinctive, colorful pattern as their collection bins. It was usually kept locked, with a PLEASE USE OTHER DOOR sign on the sidewalk side.

"The original owners expanded the Laundromat into the space next door so they could put in oversize washers," Nieca said. "That's why we have two entrances. I looked it up."

"*You* looked it up?" Franco gawked at her. "Since when do you read? Anything except *Vogue,* I mean."

"Har, har. Let's just say I was inspired. I'm into bookish things lately." Nieca studied Lucy expectantly. "Well? What do you say?"

"I say we should make a go of this place first," Lucy demurred. "Then we can think about expanding."

"But designer stuff is what brings in the money!" Nieca protested, giving an impatient gesture. "Without the income we get from it, who knows how long we'll survive."

"We're doing fine," Lucy insisted. "If you need another advance on your paycheck—"

"No, thanks." With dignity, Nieca raised her chin, making her dangling earrings catch the light. "It just so happens I've got a slammin' budget going on. I don't need an advance."

Lucy blinked. Franco gaped. "Are you sure? Even counting those vintage sunglasses you bid on on eBay?"

Nieca gave him a *shut up* look. They all knew she had a weakness for retro eyewear. "I'm having them refitted with prescription lenses. That means they fall into the necessities category. Also, I can tax-deduct them as medical supplies."

This was getting bizarre. None of them had explored the tax system beyond the EZ forms available in large, non-intimidating type. With their paychecks, who itemized?

"Okay." Lucy put her hands on her hips, regrouping. There was no point grilling Nieca when she was in this mood. "Let's get started on clearing space for the runway. That grand opening isn't going to happen all by itself."

Glumly, Nieca and Franco stared at her, not moving. Franco leaned on his broom, his skinny body even more hunched than usual.

"What's wrong with you two?" Lucy asked, puzzled.

"I don't know what's wrong with Ms. Budgeting Genius over there," Franco said, hooking his thumb at Nieca, "but *I* want to be in the fashion show."

"In the fashion show?" Lucy repeated, wrinkling her brow.

He nodded. "You know. The one Max set up for the grand opening, with the Dragon Lady and her friends modeling their donatable outfits. I want to do it too. You need someone for menswear, after all."

Lucy examined him. Franco straightened his faux-hawk, then peered at his black-painted fingernails with apparent unconcern.

"There's more to it than that, isn't there?"

"Well . . ." Franco hesitated. A goofy, self-conscious look sprawled over his features. "I *may* have bragged to one of my *many* recent dates that I was going to model."

"Seriously?" Nieca guffawed. "And they believed you? Are you dating Mr. Magoo?"

"Thank you, Captain Sarcasm." Looking wounded, Franco stiffened his spine. His studded belt weighed down his angular torso, preventing the motion from becoming habitual. "All I'm saying is, I think I could do it."

Lucy smiled. "Me too. You're in."

"Yay!" Franco grooved a happy dance. "I already invited three dates to this thing!" He sobered. "What if they see each other? Oh shit. I'm screwed!"

Nieca ignored his whiplash transition from gleeful to panicked. "What? If he's doing it, I'm doing it!"

"Okay." Lucy waved. "You can both choose something to wear. Something representative of our stock—hopefully something that will bring in donations via the charitable silent auction."

"Me too!" Penny cried, scurrying over from the cash register. An expectant look brightened her gamine features. "I want to wear something Goth. With chains and spikes. Okay?"

Lucy surveyed her staff, with their eager expressions and can-do attitudes. Despite their quirks, they really knew how to pull together in a crunch. "Awww. I love you guys! Of course you can model, Penny. The more the merrier. We'll all do it!"

They all hugged.

"In that case," came a voice from the shop's entrance, "I want to join in too."

Max. He stood a short distance away with both hands shoved in his shorts pockets, looking . . . apart. In his eyes, Lucy glimpsed the same longing she had before, coupled with something close to hopefulness. She couldn't resist.

"*He* can model his birthday suit." Penny wolf-whistled.

Lucy grinned. "Sure," she said. "The price of admission is that you join in this group hug." She waved him over.

Max stepped back, looking aghast. "Oh. Hell, no."

Conspiratorially, Lucy glanced to her staff members, all of them huddled together. Seconds later, they'd surrounded Max.

"No! Arrgh!" he cried as they closed in. "Stop!"

But before long, Max surrendered completely, buried in a genuine Successfully Dressed group hug. And he even, Lucy noticed with a grin, brought up both brawny arms . . . and, surreptitiously, hugged them all back.

"Okay. So you didn't like my *other* choice of a new baseball player for your team," Max said as he caught Lucy by the hand and guided them both up the bleachers to find seats. "I can handle that. But I've been doing some scouting. I think you'll like what I've come up with this time."

Lucy sighed, settling herself on the sun-warmed aluminum bench. All around them, people gathered in clumps on the bleachers, toting six-pack coolers, bottles of Aquafina, and hot dogs from the vendor near the park's entrance. Although this wasn't a major league venue, several women waved banners featuring the names of their favorite players.

"I meant what I said before," she explained earnestly. "I may have overreacted about your Diamondbacks recruit. Everyone on the team *loved* him. We've never had such a good practice before. Franco even learned where left field is."

"No, I insist." Max squeezed her hand, then offered her the sunscreen. In Arizona, wearing something near SPF one million was crucial in the summertime. "I get what the problem was, and this time I'm going to fix it. You'll see."

Bending over, Lucy rubbed sunscreen on her exposed calves. Conversations buzzed nearby. The sun blazed overhead, but a breeze kept the afternoon from feeling too stifling. This was the kind of desert weather she loved—a cloudless sky, pristine air, and sunshine for miles.

Even better than that, though, was Max. He was really *getting* it. He was trying to understand her, and succeeding. That meant a lot to her, especially knowing how very different they were. She loved it.

Trying to convey that fact, she adjusted her floppy sun hat and smiled at him. "I believe you. When does this baseball whiz of yours come on the scene?"

"In a few minutes."

She regarded Max, sitting there happily with his forearms clasped loosely between his knees. Dark hairs curled at the back of his neck, and his skin took on a faint sheen in the heat. His T-shirt and shorts were casual and—on any other man—unremarkable. But on Max they were perfection.

He leaned closer, eyeing the empty baseball diamond. A sense of urgency emanated from him . . . that, and impatience. It really mattered to Max that she approve of his choice, Lucy realized.

The warmth she felt next had nothing to do with the summer weather. She put her hand on Max's muscular thigh and smiled up at him.

"After this, maybe we'll go to my place," she said.

"Mmmm-hmmm." He squinted more intently as players entered the field. He patted her hand. "Okay. Sounds good."

"I'll make you dinner. Bean burritos *especial*."

He mustered another *hmmm*. "What makes them *especial*?"

"I unwrap them before putting them in the microwave to defrost. That's the extent of my cooking abilities." Grinning, Lucy snuggled closer. She stroked his thigh with her thumb, then seductively kissed his earlobe. Erotic images swam in her head, conjured by her affectionate feelings toward him. Huskily, she lowered her voice. "After that—"

"Look. They're starting."

She sat back, flummoxed. Why was Max more interested in baseball than in her *especial* invitation?

That was *so* unlike him.

"There he is." Max pointed. "Look."

Lucy did. But she didn't see anything of note. "Those are kids," she puzzled. "Hey, this is a Little League game."

"Yeah. I've been coming to them for the past couple of weekends. It occurred to me that I'd overlooked the perfect addition to your team."

"Max, I don't need another player."

"This one is really special. Look. Number thirty-two."

Gamely, Lucy did. She saw tousled brown hair beneath a ball cap, an eager grin, and the name RUIZ above the number on his jersey. "He's—"

"Awesome, right? Look at that positive attitude. Nothing gets him down, not even missing a catch." Max gave an admiring whistle as the player *almost* fielded a practice grounder between his ankles. "I told you he's perfect."

"He's eleven years old," Lucy pointed out. "And about two feet shorter than the opposing players we'll be facing."

"Like I said. Perfect."

Max offered her a boyish grin, handing over a chilled cranberry juice bottle. Lucy was still gawking over the words *fresh, all-natural,* and *organic* on the label when she heard Max's next words.

"He'll sneak in right under the opposing team's noses."

He guffawed, obviously relishing the image.

The game started. Everyone in the stands turned their attention to the players as they took their places. A few women—mothers of players, Lucy guessed—hooted

encouragement. Several men—fathers, she calculated—wielded camcorders.

This was full-on suburbia.

They were unlikely to find another "ringer" here.

"Max," Lucy said gently, after the game had reached its
fifth inning, "I'm not sure how to tell you this, but . . .
your top pick is—"

"Not very good. I know." Cheerfully, Max waved.

The kid—Ricky Ruiz, she'd learned—waved back. His
grin shone all the way to the stands. He was cute, but . . .

"He's struck out," she whispered, "every time at bat."

"I know. He needs to choke up on the bat more.
Loosen his shoulders and bend his knees."

Complacently, Max went on watching the game. Didn't
this bother him? Max, who was all about winning?

"He dropped two fly balls and ducked from the third."

"Yeah." Max gave her an enthusiastic one-armed hug.
"A few games ago, I heard he hit one straight up over his
head, caught it without thinking, and got himself called
out." Max whistled. "I wish I could've been here for that
one."

Lucy stared. "Then why do you want him for our
team?"

"*Our* team?" Max's sharp gaze caught hers. "You've
never called it that before."

She remembered the way Max had brought everyone together for the remodel, the grand reopening preparations,
and the increasingly popular seminars at Successfully
Dressed. Until he'd come to the shop, Lucy understood
then, they hadn't been as united or effective as they could
have been.

Max had changed that.

"We're in this together." She smiled, and for the first
time, honestly believed it. "Which is why I'm curious to
know . . . why him? Why Ricky Ruiz?"

"It's simple." Max diverted his attention from the game

to her face, and the sincerity in his expression struck her. "Ricky is perfect for your team because he's just like you. He plays with heart, win or lose. Watching him is like holding sunshine in your hands." Max hesitated, seeming at a loss to describe it otherwise. "I'm sorry I missed it all this time."

All this time, Lucy realized then, *she'd* missed something too. She'd missed the real Max.

She'd missed the fact that she loved him.

She knew it then, the same way she knew she'd hold his hand during the game. The same way she knew she'd invite Ricky to her charity game, strike out a few times herself, and, in a few days' time, live to see Franco "strike a pose" on the runway.

The same way she knew she had to tell Max how she felt.

"About that invitation to my place," she began, leaning closer so only Max could hear her. "How about an RSVP?"

"You're a stickler for propriety now?" He touched her forehead as though checking for a fever. Grinned. "You've had too much sun. You need a cold beer and an ice bath. Nude. With nurse Max on the cold compresses." He winked.

That wasn't *exactly* what Lucy had in mind. But it was close enough to count. And as she watched all the Little Leaguers scurry around the baseball field, she began to hatch a plan. A plan to show Max how much she loved him.

Starting tonight.

17

It was going to be amazing. Lucy knew it.

She hurried around her house, a pair of beeswax candles in hand, arranging everything just so. Extra pillows on her bed? Check. Filmy chiffon scarves tossed over her lamps? Check? Mood-setting music on her tinny radio? Check. Rows and rows of lighted candles? Check.

She stepped back, surveying her bedroom. There were so many pillows plumped along her headboard, the coverlet was barely visible. Perfect. She dipped her finger in the bowl of cinnamon massage oil on the nightstand, then rubbed some over her forearm. Mmmm. She could just imagine Max doing the same thing, rubbing the slippery oil over her shoulders, her back, her chest. He'd caress her breasts, her belly, her thighs, using those slow, wonderful strokes of his, and she'd—

Ding. Her microwave's timer spoiled the fantasy.

Feeling breathless, Lucy zipped to her cluttered kitchen, ducking beneath the wind chimes and the mobile sculpture. Her Chinese dressing gown trailed behind her, flowing over her legs in a way that reminded her of the lengthy bath she'd taken to prepare. No woman had ever spent so long buffing, scrubbing, shaving, and moisturizing as she had.

She pulled out the dinner supplies. Frowned at them. She wasn't entirely sure about the dinner thing, but everyone said the way to a man's heart was through his stomach, right? Lucy wanted to leave no stone unturned. She'd assembled all of Max's favorite things. Preparing them had been a little trickier.

But she wasn't worried. Smiling with anticipation over the night to come, Lucy twirled to grab a box of matches. She carried it to her cast-off dining table and set it next to the plates, bowl, silverware, glassware, and twin candles already arrayed there. Nothing matched, really, and none of it was as luxe as the stuff at Max's place. But the plate she'd chosen for Max was deep red, for love, and the handwoven placemat beneath it depicted a crazy pattern of intertwined hearts.

He'd be sure to get the message.

She took a dainty slug of red wine, then breezed through the living room with the bottle still in hand. Here, everything was as neat as she could make it—not that that fact was immediately apparent, given the quantity of collectibles crammed in the room. But Lucy knew Max would appreciate it. Tidying up was her way of acknowledging the changes he'd made in her life—the changes he'd prompted in her. Just yesterday, in fact, Lucy had actually bought Jade a birthday card almost *two weeks* in advance. She'd *never* been given to strategizing like that before Max had come into her life.

Making her way to her freshly scoured and potpourried bathroom, she thought about him. He was kind, underneath all his macho talk. He was funny, smart, generous. He was eager to help and to come up with new ideas. He listened to her. He snuggled and laughed and held her hand at all the right moments. And although he'd started out as a casual fling, over the past weeks Max had come to mean so much more to her.

So much more.

Suddenly panicked at the thought, Lucy gripped the spare toothbrush she'd bought. She stared at her reflection in the bathroom mirror. Two huge, round eyes looked back at her from a paler-than-usual face, surrounded by a shock of lavender hair. Her gown's mandarin collar framed her features in its vivid red silk print. Her silver eyebrow ring gleamed.

Red and lavender? Together? What had she been thinking? Max would never go for a woman who *clashed*. He was subtle. Sophisticated. Worldly. He would want a woman who looked classy, not a woman who looked like an Easter egg propped up in a take-out kung pao chicken box.

She was all wrong for him. Nearly hyperventilating, Lucy bolted, barefoot, for her closet. Its dinky confines were packed with clothes and shoes of every description, swathed with scarves and handbags and belts. But somehow, everything looked wrong. She hurled items right and left, searching for exactly the garment that would say *I love you, Max*. The ensemble that would remain in his memory forever whenever he recalled this night.

She turned up squat. Draping a sari despairingly over herself, Lucy sprinted to the bathroom and stood on the closed toilet lid to get a better view in the mirror. She looked like a bohemian panhandler with ADD, like a color-blind gypsy who couldn't *quite* get the knack of fortune telling.

It was over. Max would take one look at her and realize he could never, ever love her back. Not while she had—oh crap! Was that an actual *hair* sprouting from her chin? She was halfway toward becoming a bearded lady! Tonight, of all nights! Desperately, she grabbed her tweezers—no, a razor would be faster—and squinted in the mirror, angling her jaw to the light.

Ding.

The doorbell. Jerking in surprise, Lucy glanced toward

the sound. *Max was here.* Was it too late to sneak out a window?

No. That would never work. Thanks to the painting party she'd hosted last spring, several of her lovely periwinkle blue windows were permanently painted shut. She was stuck.

Several excruciating and panic-stricken minutes later, she opened the door wearing a brave smile. Max stood on the other side, dressed in jeans and a buttoned shirt under a dark blue jacket that nearly matched his eyes. He looked good enough to drag inside and tie to the bed. Probably she'd have to use force, Lucy realized, to make him stay.

Why, oh why, hadn't she grasped the truth before? She was simply too weird, too different, too oddball for him . . . the man she recklessly, *urgently* loved.

"Come on in." She waved him inside, then led the way to the sofa. The least she could do was provide him dinner. He *had* come all this way from Big Shot Central to Hairy Girl Town.

"Mmmm. Smells good in here," Max said. His gaze shot to her leg. "Are you limping?"

"Minor bathtub-scrubbing injury." He would never fit in her teeny tub, Lucy realized with growing despondency. All those muscles, all that machismo, all those strong, sure movements Max made . . . they couldn't be contained. She got distracted for a minute trying to picture squeezing his naked, buffed-up, soapy body into her pink-tiled tub, then gave up. "Want some wine? It'll be a few minutes till dinner."

She sloshed the bottle up from its position at her side. There seemed to be surprisingly little vino left inside. Confused, Lucy peered at it.

"No, thanks." Max reached to draw her onto the sofa beside him. He smiled. Then his gaze focused on her chin.

Oh God. Oh God. Here it comes . . . the moment he realizes he's dating Sasquatch.

"Hurt yourself?" he asked, his smile quirking on one side.

Lucy fingered her chin. *I cut myself shaving,* she considered, but couldn't bring herself to actually say the words. Too late, she remembered that the only bandages available on a quick, doorbell-induced grab had been her usual. "I'm totally into SpongeBob SquarePants."

Max raised his brow.

"It's decorative. I'm into the hip-hop style. Yo."

He guffawed.

Even laughing, Max looked scrumptious. His jaw was clean shaven, his hair wonderfully tousled. He smelled of something masculine and delicious and vaguely soapy, as though he'd come straight from showering with soap on a rope. She bet he had no idea how amazingly sexy he looked, with his hands clasped loosely near his thighs and his gaze turned directly on her.

It occurred to Lucy that Max probably thought he was having a normal dinner with her. He probably thought nothing had changed, probably thought they were still having a casual fling—when Lucy knew that, for her at least, everything had changed.

I love you, she considered blurting out.

"I'll check on dinner," she said instead.

Max rose. "I'll help."

She shoved him back down. The last thing she needed was for him to see how hopeless she was with all things culinary. Didn't men want women who could cook? Or was that totally archaic? Lucy had always figured getting food was pretty free of gender bias. After all, nobody speed-dialed for take-out pizza with their penis.

But Max was a traditional guy. Maybe . . .

She rammed the wine bottle toward him, then made her getaway—straight into the Dumpster-liberated armchair she'd helped reupholster with vintage fabrics last fall. She grabbed her toe, yelping.

"Are you okay?" Max asked, concerned. "That looked—"

"Fine," Lucy gritted out. "That chair must have moved."

Right. On its own. It had stood in that spot for the past thirteen months, too heavy for her to rearrange by herself.

She groaned and hobbled to the kitchen, intending to have a showdown with her nemesis, the stove.

Lucy found herself quivering with mortification instead. Hugging herself, she stared at the metallic stars painted on her deep blue kitchen ceiling. She thought she might cry, laugh, dance a tango. Her stomach quaked and her heart pounded. She looked at her hands and found them shaking. This was supposed to be a romantic night of seduction. She'd planned it all down to the last detail. What was wrong with her?

It wasn't as though she'd never loved anyone before.

Although Max was strictly *not* an abandoned kitten, a longtime pal, or an official member of her far-flung family. Those were the only people she'd *really* loved until now. And none of them had ever made her feel this way—giddy, gawky, prone to wild imaginings and even wilder yearnings.

Wishing she still had possession of the vino, Lucy peeked around the corner. Max still lounged on her sofa, looking fairly at home and absolutely edible. She wanted him so much it made her ache. Fear that he'd see her— *really* see her—locked her in place beside the dinner supplies, biting her lip.

What if he didn't love her too?

The only thing to do was find out. After a few revitalizing yoga breaths and several minutes of haggling with her home appliances, Lucy emerged. Her Chinese gown still trailed clashingly behind her, but Max's gaze skimmed to her legs, exposed by its daring slit. He didn't seem to care much about the principles of color coordination.

His appreciative smile made her tingle.

"Okay, here we go," she announced. "Have a seat."

She nodded to the table, its romantic accoutrements seeming suddenly abysmal. She should have gotten flowers! Roses were romantic, although she preferred daisies. But the candles were still . . . unlit. There went her seductive aura.

Max wandered past her, craning his neck. "Ummm . . . what are you doing? Are you going to be all right? You look a little . . . green."

Terrific. Sasquatch in need of concealer.

"I'm fine." Mustering a smile, she gripped her serving board. "But if you don't take your seat, I might drop this."

Max eyeballed the long-handled pizza peel she'd carried from the kitchen. On its far, *far* end rested a T-bone.

His grin was adorable, if confusing. "Are you planning to serve that steak or *serve* that steak? I don't see a net."

"Har, har." For a minute, looking at his familiar and beloved face, Lucy felt her anxiety ease. "It's been awhile since I've handled red meat. I liked it better . . . over there."

She craned her neck, indicating the steak.

It seemed, thankfully, a long way away.

"It's for you!" she blurted. "Your favorite! So just—"

"Let me help you." Wearing a strangely affectionate expression, Max took the pizza peel. He gave it an expert shuffle. The steak slid onto his plate. "Voilà."

Lucy raised her brows.

"Oliver and I once started a chain of coal oven pizza joints. We were pretty hands-on in the beginning."

"Ahhh." Lucy bobbled her head in idiotic agreement, then speed-walked to the kitchen for the beer, the mashed potatoes, and everything else. They both sat.

The candles refused to light until Max fiddled with the

wicks, then held a match to them. He smiled at her. She thought she might die of unrealized romantic intentions.

For a while, the only sounds were cutlery clinking, glasses being filled, and occasional shuffles. Also, mood music that did not seem to be setting the desired mood. For Lucy, eating was impossible. Not because she'd attempted a T-bone for herself, since she'd also prepared (via can opener) a perfectly tasty lentil soup, but just because all her attention was focused on Max.

She gazed at his face, angular and hard jawed and stunning. At his shoulders, broad and spiffy beneath his jacket. At his chest and arms, solid and—she knew from vivid memories—enhanced with exactly the right amount of muscle. At his hands, deft and masculine, with blunt fingers that could work magic.

Lucy swallowed hard, feeling desire prickle to life again within her. All day she'd been thinking of this night—thinking of the time when she'd have Max alone, all to herself, hers to show how much she cared about him, wanted him . . . loved him. As soon as he finished cutting his next bite of steak, she told herself, she would take his hand and begin her seduction.

Max sawed at his steak. And sawed. And sawed. Lucy was hardly an experienced carnivore, but it began to seem abnormal for a hunk of meat to require so much effort.

"Is everything all right?" she asked.

"It's a little well done." Valiantly, Max chewed.

And chewed. At this rate, he would have jowly chipmunk cheeks before the night was through.

"I've got strong teeth," he volunteered. "Don't worry."

Oh God. She would love him with dentures, sure, but—

"Hey, aren't you hungry?" He examined her soup bowl.

"Famished." Lucy spooned up some of the thick lentil soup, redolent of garlic, onions, and curry. It was halfway to her mouth, strictly on autopilot, when she realized Max would never kiss her garlicky, Sasquatchian, mismatched self if she actually ingested any of it. She offered him a pained smile and dribbled the soup surreptitiously back into her bowl. "For this."

She grabbed one of the beers and wrestled it open.

"Wait." Max touched her wrist. "Before you drink that . . ."

"Yes?"

"I just wanted to tell you . . . there've been some things I've been thinking about, and I—" He paused, looking a little green around the gills himself. "Thanks for dinner. It's terrific. And your place." He glanced around. "It looks very orderly."

He'd noticed. Absurdly grateful, Lucy slid her hand sideways and down so she could grasp Max's hand. He intertwined their fingers, offering her another smile. It was time.

"I did it for you." Her heard thudded madly.

"I know."

"Because I . . ." Lucy gulped, trying to muster the courage to say the words. *Because I love you.* Her throat clogged with emotion and her heart attempted to karate chop its way out of her chest. Her fingers wobbled within Max's. "I want you to be powered up. You know, for the night to come."

She tried for a seductive grin, then stroked his fingers. Max only watched her quizzically.

"I could have sworn you were going to say something else."

"I could have sworn *you* were," she replied.

For a minute, they only stared at each other, questions whirling unspoken between them. The mood music swelled, then crackled with static. The candles flickered.

"Are you going to fight your way through that charcoal steak," Lucy asked, "or shall we go for it right here?"

"Go for it?" He raised his brow.

"I want you, Max."

And even though it was *so* much more than that, even though it was *love* she wanted to show him, stepping onto the familiar turf of naked bodies, hot kisses, and under-the-tablecloth groping somehow felt a whole lot safer to Lucy just then.

His mouth quirked again. His gaze met hers, and she could have drowned in the warm, welcoming desire she saw there.

"Are you going to clear the table," Max asked, "or shall I hurl off the dishes and take you right here?"

In the end, they left the dishes—and the table—as they were. At Max's prompting, Lucy rose and took his hand. Taking the few steps toward him felt different. Meaningful. Like the few steps down the wedding aisle probably felt to a bride. Only a few feet's distance to trek . . . but a whole new life waited on the other side.

Drawing in a deep breath, Lucy raised her hands to Max's face. She felt the smooth, masculine texture of his skin, the hard length of his jaw, and smiled. Her whole body eased toward him, as accustomed to the motion as her wind chimes were to dancing to the breeze.

"Hold still," she murmured. "I have plans for you."

She stretched upward and kissed him, a soft press of her lips against his. She wanted that kiss to convey longing, love, surety . . . but the moment their mouths met, long-standing need took over. Lucy found herself clinging to Max in the end, both arms around his neck, panting for breath.

"I have plans too," Max announced, a smile on his face as he ran his hands down the sides of her silky dressing gown. "Definite plans. If only I could remember what they were. Seeing you made them all fly out of my head."

"It's not important. I'll handle everything."

Lucy kissed him again, angling her head sideways to

accept more of him. Kissing Max was like stepping off a cliff, like freefalling through the sky while bungee jumping. It was wild and free and addictive. He groaned and thrust his hands in her hair, holding her closer, and she knew that in another minute, they'd be dropping to the floor, the sofa, or the kitchen table, typically unwilling to wait for each other.

Max pressed his mouth to her neck, urgently moving aside the banded collar of her gown. Lucy squirmed and gasped, and this time she was the one clutching him. His hair tickled her fingertips, lush and thick and longer than when she'd met him.

"Come with me." She took a moment to nibble his earlobe, to savor his gasp of surprise when she bit gently, then grabbed his hand. She tugged. "This way."

The path to her bedroom had never seemed so long, so strewn with opportunities to lounge against a wall and be kissed again, to sink onto a chair arm and feel her dressing gown slide from her shoulders, baring her skin inch by inch. Lucy didn't know where she found the fortitude to resist falling to her handwoven Navajo rug, pulling over one of her many floor pillows, and letting Max have his way with her. She only knew that eventually, hazily, they made their way to their destination.

Just inside her bedroom, Max paused. His hands, cupping her breasts from behind, quit caressing. His breath panted across her bare shoulder in the spot where her gown had slipped. The hard, hot length of him pushed adamantly against her backside, not at all concerned with where they were.

"Hmmm," he said. "Nice. Just like you."

He'd never been here before, Lucy realized then. They'd never made it this far. And she tended to keep this room private, to herself, without really meaning to.

But seeing it now, revealed through his eyes, she had to agree. It was hard to think coherently when her nipples insisted on tightening beneath Max's fingertips in blatant invitation, but she could still discern that her old wooden bed looked cozy and appealing, and her familiar rug and curtains and plants and keepsakes and photos and table and lamps looked homey and warm. Lighted candles squatted along her bureau, casting the whole place in a flickering glow.

"Yeah. I took out the trapeze and the jungle gym this morning," she deadpanned. "They can be kind of intimating for first-timers."

Max nudged her, giving a low, seductive laugh. "I'm up for anything you are."

Even love? Lucy wondered instantly, but she only clasped her hands over his and squeezed them more tightly together. She finally felt ready. Ready to show Max those emotions, even if she couldn't quite express them aloud. Not yet.

"Then follow me," she said, and inched forward.

Surprisingly, Max didn't come with her. The night had been going pretty well up to this point—all things considered—but when Lucy whirled to find out what was wrong, she saw Max staring at her bedroom with dawning revelation on his face.

"My family is busy," he said decisively—if mystifyingly. He looked at her squarely. "My parents both have demanding jobs—my dad as an attorney and my mom as a technical engineer. I suspect that's why I'm an only child."

Utterly baffled, Lucy went on staring.

"I grew up in Austin, but before I came to Phoenix, I lived in Miami, Manhattan, Seattle, San Francisco, and Philadelphia."

"Max . . . ?"

"I moved into Big Shot Central because I liked the view of the mountains." He smiled at her, then gazed down at his suit jacket. "And yes, sometimes these things *do* chafe."

She felt completely confused now. Especially when Max shucked his suit jacket and dropped it on a nearby chair, then made absolutely no move to undress her in similar fashion.

Her body still thrummed with the feel of his hands on her, his palms skimming over her hips, her thighs, her derrière. It turned out that her clashing, gaudy dressing gown had one spectacular advantage—its silkiness. Its softness had multiplied every caress, working with Max's kisses to amplify the desire she'd kept simmering all day long.

"What are you *talking* about?" she asked.

"You asked me some questions once," Max mused, as though his detour were perfectly natural. "Things you wanted to know about me. I've been thinking about the answers."

"Thinking? Now?" Lucy gaped. "No. Stop it."

She tucked her hand in his belt buckle and hauled him forward. It was her favorite move, and so far had never failed to yield magnificent, love-me-now kinds of results. She fisted her hand in his shirtfront and tugged, deciding it might be better to use both hands in this situation. She kissed him.

"Mmmm." Dreamily, Max gazed at her. He smiled, then visibly regrouped. "My hair is cut so short because it's fast and efficient. And no, it wasn't an accident. Or a drunk haircut."

Okay. So maybe she *did* want to know all these details about him. But not right now. Stifling a groan, Lucy started unbuttoning his shirt. She inhaled at the resulting view of his bare skin and defined chest muscles, as intoxicated by the sight of him as she'd always been. "Mmmm-hmm. That's nice."

"I'm a TV person *and* a book person—so long as the TV is SportsCenter, CNN, or that Emeril guy, and the books are—" At her questioningly raised eyebrows, Max shrugged. "So shoot me. I surfed past it one night and liked the whole *bam!* part."

Lucy found that goofily endearing. But not enough to make her quit unbuttoning. She spread his shirt wide, letting it fall from his shoulders. She nuzzled his chest, lowering her hands to his taut belly. She grazed circles there, feeling Max's muscles flex beneath her palms.

He wasn't as immune to her as he pretended.

"And, uhhh . . ." Max gave a husky moan, seeming to forget what he'd been talking about. To her disappointment, he remembered. "I don't like champagne. I *have* been moshing—"

Just like that, Lucy realized what this was all about. She'd asked Max every one of these questions that day in the shop. That day he'd overloaded all the washing machines and flooded the place. That day she'd tried to make him talk about himself for a change.

Lucy gazed up at him in astonishment. She couldn't believe Max had actually remembered everything she'd wanted to know.

He *had* been listening. Even then.

Her heart turned over with happiness, leaving her even giddier than before. Max cared about her. He really did.

". . . getting used to the tofu, especially barbecued," he was saying, earnestly trying to get through the list. "I'm usually too busy for celebrating holidays, but—"

"*That* can't go on." Lucy smiled and dropped his shirt to the floor. She took his hand and led him toward the bed, kicking aside the discarded runner-up clothes she'd desperately strewn all over the place. "I love holidays. I'll help you."

Max paused. "I don't do birthdays. Or Groundhog Day."

Lucy scoffed. That's what *he* thought. "How about naked holidays? Because I feel pretty celebratory right now."

She lifted her hands to her dressing gown's front and leisurely unlooped the first gilt fastener.

As though prodded by her actions, Max talked faster. "I hugged my mom when I visited Austin last month. I like puppies, especially Spike, unless he's peeing on me. The stock market is not phony, and of course I own stock. I have several diversified investments in my portfolio."

Three fasteners down. Three to go. Lucy felt a whoosh of anticipation as her gown drooped lower, catching Max's eye. The silk draped over the back of her hand, heavy and luxurious.

"Stop," Max blurted. "Don't move a muscle."

Perplexed, Lucy did stop. She felt doubly puzzled when Max moved nearer, seeming to forget about his Q&A session, and covered her hands with his own. Rapidly, he slipped all her fasteners in place again, a concerned look on his face.

Terrific. She was the only woman in history who'd set out to seduce a man . . . and wound up getting *more* buttoned up than before. At this rate, she'd be twice as hot and bothered by the *end* of this night than at its beginning.

Max saw her undoubtedly disappointed look. He gave her a gentle kiss . . . one that rapidly morphed into a toe-curling, rapidly clutching, breathless extravaganza. Dizzily, Lucy wobbled in front of him. Fortunately, she still had his belt buckle to anchor her.

"I've been wanting to do this for a long time." Wearing a wicked anticipatory look, Max lowered his hands to her gown again. Slowly, he pushed the first fastener through its loop. "A woman like you should be undressed properly. And often."

Lucy *loved* being undressed! The gentlemanliness of it spoke to all the traditional, womanly parts of her. If she'd loved Max before—and she had—she felt wildly in love with him now.

"You're doing a fine job of that." Her gown slipped more.

"Mmmm." Concentration roughened his features.

Seeming determined, Max started talking again. "My business partner's name is Oliver, and I met him in third grade. Public, not private school. I was never a frat boy. By college, Oliver and I had already invented a set of auto-refilling beer glasses we sold on campus. The profits financed our first real venture."

"Interesting. Done talking yet?"

He grinned. "You're the one with all the questions."

But just now, Lucy didn't care. "I couldn't possibly have had this many questions. Who *talks* this much?"

She kissed him again, hoping to dissuade further answering. To her surprise, Max threw himself wholeheartedly into their kiss, and when it was finished, he focused on finishing unbuttoning her. He fisted the pieces of her gown together, leaving Lucy desperate for him to just take it off.

"What? No more questions?" It was too much to hope for.

"No more questions. I did it. All of them."

He seemed inordinately pleased with himself. It occurred to Lucy that all those answers were what Max had started telling her when he'd arrived. When she'd almost told him . . .

"I love you, Max. I really, really do."

His eyes darkened. He absorbed her trembling energy, her quivering smile, her tentative touch to his cheek. He brought his forehead to hers, the gesture intimate and right.

"I should have let you talk first," he said, and dropped her dressing gown to the floor.

From that moment on, there was nothing but love. Lucy felt it in the way Max touched her, running his hands tenderly over her skin as though marveling at its softness and warmth. She sensed it in the way he carried her down to her bed, as though holding something precious and rare. She reveled in it as Max followed her there, shedding his clothes until nothing stood between them but . . . nothing. No barriers, no hesitancy, no secrets. All Lucy needed on this night was Max.

All she wanted was to love him.

Her whole body quaked beneath his caresses. She arched upward to meet him, skin to skin, and knew that loving did not get better than this. Max cupped her breasts in his big, strong hands, stroking her with exquisite care. He kissed his way from her collarbone to her knees, lavishing attention on every place in between. Lucy moaned and begged, and whenever she could, she loved him back. Beneath her hands, his muscles turned harder than ever, his groans deeper, his needs fiercer.

"Be with me," she whispered, both of them tangled in the coverlet. Pillows strewed the mattress, all shapes and colors cushioning them. "Love me," she encouraged, every moment enriched by the knowledge that she loved him . . . loved him.

"Not so fast," Max said, and made true his word in every instant that followed. He kissed her as though he had all day to enjoy it. He licked her as though he had all day to savor it. He stroked her and tickled her and even made her laugh in the midst of all his sensual torture, and Lucy knew then that they were perfect for each other. If she'd had any doubts, they were banished. Any man who could withstand her giggles and understand that they were expressions of sheer joy, bubbling over, was the man for her.

She opened herself to him the same way she'd opened her bedroom to him, generously and bravely. Max gave back to her in kind, and as he kissed her again with his hand cradling the back of her head and his hips grinding against her, she knew she would need more and more and more of this.

"Please," she begged, squirming to reach him. He filled her hand, hard and hot, a perfect match for the slickness she felt. "Please, please . . ."

Finally, Max made them complete, holding himself above her with intense absorption and fierce tenderness.

Lucy gasped, loving the overwhelming unity of their bodies together. Nothing had ever felt this good. This right. This lovely. Max groaned and thrust with incredible slowness, making her curve higher and higher, striving for an orgasm that felt . . . *ahhh*. Like heaven.

Still quivering, still panting, Lucy felt him stiffen in his own release. She clutched his damp muscled back to bring him closer.

"Yes, Max," she whispered. "Don't hold back. I want everything. I love you. Love you, love you."

Max widened his eyes, his body racked with tremors. His lusty groan filled the room, imbuing Lucy with a satisfaction she'd never experienced before. All that mattered now was her and Max, together. All that mattered was this . . . forever.

"Ahhh, Lucy. You're amazing." Max turned his head against the crook of her neck, then kissed her. He slumped with a beatific smile. "How did I get this lucky?"

"The same way I did, I guess." She snuggled against him, her palm spread over his chest. Long moments passed while, beneath her hand, his chest rose and fell with contented breaths. "We're just lucky together."

"Hmmm." His voice rumbled against her, touched with amusement. "I thought you said 'lucky' was a bunch of hooey."

"Did I? I must have never experienced it properly before, then." Lucy smiled, reveling in the tender way Max sifted his fingers through her hair, arranging the strands across his shoulder. "I'm a convert now."

"Good. But I've got to warn you." Max gave her a mock serious look. "There's no going back." And all night long, he showed her exactly how wonderful getting *lucky* could be.

18

"You have *got* to be kidding me." Max looked at the baseball uniform in Lucy's hands, then shook his head. "No way."

"Way." Proudly, she brandished the thing. "This is a one-of-a-kind, original creation designed especially for the Successfully Dressed Bombers. Pretty sweet, right?"

Not quite. His eyes hurt from looking at it. Tie-dyed in the shop's signature colors, fringed, and tight fitting, the ensemble looked like something Britney Spears would wear to a Grateful Dead concert. If she were color-blind. And a man.

"This version is for you," Lucy continued. "The girls have cute skirts with Spankys. You know, those spandex short-shorts cheerleaders wear under their uniforms?"

Invoking cheerleaders cheered up Max. A little. But he couldn't quite picture squeezing himself into those pants.

"Come on. Don't look so skeptical. This uniform is practically custom fitted." Lucy sashayed nearer and held the pants to his bottom half, demonstrating. She nodded, approving. "What did you *think* Penny was measuring you for?"

"Cheap thrills?"

"Har, har." Lucy tossed him the uniform. "Get going, hot stuff. We're due at the field in an hour."

Clutching an armful of fabric, Max glanced toward the fitting room at the other side of Successfully Dressed. They'd closed the store early today, in honor of the game, but several team members had assembled here for an impromptu pep rally.

"What are we gonna do?" Nieca yelled, wielding a clipboard.

"Have fun!" everyone screamed back, cheering.

"Beat the crap out of 'em!" Penny shouted, oblivious.

"How are we gonna do it?" Nieca prodded.

"Fair and square!" the crowd replied.

"Any way we can!" Penny piped up, waving her banner.

Franco separated himself from the others. "Hey, check me out, you guys. I'm totally ready, right?"

His uniform bagged from his lanky body, customized with a black leather armband and Franco's usual studded belt. On his feet were kick-ass cowboy boots, into which he'd tucked his pants. The whole effect was very Mötley Crüe-meets-Babe Ruth.

"Nice." Lucy nodded. "You even put on your game-day eyeliner."

"I know!" Widening his gunmetal gray-rimmed eyes, Franco shook his faux-hawk. "Fierce, right?"

Max watched him trundle to the Gatorade stand set up at the cash register. Everybody had been quaffing the stuff as though it were magic. Max knew the only magic to be found was in his lucky Astros cap, which he'd worn to the shop today.

"Go on! Get ready!" Turning from her perusal of Franco, Lucy gave Max a gentle shove. Her face beamed with enthusiasm. "I can't wait to see you."

"I can't wait to see *you*." Max gave her a goofy smile, remembering waking up with her this morning, all cozy in her cramped, saggy, nondesigner bed. Despite the girly bedding, the flea market lava lamp on the nightstand, the multiplying pillows, and the patchouli-scented bohemian surroundings, being there had felt right. It had felt perfect. It had felt like something Max wanted to experience again and again and again. "Where's your uniform?"

"Fitting room. I'm going in after you."

"Let's go together."

"We can't!" Lucy gave him a scandalized look. "You know what will happen."

"Our uniforms will mutate, get together to spark a doobie, and hitchhike to the grocery store for some Chubby Hubby?"

"Very funny."

"Come on." He took her hand. "I don't want to be apart."

And even though Max realized as he said it exactly how sappy and lame-ass that was, he also realized it was true. He wanted to stay with Lucy, to bask in her warmth and her smile, to hold her close and maybe, if he found an opportune moment, tell her how much she had changed things for him. Because of Lucy, he was a different man. A man who was about to destroy his tough-guy rep by appearing in public in tie-dye, sure. But also a man who suddenly found himself wanting to stay in Phoenix, settle down, and maybe even start up a whole new kind of venture. With Lucy.

"Awww." Lucy beamed at him, her face bright and happy and suffused with the kind of blindingly obvious affection any other woman would have tried to hide. "How could I refuse an invitation like that?"

"You can't," Max told her, reasserting his machismo. He lowered his voice and gave her a wicked grin. "Come on. Come help me tie up these damned lace sleeves."

* * *

At the baseball field, Max got his first view of their op-
position. The other team looked like a bunch of pantywaists.
That fact would have been more reassuring had the Successfully Dressed Bombers been a little less delusional.

"This year's gonna be different," one of Franco's bandmates volunteered as he slung a mesh bag of balls into
the dugout. "I can feel it, dude."

"Yeah," Franco agreed, pacing. "This is going to be
epic. I had sixteen espressos to power up. I'm totally
ready." He smacked his fist in his palm.

He winced.

"With uniforms like these, we'll dazzle 'em just going
in," Nieca observed, flouncing into the dugout with her
braids half-covered by a custom newsboy cap. She'd announced, as head designer, that baseball caps were "so
expected." Only Max wore a traditional cap—a maneuver that had required some fancy footwork on his part.
"The crowd will love us."

"Totally. Nice work, Nieca," said another band
member.

"Really excellent," Lucy gushed. "Nicely retro too.
You've outdone yourself this year."

More appreciative and supportive murmuring followed.

"Ha! No mercy!" Penny cried, hefting some bats as she
muscled her petite figure into the dugout. "Winner take
all!"

"Actually," Lucy pointed out, "we all 'take all.' Since
the pledges get paid win or lose. As long as we play."

She tossed Max a grin, brimful with energy for the impending game. She grabbed his hand for balance while
she performed a quadriceps stretch. Somehow, on Lucy,
the tie-dyed monstrosity of a uniform looked cute. Probably because the girly version showed off her spectacular
legs. She stretched on the other side, then clapped her
hands together.

"Let's go, everybody! Woo-hoo!"

They fanned out on the field, going through their warm-ups. The late-afternoon sunshine sparked off their vibrant uniforms and highlighted the sparse crowd of onlookers. Several spectators carried banners, a few hefted beers, and more than one had turned the game into a full-on event, complete with umbrella, blanket, picnic, and pillows.

"Pillows?" Max asked, lingering behind to help finalize the batting order. "What's that about?"

Nieca shrugged. "Our games tend to run into extra innings. Sometimes it can take awhile before somebody scores."

"Before somebody . . ." *Scores . . . at all?* She couldn't be serious. On the other hand . . . "Never mind. It'll be fun."

That was just how much Max's attitude had changed. Thanks to Lucy.

Relaxing, Max spotted Oliver in the stands, nearly hidden by a sun shade. He had Spike on his lap and was smearing on some of the experimental pet sunscreen they'd ordered for their boutiques. Max hadn't expected his partner to show up for this game, but now that he had, Max was glad. He hadn't seen much of Oliver lately. He'd been too wrapped up with Lucy.

He waved. To his surprise, so did Nieca.

Max did a double take.

Especially when she blew his partner a kiss.

Oliver didn't even pass out, or blush, or anything.

"Seriously?" he asked, tipping his head toward the stands in a you-and-him? gesture. "You and Oliver?"

Nieca raised her chin. "You want to make something of it?"

"No." Max raised his palms, feeling a stupid grin spread over his face. So *that's* who Oliver had been preoccupied with lately. Nieca, not Andrea. "I'm happy for you both."

That was the way of true love, he figured. Now that

he'd found some for himself, he wanted to see it spread all around.

Ricky Ruiz arrived next, accompanied by his parents. He'd even donned the special Bombers uniform, probably at risk of having the crap beat out of him by any passing fifth graders.

"We told him it's a sneak preview of what the Diamondbacks will be wearing next year," Mrs. Ruiz confided in a whisper as Ricky trotted off to warm up. "Once he heard that, he couldn't wait to play."

"We're lucky to have him," Max said. "Thanks."

"No, thank *you!* It's not every businessman who'd take the time to include Ricky, you know. We appreciate that."

All the Ruizes nodded. Around them, the warm-ups took on a more intense quality as game time neared. The other team chanted a start-up cheer . . . something to do with tie-dye. Max didn't care. It was a beautiful day, he was part of something new, and Lucy was waving at him from center field. She bobbled the ball, but hey— priorities were priorities. He'd rather savor her smile than come up a winner.

It was a major first for him.

"Enjoy the game," he said, then tipped his hat to the Ruizes and jogged out to join his team . . . the first one he'd really felt a part of in a long time.

Several catcalls followed. They were all from his teammates. Max couldn't help but grin as he took his place beside Lucy in the infield. "Let's go, everybody!"

"Goooo, Bombers!" his team shouted.

If a winning spirit counted for anything, the Bombers were a shoo-in.

"Hey," Lucy called, squinting at his head. "Where's your lucky Astros cap?"

"I ditched it." Max tugged down his personalized tie-dyed cap, courtesy of Nieca. He hunkered in place, ready to play. "Who needs luck with a team like this?"

* * *

It turned out, Lucy thought as she lounged in Max's spotless stainless steel and glass loft kitchen after the game, that *everyone* with a team like theirs needed a shot of luck.

As usual, the Bombers had lost the game in extra innings, 1 to 0.

But their pledges had paid out, raising much-needed funds for their designated charities. And, as an extra incentive, Max had opened his whole deluxe bachelor pad to everyone on the team for a swanky after-party. Even now, music thumped from the sleek sound system across the room, hors d'oeuvres sat spotlit on the living room console table, and the whole place swelled with tie-dye-wearing Bombers.

Lucy grinned, thinking of their reception by the doorman, Hank. He'd politely admitted the first few team members, but as their ranks had grown, he'd looked pretty worried. By the time Franco and his punk-haired band members had arrived, Hank had begun popping antacids and calling for reinforcement.

But Lucy knew theirs was a gentle crowd, from the players to their inevitable boosters. Across the room, Jade pressed Oliver—with a shaggy Spike in his arms—to stop by her health food store for some of her homemade dog treats. Near them, Victor showed his henna mehndi body art to a couple Lucy thought were the Ruizes—they hadn't been introduced.

Ricky chomped mini hot dogs and punch, unconcerned with the expensive furnishings beneath his grass-stained butt. He swung his cleats and bobbed his head to the music, apparently thrilled with the two strikeouts and one grounder he'd hit today.

Nieca chatted with another spectator, whirling to show off her uniform's skirt. Lucy recognized Andrea Cho, the publicist. Apparently, there was nothing like a bond formed over fashion to really cement a new friendship. The two women looked as if they could talk handbags and couture all night.

Penny stood chatting with her husband and one of Franco's band members, her silvery hair gleaming now that she'd removed her cap. She hadn't taken losing as hard as Lucy might have expected. There was always next year. They all knew that.

She couldn't believe how amazing Max's loft looked. He'd really gone all out for the party, but the place had a special appeal on its own, too, she realized. At the edge of the crowded room, the wide windows showcased a spectacular, dusky view of the Phoenix sprawl. Lights had just begun to glimmer across the valley, and Camelback Mountain loomed like a mysterious, purple creature of the dusk.

I liked the view of the mountains, Lucy remembered Max telling her as his reason for moving here. Just then she felt perfectly in sync with him. Ever since last night—and this morning, waking up together for the first time—she'd been absolutely giddy with happiness. Finally, they understood each other. She and Max had reached an accord, worked out a relationship that actually thrived on their differences.

Not long ago, Lucy wouldn't have believed it.

Now, she absolutely did.

Joyfully, she strode to the window, pausing to joke with Franco and wave to her astrologer friend. She gazed outside, hugging herself. Max's loft had its advantages—chiefly, him. But it was an ideal setting for a postgame celebration too. How Max had realized this would be exactly what everyone needed, Lucy didn't know. But the fact that he had . . . well, it made all the difference in the world.

Max was giving. He truly was. No matter how he tried

to hide it or shrug it off. He hadn't had to throw a party—especially for a (technically) losing team—but he'd done it.

She spotted him across the room, wedged in near the low-slung sofa. He had his head down, talking to Oliver. Not far away, Nieca held his furry puppy in her arms, crooning to it. Lucy knew about Nieca and Oliver, but she'd been too wrapped up in Max to really pay their relationship proper attention.

Well, there was no time like the present to remedy that. Clutching her martini glass—Max still hadn't mastered the art of sangria—Lucy wove her way across the room. She would officially meet Oliver, give him and Nieca her blessing, then spirit Max away to a more secluded area of the loft—maybe the balcony—for a private tête-à-tête. She wanted to thank him for the party, for playing baseball today, for drafting Ricky Ruiz, and for just being himself. The man who'd made her realize there could be good things everywhere—even at Big Shot Central.

Partygoers clogged the room, blocking her path. Feeling happy-go-lucky, Lucy detoured around the partial wall that formed the foyer, then veered through the kitchen, approaching Max from behind. She drained her martini glass and set it down. She would tiptoe behind him, put her hands over Max's eyes, and make him conjure up an answer to "Guess who?"

Lucy glimpsed the back of Max's head, still bent as he talked with Oliver. Perfect. He'd never see her coming.

"I'm just relieved your damned volunteering is over with."

Oliver's voice drifted toward her. Lucy paused.

"It was a major time sink, that's for sure," he went on.

She frowned. Well, she wouldn't hold it against Oliver. Probably he needed a dose of volunteering himself to really understand it. Judging by Oliver's fancy suit and high-gloss shoes, he wasn't exactly a hands-on guy. Although Nieca, unlike Lucy, typically had excellent judgment when it came to men. She wouldn't have fallen for Oliver if he wasn't worth it.

"It wasn't so bad," Max said, his voice carrying. "You should be happy I was out of your hair."

Lucy started forward again.

"Besides," Max added, "I made plenty of contacts."

She froze, suddenly struck with the thought that she probably didn't want to hear what was coming next.

"Right," Oliver agreed, his drawl suggesting otherwise. "You made them—about a third of them, if I recall correctly. But I haven't seen any of them trooping down to the offices to sign on as investors. The Ruizes are getting antsy."

The Ruizes? Lucy scanned the crowd, looking for them. What did they have to do with this?

"The Ruizes are fine." Max's voice was sure. "They're still on board to go forward with selling their properties."

"They'll be more 'on board' when you get your butt in gear again," Oliver informed him. "Now that your little vacation in BoHoVille is over with, maybe you can—"

"Hey—"

"—get back to work for a change. I mean it, Max. Don't be a dickhead. You promised."

Max's head slumped in acknowledgment. A trickle of dread poured down Lucy's spine. What had he promised?

"At least some of those Successfully Dressed benefactors ought to be willing to invest in our pet boutique venture," Oliver prodded. "The ones who won't must have friends—or husbands—who will. You told me so yourself."

Max had? Lucy stood unmoving behind them, shielded by the ever-flowing party traffic. Revelry surged all around her, but all at once she felt far from celebratory. Something was going on here. Something big and ugly.

"Knock it off," Max growled, his voice louder. "I said I'll deliver your damned investors."

"We need them soon. The contracts . . ."

Whatever else Oliver said was lost in the music.

"I said I'll do it." Max slapped his hands on his thighs, shooting Oliver a sideways glare. His shoulders stiffened. "Have I ever let you down before?"

Oliver's pointed stare hurt Lucy to see. It must have hurt Max doubly so . . . except she felt too confused, too desperate to deny what she seemed to be hearing, to go to him.

"The grand reopening is coming up soon," Max gritted out, sounding as though he was fighting for patience. "All the power players will be there. CC Burnheart's already a shoo-in. I'll put everything else in motion then."

Oliver's reply was drowned out by party noise.

What did Cornelia Burnheart have to do with this?

Why was the shop's grand reopening involved?

Before Lucy could puzzle it out, Max stood in one swift motion. His gaze fixed on Oliver. Something like regret, or maybe anger, flashed over Max's face.

Lucy had never seen him look that way before. So intense, so commanding, so formidable. So apart from her.

Max turned, his whole body tensed.

He saw her. The dismay on his face was what made Lucy finally understand.

"*Oh, Max,*" she said, realization dawning. "Not you too."

Benefactors. Investors. A man who would bribe her upon first meeting for the return of his "lucky" suit.

"How much did you hear?" Max asked, frowning.

"You used me." Lucy's whole body trembled. He looked like a stranger to her then, someone she couldn't possibly have known—or loved. "You used me to get to the DL and her cronies. Didn't you?"

"Lucy, come on. Don't get all melodramatic on me." He

stepped forward, wearing one of his patented charming smiles. His dimple looked a little shaky, but that was to be expected, given the circumstances. "You don't understand."

But she did understand. All too well. Oliver's face, gawking at them both, swam in Lucy's vision. So, as a matter of fact, did Max's face. They both seemed wobbly and watery and heartless. How could she have been so blind?

"I think I do understand. Finally." Hurt shoved at her, penetrating the denial she'd been practicing until now. "I can't believe it took me so long."

You're easily hurt, she remembered Nieca and Franco telling her. *Remember Seth?* And just then, Lucy did.

She remembered that when it came to men, she was pathetically gullible sometimes, too willing to believe the good in people to notice the bad.

Except *this* . . . this was a million times worse than Seth.

Sure, Seth had used her to get closer to the Dragon Lady—and Mr. Dragon Lady—in an attempt to further his own job opportunities with the local tycoon types. But Lucy had never loved Seth. She'd never let him in, trusted him, hoped for a future with him. With Max . . . she had.

All the way.

"Lucy, Lucy." Max was beside her, catching hold of her chilly hand. He rubbed it between his palms, looking concerned. He really had that *concerned* expression nailed. "You're overreacting. Listen to me. I have a business to run. It's nothing personal. You know me—I have commitments, promises, things I have to do—"

"People you have to betray?" She lifted her gaze to his.

"No! Jesus, Lucy." He dropped her hand, his frown deepening. "What's the matter with you? So what if I met a few people while I was volunteering? What difference does it make?"

"What *difference* does it make?" Her voice cracked. A few people stared, but Lucy didn't care. "What *difference?*"

Max nodded, stubbornly silent.

"You never wanted to volunteer at all," she accused.

"So? You knew that going in." He crossed his arms over his chest. "I still did it. I *did* it."

"But you did it for all the wrong reasons! You did it to *gain* something from it—to meet Cornelia and schmooze investors." Something else struck her, and Lucy gestured wildly toward little Ricky Ruiz. "Even our baseball game wasn't exempt! I heard Oliver talking about the Ruizes. I'm not stupid, Max. I know you must have drafted Ricky to impress them." She lowered her voice, pain seeping through her. "I should have known you wouldn't lose on purpose. Not without a reason."

"Nobody wants to lose." Max said so impatiently, as though it were blatantly obvious. "Are you done yet? Because there are a few things—"

"Am I *done* yet?" Through teary eyes, Lucy gaped at him. She didn't even know this man. This Max. "No, I'm not done! You *knew* how much good intentions mean to me, and you took advantage anyway. You didn't even care about—"

"No. Don't pull that 'good intentions' bullshit on me. You got something out of this too."

"What? A—" *A broken heart?* a part of her cried, but she refused to wail it aloud. "What did I get, Max?"

A simmering look passed between them. Instantly, she knew he was remembering all those times they'd spent together—in the storeroom, at her tiny house, at the baseball field, on the sofa only a few feet away. All those sexy, irresistible, *foolish* times. Lucy couldn't believe he had the gall to remind her of how gullible she'd been. She'd treasured all of those times.

Until now.

"You got weeks' worth of perfectly good volunteering," Max stated, his posture rigid. "Weeks' worth of consulting, of free PR work, of washer repairs and sales pitches. You benefited, damn it. So don't stand there and give me that wounded look, because you know damned well I'm right. I did what I promised."

"What you promised me? Or what you promised Oliver?"

Max gritted his teeth. Exasperation fell from him in waves. "Mostly? What I promised you."

"No. I never asked you to use me." Tears choked her voice, making it hard to speak. The party spun before her eyes, growing quieter now as people realized what was happening. A low buzz hummed through the room. "I never asked you to make me love someone who couldn't love me back."

"Couldn't—" Max threw up his hands, his face darkening. "Damn it, Lucy. This is who I am. Don't pretend you didn't know that from the beginning."

"*I* was never pretending. I guess that's the difference between us." She waited a minute, then realized she was actually—stupidly—hoping he would contradict her. Tell her he hadn't been pretending to care about her either. But Max only stood there, glaring at her as if *he* were the wronged party. "I've got to go. Bye, Max."

Lucy turned, shoving past a clump of people. She had to get out of there. To leave before she fell apart completely. Partygoers—her friends and neighbors—reached out with hugs and questions, but she couldn't handle sympathy right now.

At the door, Max caught up with her. He slammed it shut the moment she opened it, slapping his big hand on the wood.

"Where are you going?" he demanded.

She couldn't believe he couldn't guess. "Home."

"Not alone, you aren't." He reached for his keys from the foyer table. Fisted them. "I'll drive you."

"You have a party to see to."

"I don't care." Mulishly, Max waited for her to agree. "I'd rather be with you."

"Oh, Max." Lucy gazed up at him, and suddenly all the anger, all the hurt, eased a fraction. She remembered the good times they'd shared, and she didn't want to ruin them with a horrible good-bye now. "You don't get it, do you? I'd rather be with you too. But now I never can be. Not with a man who'd hurt me on purpose."

"Hurt you on—" He fisted his keys harder, shaking his head. "Damn it, Lucy. I never meant—"

"No," she interrupted, raising her hand to his cheek. "You never meant any of it. And that's the whole problem. I needed you to *mean* it. Really mean it." Tears threatened again, leaving Lucy struggling for composure. She blinked, then lowered her hand. "I'm sorry, Max. We could have been really, really great together."

A smile quirked her mouth, in spite of everything. For a while, at least, they *had* been really great together. That, Lucy realized, was what she had to hold on to now.

"Good-bye, Max," Lucy whispered.

Then she slipped out the door, leaving him standing on the other side—not nearly as alone as she would be from now on.

19

Max hurled a dart at the sleek board hung from his living room wall. It zinged with faultless precision to the center of the target, making a satisfying *thunk* as it struck home.

"You ought to call her," Oliver said.

Max grunted a refusal. "She doesn't have a phone."

Thunk went the next dart. Max hadn't had time to use the board—a FedExed birthday gift from his absentee parents several months ago—until now. But all of a sudden, playing darts seemed like a fantastic use of his time.

"Visit the shop, then," Oliver suggested.

"Fuck the shop. Let them see how well they'll do on their own." *Thunk.* Narrowing his eyes, Max frowned. Off center. "They can sing folk songs and hold hands to pay the bills."

He waited for Oliver's inevitable comeback. But this time, unlike the past seventy-six minutes, his partner and closest friend remained silent. In unison, they stared at the dartboard. Deepening gloom cast the apartment into steely industrial shadows, forecasting a summer storm. The windows lurked gray and empty. Max didn't care.

"I'm really sorry," Oliver finally said, his voice low. "I

didn't realize Lucy didn't know about your networking or—"

"Shut it."

"How was I supposed to know? It's all you do. Working, I mean." His partner regrouped, displaying a tottering kind of tenacity that had served him well over the years. "It just didn't occur to me—"

"Give me those other darts."

"Although you *have* been different lately," Oliver mused. "Kinder, gentler—"

"Screw off." Max flipped Oliver the finger, then heaved from the sofa to get the darts himself. All around, the festive remains of the postbaseball nonvictory party seemed to mock him. He hadn't had the energy to clean up last night.

Or, frankly, the desire. For anything.

"Which is why I had to prod you about those investor contacts," Oliver persisted. "You were having so much fun with Lucy, hanging at the shop so much, that—"

Thunk. Darts were the most awesome game ever. If Max stayed focused on the board, he could forget everything else.

"—you weren't paying much attention to business. But now . . ." Oliver trailed off. Max felt his speculative gaze trained on him. "I'm not sure this is good for you."

Thunk. Hearing this crap from Mr. Lovestruck himself was not the way Max wanted to spend the day. He didn't need pity.

"If you're thinking of pulling that puppy trick on me, you punk, think again." *Thunk.* "Maybe you didn't get the memo last night. I'm a selfish asshole, remember?"

"Lucy never said that."

No, Max agreed silently, weighing the heft of his next dart between uncharacteristically shaky fingers. She'd only said that he wasn't enough. Exactly the way he'd feared.

"Aren't you late for the Dr. Phil fan club meeting?" he asked. "I hear they're giving out HUG ME pins."

"Oh, bite me, Nolan." Oliver sighed, casting his gaze around the room. "I'm trying to help you, you stubborn bastard, but if you'd rather feel sorry for yourself, you go right ahead. I've had it. I'm finished. I'm through. I've got better things to do."

Max offered him his choicest expletive. Then he offered him a fistful of darts. Again.

Oliver studied them. "You really *are* a selfish asshole, you know that?"

But he took the darts all the same. And as the first one sailed through the air—pathetically off target and aimed at his HDTV plasma screen—Max felt a little better. Maybe he couldn't have Lucy anymore, he told himself, but he still had . . .

Hell. Nothing that felt real.

Christ. His next three darts wobbled off target, despite Max's gritted-teeth efforts. He tried again and almost punctured his big toe. If he kept this up, he was going to hurt himself.

Max considered it, then threw again. Who was he kidding? It sure as hell didn't get any more *hurt* than this.

"Are you sure you're going to be okay?" Nieca asked.

Lucy rolled her eyes. "Don't I *look* okay?"

She gestured to her outfit, an ensemble composed of Day-Glo tights, fluorescent orange T-shirt, acid green skirt, and purple Converse sneakers. She'd even stuck a fake magenta flower in her hair, desperately striving for a cheery note.

Nieca shook her head. "You look desperate."

Damn that Magic 8 ball effect.

"Desperate to prove you're not heartbroken," Franco added.

"I'll be fine, you guys." Struggling toward *carefree,* Lucy shook out the donated bowling shirt she'd been examining and wrestled it onto a hanger. "You know me. Happy go lucky. Live and let live. Just taking things easy."

Franco and Nieca gave her identically skeptical looks.

"Okay, sure," Lucy blathered on, thinking she sounded almost convincing as her formerly happy hippie self, "so things kind of went south with me and Max, but those are the breaks, right? It's probably my karma. There's no fighting that."

Franco and Nieca uttered identically disbelieving snorts.

"And right, okay, sure. So you have a point about how much I cared about Max," Lucy continued, "but isn't it better that it ended this way? While I can still put Successfully Dressed back the way it's supposed to be?"

Franco and Nieca let drop an identically disapproving silence. It lingered painfully, niggling at Lucy's recent decision to cancel the brouhaha around the shop's remodel.

"You should reconsider the grand reopening," Nieca said.

"And the fashion show," Franco added. "We need it."

Lucy scoffed, choosing another donated item to hang. "We don't need anything! We're doing fine." She deliberately did *not* glance around the conspicuously vacant shop. "This is just the summer slow season, that's all. Things will pick up."

Although she didn't care, just then, if they ever improved.

She'd spent several sleepless nights in her big, empty bed, helplessly reliving all the moments she'd spent with Max. All the times she'd thought he'd been sincere . . . when he'd really just been schmoozing. No wonder he and the DL had gotten along so well. They were both two of a kind, equally opportunistic.

"I hope you made those cancellation phone calls," Lucy told Nieca, not glancing up from the dowdy skirt she'd been hanging. She tucked the whole shebang beneath her chin and tried again. "The last thing we need is for the grand opening to go ahead, just when I've decided to go back to doing things the way they used to be. Before we got all power hungry and crazy."

Before Max.

More silence.

"I know you're bummed about not modeling in the show," she added to Franco, briskly hanging the skirt on a nearby rack. Lucy shook out her hair, realizing just then that a post-breakup haircut might be just the ticket to make her feel better. "But your dates will understand. Unless, you know . . . they're just using you to meet other fashion show models or something."

Franco uttered a wounded sound. Lucy rationalized that he needed to toughen up, the way she'd had to. At least she hadn't blurted out the truth—that his dates would probably only take advantage of his trust and betray him somehow.

"That's low, Lucy," Nieca said, sounding appalled.

"Hmmm. Sorry." *Free, easy, breezy,* she reminded herself.

Clapping her hands together, Lucy looked around, at a loss for what to do next. Ordinarily, she'd have . . . hung out with Max, learning how to actually understand bookkeeping or how to write good advertising copy. Or slipping off to the storeroom for a cuddle. But today the shop she'd always loved squeezed in around her, feeling empty and bleak.

Empty and bleak . . . without Max.

No, no, no. Panicking, Lucy flapped her arms, searching for something else to occupy her time. She'd done so well. Staying busy, staying Zen, staying numb. But now—

Suddenly, two pairs of safe, comforting arms closed around her. Nieca and Franco shuffled nearer, murmuring consoling things and holding her close. Wrapped in their combined embrace, Lucy did the only thing that seemed reasonable.

She burst into tears and finally, *finally* let it all out.

Max strode into his office, briefcase in hand. He barked at Marlene for a cup of coffee, then took refuge at his desk. He was sick of wallowing in misery at home. He was pretty sure staring at his luxury loft walls was screwing with his head.

Besides, playing darts sucked.

As a replacement for living, at least.

He whipped off his sunglasses. They skittered across his desk, coming to rest near his out-of-date calendar, just as Marlene entered the room. She set down his coffee.

"Hey, are those vintage aviators?" she enthused.

Max grunted. He'd gotten them at Successfully Dressed, at Lucy's urging, but right now he didn't want any talking.

Or feeling. Or hoping. Or wanting.

"My uncle had a pair like those," Marlene nattered on. "My mom used to say he looked just like Steve McQueen whenever he wore 'em. Do you mind?" She pantomimed trying them on.

He downed half his coffee in one gulp. *Come on. Make me feel normal, damn it.* Marlene, obviously interpreting his silence as acquiescence, slid on his sunglasses. She pranced to the window, using its reflection of the still-overcast city to primp. Max fortified himself with more java.

"I want to start lining up appointments for potential investors to meet with me and Oliver. Here at the office. I'll give you the names." He eyeballed the binder he'd brought.

His terse pronouncement did not have the desired effect. Instead of hopping into motion, Marlene merely let her gaze meet his via the window reflection. She studied him.

"I thought you said you were making those contacts at the grand opening of Successfully Dressed," she finally said.

Max stared her down. Marlene already knew too much about his former plans, thanks to their friendly relationship. He shouldn't have to explain himself. At work, at least, everything should run the way *he* wanted it to.

Marlene broke eye contact first.

"Okay, okay." Shaking her head, his admin held up her manicured nails. "You don't have to go all Incredible Hulk on me. I'll do it, whatever you want."

"Good."

She brought back his glasses, then paused in the midst of putting them on the desk. She peered at him. "Are you okay?"

He tried another staring contest. This time, nada.

"You look like hell." Abandoning his sunglasses, Marlene came blithely around to his side of the desk. Her nylons swooshed in the stillness. Her ever-present perfume cloud wafted toward him. She examined him with concern. "Yup. Really awful. I should make a doctor's appointment for you. God knows, you macho types don't take care of yourselves."

Max shoved away her fussing hand. "Allergies. This damned dry desert air is bothering my eyes."

He'd felt it for days now—a scratchy, hellish burning that didn't quit. Eyedrops didn't soothe it, cold compresses didn't help, and chilled glasses of Scotch only went so far. Clearly, Arizona didn't agree with him.

Marlene's testy expression softened. "Allergies, my ass."

Her compassion only made it worse somehow. "Go . . . do something." Max gestured impatiently toward the reception area. "Leave me alone. I've got work to do."

"But Max—"

"Christ, Marlene! You're making it worse!"

Every time he looked at her motherly, worried expression, some kind of . . . *emotion* he didn't want to feel struggled to surface. And those allergies—any second now, his eyes would burn right out of his skull. Max covered them with his spread fingers, pressing hard at his temples. Blindly, he waved Marlene away with his other hand.

She didn't move. He knew it because her perfume still smothered him with its musky sweetness, as cloying and comforting as the kind his mother wore back in Austin.

Hell. He didn't know where his sense of authority had vanished to. Max wanted to make it clear that he didn't need sympathy—that sympathy only made it hurt more—but for once in his glib, guiltless life, he just didn't have the words.

He sat there helplessly, jaw clenched. Waiting.

Marlene's soft, wrinkled hand descended to his shoulder. She gave him one firm squeeze. "Don't you know? You can't go backward, hot stuff."

He didn't know what the hell that was supposed to mean.

"Just talk to Lucy. Tell her how you feel," Marlene urged.

Then she quietly crossed the office and left him alone.

To his dismay, Max realized he was almost getting used to that *alone* sensation . . . all over again.

* * *

"Yes, thanks Mrs. Callahan," Lucy said into her office phone, forcing herself to sound cheerful. "It's lovely to speak with you too. Yes, it *has* been a long time."

She paused, listening to the Successfully Dressed benefactor, one of the DL's closest pals, describe her recent trip to Antigua. As politely as she could, Lucy steered their conversation toward business again.

"That's right. The reason I called is to assure you that the pet boutique venture Mr. Nolan was sponsoring had nothing at all to do with Successfully Dressed. In fact—"

Lucy gripped the phone tighter. In her cultured voice, Mrs. Callahan expressed her confusion about Max's plans. Which was weird, because Lucy felt certain the resort-spa heiress would have been at the top of Max's schmoozing list.

"But I'm *sure* you must be familiar with it. Maybe you've forgotten." Lucy paused. "No, of course I'm not suggesting you're senile. Not at all. It's only that—"

She went on explaining. Mystifyingly, Mrs. Callahan didn't seem to know anything about Max's plans.

"Yes, we did receive your de la Renta donation," Lucy assured her, struggling against her growing confusion. "It's a lovely gown, and we do appreciate it."

No matter how deftly or persistently Lucy worked her way around to the subject of Max, Mrs. Callahan had nothing but kind things to say about his efforts—on behalf of Successfully Dressed. It was downright perplexing. Either Max was even more of a smooth talker than she'd thought or he hadn't been poaching her benefactors at all.

After a few minutes' chitchat, Lucy hung up the phone.

"Well?" Nieca sat on the edge of her desk, scanning the indie movie listings in the *Arizona Daily*. "What did she say?"

"The same thing everyone else did."

"Told you. Oliver said Max hadn't turned up anything."

Dazed, Lucy lifted her hand from the receiver. After the number of calls she'd made today, her ear felt permanently phone shaped. "Mrs. Callahan insists she's never heard of Max and Oliver's pet boutiques."

"Well, she *will* be hearing about them. I can guarantee that," Nieca said loyally. "They're going to be fantastic."

She turned another page, brow furrowed.

"But I don't get it." Lucy squinted down at today's choice of ineffectually vivid clothes. No matter how bright the hues she wore, they still hadn't put a dent in her weepy moods. "If Max wasn't schmoozing for clients while he was volunteering, what was he doing?"

Franco's exasperated sigh filled the room. "Duh. Falling for *you*. That's what he was doing."

"Yeah," Nieca agreed. "From what Oliver said, Max didn't even *want* to try to find investors here. Oliver pressured him to do it, for the sake of their new venture, but Max was reluctant. And he was here for *days* before Andrea and Oliver even got the idea to hit up our benefactors for . . ."

Lucy didn't want to hear it. *Couldn't* hear it. Nieca's voice droned on, defending Max, but Lucy couldn't stand it. She swiveled in her cast-off hair dryer chair, nearly clonking her head on the perforated plastic bonnet.

She stared at her cluttered office, overflowing with all its usual knickknacks and collectibles.

She wondered, suddenly, if Max's apartment still had all those pictures she'd given him. All those candles, all those pillows, all those handmade pottery bowls and cozy throws.

Max had really seemed to like all that stuff.

When he'd looked at the picture of him and Lucy and Nieca and Franco in their funny hats, he hadn't seemed the least bit a hard-bitten businessman, out for success at all costs.

He'd only seemed . . . vulnerable. And lovable.

Lucy leaned her head back, despair swamping her. When would she ever develop good judgment about men? She'd really believed Max was the one. The one she could trust. And love.

"Uh-oh." Nieca stiffened, rustling her newspaper. "Lucy, do you know a Beryl Naughton?"

"Beryl Naughton?" Instantly alert, Lucy looked up. She whipped her gaze to the newspaper. "We got some press?"

"If you can call it that." Nieca frowned. "There's an article here in the living section. But it doesn't look good."

Leaning over, Nieca showed her. All Lucy could do was agree. Just when she'd thought things could not get worse.

Max didn't understand it. He was doing all the right things—working hard, working out, chatting with clients, and lounging around his posh apartment—all the things he'd always done. But somehow, his life didn't feel right.

He was the same man he'd always been. Capable, smart, lucky. So he'd made a detour into touchy-feely bohemianism. It hadn't been for him. It was over. As far as Max was concerned, things could go back to normal any day now.

Except they didn't.

He wandered around his apartment, feeling frustrated and wrung out. Also, hideously allergic. The array of drugstore remedies lined up along his countertop hadn't put a dent in his symptoms. Max swept them into the trash can. His gaze fell on the framed photo beside his cell phone. He stopped.

Lucy's smiling face beamed at him from the photo.

God, he missed her.

"You know," Oliver said from the other side of the counter, "you could just go over there. Have a talk. Mend fences. Nieca says Lucy is working just about all the time these days."

"Butt out," Max returned automatically.

As he passed by the sofa, Lucy's hideous puke-green tasseled pillow fell off the cushion. He'd been carrying it around, Max recalled shamefacedly, and had shoved it there when Oliver had arrived. Without thinking, he picked it up again.

"A guy like you could easily explain himself," Oliver prompted. "With a little effort. And some understanding. True love is worth fighting for, you know. Sixty percent of—"

"Spare me. Just because you're all goo-goo eyed over Nieca doesn't mean I have to lay down and get walked on."

But Oliver's words sunk in, despite Max's resistance.

"You were nicer when you were with Lucy," his pal observed.

"Screw nice." But Max squeezed that ugly pillow all the same. And although he'd planned to pack up all the things Lucy had given him and return them, he still hadn't done it. "She didn't even give me the benefit of the doubt. *You* know damned well I got too carried away with that stupid shop to stump for my own business. *Our* business. I spent all that time fixing things and collecting shoe donations. What a waste."

"Lucy doesn't know that."

"She ought to." Reluctantly, Max stepped in the hall and hurled the pillow toward his bed. After a moment's stubborn pause, he leaned sideways to make sure it had landed safely. It had. "She ought to trust me, damn it. I did the right thing."

Oliver was silent. Thoughtfully, he flipped open the

leather-bound notebook he'd brought and scribbled something in it. He gazed at the page, a certain pleasure suffusing his face. He tilted his head sideways, smiled, wrote another line.

He snapped his notebook shut again.

"Maybe you're right," Oliver said. "Maybe you did do the right thing. But did you do it for all the right reasons?"

Max glared at him. Then the truth struck him.

"Yeah. I did, damn it. I might have started off using volunteering as a springboard, but in the end . . . in the end, it was all about Lucy." *About making her happy,* he realized.

Because he loved her.

Loved her!

"Hmmm," Oliver said, giving him a knowing look. "I knew you'd get it. Eventually."

His friend's smug grin didn't even bug Max. Because in that moment, he realized what he had to do. He had to win Lucy back. He had to tell her the truth and win her back.

Maybe then, with Lucy, he would feel right again.

He could do it, he assured himself, pacing with new vigor across his loft. He was still himself, wasn't he? Lucky Max, capable of persuading anyone to do anything. It would be a piece of cake. It would be amazing. It would be, to coin a phrase, the best thing he'd ever accomplished in his life.

He turned to Oliver.

His partner tapped his ballpoint against his temple, lost in thought, one finger keeping his place in his notebook. "I'm stuck. What rhymes with 'beautiful smile'?"

Max waved him off, too excited to be sidetracked. He headed for his closet and emerged a few minutes later, fully outfitted. A man didn't go into battle unprepared. Especially a man like him.

"Okay," Oliver persisted, probably not having noticed Max's absence. He squinted at his notebook, almost sweating. "How about 'goddess of my heart'? I'm stuck on that one too."

"What is that?" Max peered closer. "Mad Libs O' Love?"

"It's a surprise for Nieca." Oliver crossed out a line, then scribbled something else. "She likes poems, so I'm writing her one." He looked determined. "But I'm really not a flowery language person. I keep wanting to put in statistics."

"Yeah. Good luck with that. You'll write the first differential equation mash note." Sudden hopefulness surged within Max. He grabbed his keys. "Let yourself out when you're done there, Sir Rhymes A Lot. I've got to run."

"*Improprieties?*" Lucy screeched in disbelief. She rattled the newspaper. "Tax shelters? Bogus donations? High-society clothing swap for the Valley's elite?"

She gawked at Nieca. Franco too. Her initial shriek had brought him galumphing from the sales floor to the office, wielding an especially sturdy polka-dotted umbrella as a weapon.

He lowered it, reading over her shoulder. "What does 'charitable flimflam' mean?"

"It means that Beryl Naughton thinks we're the DL's cover-up," Nieca said, her voice shaking. "That Successfully Dressed is a place for Cornelia and her Botox posse to 'donate' their old designer duds and claim those contributions as tax deductions . . . while secretly hosting a high-end clothing swap."

Given Nieca's newfound income tax acumen, none of them doubted her interpretation. Since hooking up with Oliver, she'd really begun appreciating the brainier side of life. She'd even taken to reading the business section before flipping to her daily *Zippy* comic strip.

Still stunned, Lucy stared at the damning newsprint. She'd never even met Beryl Naughton. How had this article happened?

"Clothing swap?" Franco prodded, clearly confused.

"You know. The DL's last-season Armani, traded for her best friend's resort-wear Gucci," Nieca explained. "Or Mrs. Callahan's old Manolos for one of the Lopez sisters' Takashi Murakami handbags. Kinda shady, I'd say, and pretty obvious . . . unless you have a 'vintage charity shop'"—she formed air quotes on the words, looking disgusted—"to funnel everything through."

"No way!" Franco exclaimed. His mouth gaped. "We don't do that. What about everybody else? Tracee? All our other interview-suit customers?" He paused. "What about that guy yesterday? The one I spent two hours finding a Cable Technician School graduation suit for?"

"What about our résumé tip sheets?" Lucy protested, equally upset. "Our interview hint flyers? Our—"

Seminars, she almost said, but didn't.

"They're not mentioned," Nieca said. "There's a fleeting reference to you, Lucy." She pointed. "And to our charity baseball game. But the rest of it . . ."

"This makes it sound as if the DL did *everything* for Successfully Dressed!" Lucy wailed, scanning the article again. Anyone who read it would swear Lucy was a hired laundress. "I mean, sure, Cornelia started the place, but *we're* the ones—"

"Who've worked our asses off," Franco put in.

"To make a success of it," Nieca finished.

They stared at each other, wearing matching frowns.

"Where does she get off?" Nieca fumed, jumping down from the desk. "That article is completely misleading. And it's on the front page of section B! Everyone will see it."

"It mentions the grand reopening," Franco added. "The fashion show too." He peered. "Nice picture of the DL. Not."

They all glared at it.

"The real kicker is, Cornelia wouldn't even have bothered with that stupid fashion show if Max hadn't talked her into it," Lucy mused. "*He's* the one who—"

She stopped. She frowned at the paper.

Max had done an awful lot of talking with the press.

"Max did this," she said, suddenly sure of it. "He got this article in the paper. It *had* to have been his idea."

She couldn't *believe* he would plant such an incriminating piece. Hadn't he known how bad it would make the shop look?

"No way." Franco shook his head. "I don't buy it."

"Neither do I." Meditatively, Nieca bit her lip. "And even if Max *did* talk to the paper . . ."

Alerted by something in Nieca's tone, Lucy looked to her friend. "Even if he did . . . *what?*"

"Well, Max isn't the only one who thought this place could use a little publicity," Nieca admitted. "I did too. What did you think Andrea Cho and I were talking about all that time?"

"Handbags," Lucy said, mystified.

"Vintage designer stuff," Franco added.

"And PR." Nieca's chin jutted at a defiant angle. "I mean, seriously—we all agreed we could use the press. Like in the *New Times*. Or magazines." Quickly, she went on. "Maybe Max was just getting a jump on things. Judging by what Andrea's told me about Max and Oliver's PR skills . . . it's believable. But he couldn't have known it would backfire like this. Could he?"

They stared at each other. Contemplatively.

"Nieca's right," Franco said finally. "This Beryl woman took advantage of Max. That's got to be it. I mean, come on. Max is a good guy!"

"Yeah. Good enough to break my heart," Lucy muttered.

That stopped the conversation cold. She gazed at her friends through wide eyes, feeling flattened. She'd loved Max, and he hadn't loved her back. She'd trusted him, and he'd done . . . this. She picked up the paper for a final time.

"That's it. I've had it." Lucy veered toward her office door, determined to do whatever it took to save her shop. After all, Successfully Dressed was all she had now. She had to protect it. "I'm getting to the bottom of this. You guys close up for me, okay?"

She wrested her shop keys from the clip at her hip and tossed them to Nieca.

"No, Lucy. Hang on," Nieca pleaded, catching them with a worried frown. "Don't jump to conclusions."

"Yeah, stop," Franco added, grabbing her arm. "Even if Max *did* talk to that reporter, he couldn't have known what kind of spin she'd put on the story."

Lucy surveyed them both impatiently.

"Don't do something you'll regret," Nieca prompted, trying to snatch away the *Arizona Daily*. She missed. "Max cares about you. I'm sure he must have meant well!"

That was exactly the wrong thing to say.

Lucy shook her head. "Max *never* means well," she said. "He wouldn't begin to know how."

Then she strode to the door with the newspaper in hand, ready for the showdown that would determine her future, once and for all.

20

Max strode through the deserted shop, noticing the changes in Successfully Dressed since he'd been there last. The Christmas lights were back, and so were the paper lanterns strung overhead. The special sales rack he'd initiated had been turned into a display of ladies' interview suits. The bulletin board for announcing upcoming seminars boasted a recipe for "job seeker's cheer-up brownies" instead, along with a scribbled card advertising pet-sitting services.

Pet-sitting services. Hmmm. That would be a perfect adjunct to his and Oliver's pet boutiques.

But he didn't have time for that now. He had to find Lucy. He had to find Lucy, explain, and pull her into his arms again. The past few days, he'd felt downright empty.

Wracked with unaccustomed nervousness, Max frowned and kept going. He didn't have time for nerves either. So what if he'd spent his whole life *doing* things and never actually focusing on the *meaning* behind them? So what if he didn't have practice being authentic, being touchy-feely, being heartfelt? If that was what Lucy needed, damn it, he'd reach down inside himself and find those things.

That was how much she meant to him.

Optimism burgeoned within him as he neared the rear of the store and spotted the closed office door. Lucy had to be in there. Max pictured the scene, imagining the two of them enjoying a romantic reunion. He should have brought flowers, he thought in a sudden panic. Roses, maybe. They were romantic.

Although, somehow, he pegged Lucy as more of a "bundle of daisies" type. Still—

Whap. The door whooshed open and clipped him.

His forehead pinged off the heavy wood.

"Oh my God!" came Lucy's breathless voice.

Her shoes clattered over the floor. Woozily, Max felt her rush to his side as he stumbled backward in reaction. Her hands probed his back, tousled his hair, squeezed his shoulders in an attempt to discern his injuries.

"Max, are you okay?"

This wasn't starting off well. He tried to straighten. To be manly—and simultaneously sensitive, the way she wanted. But his body demanded he clutch his forehead. It throbbed, cutting off all rational thought. All he knew was that Lucy's hands were on him. If Max hadn't felt as if his forehead were about to fall off, he'd have savored every minute.

Carefully, he pressed his fingertips to his head, then peered at them. No blood. No foul. Okay. After a few hours, he figured the double vision would go away on its own.

It occurred to him that Lucy had *really* been motoring out of her office.

She *never* moved that fast. She said it upset her chi.

Whatever. Onward, to winning her back. To that end . . .

"Hey, I'm glad you're here." Stifling a groan, Max rallied. He offered her a wincing smile. Yeah. He was going to be fine. Just looking at her—at *both* of her—made him feel better already. "I'm glad I caught you."

"Are you okay?" she asked again, peering at him. "I didn't even know you were out here."

"Yeah." He hooked a thumb to the door. "I just got here."

He spied Nieca and Franco, curiously watching from within the office. He gave them a halfhearted wave. They frowned.

Then they huddled together, talking. What the hell?

Max regrouped. He had to focus on the reason he was here. Lucy. Winning her back. "The thing is, I came to—"

"But you're okay?" Lucy interrupted.

"Yes." His smile broadened. She cared. She really cared, even after everything that had happened. "I'm fine. Now."

The subtle nuances of that *now* didn't seem to hit her.

"Good," Lucy said. "I'm glad to hear it."

She didn't, it occurred to Max suddenly, *seem* very glad to hear it. Thunderclouds rolled over her face, obliterating her normally happy-go-lucky expression. He'd never seen her mad before. Hurt, yes. Angry, no. It was surprisingly scary.

"You don't sound very glad to hear it," he ventured.

It didn't take a rocket scientist to recognize the need to tread carefully here. Something was going on.

"Oh, I am," Lucy assured him, that weird look still suffusing her face. "I'm very glad."

"You are?" Max's smile returned.

"Yes. Because you saved me a trip to do this."

Whap! Lucy smacked him with the newspaper in her hand. She went on beating him with it, walloping his shoulder, his arm, his belly. Max shied away, too surprised to stop her.

For a beatnik wannabe, she really packed a punch.

"What—" *whap!* "—were you thinking—" *whap!* "—when you did *this?*" *whap!* "I can't believe—" *whap!* "—you would—" *whap!*

Max grabbed her arm, trying to stop her raining blows. "What the hell is the matter with you?"

"I was going to talk to you," she panted, "but now that I see you, your stupid philosophy finally makes sense to me. Taking action *does* feel better! 'Just do it' is right!"

Whap! Her eyes gleamed with a baseball-pitching fervor.

"This is for 'charitable flimflam'!" *Whap!* "This is for 'high-end clothing swap'!" *Whap!* The newspaper buckled, forcing her to re-roll it. She waved it at him. "This article is absolutely evil, Max. Even for you, this is low."

"Even for me?" Okay. A man had to draw the line someplace. Also, "What article? Give me that."

He pried the rolled-up newsprint from her demonic grasp. Lucy huffed and shook her hair from her eyes, every inch of her prepared to wrestle him to the ground.

At least now Max saw only one of her. The bad news was, she was pissed enough for two.

Something told him winning Lucy back wasn't going to be as easy as he'd expected.

"It's fine if you're mad at me," she cried, her voice shaking. "I can handle that. But you'd better just leave my shop out of it! People depend on this place for their livelihoods, you know."

Reminded of those "people," Max slanted a glance toward Nieca and Franco. They eavesdropped unashamedly from the office. Nieca gave him a bewilderingly encouraging thumbs-up sign. Looking slightly less buoyant, Franco pantomimed something and pointed to the newspaper.

Taking the hint, Max unfolded it. The damning article leaped out at him immediately, highlighted as it was by Max-shaped dents and wrinkles. Holy shit. It looked bad.

"You're ruining *everything!*" Lucy said, standing toe to toe with him. Her teary eyes accused him. "Everything! It's not enough that you broke my heart, is it? You

had to wreck my shop and my friends, too, didn't you?
Everything that matters to me! You mean, heartless—"

"I didn't do this."

"—PR-sucking excuse for a—"

"I swear, Lucy. I thought this would be a good thing."

"—nonvolunteering, no-good liar!"

"I only wanted to help you. That's all this was about."
Max lifted the newspaper in indication, sorry he'd ever
spoken with Beryl Naughton. "You take your chances
with the press, I'm afraid. Sometimes their idea of a
newsworthy slant isn't the same as yours."

"I'll say." Lucy sniffed, her eyes red rimmed.

Max drank in the sight of her anyway.

Damn, but she looked good. Even deflated, deprived
of ammo, and hankering for another whack at him, Lucy
looked good in a way he couldn't even explain. Looking
at her made Max feel . . . full again. Whole.

"I missed you," he heard himself say. "God, I missed
you. Lucy . . . I'm sorry."

Everything went still. The drone of the shop's multiple
oscillating fans fell away, along with the rustle of the paper
lanterns. The crinkle of the newsprint muted. The newspaper barely made a thud as Max tossed it to a nearby basket
of shoes, desperately wanting to be rid of it.

"I'm sorry for everything," he said, stronger now.

Lucy stared at him. He felt balanced on a precipice,
ready to soar skyward or plummet in despair on a single
word from her. He didn't know how or why he'd reached
this point. He only knew that he needed her. He would do
anything to have her back.

"Please say something," Max said, feeling desperate.

Her gaze roved over him. She crossed her arms, and
his feelings of desperation grew. Maybe Lucy was only
drawing this out to make a point, in that freaky, indirect
way women had. If so, Max knew he could take it. He
could take anything.

"It's too late, Max. You're out of luck."

Anything except that.

"Is it always this loud?" Oliver asked.

"No," Nieca said, bobbing her head beside him. They'd spent the last half hour in an eastside garage, listening to Franco and his band practice 80s cover songs. "Sometimes it's even louder!"

Enthusiastically, she grooved in her chair—an upturned five-gallon bucket of spackle that matched Oliver's five-gallon bucket of spackle. Franco's retro punk wasn't exactly her scene, but she'd thought Oliver might like it. Given how stodgy he was sometimes, he probably thought this was new music.

"You really like this?" he asked her.

"Sure!" she yelled back. "I love it!"

Plus, it was nice to support Franco. He posed near the drum kit, faux-hawk vibrating, playing guitar with enthusiasm. A broad smile broke over his face. Then he remembered he was in an official rock band and put on a sneer.

It looked completely unconvincing against his lanky, good-natured, black-studded-leather-belted self, but Nieca figured that was part of Franco's charm. Inspired, she put both hands to her cheeks and howled like a groupie.

"Yaaay! Franco! Wooooo!"

He guffawed and went on playing.

Happily, Nieca glanced at Oliver again. Uh-oh. He was studying her with that smarty-pants expression of his. The one that usually preceded a bizarre announcement like, "You definitely need an IRA," or "Lucky Charms do *not* constitute 'dinner.'"

"What?" she asked.

He smiled. It was a smarty-pants smile too. The kind

that made her feel all girlish and fluttery and uncertain
Nieca hated it. And she loved it. She didn't understand it
which was her least favorite thing of all.

She wanted to be master of her universe. In every way

"Cut it out, smarty-pants." She nodded to the makeshift
oil-stained stage. "Listen to the music."

As *if* Oliver could have resisted at this decibel level.

But despite her explicit—if unnecessary—instructions, Oliver only went on watching her. He also took her
hand. He wove their fingers together and squeezed, ther
dragged their joined hands to his thigh.

He let them rest there. Comfortably. The way an old
man would have done with his beloved old wife.

Nieca knew she shouldn't allow that. She wasn't old.

She probably wasn't even beloved.

Probably.

After all, she never had been before. She'd been admired, sure. Lusted after, feared, or fooled. But she'd
never been beloved by anyone.

"I see you," Oliver said in a low voice, leaning nearer
to be heard above the thundering bass. "You're not so
tough. Underneath it all, you're *nice.*"

"Nice?" Affronted, Nieca reared back. *Nice* wasn't
part of her mystique. It wasn't something she aspired to
or even considered. "I'm not 'nice.' *You're* nice."

As she said it, she realized it was true. He was.

"We're pretty nice together," Oliver told her.

There. Things were back to normal. Oliver was being
mushy and she was being sassy. Reassured, Nieca tapped
her toes to the music, bobbing her head again.

"But mostly, *you're* nice," he added.

She whipped her head around, intent on putting this to
rest once and for all. She couldn't let him think she was
nice. He'd walk all over her. Take advantage of her.

Understand her.

"Quiet," Nieca demanded, but there was something in

Oliver's steadfast expression. Something wonderful. She'd have thought she'd imagined it, except it just kept on happening. "You're missing the music."

Oliver smiled. He didn't look like a guy who missed anything, just then. He went on watching her, then lifted their joined hands and kissed her knuckles. It was exactly like him to be so traditional, so gallant, so . . . wonderful.

She couldn't believe she liked knuckle kissing.

Maybe she really *was* nice.

Underneath it all. Reluctantly.

Nieca knew she needed to put an end to this. To slam on the brakes before Oliver, a bona fide thoughtful man, got hurt. She didn't want to be responsible for heartache, especially given the brouhaha she'd witnessed between Max and Lucy today.

But when she tried to summon up her usual "It's not you, it's me" breakup speech, nothing happened.

Panicky, she focused on Oliver's crazy, curly hair. She didn't even like men with dark, curly hair, she reminded herself. Yet when she looked at Oliver's, she felt all cozy inside.

Nieca frowned.

"What's wrong?" Oliver asked.

It was exactly like him to discern trouble and ask her about it. He was considerate, tender . . . even, yes, geeky. That side of him had never disappeared. Between kisses, he quoted percentages and obscure facts. While playing with Spike, he described all the developmental phases the puppy would be going through and when. Oliver danced like a disjointed man-puppet, laughed like a deep-throated loon, and was never far from his multi-function Swiss-made calculator watch.

But all the same, Nieca loved him.

It was, she realized, the wildest thing she'd ever done.

"Everything is right." She smiled her most radiant smile, unable to help herself. "All because of you."

Oliver smiled back, and she knew she was lost for good.

She even loved his goofy, cornball grin.

"I hope you think so," he said, "after your surprise."

"My surprise? Give it to me now. I can't wait."

"Yes, you can." He patted her. "It's not done yet."

"So?" Nieca couldn't believe he had the gall to keep a surprise from her. Now. After she'd officially declared her feelings for him. "I'll take whatever you've got."

Oliver's smile turned mysterious. "In similar circumstances, especially with regard to keeping secrets, women are three times more patient than men. Did you know that?"

"You're making *that* one up."

"Never." He kissed her knuckles again, smiled, then changed the subject completely. "So . . . how come Lucy isn't at this shindig? I'd have expected her to be here for Franco."

"She's, umm . . . tied up." Nieca flashed a semiguilty look at Franco, her partner in crime. "Maybe she'll be here later."

If we're lucky, she added to herself. *Or Max is.*

Worn out from pacing, Lucy kicked off her metallic bronze sandals and trod barefoot across the storeroom. The concrete floor felt gritty and cool against the soles of her feet. She sensed Max's contemplative gaze on her the whole way.

"You're in cahoots with them, aren't you?" she asked.

Max's careful regard simply continued. It was just like him to neither admit nor deny culpability. Although, given that, Lucy couldn't quite reason out the apology he'd offered earlier. After she'd walloped him with the newspaper.

"The three of you planned this, didn't you?" she went

on, exasperated and confused. She'd been trying, stubbornly, to remain silent for the past hour, but she just couldn't stand it anymore. "You got together and you planned this. I *knew* Nieca's new braininess would come to no good. You've dragged her over to the dark side."

Max's laughter rang out, husky and strong, stirring up feelings better forgotten. It echoed from the storeroom's walls, only faintly muffled by the cardboard boxes, stacks of hangers, and mounds of clothes surrounding them. She'd been trying, stubbornly, to avoid looking at him, but his presence was inescapable.

"The dark side?" he repeated.

"Yes! How else could she have *tricked* me like this?" Lucy gestured to the storeroom, remembering the ignoble way they'd wound up here. "I never even saw it coming."

Hey, you guys! Nieca had yelled urgently from inside the storeroom, interrupting Lucy and Max's argument over the article. *Hurry up! It's Franco!*

Naturally, they'd both rushed in to help.

Only to find the storeroom empty—and the door slamming shut behind them. Franco and Nieca had hastily locked it, shoved some furniture against it—probably Lucy's desk—and shouted from the other side: "Now both of you, *talk* to each other! Because you're not getting out until you do!"

"Neither did I." Max shook his head with not-quite-convincing regret. "I didn't see it coming."

"Yeah, right. And Franco's favorite movie is *The Sound of Music*."

"It is?"

"No! I'm making a point."

"Ahhh." Max didn't sound convinced. "Come on. Why don't you sit down. Talk to me. You're wearing a path in the floor."

Lucy glanced at him, sprawled comfortably on a set of

boxes he'd rearranged awhile ago. Resourcefully, Max had propped them up Barcalounger style. His big body looked utterly at ease. He patted the box beside him—an invitation.

She stuck her nose in the air.

"You're making this harder than it has to be," he said.

She was making this harder than it had to be? *She* was? Stifling an answering growl, Lucy wondered how Max could sound so confident. So patient. So . . . she admitted, very, very *sorry*.

Just like he had during their argument.

Well. Maybe he was willing to wait all day for them to *talk to each other,* as commanded. But Lucy wasn't.

"No, I'm not." Deliberately, she strode to the set of metal gray shelving at the other side of the room. She rummaged through its contents and came up with a suitable prop. "In fact, I'm quite happy here." She brandished the package she'd found. "Look. Sustenance."

"Cheez Doodles?"

"That's right. Nutrition from both the dairy and the . . . Doodle food groups. So, personally speaking, I could stay in this storeroom for quite some time." Lucy sat primly on an unopened hanger box, then crossed her legs. She pretended to relish a stale Doodle. "Mmmm. Too bad about you, though."

"You're not sharing?"

"With a big, strong guy like you? Nah. I'm pretty sure you can fend for yourself."

Her fingers trembled as she plucked another orangey snack from the bag. Day-Glo cheez dusted her clothes. She didn't even like Cheez Doodles—these undoubtedly belonged to Franco—but Lucy couldn't let on. She couldn't show any weakness.

"As a matter of fact, I might *have* to stay in the storeroom pretty soon. Live here. You know, after I lose my job— thanks to your talent for PR—and wind up homeless." Lucy

eered thoughtfully around the storeroom. "I could make
urtains from the donated clothes and do it up right. Pink,
naybe."

Max sighed. "Sarcasm isn't your thing."

"No? What is my 'thing,' Max? Letting people walk all
ver me? Letting people take advantage of me?"

His gaze leveled on her. "I didn't approach anybody
or investments. I swear."

Guiltily, Lucy stared into the Doodle bag. He was right
bout that. She knew that now, after her phone calls. And
fter the things Nieca had explained. But still . . .

"You certainly developed a sudden 'interest' in volun-
eering, though," she pointed out. "At first, I could barely
rag you in here. You tried to bribe me to get out of it!
Then, all of a sudden, you couldn't *wait* to volunteer."

His gaze met hers. "I was interested in you."

"You mean you were interested in my contacts."

"No. In you." Max propped his head in his hands and
vatched her, all his attention focused on her face. "You
vere outrageous and colorful and fascinating. Also,
lrop-dead sexy. I couldn't help it."

Lucy couldn't stand his scrutiny. Or the unwelcome,
incomfortable truthfulness in his voice. She let her gaze
kitter away, bouncing along to the mound of crushed
loxes propped carefully behind a shelf. *Oh God.* Those
loxes looked awfully familiar. Almost as though they
vere the same ones she and Max had arranged to . . .

Arrgh. Memories swamped her, making the Cheez
Doodle she'd been eating taste like orange chalk. She had
o get out of here. Homemade pink curtains would be no
:ompensation for this.

Damn Franco and Nieca. Damn their parting shot too.
Remember, he passed all our love-worthiness tests!

Her friends didn't know everything. They didn't know
low hurt Lucy felt, how hopeless and needy and con-
used. Seeing Max today had whirled up those feelings

all over again, and her article-induced tantrum hadn't done much to abate them.

Now, remembering it embarrassed her. But at the time, giving Max a dose of his own "just do it" philosophy had felt pretty liberating. She sneaked another glance at him.

"You're right," he said, as though he'd been patiently waiting to explain himself. "I was supposed to make contacts while I was here. I promised Oliver I would. But I didn't."

"Oh yeah? What about Cornelia Burnheart?"

"CC is a lonely woman who feels shunned every time she walks in here. I can't believe you can't see that."

"I can't believe *you* can."

Silence. "I'm not as shallow as you think, Lucy. Not anymore." Max's gaze stayed on her. "Not since you."

She stood, crumpling her Cheez Doodle bag. "I don't want to hear this."

"You might as well. We've got nothing else to do."

"That's what you think. *I'm* getting out."

Determinedly, she went to the door again. Shoving it didn't work, and neither did wrenching on the knob. The dead bolt—installed for inventory security—held fast. It locked from either side . . . with the keys Lucy had impulsively given Nieca.

She kicked the door.

"What are you even *doing* here?" she demanded, whirling in frustration to confront Max. "You're not volunteering anymore—"

"I came for you."

She gaped at him. "You expect me to believe that?"

His unwavering, steadfast patience said he did.

The worst thing was . . . she wanted to. A little bit.

"No." Lucy held up her palm, feeling herself shake. She couldn't believe he dared to say such a thing. "Don't even start. Even *I'm* not that gullible."

"I came for you," Max repeated, just as firmly.

"Stop it, okay? Just . . . stop it."

"Not until you listen to me."

He stood, moving with easy strength. Beneath his black suit jacket, his shoulders loomed broad and confident. When contrasted with the grungy surroundings, Max looked twice as polished, all of a sudden. Twice as suave. Twice as irresistible.

Twice as out of place.

He also looked fairly overdressed, Lucy noticed for the first time, for a simple thrift-store visit.

"I've made some mistakes," he said bluntly. "But I need you, Lucy. No matter what you think, that's the truth."

She wanted to believe him. Wanted to listen to him, to go to him, to make their differences fall away. But after all that had happened . . . Lucy just didn't know how she could risk it.

"Is that suit new?" she jabbered, feeling herself waver and fighting against it. "I've never seen it before."

Max stepped nearer. His meaningful look puzzled her.

"No, it's not new," he said. "I've just never needed it before. Not until now."

"Why not? A suit like that has *got* to impress investors."

Her flippant, baited remark didn't even faze him. Max only went on watching her, sincerity in his face and in his voice. She'd never seen him look quite so . . . steadfast before.

"I don't care about impressing anyone." He lifted his shoulder in a shrug. "I wore this suit for another reason."

"Well," Lucy admitted grudgingly, "you *do* look nice in it." She gave him another, more lingering look. She just couldn't help it. He was, aggravatingly, the most wonderful sight she'd glimpsed all day. All week. "So I guess if you were *really* coming here to see me . . ."

Max's eyes lit up, bringing her to a stop. Something in his expression, something hopeful, made her hesitate.

". . . then it was a good choice," she managed. "I guess."

"You guess."

"Mmmm-hmmm."

God, what was she *doing*? She was playing right into his hands! Feeling scattered, Lucy looked at those hands, for want of a better subject to occupy her thoughts. It was a bad move. It only reminded her of all the things they'd shared . . . all the things they'd given each other. She still wanted Max.

Even after everything.

And this storeroom—the site of their first real, intimate encounter—wasn't helping matters any.

"Cheez Doodle?" she blurted, holding out the bag.

But Max knew. Somehow, he knew.

"No, thanks." His smile reached down inside her, touching her heart, making her soften toward him still further. "All that orange stuff will wreck my lucky suit."

"Your . . ." It couldn't be. "Lucky suit? Really?"

Lucy stared at him, unreasonable hope fluttering to life inside her. If that was *really* his lucky suit, then that meant . . .

"Yeah." Max moved nearer, spreading his arms to showcase his expertly tailored black wool. "And if I'm very, *very* lucky—you still don't believe in giving up on people."

21

Saying it out loud was a gamble. Max knew that. Saying what you wanted went against all the rules of garnering good luck. Hell, it practically invited a cosmic body slam. But if anyone had ever been worth taking chances on, it was Lucy. Purple hair and all.

"Don't give up on me," he begged. "Just let me explain."

And it *was* begging, plain and simple. The first pleading he'd ever tried in his life. But Max could no more resist trying it than he could stop looking at Lucy, staring at him with shock on her face.

She didn't say anything.

His sense of desperation deepened.

He'd thought he'd had a reprieve when they'd wound up in the storeroom together. A chance from out of the blue. But Lucy had proved more obstinate than he'd expected. She'd munched those damned Cheez Doodles as though they were a gourmet feast and done her utmost to ignore him.

"I wanted to give you something," Max told her, his voice hoarse with days of holding everything inside. "Something more than just *me.* So when I saw I could help you with the shop . . . it was an opportunity. I grabbed it with both hands. And I hoped like hell you

would see I was better than you thought. Better than just
some guy who tried to bribe you in his underwear."

A flicker of remembrance passed over her face. Lucy
chanced a glance at him, then quickly looked away.

"It started to work too. Things here picked up, customers started coming in. You were happy." He shoved his
hand through his hair, wanting to go to her but knowing
he couldn't. Not now. Not yet. "*I* was happy. I was making
a difference. For you. And for me too. A little bit."

She folded her arms, not meeting his eyes.

This honest, good-intentions thing was going to kill
him.

"Hell, I know it sounds cheesy," Max said, stiffening
his spine. "Especially out loud like that. But it's true.
There's something about you, Lucy." He couldn't believe
he was going to say this. "Something that makes me want
you to be proud of me."

Her face lifted. The sadness there hit him like a punch
to the gut. He was too late. But he had to go on.

"I know it's a lot to ask," he admitted, desperate to
make her see this wasn't her fault. "Christ, my own
family—"

"I *was* proud of you."

For an instant, he almost fell for it. Then he remembered this was Lucy. Lucy, who palled around with her
mail carrier and helped out jobless women and subsi-
dized all her artist friends' careers, even though she
couldn't afford to.

"You don't have to say that." Max waved her off, shaking his head. "The point is . . . I came here with bad
intentions. I came here hoping to make some contacts,
make a fast deal, and get out. It's true. But I left here—"

She shook her head, biting her lip. Was she crying?

"—with something else. Something better. I left here
with a bunch of people who were like another family to
me. I left here with baseball again. With veggie burgers

and tofu and more laughs than I even knew existed. I left here—"

"I didn't give you anything. Not enough."

"—with *you*," Max persisted doggedly, needing to make her understand, somehow, exactly what she'd meant to him. "And then I screwed it all up, and I lost you. And even if I can't forgive myself for that . . . damn it, Lucy. I just need *you* to understand. And maybe someday you'll see that I really didn't mean it. All I meant, all I ever *really* meant, was loving you."

All of a sudden, her hands were on his, and she *was* crying, but Max couldn't quite figure out why. For the first time ever, a woman was a complete and utter mystery to him. Now, when he so urgently needed to make things right. So he only went on, talking as though words could save his life.

"I love your smile, and your laughter, and your purple hair." Like magic, her crazy hair was close enough to touch, so Max did. He buried his fingers in it, wondering how he'd ever done without its silky feel, its vivid color. "I love your stubbornness and your weirdness. I love the way you help everybody else and act as if that's *not* incredible. I love the way you feel and the way you look, and I love waking up with you. From the minute you smiled at me on that street, then drove over the curb in your truck, it was all over, Lucy. It just took me awhile to realize it, that's all."

Max paused, his hand still buried in her hair. He breathed in Lucy's sweet, spicy fragrance, savored her upturned face and her dazzled expression. He was babbling now, he was sure of it, but she didn't seem to mind, so he just kept on.

"When I'm with you, everything feels better," Max said. "I didn't even know . . . the baseball, the field, the T-bones . . . they were all you. The uniform and the party and the laundry . . . that was all you too. And I know I screwed it up for good. But you've got to believe me. I never, *never* meant to hurt you. If I could take it all back"—God, if he could only quit seeing her wounded expression in his dreams—"you *have* to know that I would. Right now. I'm strong enough." Max thumped his chest in proof, hearing his voice grow even hoarser. Christ, was *he* going to cry too? "I could take it, Lucy. You know I could—"

Her fingers touched his mouth. "You love me?"

The tremulous look on her face finally made sense. No, no, no. She didn't believe him. He was messing this up too.

"Yes, I love you," Max told her urgently. He brought his hand to her cheek. "I love you. I thought I was saying—but maybe—you're right. No, you're right. Simpler is better." He shook his head, sucked in a breath. "I love you, Lucy."

The words boomed, echoing around the storeroom.

"I love you too," she said, more quietly.

So quietly that Max knew he was only imagining it. But damn, it felt incredible. He blinked. "My head injury is back. I thought I heard you say—"

"I love you," Lucy said again, and this time she brought her mouth to his.

His head injury wasn't so bad after all, if it could conjure this. Stunned, he kissed her back. All by themselves, his arms reached around her. Max found himself holding her, squeezing her tight against him, and he realized that his body knew better than he did what was really happening here.

But then, his body had loved her all along.

"I love you," they said together, and their next kiss was a mishmash of smiling and smooching and relieved laughter. This was probably, Max thought in a daze, what the whole world was like for poor Oliver—muddled and confused and going in both directions at once. Tension melted from him in a rush, and he couldn't believe any one man could be this lucky.

Lucy loving him back was more than he'd ever dared to hope for.

After all, there was only so much power in a single lucky suit.

But there was Lucy, still in his arms. And there was Lucy, smiling at him. And there was Lucy, with her whole body pressed close-close-closer against him. He didn't need any more proof than that.

"I'm sorry, Max," she said. "So sorry. I should have asked you. I should have known. But I loved you so much, and I . . . well, I'm me. And you're you." She gestured at the two of them, as though that explained it. "So different. And I thought, how likely is that? So when the first doubt came along, I just . . ." Lucy stopped. Gazed up at him seriously. "It was worse than trying tofurkey for the first time. Worse than almost losing this place. Worse than anything. I didn't know what to do. So I didn't do anything. Except leave."

They both fell silent. The storeroom squeezed in around them, feeling suddenly cozy again—like the place Max remembered from his times here with Lucy. He would never again view cardboard impartially. Or without a certain fondness.

"I talk a good game," Lucy admitted, leaning back with a rueful expression. "And I honestly do mean well. But when it comes to action . . . sometimes I'm not so spectacular. I didn't realize it before. But I'm working on it now."

"You don't have to do everything all by yourself," Max reminded her, stroking her hair. "You've got Nieca and Franco and Penny. And me."

"No, there are certain things only *I* can do."

"Like what? This place runs like a champ now, and—"

"Like loving you." Lucy put her arms around his neck again. Kissed him. "I can't believe I almost lost you."

"I can't believe I almost lost *you*."

They beamed at each other. The storeroom turned even cozier, even warmer, even more intimate. Now that things were okay between him and Lucy, Max minded being stranded here alone with her even less than he had before.

"So, hmmm. We've still got Cheez Doodles," Lucy mused, pursing her lips prettily. "And we've still got that case of Gatorade over there."

"You were hoarding a case of Gatorade?"

"And there's enough cardboard for us to sit on, and enough donations to keep us warm."

"I forbid you to put on another stitch of clothing."

"So I figure we can hold out here pretty comfortably," she finished, looking around. "All we need now is love."

Max tipped her chin up. Gazed at her with wonder and no small amount of gratitude. "For you? I've got plenty of that."

"Me too." Lucy smiled at him, then took his hand. She pulled him against her. "Let me show you."

And then, just then, Lucy demonstrated exactly how actions, sometimes, could speak louder than words.

"We should *never* have left them here alone!" Nieca said, hurrying through the darkened sales floor of Successfully Dressed. "They might be unconscious by now. Injured while trying to escape. Starving. Or worse!"

"Yeah. Bored," Franco offered from beside her. "There isn't even a CD player in there."

"Be serious," Nieca snapped. "We locked Lucy and Max in the storeroom, remember? The smell of unwashed donated golf pants alone might asphyxiate them."

Oliver, shining his trusty Swiss Army flashlight,

brought up the rear. "I can't believe you waited until *after* Franco's band practice to tell me this."

It was true that he would love Nieca no matter what, but this impromptu rescue mission was putting a drastic crimp in his plans for the evening. He still had a poem to finish for her. He didn't have time to play white knight.

Although the idea of *his* being the one to come to Max's rescue—for a change—did have a certain appeal.

"Wait." Franco tilted his head, his piercings shining in the flashlight's glow. "I think I hear something."

They all stilled. Then Oliver heard it too.

Laughter burbled from within the depths of the storeroom. It floated through the office to their position near the shop floor's Christmas lights, sounding—to Oliver, at least—carefree and intimate. Playful and private. Romantic and yearning.

"Mmmm," came next, husky and low. "That's more like it."

"Even better than Doodles. Ahhhh."

Nieca straightened, her eyes wide. "They're hysterical. They've snapped! Hurry up, you two."

Franco and Oliver hesitated.

"I dunno, Nieca," Franco said. "That sounds like—"

"*Nobody* could have made up with Lucy this fast." Nieca squinted at her oversize antique men's watch. "Under three hours? You've got to be kidding me. Lucy was *really* hurt. Max had some major heavy lifting to do to make it up to her."

Another moan floated past. Then a girlish squeal.

"Heavy lifting, huh?" Franco guffawed.

"*Nobody?*" Oliver arched his brows, gesturing for them all to turn back. He tiptoed a few feet. "You've forgotten, this is Max Nolan we're talking about. Statistically speaking, the luckiest guy *ever*. Come on, Nieca. Let's get out of here."

Nieca propped her hands on her hips. She rolled her eyes. "No way. I'm not leaving them stuck in there."

A conspicuous silence filled the sales floor.

Oliver, Franco, and Nieca exchanged glances.

"Whoa." Franco paused, his skinny body poised in uncertainty. "Do you really think they passed out?"

Nieca frowned. "Golf clothes? Hello? Pee-yew." She shouldered her way forward, then stopped in front of the storeroom door. "I've sorted that stuff. It's a fate worse than death. I don't know *what* we were thinking."

With a grunt, she shoved at the desk blocking the door. It slid sideways without much effort. So much for their makeshift barricade. Oliver would have devised something much sturdier.

Nieca patted herself down in search of the shop keys. She cast Oliver a puzzled glance.

"That's bizarre," she said. "I can't find the keys."

A click. The door burst open. Max stumbled out, blinking in the flashlight's glare. Beside him, Lucy shaded her eyes, peering out at them all. They both giggled.

They both wore completely mismatched clothes.

Clothes they'd obviously just thrown on.

"That's because I've got them," Max said, jangling Lucy's missing key ring. He waggled his eyebrows mischievously. "I lifted them from you when your back was turned, Nieca."

"You *what?*" Nieca gawked.

"You did?" Lucy asked, mouth open. She clutched her shirt, which slipped precipitously from her shoulder. She stared at Max. "You could have gotten out of the storeroom all along? Anytime? All along?"

Max shrugged. "A guy can't count on luck alone. Besides," he added with a kiss, "I loved the company."

Lucy smiled. "Awww. Me too."

They murmured and kissed again, plainly reunited.

Nieca took one look at them and pumped her fist in the air.

"I *knew* it!" she cried. "My foolproof strategy *totally* worked. How could it not? Like I said—foolproof."

Franco hit the overhead office lights. They illuminated his puzzled look. "But a second ago you just said—"

"I'm *so* happy for you two," Nieca went on, oblivious to Franco's dissent. Giving a little squeal of delight, she skipped forward, then hugged Lucy and Max. "This is the *best!*"

She jumped up and down, girlishly enthusiastic.

"But—" Franco protested again, looking mystified.

"Just go along with it," Oliver advised, sotto voce. He leaned closer, man-to-man style. "And tomorrow? Pretend that squeal—and the hopping—never happened. For both our sakes."

After a second, his counsel sank in.

"Ahhh. Gotcha." Franco gave him an approving look. "Hey, do you do consulting? On dating stuff? Because I've got this situation with three dates at once, and . . ."

But Oliver knew Franco had to be joking. *Him?* Advising anyone on love-life issues? Ha. So he only slapped Franco heartily on the back and turned to watch his friends.

Lucy glowed, clearly overflowing with happiness. Max, too, looked happy—a lot less grumpy, a lot less whiskery, and a whole lot less likely to force more dart playing on Oliver. That was a relief. Much more of that and he'd have been compelled to buy Max a new HDTV plasma system. Although they *were* going for markdowns up to twenty-three percent. That was pretty good.

He'd get one himself. To watch Animal Planet on.

Spike would love it. He was a freakishly smart dog.

"Seriously," Franco urged as Lucy and Max and Nieca chattered in the background. "Do I look like a male model to *you?* Because I'm thinking the fashion show is going to be back on, which means my dates—"

"Oh no," Lucy interrupted, overhearing. She turned to them, her eyes wide. "The fashion show. The grand reopening. The newspaper article!" She gestured to the sales floor. "It mentioned both of them—and got that wrong too, I might add, since they've both been cancelled."

"Uhhh, Lucy?" Nieca began.

But Max overrode her. "You cancelled the reopening? Because I had some other ideas—"

"What newspaper article?" Oliver asked, feeling confused. Ever since meeting Nieca, he'd started turning to *Zippy* before reading the business section. He should have known slacking off would backfire. "There was an article about Successfully Dressed?"

All four of them glared at him.

"Yikes. Sorry." Oliver held up his hands. "Never mind the new guy. I'm just here for the rescuing."

They chattered again.

"I was dying to wear those leather pants," Franco moaned.

"Penny was *so* ready to go Goth," Lucy added. "And Jade was going to supply refreshments—and invite her organic alfalfa sprouts delivery guy too. What have I done?"

"Why did you cancel the reopening?" Max persisted. "It was going to launch this place. Nieca even had an idea for a whole 'silent auction' fashion tableau in the window, starring Suzy and Rocky. It was going to be spectacular."

They all gawked at him.

"Tableau?" Oliver mimicked, grinning.

Max shrugged. "So shoot me. I like Nieca's mannequin displays. So do a lot of other people."

"Still. *Tableau?*"

"Keep up. It's fashion industry talk."

"Ummm, about the cancellations," Nieca broke in.

They all swiveled toward her. Lucy arched her brow.

still holding hands with Max. Her shirt drooped, baring her shoulder.

"I kinda . . . sorta . . . never made the cancellation phone calls," Nieca admitted. She ground her toe against the floor. "I was hoping you two would patch things up before I had to."

Lucy looked stunned. Max looked thoughtful. Franco looked knowing. Oliver figured he still looked perplexed.

"What article?" he asked. He loathed being uninformed.

Nobody humored him with an answer.

"You cancelled the shop's grand reopening?" Max asked slowly, looking at Lucy. "Because of me?"

"Dude." Franco made frantic hush-hush signs with his scrawny arms, frowning. "Let sleeping dogs lie, okay?"

"I didn't have the heart to go through with it," Lucy explained—seeming, as she might have said, pretty Zen about it all. "Plus, I was mad. I know it's childish, but there you go. I'm not perfect."

"I'll say," Nieca grumbled. "You couldn't even pick-pocket your own shop keys back from Max. What did you *think* that bulge in his pants was?"

They all gawked at her.

"Do you seriously want her to answer that?" Max asked.

Franco guffawed. Oliver rolled his eyes. It was just like Max to brim over with machismo, even in the midst of a crisis. Although Oliver still didn't know quite what the nature of the emergency was.

"What article?" he prodded. "What cancellations?"

Everyone was too busy pretending *not* to contemplate pant bulges to reply.

Visibly rallying, Lucy went on. "So I asked Nieca to cancel all the fashion show arrangements and take down the grand reopening announcements," she told Max. A frown tugged at her lips. She paused. "Hey, speaking of that, where are all the—"

"Jade's store," Franco supplied as though reading her thoughts. "Victor's studio. The post office. The FedEx counter. The club where my band's next gig is."

"I gave all the announcement posters to Franco," Nieca explained. "Right after I decided not to cancel the show."

Lucy stared at them both. "You conspired against me?"

"*With* you," Nieca and Franco said loyally. "We knew you'd change your mind after things got worked out."

"Right," Oliver agreed dryly, finally putting the pieces together. "Or live in the storeroom forever."

Max didn't seem to mind. "We had Cheez Doodles."

"Are you mad at us?" Franco asked Lucy.

"Nah." After some thought, Lucy shook her head. "You guys meant well. It's okay. And—" She turned to Max. "Everything's great with us now too."

She gestured between herself and Max, beaming widely. They paused for a kiss, complete with murmured "I love you's" and plenty of lingering eye contact. It was sweet, but . . .

"Get a room," Oliver suggested.

Max squeezed Lucy's hand and offered her a whispered promise. She giggled, blushed, then nodded.

"Anyway, things are great now," Lucy said, "but what about that article? It's going to completely destroy the shop!"

Oliver contemplated another query about the article, then gave up. He'd Google it later. Research was one of his favorite things. Aside from Nieca. Speaking of whom . . .

He grabbed her hand and pulled her closer. She came willingly, probably intoxicated by all the gushy, adoring love in the room. Wait till she got a load of his poem.

Max pulled Lucy near too. "Don't worry about that article," he told her. "We'll handle it. Together."

22

The only thing crazier than a fashion show, Lucy realized later that week, was a fashion show combined with a gala thrift-store grand reopening; a giddy, loving reunion with Max; a window designer preoccupied with her *own* thrilling love connection; a pouty Goth-grandma wannabe; and a worried faux-hawked punkster who couldn't decide what to wear.

"I loved these leather pants before." Anxiously, Franco peered over his shoulder into the mirror set up in the office turned staging area at Successfully Dressed. "But now I'm not so sure. Tell me the truth." He paused for impact. "Do these pants make my butt look big?"

"Only if you pair them with Cheez Whiz chaps, a fur chubby, and knee-high mukluks." Nieca strode past with a mouthful of safety pins and an agitated expression. "Relax, Zoolander. You're going to be awesome."

Lucy patted him. "You look great. More eyeliner, though."

Franco hurried away to grab a kohl pencil from one of the volunteer makeup artists. His triple-wrapped, studded leather belt bobbed with the movement, accenting his vintage T-shirt. With a little luck, someone would bid on the whole look.

Murmured conversations flowed from the shop sales floor to the staging area, punctuated by champagne corks popping and music playing. Almost time for the show. Franco had programmed the sound system already, and during the runway event itself, one of his band members would man the turntable. Another band member was handling the lighting system they'd rented for the occasion. It turned out that the band—which had been forced into being their own roadies on more than one occasion—had hidden talents. Talents that were perfect for today. Sometimes it really paid to have unusual friends.

Lucy wrung her hands, then dragged her palm across her forehead, trying to focus. Crowd? Check. Catwalk? Check. Food, drink, and hand-calligraphed programs? Check.

"Models? Check." Nieca stopped, her safety pins all used up. She consulted her clipboard, then glanced up at Lucy. "You *know* I'll be working that Magic 8 ball effect from now until forever, don't you?"

Lucy gave her a serious look. "I hope so. Thanks for organizing all this, Nieca. You've been a whiz."

"Hey, I didn't do it all by myself. You deserve some credit, too, you know. An eensy-weensy, *tiny* bit of—"

"Very funny." Lucy hugged her, squashing them both together, clipboard and all. She felt very lucky to have such good friends. "Are the clothes all arranged? Everybody's in place?"

They both examined the women and men scurrying through the cramped office, some in varying stages of undress. A rack of appropriately tagged clothes waited, mostly ravaged, to the side. Several hats perched on the plastic bonnet of Lucy's hair dryer office chair. Shoes lined her desk—which had been shoved against the wall in violation of all the principles of feng shui—and a number of handbags hung from the lockers.

Nieca saluted. "Ready to go. Give or take a few dithering socialite types." She nodded to Cornelia Burnheart and her cohorts at the other side of the office, still fussing to make their ensembles perfect. "But everyone was totally on board with your ideas about what to wear. And the accessories too. It's going to be fab."

"I hope so." Lucy nudged aside the runway-entrance curtains—temporarily hung in place of the office door—then peered at the gathering crowd. For a measly silent auction and fashion show, the place was really packed. People overflowed the rows of chairs Franco and Max had aligned along the makeshift runway, packing the standing-room-only space. "I guess controversy really has a way of bringing folks out."

"Yeah," Franco agreed, joining them. His faux-hawk looked pointier and more splendid than ever. "We should have gotten a bogus article written about us a long time ago."

Lucy frowned. "Speaking of which . . ."

"She's right over there." Max arrived, handsome in a suit and tie—his full-on impress-everyone regalia. He gave Lucy a welcoming kiss, leaving her breathless. "Beryl Naughton." He pointed. "Front row, third seat from the left."

They all squinted through the sliver of velvet curtain.

"She doesn't *look* like evil incarnate," Nieca observed.

"Those shoes are to die for," Franco added admiringly.

"A little louder," Max suggested. "Maybe she'll write that in her notebook and feel all warm and fuzzy toward us."

"Hmmm." Lucy stared thoughtfully at the reporter who'd all but torpedoed her beloved shop. There had to be more to this story than met the eye. Maybe if she simply made friends with Beryl, they could work this out. "I'm going to go talk with Beryl," she announced. "Make her understand."

Everyone stared at Lucy, obviously aghast.

"No!" chimed Nieca and Max.

Franco paused. "Find out where she got those shoes."

"Okay. Will do." Feeling determined, Lucy started forward. She still had a few minutes before the show began, and everything was shipshape backstage. This wouldn't take long. "Don't worry, you guys. I'll be right back."

"Just a minute," came a familiar feminine voice. A manicured hand dropped to Lucy's shoulder, then gave an authoritative squeeze. "I think *I'll* do that."

Lucy turned. Cornelia Burnheart stood there, an unaccustomed expression of—well, an unaccustomed *expression* on her face. She must have backed off the Botox bandwagon.

"You have enough to handle here," CC said gently. "It's about time I did something to help you. To thank you."

They all stared. Generosity? From the DL?

"But—" Lucy began. "You never—"

"That's right. And it's about time I did," CC agreed. "Especially if I want this place to succeed—and I absolutely, positively do." A battle-ready gleam came into her eyes. Strangely enough, it looked slightly less terrifying when targeted at a common adversary. She actually smiled. "Besides, Beryl Naughton and I go way back. I think I can make her see reason."

Oliver gazed up at the runway, mentally calculating the odds of this fashion show changing people's minds about Successfully Dressed. He wasn't convinced that trotting out socialites in their best throwaway couture would garner much sympathy for Lucy and Company's cause. But Max had seemed certain this would work. After a lot of effort on the part of him, Lucy, Nieca, and Franco, it was finally crunch time.

Oliver knew a little about the show plans. He'd been involved, but his part was miniscule compared with everyone else's. From here on, he was just a spectator, like all the people crowded into the shop. He'd never felt more helpless.

Nervously, he scanned the room. Several reporters jammed the front row—Beryl Naughton among them. A journalist from the *New Times* talked with her, their heads bent in concentration.

Moving on, Oliver spotted some of the tattooed and pierced people from Successfully Dressed's weekly happy hour sessions. He saw some job seekers from his financial seminars and Max's interview workshops. He spied the Ruizes and waved to them.

He thought he glimpsed a few of the potential investors he and Max had been thinking of approaching for their pet boutique venture, but spotlights suddenly danced over the crowd and disrupted his line of sight before he could be sure.

Music thundered from the hidden speakers. The show began.

The first model sashayed out, wearing a full-length couture gown. Oliver recognized her as Tracee, one of the women who'd attended his seminars. Then, she'd worn a beleaguered expression and held hands with her two children. Today, she smiled nervously and carried an arrangement of organically grown daisies (courtesy of Jade's health food store, according to the program). Applause greeted her, and she smiled more widely.

She waved shyly to her children in the front row, then turned and headed backstage again. The velvet curtains parted to admit her and to reveal the next model.

Nieca followed, wearing a tight knee-length skirt, a sweater set, and pumps. Ropes of beads dangled around her neck, plainly costume jewelry and plainly handmade (courtesy of Meggy and Lou's All-Natural Boutique). This was, according to the program, a "sexy secretary look," inspired by midcentury retro designs. Nieca worked it with a flourish, pretending to take dictation as she swiveled her hips down the runway.

"Wow," Oliver couldn't help saying. "That sexy secretary look is so hot."

Beside him, Marlene nodded. "Tell me about it. I've *got* to put a bid on that leopard-print skirt!"

She scribbled on her notepad. Several women around her did, too, Oliver noticed. Pleased, he blew Nieca a kiss.

She puckered right back at him, her eyes shining. She seemed almost as happy as she had last night—when she'd read his finished version of "Ode to Nieca, Version 2.0."

The music pumped louder as the show progressed, setting a revved-up mood. More models strode down the runway, some wearing designer exclusives and others wearing donated items suitable for office jobs or interviews. All carried surprising accessories—a hand-painted handbag (courtesy of artist Victor Kowalczyk), a bracelet of colored blown glass (courtesy of local artisan Lylia Twarp), a tailored hemp tote (Meggy and Lou).

"I *wondered* how this 'A Neighborhood Comes Together' theme was going to play out, fashion-wise," remarked a woman seated one row up from Oliver. She nudged her friend, pointing out the introductory portion of the program. "I've never seen anything like it."

"Me either," her friend replied. "I had no idea there were so many one-of-a-kind shops downtown. This makes the mall stores look so cookie cutter!"

They turned their attention back to the show as another model emerged, clad in a sensible suit and carrying a beagle. The dog sported a rain hat and mini galoshes (courtesy of The Unique Pet Boutique, coming soon) and, to Oliver's immense relief, seemed to enjoy all the attention. His tail wagged, thumping happily against his escort's jacket.

Several more models with pets came out next. All of the dogs and cats—and one ferret—were decked out in accessories, inventive leashes, or feline jewelry. A few of the models, more comfortable in the spotlight, created miniscenarios with their animal companions, brushing their fur with special brushes, pretending to squirt on cat perfume, or offering sips of poultry- or bacon-flavored antioxidant water.

Penny appeared next, dressed in head-to-toe black (vintage Jean Paul Gaultier, according to the program), with her eyes heavily shadowed in a pale face. She sported black lipstick and a studded dog collar around her neck. Several chain-link pet leashes (courtesy of The Unique Pet Boutique) swung from her hips in place of a belt. She seemed considerably less sullen than the teenaged Goths Oliver had seen hanging out—especially when a little boy a few rows back yelled, "Yay, Grandma!"

Penny flashed him a grin and a two-fingered "rock on" sign, then sashayed backstage.

"Wow. I *love* that outfit!" Marlene gushed, scribbling on her notepad. "I've got to bid on that one too."

Oliver felt concerned. But before he could confer with his administrative assistant about her unusual free-time dressing predilections—and her apparent overload of high-salary disposable income—Franco emerged from behind the curtain.

Amid the resulting hoopla, he struck a pose, one hand on his skinny hip. His hair pointed higher and stiffer than ever, and his eyes were almost as heavily lined as Penny's had been. But his delighted grin was one hundred per-cent Franco, and so was his clomping, pants-drooping progress down the runway.

He paused dramatically. The music hit a crescendo.

Franco gave the applauding, yelling crowd a patented Zoolander pout, then turned and headed back.

"Woo-hoo!" screamed someone from behind Oliver.

"You're the best!" came another voice.

"Call me!" cried the third. "Call me!"

Oliver grinned. He guessed Franco had managed to finesse his three-dates-at-once problem.

The show went on, a steady stream of models, artsy accessories, vintage designer wear, and pets of every kind. It had turned out that almost everyone involved had an animal companion, and after Oliver had approached the models about having them outfitted by his and Max's boutiques, they'd all been receptive to including their beloved "kiddies" in the show.

"You know," said the woman in front of Oliver, leaning toward her friend again, "I can't even tell which ones are the snooty socialites and which ones are the regular women."

"I know!" her friend agreed, perusing the program. On her lap lay a scribbled-on notepad full of potential bids. "I thought I'd be able to tell them apart, but I can't."

Oliver and Marlene exchanged a look. Then Oliver realized what Lucy's innovative, last-minute idea must have been.

All the socialites—Cornelia Burnheart included—had appeared in ordinary donated interview suits from Successfully Dressed, while all the other models—regular folks and interview-suit clients and staff—had been outfitted in vintage couture. With everyone accessorized and happy to be doing their part, it really was impossible to tell the "haves" from the "have-nots."

Oliver had to give Lucy credit. She truly had a knack for bringing everyone together.

Settling back, Oliver let himself relax for the first time in a long time. All of a sudden, the odds of this show being a rousing success looked pretty damned good. Even if he did say so himself.

* * *

Max stood tapping his feet backstage, the roar of the beyond-the-curtain crowd filling his ears. All around him, models rushed to and fro, some of them carrying bulldogs or Siamese cats or poodles, and others sporting arts-and-crafts, one-of-a-kind accessories.

Max couldn't believe the grand reopening was already happening. After a lot of brainstorming, he and Lucy had come up with the revamped idea for the show together, and it had turned into a magical merging of her knack for bringing people together (via the outfits and pets and accessories) and his talent for keeping things exclusive (via the hand-delivered invitations they'd sent to key people in the Valley). Working in unison, they'd concocted an event unlike any other.

He only wished Lucy hadn't included *him* as a participant.

Stiff in his assigned outfit, Max yanked his collar, awaiting his cue. He didn't know where Lucy had flitted off to. If she didn't get here soon, she was going to miss everything. She'd worked so hard for this. He wanted to see her succeed.

Someone tapped his shoulder. Expecting to find Lucy there, wearing one of her patented grins and a kooky ensemble—she hadn't allowed Max to see what she planned to model—he was surprised to find someone else waiting for him.

"Mr. and Mrs. Ruiz." Caught off-guard, Max extended his hand. "And Ricky too. Good to see you." He smiled, nodding to their brightly painted, handwritten passes strung on macramé lanyards. "I see you decided to take advantage of those 'backstage passes' we gave you."

"Yes, yes. We did," Mrs. Ruiz said, smiling at him. "We hated to miss any part of the show, but I was afraid we wouldn't be able to catch you afterward. Especially with all that press out there. We knew you'd probably be swamped."

Max nodded. He still didn't know what had happened between CC Burnheart and Beryl Naughton. Or where Lucy was. Or what the follow-up story in the *Arizona Daily* might be.

Now, waiting to discover what the Ruizes so urgently needed to speak with him about, he felt a new pang of unease. Were they here to tell him they'd decided to pull out of his and Oliver's pet boutique venture?

It was true that Max had neglected making the local contacts they wanted. But without the Ruiz family's Valley-wide, former-convenience-store properties, launching the franchise test-marketing stores he needed would be next to impossible.

On the other hand, Max had never been one to wait for fate to wallop him. Besides, he was wearing his lucky tighty-whities—the pair he'd had on when he'd first met Lucy. They couldn't possibly let him down.

"I'm glad you came to see me." Newly determined, he steered the Ruizes to a slightly quieter corner of the staging area. "I know we've taken longer than expected to gear up for the pet boutiques. I'm sorry about the delay. I didn't expect to get so caught up in the community, or to—"

"But *that's* what convinced us about the whole thing!" Beaming, Mrs. Ruiz elbowed her husband. "Tell him, Jorge."

"That's right." Mr. Ruiz cleared his throat. Ricky looked on, clearly already aware of his parents' decision. "We were talking about it, and, well—" He paused, giving Max a straightforward look. "We figure anybody who's as invested in the community as you are is a good bet for our properties."

"We originally wanted local investors," Mrs. Ruiz rushed in, "to make sure you and Mr. Pickett wouldn't come in, buy our old store locations, and wreck all those communities. They're some of the oldest neighborhoods in Phoenix. We wanted them preserved, if we could."

"But it's obvious from all this"—Mr. Ruiz gestured to the fashion show bustle all around them, and to the accessories contributed by local artisans and shops—"that you respect *people* more than profits. That's an attitude *I* respect. That's why we've decided . . . our properties are yours, Mr. Nolan. We've already told our lawyers. We're ready to sign the deal contracts whenever you are."

Dazed, Max stared at their shining faces. He and Oliver had gotten the properties they needed after all? Just by being a part of things? Without wrangling for investors and benefactors and newer, showier ideas?

Another look at the expectant Ruizes convinced him it was true. They'd really done it.

"Thank you," Max said humbly. And he *felt* humble too. He'd thought he'd been lucky before . . . but until meeting Lucy, all his luck had been empty. From now on, things would be different. Better. Happier. "I promise we'll do our best."

They all shook hands on the deal, heedless of the commotion surrounding them, and made arrangements to meet at Max and Oliver's offices in a few days. Ricky gave Max a high five.

"Sweet!" he said. "Now that everything's set, maybe you can coach my Little League team next season. You've got a wicked batting arm, you know."

"We'll see," Max replied automatically, ruffling Ricky's hair fondly. He didn't want to disappoint the kid. Besides, experience had taught him it was better not to refuse outright—particularly when it came to the child of business contacts.

Then he realized—maybe he *would* do it. After all, he planned to stay in Phoenix. Maybe forever. Or until Lucy, with her nouveau hippie ways, decided she wanted a change of scenery.

Although now that he pondered it, Max couldn't quite imagine how they would travel very far. Especially with an entourage consisting of Nieca, Oliver, Franco, Jade, Victor, the mail carrier, Charlie the FedEx guy, the artisanal baker down the street, Meggy and Lou, Lucy's astrologer friend, her feng shui hairstylist, the alfalfa sprout delivery guy . . .

Oh well. They'd work it out when the time came.

"If you'll get me the coaching information," Max assured the Ruizes with a grin, "I'll see what I can do."

"You've got it," Mr. Ruiz said.

"Absolutely," Mrs. Ruiz added. "Plus, I—*oh my goodness.*"

She stared at something just beyond Max's shoulder, her expression rapt. Then she smiled and squeezed Max's hand.

"We'd better let you go," she said. "Come on, Jorge. Let's go, Ricky. Something tells me we don't want to miss the finale of the show."

They hurried away, offering parting waves.

Ricky giggled.

That was weird, Max thought. A fashion show wasn't *that* funny, especially to an eleven-year-old baseball nut. But he felt too relieved just then to give the Ruizes' hasty exit much thought. His new venture with Oliver was secure, his future with Lucy looked bright, and all that remained now was a particularly dreaded runway walk.

He can model his birthday suit, he remembered Penny saying.

Thank God she hadn't assigned the outfits.

"Hey, Max," came Lucy's voice from behind him. There was a rustle of fabric, then a mewling whine that sounded a lot like Oliver's screwball neurotic dog, Spike. "Ready to go?"

Max turned. The minute he saw Lucy, she took his breath away. He knew he was ready for anything.

"With you?" He held out his hand. "I wouldn't miss it for the world."

* * *

"So it turns out that Cornelia and Beryl Naughton *do* have a history together," Lucy reported breathlessly, crowding nearer to Max as the time for their entrance neared. She puzzled Spike, hardly able to believe all that had happened today. It just went to prove that when you took life easy, life took it easy on you. "Apparently, a few years ago Beryl uncovered some dodgy business dealings involving CC's second husband, Rex. Naturally, she did a story on it. Ever since then, Beryl's been suspicious of Cornelia and her whole crowd. So *that's* why Beryl assumed the shop was just a front for—" Lucy broke off, waving her hand in front of Max's face. "Hey. Are you listening?"

"Huh?" He blinked. His gaze refocused, moving in a leisurely arc from Lucy's toes to the neckline of her outfit. "Yes. Right. Beryl. Suspicious. Dodgy business dealings."

"Uh-huh." Lucy tilted her head, still not convinced Max was *really* paying attention. He seemed . . . preoccupied, all of a sudden. "Anyway, in the end, all it took to convince Beryl that Successfully Dressed really is on the up and up was a simple heart-to-heart!"

Sidestepping to avoid a model returning from the runway, Lucy grinned at Max, immensely relieved the whole ordeal was over with. She'd always known people really *were* good and really *could* be counted on to do the right thing.

Including, according to Beryl and Cornelia, a positive follow-up piece in tomorrow's *Arizona Daily*.

"A heart-to-heart?" Max repeated. "Really?"

"Yes, really. Oh, that *and* a little glance through our bookkeeping records." Lucy dismissed that technicality with a wave. She still didn't see how anybody could find a bunch of numbers and mind-numbing inventory details enlightening. "I guess it's a good thing you gave me all those bookkeeping and inventory tutorials."

"Hmmm. I guess so."

Max's grin spread wide, kicking his dimple into gear. Lucy found it enchanting. Found *him* enchanting. All around them, the hustle and bustle of the fashion show and gala reopening continued, but she only had eyes for Max. The man who'd helped save her shop, who'd helped restore her faith, who'd helped her see that there was a lot to be said for *luck* in all its forms.

"What are you grinning about?" she asked, running her hand over Spike's shaggy fur. The puppy wore an adorable argyle sweater and booties ensemble she'd chosen herself from the cache in Max's downtown office. "I'll have you know I had to arm wrestle with Nieca to be the one to carry Spike down the runway. I swear, she's like a mother with this dog."

The puppy squirmed and licked her hand. Lucy smiled.

"I'm thinking of you, demonstrating your bookkeeping acumen." Still wearing a handsome, dazzling grin, Max touched his fingertip to her eyebrow ring. He lowered his gaze to her lavender hair, to her tattoo, to the place where her navel ring ordinarily showed. "Looking . . . like that."

"Hey. Don't start on the purple hair."

"Or . . . what?" Max challenged. His gaze dipped to her outfit again, then rose to her mouth. His heated attention made Lucy's belly flip-flop. "You'll give me a tongue lashing?"

"That's right. With my bohemian-freak tongue barbell firmly in place. So you'd better watch it, mister."

"Mmmm." He leaned nearer. Kissed her. "Do you promise? I can hardly wait."

His husky voice made her quiver. She didn't know how Max could make her feel so beloved and so desired

ll at the same time. However he did it, Lucy hoped he'd
ever stop.

"I promise," she said. "With all my heart."

Max's expression sobered. Then a certain buoyancy
rossed his face, making him seem almost relieved. Or
naybe overjoyed.

But she couldn't imagine why. He dreaded modeling.

"What's the matter?" Lucy asked, crowding closer in
oncern. "All I said was, 'I promise.'"

"Yeah." Max squeezed her hand, giving her a long,
oving look. "But it was the *way* you said it."

His words swept Lucy away to all the times they'd
pent together. At her house. His place. The shop. She
elt so glad they'd found each other. So glad they'd
vorked things out. So glad they'd gotten lucky . . .
ogether.

Around them, the fashion show music picked up a few
eats, morphing into a happy-go-lucky, punk rock ver-
ion of Mendelssohn's "Wedding March." As was
aditional with authentic fashion shows, they'd decided
o end their show with the pièce de résistance—a wed-
ing dress.

"Hey, you guys!" Franco said, jabbing Lucy. "That's
our cue. Get going!"

Jolted from making goo-goo eyes with Max, Lucy hur-
iedly fluffed up the skirt of her vintage Victorian
vedding gown. Frothed with hand-crocheted lace, yards
f tulle, and carefully preserved ivory satin, it was the
inest donation piece they'd ever received. And while this
own was admittedly impractical for the Successfully
Dressed side of the shop, it might come in very handy
:—when—they decided to expand the way Nieca
vanted.

The way they'd have to, if the feature they'd been of-
:red in *Lucky* magazine panned out.

"Okay." Max stood straighter. "Are you ready?"

Wearing a broad smile, resplendent in his buccaneer style white shirt, elaborate suit coat, and fitted trousers—al assembled by the talented Nieca—he offered her his hand Lucy took it, placing her fingers in his with a surge o excitement.

And optimism. And, most of all, love.

Max cocked his brow at her. "Willing?"

The music soared a little louder.

"And able." Lucy nodded. She couldn't believe how much she loved him. "Let's do it."

They straightened together, facing the curtain. On either side of them, Franco and Nieca paused with their hands on the lustrous velvet, ready to sweep the fabric aside for their grand finale entrance.

"Wait," Max said, stopping.

"What's the matter?" Lucy gazed up at him.

"There's something I have to know." He turned toward her, his expression tender. "But first . . . you look beautiful."

Beside them, Nieca and Franco groaned. "Come *on!*"

"Thanks," Lucy said. "You look very handsome yourself."

Max gave a lusty groan and kissed her. His mouth touched hers, making the whole fashion show, all the waiting spectators, all the past and future and everything else, simply fall away. All Lucy cared about was Max Now. Them, together.

"Mmmm. I love you," he said. "So much."

"I love you too."

Nieca gave Max a kick. "That's very sweet. Now *move!*" she stage-whispered.

Max raised his head. "Okay, okay. Duty calls."

Dimple flashing, he prepped beside Lucy, straightening his shirt. He ran his hand through his rumpled hair—as i a bit of tousling could make him appear any less remark able, any less delicious, any less utterly lovable.

"Wait." Lucy put her hand on Max's arm. "What did you want to ask me? What did you need to know?"

'Oh, that." Max turned.

Beyond them, the crowd murmured on the shop floor. ticipation crackled in the air. All at once, Lucy felt it t as keenly herself.

'This dress," Max said, touching her delicate lace eve. "How would a guy go about bidding on it?"

'A silent auction bid?" Lucy blinked, feeling confused.

Max nodded. "Because given the way you look in this ss, and given the tofu-strawberry wedding cake ipes Jade has been pushing on me lately, and consid-ng the suspiciously *wedding*-oriented nature of your ligrapher friend's samples for the program today, and ing into account Victor's mysterious offer to paint a cial-occasion portrait of us—among a few other tails—I'm thinking this dress might be important to r future plans."

Lucy gasped. "Our future plans?"

'Yeah. Oliver *did* point out a certain doggie ring-arer's outfit that would be perfect for Spike," Max sed. "So if you think all that stuff would squeeze into g Shot Central, if you think it would go with you and : . . ."

'I think it would be a *perfect* fit!" Lucy cried, smiling m ear to ear. Sometimes, Max really *did* talk too ch, though. Especially when action was the thing they uired. "So we'd better get a move on. The faster we ish here, the sooner we can get started planning that u cake."

'With a deluxe champagne chaser."

'And organic crudités."

'And a lavish, first-class honeymoon trip."

Lucy grabbed Max. "Hey! I know just who can come th us!" she exclaimed, thinking of all her friends who d never done *anything* first class. Now she'd be able to at everyone she loved to the good life. She jumped up d down with enthusiasm. "Oh, Max. You're the best."

"*We,*" he said, stroking her cheek, "are the be[st]
together."

Then, holding hands as the velvet curtains parted [to]
admit them on the runway, Lucy and Max set a lan[d]
speed record for fashion show walking. Because wh[en]
life handed you a stroke of good fortune, sometimes y[ou]
just had to reach out and take it.

That was the only way, really, to honestly get lucky.

Dear Reader,

Thank you for reading *Mad About Max*! I hope you enjoyed it. I can't tell you how much fun it was for me to write about Lucy and Max—two people who *definitely* prove opposites attract! Their story is a special one for me, and I'm very happy to share it with you.

Lucy's shop was inspired by Dress For Success, the nationwide not-for-profit organization that helps low-income women make tailored transitions into the work force—and all the unique vintage stores I've visited over the years. There's nothing like snagging a real "find" to make shopping more fun. Hey . . . a girl's got to do her research, right?

Serious shopping will have to wait, though, since I'm already hitting the keyboard for my next Zebra Books contemporary romance! *My Favorite Heiress* should be arriving in a store near you sometime next year. I hope you'll watch for it.

In the meantime, I'd love to hear from you! You can send email to lisa@lisaplumley.com or write to me c/o P.O. Box 7105, Chandler, AZ 85246-7105. If you'd like to keep up on the latest insider information, please visit my web site at www.lisaplumley.com, where you can sign up for my reader newsletter, read sneak previews of upcoming books, check out reviews, and more.

Cheers,

Lisa Plumley